Between Two Kings

ALEXANDRE DUMAS

Between Two Kings

— OR —

Ten Years Later

Book Five of the Musketeers Cycle:
Being the First Part of *Le Vicomte de Bragelonne*

EDITED AND TRANSLATED
BY LAWRENCE ELLSWORTH

PEGASUS BOOKS
NEW YORK LONDON

BETWEEN TWO KINGS

Pegasus Books, Ltd.
148 West 37th Street, 13th Fl.
New York, NY 10018

Between Two Kings, by Alexandre Dumas, Translated by Lawrence Ellsworth
Translation and Original Material Copyright 2021 © by Lawrence Schick

First Pegasus Books cloth edition July 2021

Interior design by Sabrina Plomitallo-González, Pegasus Books

Library of Congress Cataloging-in-Publication Data is available.

ISBN: 978-1-64313-750-6

10 9 8 7 6 5 4 3 2 1

Printed in the United States of America
Distributed by Simon & Schuster
www.pegasusbooks.com

Contents

Introduction
by Lawrence Ellsworth

Alexandre Dumas's sprawling historical adventure, *The Three Musketeers*, was a worldwide success after first publication in 1844, and was followed in the next year by an even larger sequel, presented by this editor in two volumes as *Twenty Years After* and *Blood Royal*. Dumas then set his musketeers aside for a year before launching into his still more ambitious final sequel, the truly immense *Le Vicomte de Bragelonne*, which was serialized in weekly installments from October 1847 to January 1850.

Taking a year off to plan is understandable when one considers the mind-boggling scale of *Bragelonne:* 268 chapters, over 750,000 words, three times the size of its largest predecessor. Dumas had a vast story to tell and boldly broke free from the typical structure of the popular novel to tell it. It was an experiment in long-form narrative, and on its own terms a successful one, albeit an approach Dumas never tried again. For one thing, the market for feuilletons, the French weekly subscription papers that printed continued stories, had peaked and crashed, and the demand for prolonged serials dried up. For another, the book publishers who had to collect the *Bragelonne* mega-novel and issue it in multiple volumes strained to fit it into their usual formats.

And why had Dumas put them to the trouble? Why experiment on such a grand scale with the novel, a form that he'd arguably mastered only a few years before? Dumas had set his sights high, aiming to spin out what we now call long character arcs portraying the maturity of all four of his popular musketeer protagonists, their tales intertwined with the stories of dozens of secondary characters, and more than that, all set against the overarching saga of the early reign of King Louis XIV. It was an arc not just of people, but of a nation.

Ambitious indeed! How to make it work? The answer was to construct it from components Dumas already understood well, that is, short, punchy chapters, each built around a single dramatic scene that drove the overall narrative forward. This perfectly suited the feuilleton publication format, providing readers with enough forward momentum in each installment to ensure that they would come back eager for the next.

However, Dumas, the master dramaturge, was also telling his story in larger patterns, in acts of about eight to fifteen chapters that set up and then pay off with satisfying minor climaxes. Moreover, the entire meta-structure of *Bragelonne* is bookended (wordplay intended) by two grand sequences of fifty-some chapters each that stand alone as complete novels in themselves. These are the concluding chapters, 212 through 268, justly famous as *The Man in the Iron Mask,* and chapters 1 through 50 that comprise our current volume, which this editor has dubbed *Between Two Kings.* (See "Regarding the Title" below.)

The chapters that make up *Between Two Kings* admirably set up and lead directly into the volumes to follow, but they also tell a complete story of their own, beginning, middle, and end. And the story they tell is that of the long forging and final tempering of that once-fiery man of iron, the now mature d'Artagnan. His comrade Athos has a large role to play as well, but even more than in the earlier books in the Musketeers Cycle, *Between Two Kings* is d'Artagnan's story.

At first the tale seems to echo the structure of *Twenty Years After,* with the long-serving d'Artagnan, still only Lieutenant of the King's Musketeers, increasingly discontented with his situation and seeking a way to make a dramatic improvement in it. Dumas assumes his loyal readers are familiar with his hero's previous career and artfully plays on their expectations for him. Indeed, the author is so confident his readers know all about his protagonist that, in a neat and playful trick, he doesn't even mention the character's name until chapter fourteen, when he has the king finally utter it as a proof that he recalls his musketeer's previous services.

But then Dumas subverts his readers' expectations by showing them that this is not the d'Artagnan of *Twenty Years After* who passively awaits the assignment of a mission with which to prove himself. This, instead, is a mature and confident d'Artagnan who, once he decides the time to act has arrived, assigns *himself* a mission, and proceeds, without hesitation, to undertake it on his own account. Moreover, this is a d'Artagnan who has learned from his previous adventures and doesn't make mistakes, at least not in planning, tactics, and execution.

Not that he doesn't still have important lessons to learn. D'Artagnan, ever a man of heart—like Alexandre Dumas—is a musketeer who prefers gallant cavaliers like Superintendent of Finance Fouquet over calculating bureaucrats, which leads him to underestimate King Louis's new assistant, the intendant Colbert. And d'Artagnan's firm grasp of the tactics of intrigue leads him to believe himself equally skilled at the strategy of politics, and as a result he's more than once outplayed. Though he's nonetheless victorious in the end, there will be more lessons to come. For his new master, Louis XIV, truly king at last, will test his ingenious officer of musketeers in ways even the foresighted Gascon never expected.

Regarding the Title

Why *Between Two Kings* when that title has never historically been used for a sub-volume of *Le Vicomte de Bragelonne*?

As an author Dumas had many virtues, but he didn't have the facility for memorable titles of his great contemporary Charles Dickens. Dumas's subtitle for *Bragelonne* was *Dix ans plus tard*, and historically when the mega-novel in English translation was divided into several volumes, *Ten Years Later* has been used for the first or second book (the other titles usually being *The Vicomte de Bragelonne, Louis de La Vallière*, and *The Man in the Iron Mask*). Using the title *Ten Years Later* for a volume that follows *Twenty Years After* is obviously problematic and has confused readers for generations as to the order in which they should be read. Therefore, this editor and translator decided to restore *Ten Years Later* to its status as a subtitle, inventing *Between Two Kings* as the overall title for the first volume of *Bragelonne*, as it accurately describes d'Artagnan's adventures in this episode of the Musketeers Cycle.

A Note on the Translation

The fifty chapters of *Le Vicomte de Bragelonne* that comprise *Between Two Kings* were first published in late 1847 and early 1848 in *Le Siècle*, a Parisian weekly. They were collected almost immediately into book form by the publisher Michel Lévy Frères in Paris, followed just as rapidly by the first English translation by Thomas Williams, an American, for publisher W.E. Dean of New York. When *Bragelonne* was completed in 1851 a full translation was published by Thomas Pederson of Philadelphia, followed in 1893 by another complete version by yet another American, H. L. Williams. These Victorian-era translations, endlessly reprinted, have been the only versions of the first volumes of *Bragelonne* available for over a century. Those early translators did their work well, but they were writing for a market that was uncomfortable with frank depictions of violence and sexuality. Moreover, they employed a style of elevated diction that, though deemed appropriate for historical novels in the 19th century, seems stiff, stodgy, and passive to today's readers. It also does a disservice to Dumas's writing style, which was quite dynamic for its time, fast-paced and with sharp, naturalistic dialogue. *Between Two Kings*, the first significant new translation of its sequence in over a century, attempts to restore Dumas's edge and élan, aiming as well to recapture some of the bawdy humor lost in the Victorian versions. I hope you enjoy it.

Historical Character Note

The first time a notable character from history is mentioned in the text, their name is marked with an asterisk.* A brief paragraph describing that person appears in the **Historical Characters** appendix at the end of the book.

I

The Letter

Toward the middle of May in the year 1660, at nine o'clock in the morning, when the already hot sun was drying the dew on the ramparts of the Château de Blois,[1] a little cavalcade, composed of three men and two junior pages, was returning into the city across the Loire bridge. This produced no effect on the loiterers on the span other than a movement of the hand to the head in salute, and a movement of the mouth to say, in the purest French spoken in France: "Here comes 'Monsieur'[2] returning from the hunt." And that was all.

However, as the horses climbed the steep slope that ascends from the river to the château, several shop boys approached the last horse, which bore, hanging from its saddle-tree, several bird carcasses hung by their beaks. Seeing this, the curious lads showed with rustic candor their disdain for such meager game, and after loudly announcing that hawking was a poor sort of sport, they went back to their work. Only one of these onlookers, a chubby lad in the mood for a jest, lingered long enough to ask why Monsieur, who thanks to his vast revenues had his choice of amusements, would choose such a pathetic entertainment, and was answered, "Don't you know that Monsieur's main diversion is to be bored?"

The cheerful shop boy shrugged his shoulders in a gesture that said, plain as day, *In that case, I'd rather be plain Pierre than a prince,* and everyone went about their business.

Meanwhile, Monsieur continued on his way with an air at once so melancholy and so majestic that onlookers would surely have admired it, if there'd been any onlookers. But the citizens of Blois couldn't forgive Monsieur for having chosen their merry city to be bored in, and whenever they saw the royal sourpuss coming they slipped away, yawning, or withdrew inside, to escape the dour influence of that long, pale visage, those half-lidded eyes, and that slouching physique. Thus, the worthy prince was greeted by deserted streets nearly every time he ventured out.

Now, this irreverence on the part of the citizens of Blois was, in truth, very improper, for Monsieur, after the young king—and maybe even before the king—was the foremost noble in the realm. In fact, God, who had granted the reigning king, Louis XIV,* the happiness of being the son of Louis XIII, had granted Monsieur the honor of being the son of the great Henri IV. So, it should have been an object of pride for the city of Blois that Gaston d'Orléans* chose to hold his Court in the ancient hall of the Estates General.[3]

But it was the destiny of this exalted prince to excite indifference rather than admiration on the part of the populace. Monsieur had grown used to it. Perhaps it was even responsible for his unfailing air of ennui. It wasn't as if his early life hadn't been considerably busier; a man can't be responsible for the executioner taking the heads of a dozen of his friends without feeling some excitement. However, since the rise of Cardinal Mazarin* there had been no more decapitations, Monsieur had had to put aside his hobby of rebellion, and his morale had suffered for it. The life of the poor prince was thereafter very sad. After a morning hunt along the banks of the Beuvron or in the woods of Cheverny, Monsieur would ride across the Loire for lunch at Chambord,[4] whether he had an appetite for it or not, and the town of Blois would hear no more from its sovereign and master until he rode out for his next hunt.

So much for his boredom outside the city walls; as for his ennui inside them, let's follow his cavalcade up to the Château de Blois and the famous hall of the Estates. Monsieur was riding a smallish horse with a large saddle of red Flemish velvet and half-boot stirrups. The horse was a bay; Monsieur's doublet was of crimson velvet, the horse wore a matching blanket, and it was only by this colorful ensemble that the prince could be distinguished from his two companions, whose ensembles were purple for the one and green for the other. The one on his left, dressed in purple, was his equerry, and the one on the right, all in green, was his royal huntsman. A pair of pages followed, one carrying a perch bearing two gyrfalcons, the other a hunting horn, which he winded casually as they arrived at the château. (Everyone around this indifferent prince behaved with a casual nonchalance.)

At this signal, eight guards who'd been dozing in the sun in the inner courtyard hurried to grab their halberds and take their positions as Monsieur made his solemn entry into the château. When he had disappeared under the shadows of the gate, three or four busybodies, who'd followed the cavalcade to the château, commenting on the hanging birds, turned and ambled off—and once they were gone, the street outside the courtyard was deserted. Monsieur dismounted without saying a word and went into his apartments, where his valet helped him change his clothes; and as "Madame"⁵ had not yet sent word it was time for breakfast, Monsieur stretched out on a chaise longue and fell as fast asleep as if it had been eleven o'clock at night.

The eight guards, who understood that their work was done for the day, reclined on stone benches in the sun, the grooms disappeared into the stables with the horses, and except for a few birds, chasing and chirping merrily in the flowering shrubs, one would have thought that everyone in the château was sleeping as soundly as Monsieur.

Suddenly, into the midst of this soft silence, a bright peal of laughter rang out, which caused the dozing halberdiers to half open their eyes. This burst of laughter came from a window of the château that was now bathed by the sun, which struck it at an oblique angle for a while before giving way at midday to the shadows of the chimneys on the opposite wing. The small wrought iron balcony in front of this window sported a pot of red wallflowers, another of primroses, and an early rose, whose lush green foliage was already dappled with the red that portends blossoms.

In the chamber lit by this window was a square table covered by an old Haarlem floral tapestry, in the middle of that table was a long-necked sandstone vase holding irises and lilies of the valley, and at each end of the table was a young lady. These two lasses looked somewhat out of place, as they could easily be taken for two young maidens who'd escaped from a convent. One, with both elbows on the table and a plume in her hand, traced letters on a sheet of fine Dutch paper, while the other kneeled on a backward chair, a position that enabled her to lean over the table and watch her companion write. From this latter came a thousand jests, jeers, and laughs, the loudest of which had frightened the birds in the shrubberies and half-roused Monsieur's halberdiers.

Since we're sketching portraits, we'll present the last two of this chapter. The lass who was leaning on the chair, that is, the loud and laughing one, was a beautiful young woman of nineteen or twenty, tawny of complexion, brown of hair, and resplendent, with eyes that sparkled beneath strong arched brows and glorious white teeth that shone like pearls behind coral lips. Her every movement was a theatrical flourish, her life a vivid performance.

The other, the one who was writing, regarded her energetic companion with blue eyes as limpid and pure as that day's sky. Her ash-blond hair, arranged with exquisite taste, fell in silky curls to caress her ivory cheeks; she held down the paper with a fine, slender hand that bespoke her youthfulness. At each laugh from her friend she shrugged her white shoulders, which topped a slim and poetic form that lacked her companion's robust vigor.

"Montalais! Montalais!" she said at last, in a voice soft as a song. "You laugh too loudly, as loudly as a man! You'll rouse messieurs the guards, and you won't even hear Madame's bell when she calls."

The young woman she called Montalais,* without ceasing to laugh and sway, replied, "Louise,* you know better than that, *ma chère*; when messieurs the guards, as you call them, are taking their nap, not even a cannon could wake them. And you know that Madame's bell can be heard halfway across the river bridge, so I can hardly fail to hear it when she summons me. What really annoys you is that I laugh while you write, and what you really fear is that your worthy mother, Madame de Saint-Rémy,* will come up here as she sometimes does when we laugh too much. And then she'll see this enormous sheet of paper on which, after a quarter of an hour, you've written only two words: *Monsieur Raoul*.* And you're right, my dear Louise, because after those two words, *Monsieur Raoul*, we could add so many others, so moving and so incendiary that Madame de Saint-Rémy, your saintly mother, would burst into flame if she read them. Eh? Isn't that so?"

And Montalais redoubled her laughter and teasing provocations. The blond girl was furious; she tore up the sheet on which, in fact, *Monsieur Raoul* had been written in a beautiful hand, crumpled the paper in trembling fingers and threw it out the window.

"Look, now!" said Mademoiselle de Montalais. "Look at our little lamb, our baby Jesus, our cooing dove so very angry! Don't worry, Louise, Madame de Saint-Rémy isn't coming, and if she was, you know I'd hear her. Besides, what could be more proper than writing to a friend you've known a dozen years, especially when the letter starts so formally with *Monsieur Raoul?*"

"Fine, then—I won't write to him," said the blond girl.

"Well, there's Montalais told off, and no mistake!" laughed the brunette jester. "Come on, take another sheet of paper, quickly now, and finish up our correspondence. Ah! And there's the sound of the bell! Well, too bad. This morning Madame must wait, or even manage without her first maid of honor."

A bell was indeed ringing, a sound that signaled that Madame had finished dressing and awaited Monsieur, who was to take her hand in the salon and lead her to the refectory. Once this formality was accomplished, always with great ceremony, the couple would eat breakfast and then separate until dinner, which was invariably served at two o'clock.

At the sound of the bell a door opened in the wing to the left of the courtyard, out of which came two waiters, followed by eight scullions bearing a table-top laden with covered silver dishes. The first of these waiters, the *premier maître d'hôtel*, silently tapped with his cane on one of the guards who was snoring on a bench; he was even kind enough to hand the groggy guard his halberd, which had been leaning against the nearby wall, after which the blinking soldier escorted Monsieur's breakfast to the refectory, preceded by a page and the pair of waiters. As Monsieur's meal passed, the door guards presented arms.

Mademoiselle de Montalais and her companion watched these ceremonies attentively from their window, though they must have been quite familiar with them. They were just waiting for them to be finished so they could resume undisturbed. Once the waiters, scullions, pages, and guards had all passed, they sat back down at their table, and the sun, which for a moment had gilded those two charming faces, shone only on the flowers and the rosebush.

"Fah!" said Montalais, resuming her position. "Madame doesn't need my help to have her breakfast."

"Oh, but Montalais, you'll be punished!" replied the younger girl, sitting down again.

"Punished? Oh, right, I'll be deprived of our morning ride, going down the old steps to the big old coach, which will then bounce left and right along paths so riddled with ruts that it takes a full two hours to go a league. Then we'll return along the wall of the château under the window that once was Marie de Médicis's, where Madame will inevitably say, 'Can you believe that Queen Marie escaped through that, climbing down a forty-seven-foot drop!⁶ She, the mother of two princes and three princesses!' If that's to be my entertainment, I'd rather be punished by missing it every day, especially when my punishment is to stay with you and write such fascinating letters."

"But, Montalais! We can't ignore our duties."

"That's easy for you to say, sweetheart, when you're largely free of them. You have all the benefits of attending Court with none of the burdens and are more truly a maid of honor to Madame than I am, since you're here because Madame likes your father-in-law. You came into this sad château like a bird landing in a tower, sniffing the air, enjoying the flowers and pecking at the seeds, without the slightest duty to fulfill and no problems to solve. And you tell me we can't ignore our duties! In truth, my lazy lovely, what duties do *you* have other than to write to the handsome Raoul? And since you're not even doing that, it seems to me that you're the one who's being neglectful."

Louise took this seriously. She rested her chin on her hand and said earnestly, "Do you really have the heart to reproach me and accuse me of being the lucky one? You're the one with a future, since you're officially a member of this court. The king, if he marries, will summon Monsieur to attend him in Paris; you'll go to all the splendid festivals, and you'll see the king himself, who's said to be so handsome and charming."

"Moreover, I'll see Raoul, who attends on 'Monsieur le Prince,'"[7] Montalais added maliciously.

"Poor Raoul!" Louise sighed.

"Then now is the moment to write to him, *chère belle*. Come, start again with the famous *Monsieur Raoul* that so prettily decorated the sheet you tore up." Then she handed Louise the plume, and with a charming smile, nudged her hand, which quickly traced out the designated words.

"And now?" asked the younger girl.

"Now write what's on your mind, Louise," replied Montalais.

"How do you know something is on my mind?"

"I know some*body* is, and that's even better—or rather, worse."

"You think so, Montalais?"

"Louise, Louise, your blue eyes are as deep as the sea I saw at Boulogne last year. No, I'm wrong, for the sea is treacherous; your eyes are as deep as the azure sky above our heads."

"Well! Since you see so deeply into me through my eyes, tell me what I'm thinking, Montalais."

"First of all, you're not thinking *Monsieur Raoul*, you're thinking *My Dear Raoul.* . . . Oh, don't blush over so little a thing! *My Dear Raoul*, you'd like to say, *You beg me to write to you in Paris, where you are retained in the service of Monsieur le Prince. There you must be bored indeed to have to seek distraction by remembering a provincial girl.* . . ."

Louise rose and stopped her. "No, Montalais," she said, smiling. "That's not at all what I was thinking. Here, this is what I think." And she boldly took the plume and wrote with a firm hand the following words: "*I would have been very unhappy if your request for a remembrance from me hadn't been so warm. Everything here reminds me of our first years of friendship, so quickly passed and so sweetly spent that nothing could replace their charming memory in my heart."*

Montalais, who was watching the pen dance across the page, reading upside-down as it wrote, interrupted her with applause. "Now, that's more like it! Here is candor, here is style, here is true heart! Show those Parisians, my dear, that Blois is still the capital of our language."

"He knows that, to me, Blois has been heaven," said the younger woman.

"That's what I meant, and you write like an angel."

"I'll finish now, Montalais." And she continued: *"You say you think of me, Monsieur Raoul, and I thank you, but I'm not surprised. I know every beat of your heart, for our hearts beat together."*

"Whoa, there!" said Montalais. "Watch how you scatter your wool, my lamb, for there are wolves about."

Louise was about to reply when a horse's galloping hoofbeats resounded from under the château's gate.

"What's that?" said Montalais, rushing to the window. "A handsome cavalier, my faith!"

"Oh! It's Raoul!" cried Louise, who'd followed her friend, and then, turning pale, fell back beside her unfinished letter.

"Now there's an attentive lover, upon my word," said Montalais, "to arrive the moment he's beckoned."

"Come away from there, please!" whispered Louise urgently.

"Fah! He doesn't even know me. Let me go see what he's doing here."

II

The Messenger

Mademoiselle de Montalais was right: the young cavalier was quite handsome. He was a young man of twenty-four or twenty-five, tall and slender, graceful and comfortable in the charming military costume of the period. His tall cavalry boots enclosed a pair of feet that Mademoiselle de Montalais wouldn't have been ashamed of if she'd been a man. With one of his fine and sensitive hands he drew his horse to a halt in the center of the courtyard, and with the other he doffed the long-plumed hat that shaded his features, at once serious and naïve.

The guards, at the sound of the horse, awoke and quickly stood at attention. The young man let one of them approach his saddle-bow, bowed to him, and said, in a clear and precise voice easily heard at the window where the two young ladies were hiding, "A messenger for His Royal Highness."

"Ah ha!" the guard said, and called out, "Officer, a messenger!" However, this brave soldier knew quite well that no officer would respond, since the only one they had was in his rooms on the far, garden side of the château, so he hastened to add, "*Mon Gentilhomme*, the officer is on his rounds, but in his absence we'll inform Monsieur de Saint-Rémy,* the majordomo."

"Monsieur de Saint-Rémy!" repeated the cavalier, blushing.

"You know him?"

"But yes. Please request of him that my visit be announced to His Highness as soon as possible."

"The matter seems urgent," said the guard, as if to himself, but in hopes of obtaining an answer.

The messenger nodded.

"In that case," replied the guard, "I'll go find the majordomo myself."

Meanwhile, the young man dismounted, while the other soldiers admired the fine horse that had brought him. The first guard came back and asked, "Your pardon, Monsieur, but your name, if you please?"

"The Vicomte de Bragelonne, on the behalf of His Highness Monsieur le Prince de Condé."*

The soldier bowed respectfully, and as if the name of the victor of Rocroi and Lens[8] had given him wings, leapt back up the steps to the antechamber.

Monsieur de Bragelonne scarcely had time to tie his horse to the banister of the staircase before Monsieur de Saint-Rémy came running, out of breath, one hand supporting his bulging belly while the other pawed the air like a fisherman cleaving the waves with his oar. "What, Monsieur le Vicomte, you at Blois?" he cried. "How marvelous! Bonjour, Monsieur Raoul, bonjour!"

"A thousand regards, Monsieur de Saint-Rémy."

"How happy Mademoiselle de La Vall—I mean, how happy Madame de Saint-Rémy will be to see you. But come, His Royal Highness's breakfast, must it really be interrupted? Is the news serious?"

"Yes and no, Monsieur de Saint-Rémy. However, any delay might be an inconvenience to His Royal Highness."

"If that is so, we must make do, Monsieur le Vicomte. Come. Besides, Monsieur is in a charming mood today. So, then, you bring us news?"

"Big news, Monsieur de Saint-Rémy."

"And the news is good, I presume?"

"Very good."

"Then quickly, quickly!" said the worthy majordomo, straightening his clothing as he went along.

Raoul followed, hat in hand, a little nervous about the sound his spurs made as he marched through the solemn halls of the grand château.

As soon as he vanished into the palace, the window across the courtyard was reoccupied, and an animated whispering betrayed the emotions of the two young ladies. Soon they came to a decision, and one of the heads, the brunette, disappeared from the window, leaving the other on the balcony, half-concealed by the shrubbery, attentively watching, between the boughs, the porch where Monsieur de Bragelonne had entered the palace.

Meanwhile, the object of all this curiosity continued to follow in the footsteps of the majordomo. From ahead, the sound of servants' quick steps, the aroma of wine and meat, and a rattling of crystal and crockery informed him that they were nearing their destination.

The pages, valets, and officers gathered in the refectory's antechamber welcomed the newcomer with the region's proverbial politeness; some of them knew Raoul, and all guessed that he came from Paris. Indeed, his arrival momentarily suspended the service of breakfast, as a page who was pouring a drink for His Highness, hearing the jingle of spurs in the next room, turned like a distracted child, still pouring, not into the prince's glass, but onto the tablecloth.

Madame, less preoccupied than her glorious spouse, noticed the page's distraction. "Well!" she said.

Monsieur de Saint-Rémy took advantage of the interruption to poke his head around the door.

"Why are you disturbing us?" said Gaston, drawing toward himself a thick slice of one of the largest salmon ever to ascend the Loire and be caught between Paimbœuf and Saint-Nazaire.

"It's because a messenger has arrived from Paris. But I'm sure it can wait until after Monsieur's breakfast."

"From Paris!" the prince exclaimed, dropping his fork. "A messenger from Paris, you say? And who does this messenger come from?"

"From Monsieur le Prince," said the majordomo, using the common appellation for Monsieur de Condé.

"A messenger from Monsieur le Prince?" said Gaston anxiously, a tone that didn't escape the notice of his servants, redoubling their curiosity.

Monsieur might almost have thought himself back in the days of thrilling conspiracies, when the noise of a gate unlocking made one start, when every letter opened might betray a state secret, and every message introduce a dark and complicated intrigue. Perhaps the grand name of Monsieur le Prince roused in the halls of Blois a specter of this past.

Monsieur pushed back his plate. "Shall I ask the envoy to wait?" said Monsieur de Saint-Rémy.

A glance from Madame stiffened Gaston's resolve, and he replied, "No, on the contrary, have him enter at once. By the way, who is it?"

"A local gentleman, Monsieur le Vicomte de Bragelonne."

"Ah, yes, very good! Show him in, Saint-Rémy, show him in."

And once he had uttered these words with his usual gravity, Monsieur gave his servants a certain look, and all the pages, servers, and squires left their napkins, knives, and goblets and retreated rapidly into a side chamber. This little army marched off in two files as Raoul de Bragelonne, preceded by Monsieur de Saint-Rémy, entered the refectory. The brief moment of solitude afforded him by the servants' retreat had given Monseigneur Gaston time to assume an appropriately diplomatic expression. Rather than turn around, he waited for the majordomo to bring the messenger to a position in front of him.

Raoul stopped in the middle of the far side of the table, midway between Monsieur and Madame, where he bowed profoundly to Monsieur, bowed humbly to Madame, and then stood and waited for Monsieur to speak to him first.

The prince, for his part, waited until the outer doors were closed tightly, not turning to look, which would have been beneath him, but listening with both ears until he heard the click of the lock, which promised at least the appearance of privacy. Once the doors were closed, Gaston raised his eyes to the Vicomte de Bragelonne and said, "It seems you come from Paris, Monsieur?"

"This very moment, Monseigneur."

"How is the king doing?"

"His Majesty is in perfect health, Monseigneur."

"And my sister-in-law?"[9]

"Her Majesty the Queen Mother* still suffers from the complaint in her chest but has been somewhat better for the past month."

"They tell me you come on the behalf of Monsieur le Prince? Surely they were mistaken."

"No, Monseigneur. Monsieur le Prince has charged me with bringing Your Royal Highness this letter, and I am to await a reply." His voice trailed off in this final phrase; Raoul had been a little put off by his cold and formal reception.

The prince forgot that he was responsible for the messenger's confusion and bit his lip anxiously. He took the Prince de Condé's letter with a haggard look, opened it as he might a suspicious package, and then, to read it without anyone seeing his expression as he did so, turned away.

Madame observed all these maneuvers on the part of her august husband with an anxiety almost the equal of his own. Raoul, impassive and seemingly forgotten by his hosts, looked through the open window at the château garden and its crowded population of statues.

"Ah!" Monsieur said suddenly, with a radiant smile. "A charming letter from Monsieur le Prince, with a pleasant surprise! Here, Madame."

The table was too long for the prince's arm to reach the princess's hand, so Raoul hastened to act as intermediary, passing the letter along with a grace that charmed the princess and won the viscount a flattering thanks.

"You know the contents of this letter, do you not?" said Gaston to Raoul.

"Yes, Monseigneur; Monsieur le Prince gave me the message verbally at first, then upon reflection His Highness took up the plume."

"It's beautiful handwriting," said Madame, "but I can't make it out."

"Will you read it to Madame, Monsieur de Bragelonne?" said the prince.

"Yes, Monsieur, please read it."

Raoul began to read, with Monsieur giving him his full attention. The letter read as follows:

Monseigneur, the king is traveling to the Spanish frontier; from this you will understand that His Majesty's marriage is to be finalized. The king has done me the honor to appoint me Royal Quarter- master for this journey, and as I know how happy His Majesty would be to spend a day at Blois, I dare to ask Your Royal Highness for permission to include his château on the itinerary.

However, in the unforeseen event that this request might cause Your Royal Highness any inconvenience, I beg you to report it to me by the messenger I have sent, one of my gentlemen named the Vicomte de Bragelonne. My itinerary will depend upon the decision of Your Royal Highness, as we could choose instead to travel by way of Vendôme or Romorantin. I hope that Your Royal Highness will take my request in good part as an expression of my boundless devotion and my desire to please him.

"Why, nothing could be more gracious," said Madame, after carefully watching her husband's expression during the reading of this letter. "The king, here!" she exclaimed, perhaps a bit louder than was consistent with the demands of secrecy.

"Monsieur," said His Highness, "you will thank Monsieur le Prince de Condé and convey my gratitude for the pleasure he gives me." Raoul bowed. "On what day will His Majesty arrive?" the prince continued.

"The king, Monseigneur, will in all probability arrive tonight."

"Tonight! But how would he have known it if my answer had been other than positive?"

"I'd been assigned, Monseigneur, to hasten back to Beaugency and give a courier an order to countermand the march, which he would bear to Monsieur le Prince."

"His Majesty is at Orléans, then?"

"Closer than that, Monseigneur; His Majesty must even now be arriving at Meung."

"The Court accompanies him?"

"Yes, Monseigneur."

"By the way, I forgot to ask for news of Monsieur le Cardinal."

"His Eminence appears to be in good health, Monseigneur."

"His nieces accompany him, no doubt?"

"No, Monseigneur; His Eminence ordered Mesdemoiselles de Mancini to depart for Brouage. They are following the left bank of the Loire while the Court proceeds along the right bank."

"What? Mademoiselle Marie de Mancini* has left the Court?" asked Monsieur, whose reserve was beginning to fray.

"*Especially* Mademoiselle Marie de Mancini," replied Raoul discreetly.

A fugitive smile, a brief vestige of his old spirit of intrigue, briefly lit the prince's pale cheeks. "Thank you, Monsieur de Bragelonne," said Gaston. "If you do not wish to render the prince the commission with which I charge you, which is to tell him that I am very pleased with his messenger, I will do so myself."

Raoul bowed to thank Monsieur for the honor the prince did him.

Monsieur gestured to Madame, who rang a bell placed to her right. Instantly Monsieur de Saint-Rémy came in and the refectory was suddenly filled with people.

"Messieurs," said the prince, "His Majesty does me the honor to spend a day at Blois. I trust that my nephew the king will have no cause to regret the favor he shows to this house."

"Long live the king!" cried every member of Monsieur's household, Monsieur de Saint-Rémy louder than anyone.

Gaston's head drooped in sudden sadness; all his life he'd heard, or rather suffered through, shouts of "Long live the king!" cried out for another. For a while he'd been spared that cry, but now a younger, more dynamic, and more brilliant reign had begun, and the painful provocation was renewed.

Madame understood the pain in his sad and fearful heart; she rose from the table and Monsieur imitated her mechanically, while all the servants, like bees buzzing around a hive, surrounded Raoul and plied him with questions.

Madame saw this activity and beckoned to Monsieur de Saint-Rémy. "Now is not the time to talk, but to work," she said in the tone of an angry housewife.

Saint-Rémy hastened to break up the circle of servants around Raoul so that he could escape to the antechamber. "You will attend to this gentleman's needs, I hope," said Madame to Monsieur de Saint-Rémy.

The worthy man immediately ran to catch up with Raoul. "Madame has charged me with seeing to your refreshment," he said. "I'll assign a room for you here in the château."

"Thank you, Monsieur de Saint-Rémy," replied Bragelonne, "but you know how eagerly I wish to go pay my respects to Monsieur le Comte de La Fère,* my father."

"Quite so, quite so, Monsieur Raoul, and give him at the same time my most humble regards, I beg you."

Raoul reassured the old gentleman and went on his way. As he was passing out the gate, leading his horse by the bridle, a soft voice called from the gloom of a shaded path, "Monsieur Raoul!"

The young man turned in surprise and saw a brown-haired young woman who was pressing a finger to her lips and holding out her other hand. This young lady was completely unknown to him.

III

The Interview

Raoul took a step toward the young woman who beckoned to him, and then said, "But my horse, Madame."

"True, you can't bring the horse. There's a shed just outside the courtyard; tie your horse in there and hurry back."

"I obey, Madame."

It took scarcely a minute for Raoul to follow her recommendation and return to her. In the shadows under the vines he saw his mysterious guide waiting in a doorway that opened onto the foot of a winding staircase. "Are you brave enough to follow me, Monsieur Knight Errant?" asked the young woman, laughing at Raoul's momentary hesitation.

He replied by darting into the shadows to follow her up the stairs. They climbed three flights, he right behind her, brushing with outstretched hands, as he searched for a banister, a wide silk dress that grazed both sides of the staircase. When Raoul made a false step at a landing his guide whispered, "Hush!" and held out a soft and perfumed hand to him.

"One could climb this way to the château's tallest tower without feeling fatigue," said Raoul.

"Which means, Monsieur, that though weary from your ride, you are much intrigued but a bit uneasy. Never mind that, we've arrived."

The young woman pushed open a door, the darkened staircase was flooded with light, and Raoul saw that he stood at the top of the stairs. His guide continued, so he followed her; she entered a room, and he went in right behind her. As soon as he was fairly in the trap, he heard a loud cry, turned and saw near him, hands clasped, eyes closed, the beautiful blond young woman with blue eyes and ivory shoulders, who'd just called out "Raoul!"

He saw her and read in her eyes so much love and so much happiness that he fell to his knees in the center of the room, murmuring "Louise."

"Ah, Montalais, Montalais!" she sighed. "It's a great sin to deceive me so."

"I? Have I deceived you?"

"Yes, you told me you'd go down to learn the news, and then here you bring monsieur back up with you."

"It had to be done. How else could he receive the letter you wrote to him?"

And she pointed to the letter that was still on the table. Raoul took a step toward it; Louise, though her first step was strangely hesitant, was faster, and reached out a hand to stop him. Raoul met this hand, warm and trembling, took it in his own, and brought it so respectfully to his lips, it was as if he placed a sigh upon it rather than a kiss.

Meanwhile, Mademoiselle de Montalais took up the letter, folded it carefully, as women do, with three folds, and slipped it between her breasts. "Don't worry, Louise," she said. "Monsieur would no more take it from here than the late King Louis XIII would take her billet-doux from the bodice of Mademoiselle de Hautefort."[10]

Raoul blushed so at the sight of the young ladies' smiles, he didn't even notice that Louise's hand was still in his.

"There!" said Montalais. "You've forgiven me, Louise, for having brought monsieur to you, and monsieur forgives me for leading him to see mademoiselle. Now that peace is concluded, let's talk like old friends. Present me, Louise, to Monsieur de Bragelonne."

"Monsieur le Vicomte," said Louise, with her serious grace and frank smile, "I have the honor to introduce you to Mademoiselle Aure de Montalais, Maid of Honor to Her Highness Madame, and moreover, my friend—my *excellent* friend."

Raoul bowed ceremoniously. "And me, Louise," he said. "Won't you introduce me to mademoiselle as well?"

"Oh, she knows you! She knows everything!"

This last word made Montalais laugh and Raoul sigh with happiness, as he'd interpreted it to mean: *She knows all about our love.*

"The courtesies are complete, Monsieur le Vicomte," said Montalais. "Here's an armchair; sit and quickly bring us up to date with your news."

"Mademoiselle, it's no longer a secret: the king, on his way to Poitiers, will stop at Blois to visit His Royal Highness."

"The king, here!" cried Montalais, clapping her hands. "We'll see the Court! Can you imagine it, Louise? The real Court of Paris! But, *mon Dieu*—when will they arrive, Monsieur?"

"Perhaps as soon as tonight, Mademoiselle; certainly, no later than tomorrow."

Montalais made an angry gesture. "No time to get ready! No time to update a single dress! We live here in the past like Poles![11] We'll look like we stepped out of portraits from King Henri's reign. Ah, Monsieur, what terrible news you bring!"

"Mesdemoiselles, you will still be beautiful."

"Cold comfort! Yes, we'll still be beautiful, because Nature has made us passable, but we'll also be ridiculous, because fashion has left us behind. *Hélas!* Ridiculous! To think that I'll be mocked!"

"By who?" said Louise, naïvely.

"By who? Are you kidding, *ma chère?* What kind of a question is that? By everyone! By the courtiers, by the nobles, and above all—by the king!"

"Pardon me, dear friend, but as everyone here is used to seeing us as we are . . ."

"True, but that won't last, and then we'll be ridiculous, even for Blois. Because we're going to see the Parisian fashions while wearing the clothes of Blois, and then we'll find *ourselves* ridiculous. It's hopeless!"

"Take comfort in who you are, Mademoiselle."

"There's truth. Fah! If they find me not to their taste, that's their loss!" said Montalais philosophically.

"Small chance of that," said Raoul, faithful to his system of general gallantry.

"Thank you, Monsieur le Vicomte. So, you say the king comes to Blois?"

"With all his Court."

"Including Mesdemoiselles de Mancini, of course."

"No, decidedly not."

"But isn't it said that the king can't bear to be apart from Mademoiselle Marie?"

"The king will have to bear it, Mademoiselle. The cardinal has decided to exile his nieces to Brouage."

"Him! That hypocrite!"

"Hush!" said Louise, putting a finger to her rosy lips.

"Fah! No one can hear me. I say that old Mazarino Mazarini is a hypocrite who's out to make his niece the Queen of France."

"On the contrary, Mademoiselle, the cardinal has negotiated for His Majesty to marry the Infanta Maria Theresa."

Montalais looked Raoul in the eye and said, "Do you Parisians really believe in such fables? Come, we know better than that in Blois."

"Mademoiselle, once the marriage contract is finalized between Don Luis de Haro[12] and His Eminence, and the king goes beyond Poitiers to the Spanish frontier, you'll see that the childhood games are done."

"*Ah çà!* But the king is still the king, isn't he?"

"No doubt about it, Mademoiselle—but the cardinal is the cardinal."

"Is he not a man, then, the king? Doesn't he love Marie de Mancini?"

"He adores her."

"Well, then—he'll marry her. We'll have a war with Spain, Monsieur Mazarin will spend some of the millions he's hidden away, our gentlemen will perform feats of heroism against the proud Castilians, many of them will return to us to be crowned with laurels, and we shall re-crown them with myrtles.[13] And that's politics as I understand it."

"You're a madwoman, Montalais," said Louise, "as drawn to hyperbole as a moth is to flames."

"Louise, you are so restrained you'll never really fall in love."

"Oh, Montalais!" said Louise in tender reproach. "Consider this: the queen mother wishes her son to marry the infanta. Do you want the king to disobey his mother? Could one with a heart as royal as his set a bad example? When parents forbid love, love must be banished!"

And Louise sighed, while Raoul looked down sadly.

But Montalais laughed. "As for me, I have no parents!"

After her sigh, which revealed so much pain, Louise said, "You've no doubt already inquired after the health of Monsieur le Comte de La Fère."

"No, Mademoiselle," Raoul replied, "I've not yet seen my father; I was on my way to his house when Mademoiselle de Montalais was so good as to stop me. I hope the count is doing well—you haven't heard otherwise, have you?"

"Not at all, Monsieur Raoul, not at all, thank God!"

Then a silence ensued, while two souls in perfect harmony thought the same thoughts without even exchanging a glance.

Montalais suddenly said, "My God! Somebody's coming up the stairs."

"Who can it be?" said Louise, rising anxiously.

"Mesdemoiselles, I'm at fault here, my presence is bound to get you in trouble," stammered Raoul, flustered.

"It's a heavy footstep," said Louise.

"Ah!" said Montalais. "If it's only Monsieur Malicorne,* we've nothing to fear."

Louise and Raoul looked at each other, as if asking who Monsieur Malicorne could be.

"Don't worry," continued Montalais. "He's not the jealous type."

"But, Mademoiselle . . ." said Raoul.

"Oh, I know. But he's just as discreet as I am."

"*Mon Dieu!*" cried Louise, who'd pressed her ear to the half-open door. "Those are my mother's footsteps!"

"Madame de Saint-Rémy! Where can I hide?" exclaimed Raoul, tugging at the sleeve of Montalais, who seemed stunned.

"You're right, Louise," she said, shaking her head, "I recognize the sound of those barges—it's your worthy mother! Monsieur le Vicomte, it's a shame that the window opens on a sheer drop of fifty feet." Raoul glanced at the window as if he might try it anyway, but Louise grabbed his arm and stopped him.

"*Ah çà!* Am I crazy?" said Montalais. "Don't I have a big armoire to hold my ceremonial dresses? It's made to order for this kind of emergency!"

It was time, as Madame de Saint-Rémy was climbing more quickly than usual. She arrived on the landing just as Montalais, in a scene right out of the theater, shut the armoire door on Raoul and leaned against it.

"Ah!" said Madame de Saint-Rémy. "Are you here too, Louise?"

"Yes, Madame," she replied, as pale as if accused of a heinous crime.

"Good! Just as well!"

"Have a seat, Madame," said Montalais, offering Madame de Saint-Rémy an armchair, while facing it away from the armoire.

"Thank you, Mademoiselle Aure." Then, to Louise, "Now go, my child, and be quick."

"Where do you want me to go, Madame?"

"Why, home—don't you want to prepare?"

"Prepare? For what?" said Montalais, pretending surprise, and hoping to prevent Louise from saying something foolish.

"You haven't heard the news?" said Madame de Saint-Rémy.

"What news, Madame, could two girls hear up in this pigeon coop?"

"What? You haven't spoken to anyone?"

"Madame, you're speaking in riddles, and it's killing us," said Montalais, desperate to distract the lady from Louise, who was white as a sheet. At last Montalais caught a wide-eyed glance from her friend, one of those looks that would awaken a stone, as Louise pointed a trembling figure at where Raoul's treacherous hat sat upon the table. Montalais darted forward, seized the hat with her left hand and passed it behind her to her right, holding it behind her back.

"Well!" said Madame de Saint-Rémy. "A courier has come, announcing the imminent arrival of the king. So, Mesdemoiselles, it's all about looking your best!"

"Quickly! Quickly!" said Montalais. "Follow Madame your mother, Louise, while I see to my dress."

Louise arose, her mother took her by the hand and hurried her to the landing. "Come," she said, and then added in a lower voice, "and when I forbid you to visit Montalais, why do I find you here?"

"Madame, she's my friend. Besides, I'd only just arrived."

"You didn't catch her concealing someone?"

"Madame!"

"I saw that man's hat, yes I did, and I say to you, she's a hussy and a scamp!"

"Really, Madame!" cried Louise.

"It's that rascal Malicorne! A maid of honor to consort with such as he . . . fie!"

And their voices faded into the depths of the staircase.

Montalais hadn't lost a word of this exchange, which had been projected up the stairs as if by a trumpet. She shrugged her shoulders, and seeing that Raoul, who'd come out of hiding, had heard it as well, she said, "Poor Montalais, the victim of friendship! And poor Malicorne, the victim of love!"

She paused when she saw the tragicomic face of Raoul, who was bewildered by encountering so many secrets in a single day. "Mademoiselle," he said, "how can I repay you for your kindness?"

"We'll settle our accounts another day, Monsieur de Bragelonne," she replied. "For the moment, you'd better get moving, as Madame de Saint-Rémy is far from lenient, and a word from her in the wrong place could send us an inconvenient visitor. Adieu!"

"But Louise . . . how will I know . . . ?"

"Go! Go! King Louis XI knew what he was doing when he invented the postal service."

"*Hélas!*" said Raoul.

"And aren't I here, who are better than any postman in the realm? Return to your horse, so that if Madame de Saint-Rémy comes back up to lecture me, she won't find you here."

"She'd tell my father, wouldn't she?" murmured Raoul.

"And then you'd be scolded. Ah, Viscount, it's clear you come from Court; you're as timid as the king. *Peste!* At Blois, we know better than to ask for a father's consent to follow our passions. Ask Malicorne."

And with these words, the brash young woman pushed Raoul out the door by the shoulders. The latter rushed down to the shed, found his horse, jumped into the saddle and set off as if all eight of Monsieur's guards were on his heels.

IV

Father and Son

Raoul followed the familiar road, so dear to his memory, that led from Blois to the estate of the Comte de La Fère.[14] The reader needs no new description of this dwelling, having visited it with us before. But since our last visit the walls had assumed a grayer hue and the bricks a more harmonious copper tone, while the trees had grown, those that had formerly stretched slender arms over the hedges now towering above them, rounded, bushy, luxuriant, and bearing a lush crop of flowers or fruit for the passerby.

Raoul saw in the distance the high roof with its two small turrets, the dovecote among the elms, and around that cone of bricks the flocks of pigeons ever circling without being able to leave it, like the sweet memories that soar around a serene soul. As he approached, he heard the sound of pulleys groaning under the weight of heavy buckets, and seemed as well to hear the melancholy echoing of water pouring back into the well, a sad and solemn noise that attracts the ear of the child and the dreamy poet alike, a sound the English call *splash*, the Arab poets call *gasgachau*, but which the French, who think themselves poets, describe only with the phrase "the sound of water falling into water."

It was more than a year since Raoul had been to see his father, having spent that time as a retainer of Monsieur le Prince. In fact, after the turmoil of the Fronde, of which we formerly attempted to recount the first phases,[15] Louis de Condé had made a frank and solemn reconciliation with the Court.[16] During the entire time the prince had been at odds with the king, the prince, who had long been fond of Bragelonne, had offered him every inducement to join him that might dazzle a young man. But the Comte de La Fère, ever faithful to his principles of loyalty to the monarchy, as he'd expounded one day to his son in the vaults of Saint-Denis,[17] had refused on behalf of his son all the prince's offers.

Moreover, instead of following Monsieur de Condé into rebellion, the viscount had attached himself to Monsieur de Turenne,[18] who fought for the king. Then when Monsieur de Turenne, in his turn, had seemed to abandon the king's cause, he had left Turenne as he had left Condé. The result of this consistent line of conduct was that, though Turenne and Condé had never been victorious except when commanding under the king's colors, Raoul, young as he was, had ten victorious royal battles to his credit, and not a single rebellious defeat to tarnish his courage and weigh on his conscience. Thus Raoul, by following his father's wishes, had stubbornly followed the fortunes of King Louis XIV, despite all the factional infighting that was endemic and, one might almost say, inevitable to the period.

Monsieur de Condé, upon being returned to favor, had taken advantage of the royal amnesty to ask for the restoration of the many rights and privileges he'd previously enjoyed, including the service of Raoul. The Comte de La Fère, showing his usual good sense and wisdom, had immediately sent Raoul back to the Prince de Condé.

A year had passed since the last meeting of the father and son, during which a few letters had consoled, though not cured, the pain of separation. As we've seen, Raoul had also left in Blois an attachment other than his filial love. But to be fair, without the intervention of chance and of Mademoiselle de Montalais, those two demons of temptation, Raoul, his mission accomplished, would have immediately galloped toward his father's house—not without turning his head to look behind, however, though he wouldn't have stopped even if he'd seen Louise holding out her arms.

The first part of the ride Raoul spent missing the lover he'd just left, while the second half was spent looking forward to the father's love he'd find when he arrived, which couldn't come soon enough for him. Raoul found the garden gate open and rode right up the path, without paying any attention to the outraged gestures of an old man wearing a purple wool jerkin and a large hat of faded velvet. This old servant, who'd been weeding a bed of daisies and dwarf roses, was indignant at seeing a horse plow up his freshly raked path, growling out a surly "Hrm!" that made the rider turn his head. Then came a sudden change, for the man, having seen Raoul's face, straightened up and began to run toward the house, shouting for joy.

Raoul stopped at the stable, handed his horse to a young lackey, and dashed up the steps with an ardor that would have delighted his father's heart. He crossed the foyer, the dining room, and the parlor without meeting anyone; at last, arriving at the Comte de La Fère's door, he knocked impatiently and then went in almost without waiting for the word, "Enter!" spoken in a resonant voice both soft and serious.

The count was seated at a table covered with papers and books. He was still the noble and handsome gentleman of old, but time had given his nobility and features a more solemn and distinguished character. A brow broad and smooth below long hair now more white than black; a piercing yet gentle eye beneath the lashes of a much younger man; a slender, scarcely salted mustache framing lips strong but delicate, as if they'd never been strained by mortal passions; a straight and supple figure; and an irreproachable hand—he was still that illustrious gentlemen whom so many eminent men had praised under the name of Athos.

He was occupied in correcting the pages of a manuscript in a notebook, entirely filled with his handwriting.[19] Raoul gripped his father by the shoulders and kissed him so quickly and tenderly that the count had neither the strength nor the speed to avoid it, nor to control his upwelling of paternal emotion. "You, here, Raoul?" he said. "How is it possible?"

"Oh, Monsieur, what joy it is to see you again!"

"You didn't answer me, Viscount. Has a holiday brought you to Blois, or has something gone wrong in Paris?"

"No, Monsieur, thank God!" said Raoul, his natural calm returning. "Nothing has happened but happy events; the king is getting married, as I had the honor to tell you in my last letter, and is on his way to Spain. His Majesty will stop at Blois."

"To visit Monsieur?"

"Yes, Monsieur le Comte. And to make sure His Highness wasn't taken by surprise, and to do him honor, Monsieur le Prince sent me on ahead to warn him to prepare lodgings."

"You saw Monsieur?" the count asked eagerly.

"I had that honor."

"At his château?"

"Yes, Monsieur," replied Raoul, lowering his eyes, as he began to suspect the count's interrogation had another end than curiosity.

"Ah, really, Viscount! My congratulations."

Raoul bowed.

"But did you see anyone else at Blois?"

"Monsieur, I saw Her Royal Highness Madame."

"Excellent. But it's not of Madame that I speak."

Raoul blushed deeply but said nothing.

"Didn't you hear my question, Monsieur le Vicomte?" continued Monsieur de La Fère without hardening his voice, but with a sharper look in his eye.

"I understood you perfectly, Monsieur," Raoul replied, "and if I pause to form my answer, it's not because I'm looking for a lie—as you know, Monsieur."

"I know you never lie. But I'm surprised that it takes you this long to tell me yes or no."

"It's not that I don't understand you, but that I understand you all too well . . . and that you won't be pleased by what I have to tell you. I'm sure you won't like it, Monsieur le Comte, but I also saw . . ."

"Mademoiselle de La Vallière, yes?"

"And it's about her that you wish to speak, as well I know, Monsieur le Comte," Raoul said, humbly and gently.

"And I'm asking if you've seen her."

"Monsieur, I was completely ignorant when I entered the château that Mademoiselle de La Vallière might be there; it was only upon returning toward you, after completing my mission, that chance brought us face to face. I then had the honor to pay her my respects."

"What name do you give the chance that brought you to meet Mademoiselle de La Vallière?"

"Mademoiselle de Montalais, Monsieur."

"Who is Mademoiselle de Montalais?"

"A young person I didn't know and had never seen before. She's a maid of honor to Madame."

"Monsieur le Vicomte, I will go no further in my interrogation, and I reproach myself for having gone so far. I asked you to avoid Mademoiselle de La Vallière and to see her only with my permission. Oh, I know that what you've said is true, and you didn't seek her out! Chance caused the injury, and I won't accuse you of it. I will just content myself with a reminder of what I've already said about this young lady. I have nothing to reproach her with, as God is my witness, but it does not accord with my plans for you to permit you to visit her. I beg you once more, Raoul, to hear me on this."

It was clear from the expression of Raoul's eyes, usually so bright and clear, that he was troubled by this speech.

"Now, my son," continued the count, with his sweet smile and in his usual tone, "let's talk about something else. Must you hurry back to your service?"

"No, Monsieur, I have nothing else to do today other than to spend it with you. The prince, fortunately, made that my only other mission, and I could wish nothing more."

"The king is doing well?"

"Perfectly so."

"And Monsieur le Prince also?"

"As always, Monsieur."

The count forgot to inquire after Mazarin—but that was an old habit.

"Well, Raoul! Since you have no other duty but me, you shall have my entire day. Now, embrace me. And again! How fine to have you at home,

Viscount. Ah, here is good old Grimaud![20] Come, Grimaud, Monsieur le Vicomte wants to embrace you as well."

The old man didn't wait to make him repeat it; he ran to Raoul with open arms, and Raoul met him halfway.

"And now, Raoul, let's take a turn around the gardens. Then you'll see how I've improved your rooms for the holidays, and while I show you our preparations for fall, and introduce you to our two new horses, you can give me the news of our friends in Paris."

The count closed his notebook, took the young man by the arm, and led him to the gardens.

Grimaud gazed sadly at Raoul, whose head now nearly grazed the top of the doorway, and, fingering his white pointed goatee, he blinked damply and muttered, "All grown up!"

V

Which Speaks of Cropoli and Cropole
and of a Great Unknown Painter

While the Comte de La Fère showed Raoul his new outbuildings and the new horses in his stable, our readers will allow us to draw them back to the town of Blois to witness an unaccustomed flurry of activity in the city. The impact of the news brought by Raoul was especially felt in the town's inns.

Indeed, the king of France and his Court coming to Blois, that is to say, a hundred cavaliers, ten carriages, two hundred horses, as many valets as masters—where would everyone stay, in addition to all the local gentry who would arrive in the next two to three hours as soon as the news rippled and spread, like the widening waves from a stone thrown into the waters of a quiet lake?

Blois, so peaceful in the morning, as we've seen, the quietest pond in the world, at the news of the royal visit suddenly was abuzz with tumult and turmoil. All the château's servants, at the orders of their officers, went out into the city to fetch provisions, and ten couriers on horseback rode to the reserves of Chambord to seek game, to the fisheries of Beuvron for seafood, and to the gardens of Cheverny for flowers and fruit. Out from trunks and wardrobes came silken tapestries and chandeliers with gilded chains; an army of the poor swept the courtyards and washed the stone facings, while their wives stalked the meadows beyond the Loire to collect greenery and wildflowers.

The city, to be as groomed as the château, scrubbed itself with brushes, brooms, and water. The gutters in the upper town, swollen by the runoff, became rivers in the lower town, and the pavement, which it must be said was often quite muddy, was washed clean and gleamed in the sunlight.

Then musical instruments were brought out, and drawers of décor were emptied; merchants did a brisk business in wax polish, ribbons, and sword-knots, while the housewives laid in provisions of bread, meat, and spices. Soon the citizens, their houses stuffed enough to survive a siege, were donning holiday garb and heading to the city gate, hoping to be the first to see and announce the royal procession. They knew the king wouldn't arrive before evening, or even the next morning—but what is anticipation but a kind of madness, and what is madness if not an ecstasy of hope?

In the lower town, barely a hundred paces from the Hall of the Estates General, between the promenade and the château, in a rather pretty street that was then called Rue Vieille and was indeed very old, stood a venerable edifice, squat, broad, and with peaked gables, endowed with three windows at the street level, two on the next floor, and a small bull's-eye window on the top. On the side of this old triangle had recently been built a new parallelogram, which in accord with the practices of the time bulged right out into the street. Though the street was narrowed by a quarter, the house was nearly doubled, and wasn't that sufficient excuse?

Local tradition held that in the time of Henri III this gabled house had been the residence of a Councilor of State whom Queen Catherine had come to visit—some said for advice, and some said to strangle him. Whatever the reason, no one doubted the good lady had crossed the house's threshold with her royal foot.

After the councilor's death, by natural causes or by strangulation, the house had been sold, then abandoned and isolated from the other houses on the street. It wasn't until the middle of the reign of Louis XIII that an Italian named Cropoli, escaped from the kitchens of Marshal d'Ancre,[21] had taken the house. There he'd founded a small inn that served a macaroni so delicious that people came from leagues away to eat it or fetch it home.

The fame of the inn was further spread by the fact that Queen Marie de Médicis, when a prisoner in the château, used to send for its cooking. On the very day that she escaped from the famous high window, she left behind on her table a plate of the celebrated macaroni, tasted only by the royal mouth.

The double celebrity of this triangular house, for the strangulation and the macaroni, had given its owner Cropoli the idea of dubbing his inn with a pompous name. His own wouldn't do, as Italian names weren't well regarded at the time, and he didn't wish to draw attention to his hoarded wealth, so carefully hidden. In 1643, after the death of King Louis XIII, when he felt himself approaching the end of his own life, he sent for his son, a young man for whom he had high hopes. With tears in his eyes, he advised him to guard carefully the secret recipe of the famous macaroni, to make his name more French, to marry a Frenchwoman, and, when the political horizon had cleared of its former clouds, to have a neighboring artisan carve out a fine sign, upon which a famous artist he would name would paint a portrait of the two queens above the words, "The Médicis."

The worthy Cropoli, after delivering this advice, had only enough strength left to point his heir toward a brick in the chimney behind which he'd hidden a thousand ten-franc coins, and then he expired. The younger Cropoli, a man of heart, bore his loss with resignation and his gain without arrogance. He began familiarizing his customers and neighbors with the practice of not pronouncing his name's final syllable until eventually he was known as Monsieur Cropole, which as a name is tolerably French. In due time he married, giving his hand to a little French girl whom he loved, and whose parents provided a suitable dowry once he'd shown them what was behind the brick in the chimney.

The first two points concluded, Monsieur Cropole sought for the artist who was to paint the promised sign. This painter was soon found: he was an old Italian of the school of Raphael and the Caracci,[22] but it was a school he'd never graduated. He called himself a painter in the Venetian style, doubtless because he was so fond of color. His works looked good at a hundred paces but not at close range, and had never pleased the bourgeois—in fact, he'd never sold a one. But he boasted of having painted a bathroom for Madame la Maréchale d'Ancre,[23] though it had burned during the disaster of the marshal's downfall, and he was bitter at the loss.

The elder Cropoli, as a compatriot, had been indulgent toward this Pittrino, which was the name of the artist. Perhaps he had seen the lost and lamented bathroom. He had so much esteem and even friendship for Pittrino that he'd taken him into his home. Pittrino, grateful for a roof over his head and macaroni in his belly, had helped to spread the reputation of the savory noodles and was reckoned thereby to have done great service to the house of Cropoli.

As he grew older, Pittrino became as attached to the son as he had been to the father, and became a sort of fixture in the house, thanks he believed to his honest integrity, his acknowledged sobriety, his proverbial chastity, and a thousand other virtues that he enumerated at length, and which gave him an eternal place in the home with rights of authority over the servants. Besides, he'd established himself as the arbiter of the macaroni, maintaining the pure devotion to the ancient tradition, and wouldn't allow one peppercorn too many or one atom of parmesan too little in the recipe.

His joy was very great on the day when the younger Cropole told him of the promised sign. He was soon seen rummaging through an old box, from which he drew some brushes nibbled a bit by rodents but still passable, some dried-up colors in leather pouches, a bottle of linseed oil, and a palette that had once belonged to Bronzino,[24] that "god among painters," as the transalpine artist had called him in his once-youthful enthusiasm.

Pittrino was excited and rejuvenated by his return to painting. As Raphael had done, he changed his style to suit the subject, and painted in the manner of Albani[25] two partially clad goddesses rather than two queens. Thanks to Pittrino's effusive new style, these illustrious ladies so nobly graced the sign, where they posed as Anacreontic sirens[26] among a riot of lilies and roses, that the town's principal alderman, when invited into Cropole's parlor to view the proposed emblem, immediately declared that the two beauties were entirely too provocative to hang in the public view of passersby.

"His Royal Highness Monsieur," said the alderman to Pittrino, "who does us the honor to reside in our town, would not be pleased to see his mother in such a state of undress and would clap you in the royal dungeons, for he's not always tender of heart, our glorious prince. Either remove these two sirens or change the title, or I must forbid the exhibition of this sign. This is for your own good, Maître Cropole, and yours as well, Signor Pittrino."

What could one say to that? Cropole thanked the alderman for his consideration and advice. But Pittrino was stricken with gloom and disappointment, for he saw which way things were going. The visitor was barely gone before Cropole, crossing his arms, said, "Well, Signor, what shall we do?"

"We'll have to change the title," said Pittrino sadly. "I have some deep charcoal black that will cover the old name completely, and we can replace 'The Médicis' with 'The Nymphs' or 'The Sirens,' whichever you like."

"But no," said Cropole. "That would go against my father's wishes. My father desired . . ."

"He desired the queens' portraits most of all," said Pittrino.

"He insisted on the title," said Cropole.

"The proof that the portraits were of prime importance was his insistence that they resemble their models, and they do," replied Pittrino.

"Maybe so, but who would recognize them without the title? Nowadays the memory of the citizens of Blois is vague on their appearance. Who would know it was Catherine and Marie without the title of 'The Médicis'?"

"But what about my portraits?" said Pittrino desperately, for deep down he knew Cropole was right. "What's to become of the fruit of my artistic labors?"

"I don't want to go to jail or see you thrown in the dungeons."

"Erase 'The Médicis,' I beg you," said Pittrino.

"No," said Cropole firmly. "But I have an idea, a sublime idea . . . your artistry will appear, and so will my title. Doesn't *médicis* mean 'doctor' in Italian?"

"Yes, in the plural."

"Then we'll get another signboard from our neighbor, you'll paint six doctors on it, and below you'll write 'The Médicis'—which will be an amusing play on words."

"Six doctors? Impossible! What about the composition?" cried Pittrino.

"That part's up to you, but since that's what I want, that's what we'll have. Enough—my macaroni's burning."

This was incontestable, so Pittrino obeyed. He composed the sign with the six doctors and the designated title, the alderman approved of it, and the sign was well received by the citizenry. It just proved, Pittrino said, that poetry was wasted on the bourgeois. Cropole, to console the painter and acknowledge the artistry of the original, hung the image of the nymphs in his bedroom, which made Madame Cropole blush beneath them every night while undressing.

That was where the gabled house got its sign, and how, making its fortune, the Inn of The Médicis was able to expand in the manner described. And that was how Blois happened to have a hostelry of that name, with a painter-in-residence named Pittrino.

VI

The Stranger

Established thus on a firm foundation and advertised by a bold sign, the inn of Maître Cropole enjoyed a respectable prosperity. It's not that Cropole was likely to earn a vast fortune, but he might in time hope to double the thousand louis d'or bequeathed to him by his father, make another thousand by the sale of his house and goods, and retire as a free citizen of the town.

Cropole was eager for profit and welcomed the news of the arrival of King Louis XIV. He, his wife, Pittrino, and two scullions immediately laid their hands on all the inhabitants of the dovecote, the coop, and the hutches, so that the kitchen yard of the Hôtellerie des Médicis resounded with as many cries and lamentations as Rama.

At the time, Cropole had only one lodger. He was a man of scarcely thirty, handsome, tall, austere, or rather melancholy in attitude and appearance. He was dressed in a black velvet coat with buttons of jet; a white collar, as simple as that worn by the Puritans, brought out the fair and youthful tint of his neck; while a slight blond mustache barely covered a quivering and disdainful lip. When he spoke to people he looked them in the eye, not to intimidate, but with brutal candor, so that the brilliance of his blue eyes became so hard to bear that the other's gaze often fell before his, as the weaker sword does in single combat. At that time when men, though created equal by God, were divided by prejudice into two castes, the gentleman and the commoner, as they really divide into two races, the black and the white[27]—at that time, as we say, the man whose portrait we just sketched could not fail to be taken for a gentleman, and of the best breeding. One need only look at his hands, long, tapered, and pale, with every muscle and vein visible beneath the skin at the slightest movement, the fingers blushing at the slightest tension.

This gentleman had arrived at Cropole's inn alone. He had taken without hesitation, without even thinking about it, the best rooms in the inn, which the innkeeper had shown him right away, in the service of what some would call reprehensible greed and others just good business. It certainly showed that Cropole was a physiognomist[28] who could size people up at first glance.

These rooms occupied the upstairs front of the old triangular house: a large living room lit by two windows on the first floor up, a small room next to it, and another one above. Since his arrival, the gentleman had scarcely touched the meal that had been served to him the night before. He had said just a few words to his host to warn him that he awaited a traveler named Parry, and that when he arrived the host should show him up. Then he'd kept so quietly to himself that Cropole was almost offended, as he preferred guests who were good company.

This gentleman had risen early on the morning of the day this story began and placed himself in the window of his drawing room, sitting on the sill and leaning on the banister of the balcony, watching both sides of the street sadly and stubbornly, doubtless awaiting the arrival of the traveler he'd mentioned to his host. He had watched the passing of Monsieur's little cortege returning from the hunt, then had seemed to savor the town's sleepy tranquility as he settled into his waiting.

Suddenly there came the commotion of the poor folk hastening out to the meadows, of couriers departing, of washers scrubbing the pavement, of servants hurrying from the château, the rush of chattering shop boys, the clatter of carts, of hairdressers on the run, and pages bearing packages; this tumult and din had surprised him, but without affecting his air of impassive majesty, which resembled that which gives the eagle and the lion their supremely contemptuous looks despite the clamor and scurry of hunters and hyenas.

Soon the sounds from the street were joined by the cries of the victims in the kitchen yard, as well as the hurried footsteps of Madame Cropole, along with the bounding gait of Pittrino, who usually spent the morning smoking at the door with the phlegm of a Dutchman, a flurry of sounds that carried up the echoing wooden staircase. This all caused the lodger to start in surprise and agitation.

As he was getting up to inquire into this commotion, the door to his chamber opened. The lodger thought that no doubt the traveler he awaited had arrived at last. In unaccustomed haste, he took three quick steps toward the opening door.

But instead of the figure he hoped to see, that of Maître Cropole appeared, and behind him, in the shadows of the staircase, the rather graceful face of Madame Cropole, pointedly curious as she glanced at the stranger and then withdrew. Cropole advanced smiling, hat in hand, more bent than bowing. A silent gesture from the stranger asked him his intentions.

"Monsieur," said Cropole, "I've come to ask—but how should I address Monsieur, as Your Lordship? Monsieur le Comte? Monsieur le Marquis?"

"Just say *Monsieur,* and come to your business quickly," said the stranger in that haughty tone that admits neither discussion nor question.

"I came to find out how Monsieur had spent the night and ask if Monsieur intended to keep the apartment."

"Yes."

"Monsieur, I must say that an unforeseen event has occurred."

"What's that?"

"His Majesty Louis XIV is arriving in our city today and will spend a night here, or perhaps two."

The stranger appeared astonished by this news. "The King of France is coming to Blois?"

"He's on his way, Monsieur."

"Then, all the more reason for me to stay," said the stranger.

"Very good, Monsieur—but will Monsieur wish to retain the entire apartment?"

"I don't understand. Why would I want less today than I did yesterday?"

"Because, Monsieur, if Your Lordship will allow me to say so, when Your Lordship engaged the apartment yesterday, its price was that of ordinary times . . . but now . . ."

The stranger flushed, perhaps thinking himself insulted by an implication that his means might be limited. "And now," he said coldly, "what of now?"

"Monsieur, I'm an honest man, thank God, and though I may be only an innkeeper, within me flows the blood of a gentleman—my father was a servant and officer of the late Marshal d'Ancre, God rest his soul!"

"I'll not dispute the point, Monsieur; but I want to know, and quickly, what you have to ask."

"You are, Monsieur, too wise not to understand that our town is small, that the Court is numerous, that all our houses will overflow with visitors, and that consequently the value of a room . . . goes up."

The stranger flushed again. "State your conditions, Monsieur," he said.

"I say in all honesty, Monsieur, that I seek only fair profit from the situation and seek to do business without incivility or rudeness. Now, the apartment you occupy is spacious, and you are alone . . ."

"That's my business."

"Of course, Monsieur! I'm not seeking to turn Monsieur out."

The stranger colored red to his temples, and he flashed a look at poor Cropole that, descended though he was from an officer of Marshal d'Ancre, would have sent him crawling back under that famous brick in the chimney if he hadn't been fixed immovably by the interest of profit.

"Do you want me to leave? Explain yourself and be quick about it."

"Monsieur, Monsieur, you misunderstand me. It's a delicate situation, difficult to address properly, and doubtless I express myself badly—or perhaps, since Monsieur is a foreigner, as I can tell from his accent . . ."

In fact, the stranger spoke with that brusqueness that was the principal hallmark of an English accent, even among those of his countrymen who speak the purest French.

"As Monsieur is a foreigner, I say, perhaps it's he who misunderstands the nuances of my request. I propose that Monsieur give up one or two of the rooms he occupies, as that would reduce his rent quite a bit and relieve my conscience—for under the circumstances I see no alternative but to increase the price of these chambers, which as Monsieur must see is only reasonable."

"What was the rent for the first day?"

"One *louis,* Monsieur, including meals plus fodder for the horse."

"Fine. And the rate now?"

"Ah, that's the difficulty! With the arrival of the king, the price of beds goes up, and three double rooms cost six louis. Two louis, Monsieur, are nothing, but six louis, that's a lot."

The stranger, from red, had gone very pale. With heroic bravery, he drew from his pouch a coin purse embroidered with arms, which he carefully concealed in the hollow of his hand. This purse had a flatness, a flaccidity that didn't escape Cropole's eye.

The stranger emptied his purse into his hand. It contained three double louis, six louis altogether, as the innkeeper had asked.

Except that it was seven that Cropole required, including the previous day. He looked at the stranger as if to say, "And?"

"It's a louis short, is it not, Master Host?"

"Yes, Monsieur, but . . ."

The stranger rummaged through his breeches pocket and drew out a little wallet, a golden key, and some small change. Combining these coins he had just enough to add up to another louis.

"Thank you, Monsieur," said Cropole. "Now I just have to ask if Monsieur intends to remain tomorrow as well. If so, fine—but if not, I'll let it out to His Majesty's people when they come."

"That's fair," said the stranger, after a long silence. "But as I have no more coins, as you've seen, to keep the apartment you must take this diamond and either sell it in the city or hold it as security."

Cropole looked at the diamond with such uncertainty that the stranger hastened to add, "I prefer that you sell it, Monsieur, for it's worth three hundred pistoles. A Jew—is there a Jew in Blois?—will give you two hundred for it, or even a hundred and fifty. Take whatever he offers you, so long as it covers the rent of your apartment. Begone!"

"Oh, Monsieur!" cried Cropole, ashamed of the sudden inferiority reflected on him by this noble and disinterested disdain for money, and of having shown such ignoble suspicions. "Oh, Monsieur, I hope we're not such thieves in Blois as you seem to believe, and if the diamond is worth what you say . . ."

The stranger again pierced Cropole with a look from his azure eyes.

"I know nothing about diamonds, Monsieur, but I believe it," Cropole said.

"But the jewelers will know, so ask them," said the stranger. "Now, does that conclude our business?"

"Yes, Monsieur, and I'm very sorry, for I believe Monsieur is offended."

"It's nothing," said the stranger, with the majesty of high rank.

"Oh, but to be suspected of fleecing a noble traveler . . . please pardon me, Monsieur, I act only out of necessity."

"Say no more about it, as I said, and leave me to myself."

Cropole bowed deeply and departed with an agitation that revealed he was a man of heart who felt genuine remorse. The stranger locked the door himself, and then looked into the bottom of his purse, from which he'd drawn the small silk bag that contained the diamond, his last resource. He also searched once again through his pockets, looked through the papers in his wallet, and was convinced that complete destitution was upon him.

Then he raised his eyes to heaven in a sublime movement of calm despair, wiped a few drops of sweat from his brow with a trembling hand, and then, in a look that displayed an almost divine majesty, returned his gaze to the earth.

The inner storm had passed, thanks to a prayer that arose from the bottom of his soul.

He returned to the window, resuming his place at the balcony, and remained motionless, torpid, paralyzed, until the sky darkened, the first torches crossed the shadowy street, and nightfall signaled that it was time for lights to appear in all the windows of the town.

VII

Parry

As the stranger listened to the noises of the town and watched its lights appear, Maître Cropole quietly entered the chamber with two scullions who set the table for supper.

The stranger paid no attention to them. Cropole, approaching his guest, whispered in his ear with the deepest respect: "Monsieur, the diamond has been appraised."

"Ah!" said the traveler. "Well?"

"Well, Monsieur! The jeweler of His Royal Highness himself offered two hundred eighty pistoles."

"You have it?"

"I thought I ought to take the money, Monsieur. However, I made it a condition of the sale that if Monsieur wanted to repurchase his diamond when he could afford to, that it would be made available to him."

"By no means; I told you to sell it."

"Which I did, more or less, since without definitively concluding the sale, I got the money."

"Pay yourself," added the stranger.

"Monsieur, I will do so, since you require it."

A sad smile passed across the gentleman's lips. "Put the money on that sideboard," he said, turning to indicate the piece of furniture.

Cropole set down a bulging purse, from which he collected his rent. "Now," he said, "it would sadden me if Monsieur refused to take his supper. Already dinner was passed over, a sad reflection on the house of The Médicis. See, Monsieur, your meal is served, and I venture to say it's a good one."

The stranger asked for a glass of wine, broke off a piece of bread, and stayed by his post at the window as he ate and drank.

Presently there was a tumult of drums and trumpets, cries arose in the distance, and a confused buzz filled the lower town; the first distinct noise that struck the ear of the stranger was the sound of horses approaching.

"The king! The king!" repeated the loud and surging crowd.

"The king!" repeated Cropole, who abandoned his guest and his ideas of refined service to run and satisfy his curiosity. He collided on the stairs with Madame Cropole, Pittrino, the houseboys, and scullions.

The royal procession advanced slowly, lit by thousands of torches, some in the street, some in the windows. After a company of King's Musketeers[29] and a body of mounted gentlemen came the litter of Cardinal Mazarin, drawn like a carriage by four black horses. The pages and servants of the cardinal marched behind. Then came the carriage of the queen mother, her maids of honor leaning out the doors, her gentlemen riding on both sides. The king came next, mounted on a beautiful Saxon horse with a flowing mane. The young prince, illuminated by his pages' torches, bowed toward those windows from which came the loudest acclamations, showing off his noble and graceful profile.

At the side of the king, but two paces behind, rode the Prince de Condé, Monsieur Dangeau,[30] and twenty other courtiers, followed by a train of retainers and baggage, ending a veritable triumphal march.

This pomp had a distinctly military character. Some of the courtiers, mainly the older ones, wore traveling outfits, but most of the others were dressed as for war. Many wore the gorget and buffcoat[31] of the times of Henri IV and Louis XIII.

When the king passed before him, the stranger, who'd leaned out over the balcony to see better, but with his face concealed behind his arm, felt his heart swell and overflow with bitter jealousy. The fanfares of the trumpets intoxicated him, the popular acclamations deafened him, and he was dizzied for a moment by the clamor, the dancing lights, and the bright figures before him.

"That is a king!" he murmured with such an accent of despair and anguish it could have risen straight to the foot of God's throne.

Then, before he could return to his somber reveries, all the sound and pageantry passed on and was gone. The street below the stranger emptied out and nothing remained but a few hoarse voices calling, "Long live the king!" Then there were only six candles held by the household of The Médicis, that is, two held by the Cropoles, one by Pittrino, and one by each servant.

Cropole kept repeating, "How well he looked, the king, and how he resembles his illustrious father!"

"Handsome," said Pittrino.

"And with such a proud look!" added Madame Cropole, already turning to chat with their neighbors. Cropole added some remarks of his own to the general discussion, without noticing an old man approaching on foot but leading a little Irish horse by the bridle, trying to make his way through the knot of men and women in front of The Médicis.

At that moment the voice of the stranger was heard from the balcony above. "Make way, Monsieur Innkeeper, to let the newcomer into your house."

Cropole turned, saw the old man, and made room for him to pass, as the balcony window slammed shut. Pittrino pointed the way to the newcomer, who went in without saying a word.

The stranger was waiting for him at the top of the stairs. He opened his arms to the old man and led him to a chair, but he resisted. "Oh, no, no, Milord!" he said. "Me, to sit before you? Never!"

"Parry,"[32] said the gentleman, "think nothing of it—you, who've come so far! From England! Ah, it's not right for one of your age to exhaust yourself in my service. Rest, now . . ."

"First, I must give you my report, Milord."

"Parry . . . I beg you, say nothing for now. If the news was good, you wouldn't need to introduce it so. Your delay tells me the news must be bad."

"Milord," said the old man, "don't alarm yourself unduly. All is not lost, or so I hope. It is will and perseverance we need now, and above all resignation."

"Parry," replied the young man, "I've come here alone, past a thousand snares and a thousand perils. Do you think I lack will? I planned this journey for ten years, despite all obstacles and advice to the contrary; do you doubt my perseverance? Tonight, I sold my father's last diamond, because I didn't have enough money to pay for my lodging and my host was asking me for it."

Parry made an indignant gesture, but the young man just patted his hand and smiled. "Suddenly I have two hundred seventy-four more pistoles,[33] and I feel rich, so no despair there. Now, why do I have need of resignation?"

The old man just raised his trembling hands toward heaven.

"Come," said the young stranger. "Conceal nothing from me. What's happened?"

"My story won't take long, Milord; but in heaven's name, don't shudder so!"

"It's impatience, Parry. Come, what did the general tell you?"

"At first the general refused to see me."

"He thought you were some kind of spy."

"Yes, Milord, but I wrote him a letter."

"Well?"

"He accepted it, and read it, Milord."

"That letter explained my position and my wishes?"

"Yes, indeed!" said Parry, with a sad smile. "It faithfully conveyed your thoughts."

"Then, Parry?"

"Then the general sent the letter back to me by an aide-de-camp, who informed me that, if I was still in the general's area of command the next day, he'd have me arrested."

"Arrested!" murmured the young man. "Arrested! You, my most faithful servant!"

"Yes, Milord."

"Even though you'd signed the letter *Parry?*"

"*Every* letter, Milord," said the old man with a sigh. "And that aide-de-camp had known me at Saint James's and at Whitehall."

The young man's eyes closed and his head drooped. "Perhaps . . . that's what the general did in front of his people," he said, trying to deceive himself, "but behind their backs, in private, he sent to you? Tell me."

"Alas, Milord! What he sent me was four burly cavalrymen who put me on the horse you saw me lead in. These cavalrymen made me ride to the little port of Tenby, embarked me, or rather threw me aboard a small fishing boat bound for Brittany, and here I am."

"Oh!" sighed the young man, convulsively gripping his throat to stifle a sob. "And that's all, Parry? That's all?"

"Yes, Milord. That's all."

After this brief reply from Parry there was a long interval of silence, during which nothing was heard but the sound of the young man furiously grinding his heel on the parquet floor.

The old man decided to change the subject. "Milord," he said, "what was all that noise just before I arrived? Why were all those people shouting, 'Long live the king'? Which king? And why all the torches?"

"Ah, Parry, don't you know?" said the young man ironically. "It's the King of France who is pleased to visit his good city of Blois. All those fanfares were for him, all those shining cloaks were on his courtiers, all those gentlemen wear swords to defend him. His royal mother precedes him in a magnificent carriage encrusted with silver and gold. Oh, happy mother! His minister amasses millions and conducts him to a marriage with a rich fiancée. Thus, all his people are joyful, they love their king, they shout their acclamations until they're hoarse, and still they cry, '*Vive le roi! Vive le roi!*'"

"Now, now, Milord," said Parry, even more anxious about the tone of this new subject than the old one.

"And you know," continued the stranger, "that during all this honor paid to King Louis XIV, my mother and my sister live in poverty, without money or bread. You know that within a fortnight, when what you've just told me is generally known, I'll be an object of scorn across all Europe. Is this not a situation, Parry, where even a man of my condition might consider . . ."

"Milord, in heaven's name!"

"You're right, Parry, I'm a coward, and if I do nothing for myself, what should God do for me? No, no, I have two arms, Parry, I have a sword . . ."

He struck his arm with a fist, and then took his sword down from the wall.

"What are you going to do, Milord?"

"What am I going to do, Parry? I'll do as the rest of my family does. My mother lives on public charity, my sister asks alms for my mother, my brothers do likewise. And it's time that I, the eldest, do the same. I'm going to beg, Parry!"

And with these words, which he cut short with a nervous and terrible laugh, the young man belted on his sword, picked up his hat from a chest, and tied a black cloak around his shoulders, the same one he'd worn traveling the high roads. Then he took up the hands of the old man, who was looking at him anxiously, and said, "My good Parry, make yourself a fire, drink, eat, sleep, and be happy. Be happy, my faithful friend, my only friend, for we're rich—as rich as kings!"

He slapped the bag of pistoles, which dropped to the floor, repeated the dismal laugh that had frightened Parry so, and while the whole house was humming and hustling, preparing to receive and house the Parisian courtiers and their lackeys, he slipped out through the common room into the street, where the old man, who had gone to the window to watch him, soon lost sight of him in the darkness.

VIII

His Majesty Louis XIV
at the Age of Twenty-Two

As we related, the entrance of King Louis XIV into the city of Blois had been brilliant and boisterous, and so the young monarch had seemed satisfied. Arriving under the porte cochère of the Hall of the Estates General, the king met there, surrounded by his guards and gentlemen, His Royal Highness Gaston d'Orléans, whose demeanor, never less than majestic, boasted an added dignity and grandeur for this solemn occasion. For her part, Madame, resplendent in her grand ceremonial gown, awaited the entrance of her nephew on the interior balcony. All the windows of the old château, bleak and deserted on most days, glistened with bright ladies and lights.

Then it was to the sound of tambours, trumpets, and cheers that the young king crossed the threshold of that château in which King Henri III, seventy-two years earlier, had stooped to betrayal and assassination to keep on his head and in his house a crown that was already slipping from the Valois to the Bourbons.[34] After admiring the young king, so handsome, so charming, and so noble, all eyes sought out that second King of France, more powerful than the first, the man so old, so pale, and so bent who was called Cardinal Mazarin.

Louis was brimming with all those natural gifts that made him the perfect gentleman. His eyes were a brilliant, mild, azure blue—but even the most brilliant physiognomists, those delvers into the soul, upon fixing their gaze upon them, assuming they could sustain the regard of a king, even they couldn't see beyond into the depths that seeming mildness concealed. The eyes of the king contained the infinite depths of the summer sky, or the more sublime but frightening abysses beneath the hull of a ship on a summer's day on the blue Mediterranean, that immense mirror of the sky that sometimes reflects its stars, and sometimes its storms.

The king wasn't large, if anything shorter than average, but his youth outweighed this defect, and he moved with the grace of an athlete, shown by his easy mastery of most physical skills. In truth, he looked every inch a king, and it was no small thing to be a king who looked the part in that period of traditional respect and devotion. Until recently he'd been little seen by his people, and when he had been it was next to his mother, a tall and majestic woman, or Monsieur le Cardinal, a handsome and magnetic man, and beside those two veteran rulers few had thought much of the king.

Unaware of these belittling comparisons, which were mainly confined to the capital, the citizens of Blois received the young prince like a god, while Monsieur and Madame, the lords of the château, paid him nearly kingly honors. However, it must be said that when the king saw awaiting them in the Reception Hall a row of chairs of equal height, for him, his mother, the cardinal, his aunt and his uncle, an arrangement cleverly mitigated by their placement in a semicircle, Louis XIV flushed with anger, and looked around at the others to see if anyone was amused at his expense by this calculated humiliation. But as he saw nothing on the cardinal's face, nothing in his mother's expression, and nothing from the courtiers, he resigned himself and sat down, though he deliberately sat first and on the centermost chair.

The local gentlemen and ladies were then introduced to Their Majesties and to Monsieur le Cardinal. The king noticed that where he and his mother were rarely familiar with the names of those presented, the cardinal, on the contrary, knew all of them, and never failed to ask about their estates or absent family members, mentioning their children by name, which delighted these provincials and confirmed in them the idea that he was truly the sole king. It is the true king who knows his subjects, just as there is only one sun, for only the sun shines equally on everyone.

These lessons for the young king, who'd begun his studies some time ago without anyone noticing, were duly absorbed, and he spent some time observing those circulating in the hall, trying to draw conclusions about even the least significant of them. They were served a collation; the king, without daring to demand hospitality of his uncle, had awaited this impatiently—and this time he received all the honors due, if not to his rank, then at least to his appetite. As for the cardinal, he contented himself with touching to his withered lips a little broth served in a golden cup. The all-powerful minister, who had appropriated her regency from the queen mother and his royalty from the king, had been unable to command nature to give him good digestion. Anne of Austria,* already suffering from the cancer that in a few more years would take her life, ate little more than the cardinal. As for Monsieur, preoccupied with this great event that had overturned his provincial life, he ate nothing at all.

Madame alone, like a true Lorrainer, kept up with His Majesty, so that Louis XIV, who'd been embarrassed to be the only one eating, was grateful to his aunt, and also to Monsieur de Saint-Rémy, her *maître d'hôtel*, who'd likewise distinguished himself.

The collation complete, at a gesture from Mazarin the king rose, and at the invitation of his aunt began to circulate among the ranks of those assembled there. The ladies observed, for there are certain things that the ladies are as quick to observe in Blois as in Paris, that Louis XIV had a bold and lingering eye, which promised to those with attractions a distinguished appreciation. The men, for their part, observed that the prince was proud and haughty, and that he would hold the gaze of those who looked at him too openly or too long until they dropped their eyes, which seemed to foretell a masterful ruler.

Louis XIV had completed a third of his circuit when his ears pricked up at a word spoken by His Eminence, who was conversing with Monsieur. This word was a woman's name. Louis XIV had scarcely heard this word before he cut short the arc of his circulation and began drifting toward the cardinal, whose conversation, despite his pretense otherwise, now occupied all the king's attention.

Monsieur, as a good courtier, had inquired of His Eminence about the health of his nieces. In fact, five or six years earlier, three nieces had arrived at the cardinal's house from Italy: Mesdemoiselles Hortense, Olympe, and Marie de Mancini. Therefore, Monsieur asked after the health of these nieces, regretting that he didn't have the pleasure of receiving them at the same time as their uncle, as they must certainly have grown in both beauty and grace since Monsieur had seen them last.

The king had been struck by the difference in the voices of the two speakers. The voice of Monsieur was calm and natural, but that of Monsieur de Mazarin was strident and elevated above its usual tone. It was as if he were pitching his voice so it would carry to the end of the hall. "Monseigneur," he replied, "Mesdemoiselles de Mancini still have to complete their educations, comprehend their positions, and learn how to fulfill their duties. To stay at a young and brilliant Court would distract or even dissipate them."

Louis smiled sadly at this last characterization. The Court was young, it was true, but the cardinal's thrift and avarice ensured it was far from brilliant.

"But surely you have no intention," replied Monsieur, "of keeping them cloistered or educating them among the bourgeois?"

"Not at all," said the cardinal, emphasizing his Italian accent so that his voice, usually soft and smooth, became sharp and penetrating. "Not at all; I intend to see them married, and as well as possible."

"You'll have no shortage of suitors, Monsieur le Cardinal," replied Monsieur, like a cheerful merchant congratulating another on his bustling trade.

"So I hope, Monseigneur, especially since God has graced them with charm, wisdom, and beauty."

During this conversation, Louis XIV, led by Madame, had been making a circuit of the room. "Mademoiselle Arnoux, the daughter of my music tutor," said the princess, presenting to His Majesty a buxom blonde of twenty-two, who at a village festival might have been taken for a peasant in her Sunday best.

The king smiled. Madame had never been able to play four fair notes in a row on the viol or the harpsichord.

"Mademoiselle Aure de Montalais," continued Madame, "a young lady of quality, and my good servant."

This time it wasn't the king who smiled, it was the young woman presented to him, because for the first time in her life she heard Madame, who was usually rather brusque, speak well of her. So Montalais, our old acquaintance, made a deep bow to His Majesty, as much from respect as from the need to hide an inappropriate and quite unladylike smirk, which the king might have misunderstood.

It was at just that moment that the king heard the name that had made him start.

"And the third one is called . . . ?" asked Monsieur.

"Marie, Monseigneur," replied the cardinal.

There was, beyond doubt, some magical power in this name, for as we've said, at this word the king shuddered, and drew Madame toward the origin of the conversation, as if he wished to put some confidential question to her, but in reality to get closer to the cardinal. "My Aunt Madame," he said, in a laughing undertone, "my geography tutor never informed me that Blois was at such a prodigious distance from Paris."

"How so, my Nephew?" asked Madame.

"Because it seems it takes several years for fashion to travel that distance. Look at these young ladies."

"Well! I know them all."

"Some of them are pretty."

"Don't say that too loudly, my Nephew, or you'll drive them to distraction."

"Patience, my dear Aunt," said the king, smiling, "for the second part of my sentence outweighs the first. Because, my dear Aunt, some of them seem positively old and ugly, thanks to their ten-years-out-of-date fashions."

"But, Sire, Blois is no more than five days from Paris."

"Oh?" said the king. "Then that's, let's see, two years behind for each day."

"You really think it's that bad? I hadn't noticed."

"Look here, Aunt," said Louis XIV, still approaching Mazarin under the pretense of leading Madame toward someone else. "Look, past this ancient jewelry and these pretentious coiffures, look at the elegance of this simple white dress. This must be one of my mother's maids of honor, though I don't know her. Look at her artless finesse and graceful posture. There's no comparison: here is a lady, while these others are just mannequins."

"My dear Nephew," replied Madame, laughing, "permit me to tell you that this time your keen senses have failed you. This young woman is no Parisian, but a native of Blois."

"Really, Aunt?" replied the king, skeptically.

"Come here, Louise," said Madame.

And the girl whom we've already met under this name approached, timid, blushing, eyes dropping under the royal gaze.

"Mademoiselle Louise-Françoise de La Baume Le Blanc, daughter of the Marquis de La Vallière," said Madame ceremoniously to the king.

The young lady bowed with such grace despite being intimidated by the royal presence that the king, watching her, actually missed a few words of the conversation between the cardinal and Monsieur.

"Stepdaughter," continued Madame, "of Monsieur de Saint-Rémy, my maître d'hôtel, who oversaw the creation of that excellent truffled turkey that Your Majesty seemed to enjoy so well."

There was nothing that grace, beauty, and youth could do to overcome a vulgar association like that. The king smirked. Whether Madame meant her words as a pleasantry, or was merely naïve, the connection annihilated anything Louis might have found charming or poetic in the young woman. For Madame, and therefore at that moment for the king, Mademoiselle de La Vallière was nothing but the stepdaughter of a man who saw to the preparation of truffled turkeys.

But such is the nature of princes. The gods were much the same on Olympus, and no doubt Diana and Venus were just as condescending when they spoke of the beauty of the poor mortals Alcmene and Io, if they deigned to address the subject while taking nectar and ambrosia at Jupiter's table.

Fortunately, Louise had bent so low that she didn't hear Madame's remarks or see the king's smile. Indeed, if the poor child, the only one of all her companions with the natural good taste to dress in white, had heard Madame's words and seen the king's cold sneer, her delicate dove's heart would have stopped and she'd have died on the spot. Even Montalais herself, with all her ingenuity and ambition, wouldn't have tried to recall her to life, for ridicule is the death of everything, even beauty.

But fortunately, as we said, Louise, whose ears were ringing and whose gaze was averted, Louise saw and heard nothing, and the king, preoccupied with the cardinal's conversation, hastened to move on. He arrived just as Mazarin concluded with, "Marie, like her sisters, is bound for Brouage. I had them follow the opposite bank of the Loire from us, and if they obey my instructions, I calculate they should be across from Blois tomorrow morning."

These words were pronounced with that tact, that precision, and that mastery of tone that made Signor Giulio Mazarini the world's greatest comic actor. As a result, the words struck right to the heart of Louis XIV—as the cardinal, turning at the sound of His Majesty's approaching footsteps, could see from the effect on his pupil's face, a subtle reddening that was nonetheless noted by the eye of His Eminence.

But what was one more trick of persuasion and perception to a man who'd been hoodwinking the diplomats of Europe for over twenty years? From the moment the king heard these words it seemed he'd taken a poisoned dart to the heart. He lost all confidence and, suddenly uncertain, cast anxious looks at the assembly surrounding him. He tried again and again to catch the queen mother's eye, but she, engrossed in the pleasure of speaking with her sister-in-law, and moreover warned off by a glance from Mazarin, didn't seem to notice her son's pleading glances.

From then on, all music, flowers, lights, even beauty itself seemed hateful and tedious to Louis XIV. Back in his chair, after he'd bitten his lips a dozen times, stretched out his arms and legs as if confined, like a well-bred child who, not daring to yawn, seeks every other way possible to express his boredom, after having once more tried and failed to implore mother and minister, he turned a desperate look toward the door, that is, toward freedom.

At this door, framed by the doorway against which he was leaning, he saw, standing out in strong contrast to his surroundings, a proud and spare figure, with an aquiline nose, a severe but sparkling eye, hair long and gray, and a black mustache, a veritable model of military virtue, whose gleaming gorget, shining like a mirror, broke all the reflected lights of the hall into shimmering flashes. This officer wore on his head a gray felt hat with a red plume, proof that he was there on duty rather than for his pleasure; if he'd been a courtier rather than a soldier he'd have been holding his hat in his hand, as one must always pay a price for pleasure.

What showed even more clearly that this officer was on duty and performing a familiar task was the way in which he watched, arms folded and with utter indifference, the party with all its joys and disappointments. He seemed above it all, like a philosopher—but all old soldiers are philosophers, with a much greater understanding of disappointment than of joy, which they've had little opportunity to sample.

So, he stood there, leaning against the richly carved door frame, until the king's sad and anxious eyes met his own. And it wasn't the first time, it seemed, that the officer's eyes had met such a look, because as soon as he saw the expression on Louis XIV's face, he knew just what was passing in the king's heart, his anxiety and the desire for freedom from what oppressed him. Instantly seeing what duty required of him, the officer stood tall and said, in a voice that resounded like that of a commander on the battlefield: "On the service of the king!"

At these words, which burst like a roll of thunder above the sound of the orchestra, the singers, the talkers, and the strutters, the cardinal and the queen mother looked with surprise at His Majesty. Louis XIV, pale but resolute, supported by his thought being echoed and magnified by the voice of his Lieutenant of Musketeers, rose from his chair and took a step toward the door.

"Are you leaving, my son?" asked the queen, while Mazarin contented himself with an inquiring glance, which might have seemed concerned if it hadn't been so piercing.

"Yes, Madame," replied the king. "I am fatigued and would like to write this evening."

A smile touched the lips of the minister, who appeared, with a nod, to give the king his permission.

Monsieur and Madame hastened to give orders to their guards to present arms. The king bowed, crossed the hall, and approached the door, where a double file of twenty musketeers awaited His Majesty. At the end of the line stood the impassive officer with his naked sword in his hand.

As the king passed, the crowd stood, some on tiptoe, to watch him go by. Ten musketeers preceded him out into the antechamber, ten more falling in behind the king and Monsieur, who wanted to accompany His Majesty. Assorted servants followed, a little procession escorting the king toward his designated lodging, the same apartment occupied by Henri III when he'd convened the Estates General.

Monsieur had given his orders. The musketeers, led by their officer, entered the narrow passage that connected one wing of the château to the other. This passage began in a small, square antechamber that was dark and somber, even on sunny days. There Monsieur held up a hand to Louis XIV and said, "You're passing, Sire, the very spot where the Duc de Guise received the first thrust of the poniard."[35]

Even the king, nearly ignorant of history, had heard of this event, though he knew nothing of its context or details. "Ah!" he said, shuddered and stopped. Everyone else, both before and behind him, stopped as well.

"The duke, Sire," continued Gaston, "was about where I am, walking in the direction Your Majesty was walking; Monsieur de Loignac was where your Lieutenant of Musketeers is standing, and Monsieur de Sainte-Maline and the King's Ordinaries were behind and around him. It was there that he was struck."

The king turned toward his officer of musketeers in time to see a cloud pass across his bold and martial countenance. "Yes, from behind," murmured the lieutenant with a gesture of supreme disdain. And he turned as if to continue their march, as though uncomfortable between walls that had witnessed such treachery.

But the king, who appeared eager to learn, seemed disposed to pause and look around the lethal location. Gaston understood his nephew's curiosity. "See, Sire," he said, taking a torch from the hands of Monsieur de Saint-Rémy, "here is where he fell. There was a bed against the wall, and he tore down its curtains as he collapsed."

"Why is there a hollow in the parquet floor at this spot?" asked Louis.

"Because that's where his blood pooled," said Gaston. "The blood soaked deep into the oak and it was only by gouging out the wood that it was effaced—and yet," added Gaston, holding the torch near, "you can still see a reddish tint that has resisted all attempts to scrub it away."

Louis XIV raised his head. Perhaps he was thinking of the bloodstain he'd been shown one day at the Louvre, where the blood of Concini had been spilled at the command of his father, Louis XIII. "Let's go," he said.

The march immediately resumed, for emotion had given his voice an as-yet-unaccustomed tone of command.

They arrived at the apartment reserved for the king, which communicated with the narrow passage by which he'd approached, as well as with a staircase that overlooked the courtyard. Gaston said, "I hope Your Majesty will accept this apartment, unworthy though it is to receive him."

"Uncle," replied the young prince, "I thank you for your cordial hospitality."

Gaston bowed to his nephew, who embraced him, and then went out. Of the twenty musketeers who'd escorted the king, ten accompanied Monsieur back to the reception hall, which was still busy despite His Majesty's departure. The other ten were assigned their night posts by their officer, after he'd spent five minutes exploring all the surrounding chambers, surveying them with that cold and considering regard that was less the fruit of experience than of a certain tactical genius.

Then, with all his people placed, he chose for his headquarters an adjacent antechamber in which he found a large armchair, and next to it a lamp, some wine, water, and a half-loaf of bread. He turned up the lamp, drank half a glass of wine, curled his lip in a scornful smile, sat down in the big chair and prepared to fall asleep.

IX

In Which the Stranger from the Inn of The Médicis Drops His Incognito

Despite his air of nonchalance, the officer who was settling down to sleep was burdened with a grave responsibility. Lieutenant of the King's Musketeers, he commanded the entire company of one hundred twenty men that had come from Paris, but other than the twenty already referred to, the other hundred were detailed to guard the queen mother and, especially, the cardinal. Monsignor Giulio Mazarini was thrifty, and instead of traveling with his own guards, he economized by using the king's, taking fifty of them for himself—which, to a stranger to this Court, might have seemed an unusual escort for a foreigner. What such a stranger might have found even more unseemly, even extraordinary, was that the wing of the château occupied by the cardinal was brilliant with lights and busy with visitors. The musketeers who mounted guard over the doors of this wing admitted only couriers who brought the cardinal, even while traveling, his urgent correspondence. Twenty men were on duty outside the queen mother's rooms; thirty were resting to be ready to relieve their companions the next day.

In contrast, the wing assigned to the king showed only darkness, silence, and solitude. Even the château's servants had one by one withdrawn. Monsieur le Prince had sent to inquire whether His Majesty required his attendance, and the Lieutenant of the Musketeers, who was accustomed to this nightly question, gave the customary negative reply. After this, all prepared for an early bed, as if in a good bourgeois household. And yet, from the rooms assigned to the king, it was easy to hear the festive music that issued from the richly illuminated windows of the great hall.

Ten minutes after arriving in his rooms, Louis XIV had been able to recognize, by the grand procession that eclipsed his own entourage, the departure of the cardinal, who moved toward his bedroom accompanied by a numerous escort of gentlemen and ladies. To observe all this activity the king had only to look out his windows, whose shutters stood still open. His Eminence crossed the courtyard, his way lit by Monsieur himself, who bore a torch; they were followed by the queen mother, leaning on Madame's arm, the two whispering on their way like two old friends. Behind these two couples came columns of ladies, pages, and officers, their torches illuminating the courtyard like a walking bonfire surrounded by reflections from the windows; then the procession disappeared inside, moving toward the upper floors.

No one thought of the king, leaning on his balcony, from which he'd sadly watched this flow of noise and light—no one, that is, but the stranger from the Inn of the Médicis, whom we saw go out wrapped in his black cloak. He had gone straight up to the château and circled the main palace, watching, from behind his melancholy face, the people who still thronged it. Then, noticing that no one was guarding the main gate, since Monsieur's guards were all fraternizing with the royal troops, discreetly, or rather indiscreetly, sharing out the Beaugency wine, he entered, passing through the people lingering in the courtyard until he came to the landing of the stairs leading to the cardinal's wing.

Doubtless it was the torchlight and busy passage of pages and servants that drew him that way. But he was stopped by a horizontal musket and the challenge of a guard. "Where are you going, friend?" demanded the sentry.

"I go to see the king," replied the stranger, with cool hauteur.

The soldier called one of His Eminence's ushers, who, in the tone of a functionary directing a petitioner to a sub-minister, said, "You want the other stairs across the way."

And the usher, without sparing another thought to the stranger, returned to his conversation.

The stranger made no reply, just turned and crossed to the indicated staircase. On that side there was no noise and few torches lit the gloom, through which a single sentry paced like a shadow. It was so quiet the stranger could hear the sound of his footsteps and the noise of his spurs when his heels struck the flagstones. This sentry was one of the twenty musketeers assigned to the king's service, and he mounted his guard with the stiffness and impassivity of a statue. "Who goes there?" he said.

"A friend," replied the stranger.

"What do you want here?"

"To speak to the king."

"Oh ho! My dear Monsieur, that's out of the question."

"Why is that?"

"Because the king has gone to bed."

"To bed, already?"

"Yes."

"No matter; I must speak with him."

"And I tell you that's impossible."

"But . . ."

"Be off!"

"What about the password?"

"I don't have to give you a password. Be off."

And this time the sentry added to his words a threatening gesture. But the stranger never moved a hair and seemed rooted in place. "Monsieur le Mousquetaire," he said, "are you a gentleman?"

"I have that honor."

"Well! So am I, and between gentlemen there ought to be some measure of consideration and respect."

The sentry lowered his weapon, impressed by the dignity with which the stranger had delivered these words. "Speak, Monsieur," he said, "and if what you need is within my power . . ."

"Thank you. You have an officer, I suppose?"

"Yes, Monsieur, our lieutenant."

"Well, I would like to speak to your lieutenant."

"Ah! That's another thing entirely. Follow me, Monsieur."

The stranger saluted the sentry in a lofty manner and mounted the stairs, while the sentry called ahead, "Lieutenant, a visitor!"

This word was passed from sentry to sentry until it reached the officer's antechamber and roused him. He dragged on his boots, rubbed his eyes, threw on his coat, and then stepped toward the stranger as he came in. "What can I do for you, Monsieur?" he asked.

"You are the officer on duty, the Lieutenant of Musketeers?"

"I have that honor," replied the officer.

"Monsieur, I absolutely must speak with the king."

The lieutenant looked closely at the stranger, and in that look, brief though it was, he learned all he needed to know, perceiving a proud distinction concealed by common clothes. "I don't take you for any kind of fool," he replied, "yet it seems to me you must know, Monsieur, that no one approaches the king without his consent."

"He will consent, Monsieur."

"Permit me to doubt it, Monsieur; the king retired more than a quarter of an hour ago and by now must be nearly undressed. Besides, the order has gone out."

"When he knows who I am," said the stranger, lifting his chin, "he will withdraw the order."

The officer was growing increasingly surprised and increasingly impressed. "If I agree to announce you, Monsieur, will you at least consent to tell me what name to announce?"

"You will announce His Majesty Charles II, King of England, Scotland, and Ireland."*

The officer stifled a cry of astonishment and recoiled slightly, his pale face showing an unexpectedly poignant expression on the visage of such a man of action. He looked closer and said, "Oh, yes, Sire! In fact, I should have recognized you."

"You've seen my portrait?"

"No, Sire."

"Or did you see me at Court before I was expelled from France?"

"No, Sire, not that either."

"How could you recognize me, then, if you've seen neither my portrait nor my person?"

"Sire, I saw His Majesty the King, your father, on a terrible occasion."

"The day . . ."

"Yes."

A dark cloud passed over the prince's face, but then, waving it away, he said, "Do you still see any problem with announcing me?"

"Pardon me, Sire," replied the officer. "I couldn't imagine I was addressing a king under so simple an exterior, though as I had the honor to tell Your Majesty a moment ago, I'd seen King Charles I . . . but excuse me, I must go warn the king."

He turned, then retracing his steps, he asked, "Your Majesty doubtless wishes this interview to remain a secret?"

"I don't insist upon it, but if it's possible . . ."

"Quite possible, Sire, for I can dispense with notifying the First Gentleman on duty; but Your Majesty will have to consent to give me his sword."

"Ah, right. I'd forgotten that no one may go in to see the King of France while armed."

"Your Majesty may insist on an exception, but then it will be my responsibility to notify the First Gentleman."

"Here is my sword, Monsieur. Would you care to announce me to His Majesty now?"

"This very moment, Sire."

The officer immediately marched to the king's door, which the valet de chambre opened to him. "His Majesty, the King of England!" the officer announced.

"His Majesty, the King of England!" repeated the valet de chambre.

At these words an attending gentleman opened the inner door of the king's apartments to reveal Louis XIV without hat or sword, doublet unlaced, and advancing with every indication of surprise. "You, my Brother! You, at Blois!" cried Louis XIV, dismissing with a gesture the gentleman and valet, who withdrew into an antechamber.

"Sire," replied Charles II, "I was on my way to Paris in hopes of seeing Your Majesty when I heard of your visit to this city. I extended my stay, as I have something very important to say to you."

"Does this chamber suit you, Brother?"

"Perfectly, Sire, for it seems private enough."

"I've sent my gentleman and my valet into the next room. Outside this room is the antechamber, where you saw just one officer, right?"

"Yes, Sire."

"Well, then! Speak, Brother; I'm listening."

"I'll begin, then, Sire, and may Your Majesty take pity on the troubles of my house."

The King of France blushed, covering it by drawing together two armchairs.

"Sire," said Charles II, "I need not ask Your Majesty if he knows the deplorable details of my history."

Louis XIV colored even more, and then, placing a hand over that of the King of England, he said, "My Brother, I'm ashamed to say that the cardinal rarely speaks of politics in front of me. Worse, in former days I had La Porte,[36] my personal valet, read history to me in the evening, but the cardinal stopped these readings and sent La Porte away, so that I must beg my Brother Charles to tell me everything, speaking as if to a man who knows nothing."

"Well, Sire, I think that by starting at the beginning I may have a better chance of touching Your Majesty's heart."

"Speak, Brother, speak."

"You know, Sire, that I was called to Edinburgh by loyalists in 1650, during Cromwell's expedition to Ireland, and I was crowned at Scone. A year later, after being wounded in one of the provinces he'd subjugated, Cromwell returned to come down upon us. To meet him in battle was my goal, to get out of Scotland my desire."

"But isn't Scotland almost your native country?" asked the younger king.

"Yes, but the Scots were cruel compatriots to me! Sire, they forced me to deny the religion of my fathers, and they hanged Lord Montrose, my most devoted servant, because he wouldn't become a Covenanter.[37] The poor martyr, offered a boon when he was dying, asked that his body should be cut into as many pieces as there were cities in Scotland, so that there might be proof of his loyalty everywhere, and as a result I couldn't leave one town or enter another without passing some scrap of that body that had acted, fought, even breathed for me.

"In a bold move, I dashed through Cromwell's army and made it into England. The Protector then joined me in a strange race, with a crown for the goal. If I'd been able to get to London before him, doubtless the prize of the race would have been mine, but he caught up to me at Worcester. The Spirit of England had passed from us and into him. On September 3, 1651, the anniversary of the Battle of Dunbar, so fatal to the Scots, I was defeated, Sire. Two thousand men fell around me before I thought of retreating a step. Finally, I had to flee.

"From then on, my life became a melodrama. With my pursuers close behind me, I cut off my hair and disguised myself as a woodcutter. A day spent hiding in the branches of a broad oak gave that tree the name of Royal Oak, which it bears to this day. My adventures in the county of Strafford, which I escaped with my host's daughter riding pillion behind me, are still told around the fireside there, and became the subject of a ballad. One day I'll write all this down, Brother, for the instruction of my brother kings.

"I will say how, upon arriving at Mister Norton's, I met a chaplain from the Court who watched me suspiciously as I played a game of bowls, and an old servant who recognized me and burst into tears, nearly betraying me out of loyalty rather than treachery. Finally, I'll mention my terror—yes, Sire, my terror—when, at the house of Colonel Windham, the hostler who looked after our horses declared that they'd been shod in the north."

"How strange," murmured Louis XIV, "that I never heard of any of this. I only knew that you'd embarked at Shoreham and then landed in Normandy."

"Oh!" lamented Charles. "Dear God above, if you allow it to happen that kings don't hear one another's stories, how can you expect them to help each other?"

"But tell me, Brother," continued Louis XIV, "how, having been treated so rudely in England, you can still hope for anything from that unhappy country and her rebellious people?"

"Because, Sire, since the Battle of Worcester, everything has changed! Cromwell has died, after signing a treaty with France on which he dared to place his name above yours. He died on September 3, 1658—another anniversary to add to that date, after the battles of Worcester and Dunbar."

"His son succeeded him . . ."

"But some men, Sire, may have a son without having an heir. Oliver Cromwell's legacy was too great a burden for Richard Cromwell. Richard, who was neither Republican nor Royalist; Richard, who let his guards eat his lunch and his generals govern his state; Richard abdicated the Protectorate on May 25, 1659,[38] a little over a year ago, Sire.

"Since then England has been little more than a casino where everyone throws dice for my father's crown. The two players still at the table are Lambert and Monck.* Well, Sire, it's my turn! I'd like a seat at the game that's being played on my royal cloak. A million, Sire, to corrupt one of these players and buy me an ally, or two hundred of your gentlemen to drive them from my palace of Whitehall, as Jesus chased the moneychangers from the temple."

"So," replied Louis XIV, "you've come to ask of me . . ."

"Your aid; not just what kings owe to one another, but no more than the duty between simple Christians; your aid, Sire, whether in money or men; your aid, Sire, and within a month, whether I pit Lambert against Monck, or Monck against Lambert, I'll have reconquered my paternal inheritance without having cost my country a single guinea, or my subjects a drop of blood, because they're now so sick of the fever of revolution, of protectorate and republic, that they ask nothing more than to fall safely asleep in the arms of royalty. Give me your aid, Sire, and I'll owe my throne more to Your Majesty than to my father. My poor father, who paid dearly for the ruin of our house! You can see how desperate, how unhappy I am, Sire, since I blame my own father."

And the blood mounted in the pale face of Charles II, who put his head between his hands for a moment as if blinded by the flush of such filial blasphemy.

The young king was as unhappy as his elder brother and squirmed in his seat, unable to find the words to respond. Finally, Charles II, to whom ten extra years gave a greater ability to master his emotions, regained his voice. "Sire," he said, "your answer? I'm like the condemned awaiting his sentence. Must I die?"

"My Brother," the French prince replied to Charles II, "you ask me for a million, but I've never had even a quarter of that sum! I have nothing! I'm no more the King of France than you are King of England. I'm just a name, a figurehead dressed in velvet fleurs de lys, nothing more. I can see my own throne, but that's the only advantage I have over Your Majesty. I have nothing and can do nothing."

"Is this true?" cried Charles II.

"My Brother," said Louis, lowering his voice, "I have suffered humiliations not even my poorest gentlemen would endure. If poor old La Porte were still here, he'd tell you how I slept in ragged sheets with holes big enough for my legs to pass through; how when I was older, and asked for my carriage, they brought me a vehicle half-gnawed by the rats of the coach house; how, when I asked for my dinner, they sent to the cardinal's kitchen to see if there was any food for the king.

"And today, today when I'm twenty-two years old, today when I've attained the age of royal majority, today when I should have the key to the treasury, the command of politics, the decision of peace or war, cast your eyes around and see what leavings they give me. I am abandoned, disdained, silenced, while across the way all is light, activity, and homage to power. There! There you see the real King of France, my Brother."

"The cardinal's chambers?"

"The cardinal's, yes."

"Then, I am condemned, Sire."

Louis XIV said nothing.

"Condemned is the word, for I will never plead with the one who left, to die of cold and hunger, my mother and my sister, the daughter and grand-daughter of Henri IV, saved only by Monsieur de Retz[39] and the Parliament, who sent them wood and bread."

"To die!" murmured Louis XIV.

"Why not?" continued the King of England. "Poor Charles II, grandson like you of Henri IV, Sire, having neither parliament nor Cardinal Retz to help him, will die of hunger as his mother and sister nearly did."

Louis frowned and tore at the lace of his cuffs. This futile fidgeting as he tried to mask his internal emotions struck King Charles, and he took the younger man's hand. "Thank you, Brother," he said. "You were frank with me, and that's all I could ask of someone in your position."

"Sire," said Louis XIV, suddenly raising his head, "you need a million in gold or two hundred gentlemen, isn't that what you said?"

"Sire, a million would do it."

"That's not so much."

"Offered to one man, it's quite a lot. Convictions have been bought for far less, and I'd be dealing with mere venality."

"And two hundred gentlemen—why, that's hardly more than a company."

"Sire, there's a tradition in our family that four men, just four French gentlemen devoted to my father,[40] came this close to saving him, though he was condemned by parliament, guarded by an army, and in the middle of an angry nation."

"So, if I can find you a million, or two hundred gentlemen, you'll be satisfied, and feel I've treated you as a true brother should?"

"I'll call you my savior, and when I regain my father's throne, England, so long as I reign, shall be like a sister to France, as you have been a brother to me."

"Well, Brother!" said Louis, rising. "What you hesitated to ask of me, I will go ask for without hesitation! Though I've never asked such things for myself, I'll ask them for you. I'll go see the King of France—the other, the one who's rich and powerful—and demand this million in gold or two hundred men. And then we'll see!"

"Oh!" cried Charles. "You're a noble friend, Sire, a heart blessed by God! You save me, Brother, and if you ever need the life you hereby preserve, ask it of me!"

"Not so loud, my Brother! Hush!" whispered Louis. "We don't want to be overheard. We're not yet at our goal. To ask Mazarin for money? Why, it's like passing through the enchanted forest where each tree harbors a demon. There's nothing harder in the world!"

"But still, Sire, when it's you who asks . . ."

"I've already said that I never ask," replied Louis with a hauteur that made the King of England go pale. When he saw Charles wilting like a wounded man, he quickly added, "Please pardon me, Brother—I don't have a mother and sister who are suffering. Forgive me my pride, and I'll pay for it with a sacrifice. I go now to see the cardinal. Wait for me, I beg. I will return."

X

The Arithmetic of Monsieur de Mazarin

While the king was traversing the corridors that led to the cardinal's wing of the château, accompanied only by his valet, his officer of musketeers, breathing like a man who'd been holding his breath a long time, stepped out from the entry chamber which the king had thought empty. This little room was really part of the king's bedchamber, separated by nothing but a thin partition. And this partition, which blocked only the eyes, did nothing to prevent the ears from hearing everything that passed within.

So, there was no doubt but that this Lieutenant of Musketeers must have heard every word exchanged in His Majesty's chamber. Warned in time by the king's final words, the officer had exited into the antechamber ahead of him, to salute him as he passed and to watch him until he disappeared down the corridor.

Once the king had disappeared, he shook his head in a way that belonged only to him, and said, in voice that forty years after leaving Gascony still retained its accent, "It's a sad service for a sad king." Then, these words pronounced, the lieutenant resumed his place in the armchair, extending his legs and closing his eyes like a man who intends to meditate or to sleep.

During this short monologue and the arrangements that followed, while the king passed down the long corridors of the old château, a different kind of scene was playing out in the cardinal's chambers. Mazarin had gone to bed suffering somewhat from the gout, but as he was a man of order who made use even of pain, he made his wakefulness into the humble servant of his work. Therefore, he'd had Bernouin,* his personal valet, bring him a small travel desk so he could write while lying in bed. But gout is not an adversary that gives in easily, and as every movement stabbed him with pain, he asked Bernouin, "Is Brienne still there?"

"No, Monseigneur," replied the valet de chambre. "Monsieur de Brienne,[41] by your leave, has gone to bed. But if Your Eminence so desires we can always wake him."

"No, it isn't worth it. Now let's see. Damn these numbers!" And the cardinal gazed at nothing while counting on his fingers.

"The numbers again?" said Bernouin. "Fine! If Your Eminence is going to return to his calculations, I can promise him a fine migraine in the morning. And Doctor Guénaud didn't come with us."

"You're right, Bernouin. Well, you'll just have to stand in for Brienne, my friend. Really, though, I should have brought Monsieur Colbert.* That young man will go far, Bernouin, very far. Such orderly thinking!"

"Maybe," said the valet, "but personally I don't like the face of your young man who will go far."

"Enough, Bernouin, enough. I didn't ask for your opinion. Now sit here, take the pen, and write."

"Very well, Monseigneur. Where shall I write?"

"There, under those two lines I drew across."

"Got it."

"Write: seven hundred sixty thousand livres."

"Done."

"In Lyons . . ." The cardinal seemed to hesitate.

"In Lyons," repeated Bernouin.

"Three million nine hundred thousand livres."

"Fine, Monseigneur."

"In Bordeaux, seven million."

"Seven," repeated Bernouin.

"Ah, yes," said the cardinal with a smile, "seven." He sighed and resumed, "You understand, Bernouin, that this is all money there to be spent."

"*Ohé,* Monseigneur, whether it's to be spent or saved is nothing to me, since none of these millions are mine."

"These are the king's millions; this is the king's money we're counting. Can we get on with it? You always interrupt me!"

"Seven million in Bordeaux."

"Yes, that's right! In Madrid, four. I tell you whose money it is, Bernouin, because everyone is so foolish as to think I'm rolling in millions. I reject such nonsense! A minister has nothing of his own. Now, let's continue: general receipts, seven million. Real estate, nine million. Got all that, Bernouin?"

"Yes, Monseigneur."

"On the markets, six hundred thousand livres. Assorted properties, two million. Oh, I forgot—the furnishings of the various châteaux . . ."

"Should I add the royal crown?" asked Bernouin.

"No need for that, its inclusion is implied. Now, got everything, Bernouin?"

"Yes, Monseigneur."

"And these sums . . . ?"

"Are all lined up in a column."

"Total them, Bernouin."

"Thirty-nine million two hundred and sixty thousand livres, Monseigneur."

"Agh!" spat the cardinal. "Still short of forty million!"

Bernouin added the numbers again. "Yes, Monseigneur, short by seven hundred forty thousand livres."

Mazarin asked for the ledger and checked it over carefully. "Just the same," said Bernouin, "thirty-nine million two hundred and sixty thousand livres is a nice round sum."

"Ah, Bernouin! But I wish the king had forty million for us."

"Didn't Your Eminence say that all this money belongs to His Majesty?"

"Absolutely, that couldn't be clearer. But these thirty-nine million are spoken for, and well beyond."

Bernouin smiled to himself like a man who believes no more than he has to, meanwhile preparing the cardinal's night medicine and fluffing his pillow.

"Hmpf!" said Mazarin, once the valet had left the chamber. "Still less than forty million! Will I never achieve my goal of reaching forty-five? Who knows if I have enough time left to do it? I'm sinking fast, I'll never make it. Still, maybe I can find two or three million in the pockets of our good friends the Spaniards. They plundered Peru, those people, and there must be some of that still around."

He was talking this way, focused on his figures and forgetting about his gout, which gave way to this most important of his preoccupations, when Bernouin, upset, suddenly burst back into his room. "Well?" demanded the cardinal. "What is it?"

"The king! The king, Monseigneur!"

"The king? How?" said Mazarin, stuffing the ledger under his covers. "The king here—and at this hour! I should think he'd been long abed. What is it?"

Louis XIV heard these final words and saw the cardinal sitting up in surprise, for he came in at just that moment. "It's nothing, Monsieur le Cardinal," he said, "or at least nothing to alarm you; it's just an important discussion that I need to have with Your Eminence tonight, that's all."

Mazarin immediately thought of the attention the king had paid to his remarks about Mademoiselle de Mancini and assumed the discussion had to be about that. That was reassuring, and he adopted a charming and receptive demeanor, which in turn reassured the young king. When Louis was seated, the cardinal said, "Sire, I should by rights listen to Your Majesty while standing, but the agony of my condition . . ."

"No standing on ceremony between us, my dear Cardinal," said Louis affectionately. "I'm not the king, just your pupil, as you know, and it's doubly true this evening, as I come to you as a supplicant, a very humble supplicant both eager and hopeful."

Mazarin, seeing the color mounting in the king's face, was confirmed in his first idea, which was that thoughts of love were behind these pretty words. But this time that cunning politician, wise though he was, had it wrong: this blush wasn't caused by shy and youthful passion, but rather by the nervous rise of royal pride.

Like a good uncle, Mazarin sought to facilitate the expected amorous confidence. "Speak, Sire," he said, "and since Your Majesty will temporarily forget that I'm his subject and call me his tutor and teacher, I listen to Your Majesty with an open heart."

"Merci, Monsieur le Cardinal," replied the king, "but what I have to say to Your Eminence is not on my own account."

"Too bad, Sire," said the cardinal. "I'm just in the mood for Your Majesty to ask me for something important, even at personal sacrifice . . . but whatever you've come to ask me, I'm ready to gratify you by granting it, my dear Sire."

"Well, then! Here's what it's about," said the king, his heart beating at a rate equaled only by that of his minister. "I just received a visit from my royal brother, the King of England."

Mazarin sprang up in bed as if he'd been jolted by a Leyden bottle or Voltaic battery, while an expression of surprise, or rather deep disappointment, was followed by such a flash of anger that even Louis XIV, novice diplomat though he was, could tell that the minister had expected him to say something else.

"Charles II!" cried Mazarin, his lip curling in disdain. "You received a visit from Charles II?"

"From *King* Charles II," replied Louis XIV, according his fellow grandson of Henri IV the title Mazarin appeared to forget. "Yes, Monsieur le Cardinal, that unhappy prince has touched my heart with an account of his misfortunes. He's in great distress, Monsieur le Cardinal, and I share his pain—I, who have seen my own throne disputed, and was forced, in the time of unrest, to leave my own capital—I, in short, who understand such misfortune, was moved to help a royal brother now dispossessed and fugitive."

"Indeed?" sneered Mazarin. "Why doesn't he have a Jules Mazarin near him as you do, Sire? His crown would still be on his head."

"I know all that my house owes to Your Eminence," said the king, with some hauteur. "You must believe that, for my part, Monsieur, I will never forget it. It's because my brother the King of England lacks the minister of genius who saved me that I turn now to that same minister to come to his aid. If you extend your hand over his head, rest assured, Monsieur le Cardinal, that your hand would be able to restore the crown to his brow from where it fell at the foot of his father's scaffold."

"Sire," replied Mazarin, "I'm grateful for your good opinion of me, but we have no business meddling over there. They are madmen who deny God and behead their kings. They're dangerous, Sire, and their hands reek with the stain of royal blood. That policy offends me, and I reject it."

"Then help us to replace it with another."

"Such as?"

"The restoration of Charles II."

"What? My God!" said Mazarin. "Does that poor prince flatter himself that he can grasp such a mirage?"

"But yes!" replied the young king, intimidated by the difficulties his minister seemed to foresee in the project. "He's only asking for a million."

"Is that all? One little million, if you please?" said the cardinal ironically, his Italian accent creeping out. "One little million, if you please, my brother? Bah! A family of beggars."

"Cardinal," said Louis XIV, lifting his chin, "this family of beggars is a branch of my own family."

"And are you rich enough to give others millions, Sire? Do you have such millions?"

"Oh!" said Louis XIV with an agony in his heart that he struggled not to show on his face. "Yes, Monsieur le Cardinal, I know how poor I am. But I'm sure the Crown of France must be worth a million, and for this good deed, I'm even willing to pledge my crown. There must be a Jewish moneylender who will give me a million for it."

"So, Sire, you say you need a million?" asked Mazarin.

"Yes, Monsieur, that's what I'm saying."

"You're badly mistaken, Sire, you'd need much more than that. I will show you, Sire, how much you really need. Bernouin! Where are you?"

"What, Cardinal?" said the king. "Are you going to consult a lackey about my royal business?"

"Bernouin!" the cardinal called again, appearing not to notice the young king's feeling of humiliation. "Come here and repeat to me that sum we were discussing just now."

"Cardinal, didn't you hear me?" said Louis, pale with indignation.

"Don't be angry, Sire; I manage Your Majesty's affairs in an open and aboveboard fashion; everyone in France knows I keep an open book. What was I having you do just now, Bernouin?"

"Your Eminence had me adding up sums, Monseigneur."

"Which you did, didn't you?"

"Yes, Monseigneur."

"To figure the sum that His Majesty needs at the moment, right? Isn't that what I said? Speak frankly, my friend."

"As Your Eminence says."

"Well, then! How much did I say I wanted?"

"Forty-five million, I believe."

"And how much do we have if we combine all our resources?"

"Thirty-nine million two hundred sixty thousand livres."

"Very well, Bernouin, that's all I needed to know. You may leave us now," said the cardinal, turning his sharp eyes on the young king, who was dumb with stupefaction.

"But . . . that is . . ." stammered the king.

"Ah, Sire! You still doubt?" said the cardinal. "Well! Here's the proof of what you just heard." And Mazarin drew from under his covers the number-filled ledger and presented it to the king, who averted his eyes, so deep was his grief and shame.

"So, if you want a million, Sire, that's a million not accounted for here, and it's actually forty-six million Your Majesty needs. Well, I fear there aren't enough Jews in the world to lend you such a sum, even if you did pledge the Crown of France."

The king, clenching his trembling fists, pushed back his chair. "Then it seems," he said, "my brother the King of England must die of hunger."

"Sire," replied Mazarin, in a softer tone, "remember this proverb, which I offer you as a basis of sound policy: 'Rejoice in being poor when your neighbor is poor as well.'"

Louis thought for a few moments, while glancing curiously at the ledger peeking out from under the cardinal's bolster. "So," he said, "it's impossible to fulfill my request for money, Monsieur le Cardinal?"

"Absolutely, Sire."

"Remember that this will make an enemy of him if he regains the throne without my help."

"If that's Your Majesty's only concern, then he should rest easy," said the cardinal eagerly.

"All right, I don't insist," said Louis XIV.

"Have I convinced you, at least, Sire?" said the cardinal, placing his hand on the king's.

"Completely."

"If there's anything else, ask for it, Sire, and I'll be happy to see that you get it, having refused you this."

"Anything else, Monsieur?"

"Why, yes! Am I not in service, body and soul, to Your Majesty? Hey, Bernouin! Torches and guards for His Majesty! His Majesty is returning to his apartments."

"Not yet, Monsieur. Since I find your good will at my disposal, I'll take advantage of it."

"Something personal, Sire?" asked the cardinal, hoping that the subject would finally turn to his niece.

"No, Monsieur, nothing for me," replied Louis, "but once more for my brother Charles."

Mazarin's expression darkened, and he muttered something that Louis couldn't hear.

XI

The Politics of Monsieur de Mazarin

Instead of the hesitation with which he'd approached the cardinal a quarter of an hour before, now there could be read in the eyes of the young king a will to win, an urge that, though it might fail because it wasn't backed by true power, showed that he would at least keep the memory of a defeat deep in his heart. "This time, Monsieur le Cardinal, it's for something easier to find than a million in gold."

"You think so, Sire?" said Mazarin, regarding the king with that gaze that read what was written on men's hearts.

"Yes, I think so, and when you hear what I'm asking for . . ."

"Do you think I don't already know, Sire?"

"You know what I'm going to ask for?"

"Listen, Sire, and I'll tell you what King Charles said."

"But you couldn't!"

"Listen. He said, 'And if that stingy Italian peasant . . .'"

"Monsieur le Cardinal . . . !"

"If not his exact words, that was the sense of them. *Mon Dieu*, I can hardly blame him; everyone is driven by their passions. He said, 'If that Italian peasant refuses you the million we ask, Sire, and we're forced, for lack of money, to renounce diplomacy, well! We'll ask him for five hundred gentlemen.'"

The king shuddered, for the cardinal was right in everything but the number.

"Isn't that how it went, Sire?" cried the minister with a note of triumph. "And then he added some lovely, encouraging words, saying, 'I have friends on the other side of the Channel, friends who need only a leader and a flag to follow. When they see me, and they see the banner of France, they'll rally to my side, for they'll know I have your support. The French flag and uniform are worth more to me than the million that Monsieur de Mazarin has refused us.'

"For he knew very well that I'd refuse it. 'With these five hundred gentlemen, Sire, I will conquer, but the honor of the victory will be yours.' That's what he said, isn't it? That or something very similar, embroidering his words with brilliant metaphors and proud imagery, because they're fine orators in that family. Why, the father even gave a speech on the scaffold."

The sweat of shame beaded Louis's brow. He felt that this insult to his royal brother was an attack on his dignity, but he didn't know how to respond, especially to the man to whom he'd always seen everyone bow, even his mother.

Finally, he made an effort. "But, Monsieur le Cardinal," he said, "he didn't ask for five hundred men, only two hundred."

"You see that I guessed what he was after."

"I have never denied, Monsieur, that you see deeper and farther than others, which is why I thought you wouldn't refuse my brother Charles something so simple and easy to grant as what I ask in his name, Monsieur le Cardinal—or rather in mine."

"Sire," said Mazarin, "I have labored in politics for thirty years, first under Cardinal Richelieu,[42] then on my own. My policies have not always been entirely forthright, I admit, but they have never been inept. Now, the idea that's been proposed to Your Majesty is both dishonest *and* inept."

"Dishonest, Monsieur!"

"Sire, you signed a treaty with Monsieur Cromwell."

"Yes, a treaty on which Monsieur Cromwell signed his name above mine!"

"Why did you sign it down so low, Sire? Monsieur Cromwell found a good place for his signature, and he took it; that was his way. The point is you signed a treaty with Cromwell—or in other words, England, since when you signed that treaty Monsieur Cromwell *was* England."

"Monsieur Cromwell is dead."

"Do you think so, Sire?"

"Beyond a doubt, since his son Richard succeeded him, and then abdicated."

"So he did! Richard inherited from Cromwell upon his death, and England inherited when he resigned. The treaty was part of that inheritance, whether it was in Richard's hands or in England's. That treaty is as legal and as valid as ever. Why would you abandon it, Sire? What has changed? What Charles II wants today we didn't want to give him ten years ago, and don't want to now. You are allied with England, Sire, and not Charles II. It might have been unseemly, from the family point of view, to sign a treaty with the man who beheaded your father's brother-in-law,[43] and to have contracted an alliance with the body they call the Rump Parliament;[44] that might be unseemly, as I say, but politically it was far from inept, since, thanks to that treaty, I saved Your Majesty, who was then still a minor, from the danger of a foreign war during the Fronde[45] . . . you remember the Fronde, don't you, Sire?"

The young king lowered his head.

"A war that would have fatally complicated settling the uprisings of the Fronde. And I say to Your Majesty that to change course now without warning our allies would be both dishonest and inept. We'd be going to war without right on our side, and it would justify the same being done to us, for an attack by five hundred men, or two hundred men, or fifty or even ten, is still an act of aggression.

"A Frenchman is the nation; the uniform is our army. Suppose, for example, Sire, that you were at war with Holland, which sooner or later is bound to happen, or with Spain, which could occur if somehow your marriage fell through"—Mazarin looked closely at the king—"and there are a thousand reasons why that might happen . . . anyway! In that case, would you approve of England sending the United Provinces or the infanta a regiment, a company, or even a squad of English gentlemen? Would you think that comports with the elements of your treaty of alliance?"

Louis listened, and thought it strange to hear Mazarin invoking good faith, when he was the originator of so much political chicanery that such tricks were known as *mazarinades*.[46] "However," said the king, "unless I directly forbade it, I couldn't prevent gentlemen of our state from going to England on their own account."

"You would have to order them to return, Sire, or at least protest their presence as enemies in an allied country."

"But see here, Monsieur le Cardinal, surely a political genius like yourself could find a way to help this poor king without compromising ourselves."

"But that's exactly what I don't *want* to do, my dear Sire," said Mazarin. "For my purposes, events in England couldn't be unfolding better if I'd planned them myself. Governed the way it's governed, England is a magnet of trouble for all of Europe. Holland wants to protect Charles II? Let Holland do it; the only two maritime powers will clash, we'll watch as they sink one another's fleets, and we'll use the debris to build our own ships, if we can ever afford the nails to do so."

"Oh! This all sounds so miserable and petty, Monsieur le Cardinal!"

"Yes, quite true, Sire, I admit it. More than that: if I admit for a moment the possibility of your evading the terms of your treaty, which happens sometimes when there is a great interest at stake, or the terms bind one too closely; well! You'd authorize the engagement you request, France, or its flag, which is the same thing, would cross the Channel to fight—and France would be defeated."

"Why is that?"

"*Ma foi!* We know what manner of general His Majesty Charles II is, as we saw at Worcester!"

"He no longer has to deal with Cromwell, Monsieur."

"That's right: now he has to deal with General Monck, who is far more dangerous. Cromwell was a visionary, a man with moments of exaltation, of expansiveness during which he, that former brewer, overflowed like an overfilled barrel. Then we might taste a drop of his thoughts, which gave us the savor of his intentions, a flaw that enabled us repeatedly to penetrate to Cromwell's soul, though they claimed that soul was armored in triple brass, as Horace says.[47] But Monck! Ah, Sire, God forbid that you must come to grips with Monsieur Monck! He's the one who in the last year has given me all these gray hairs!

"Monck is no visionary, no, not he; alas, Monck is a *politician*. He keeps close, and never overflows. For the last ten years he's had his eyes fixed on a goal, but no one can figure out what it is. Like Louis XI,[48] to prevent anyone from guessing his thoughts of the night before, every morning he burns his nightcap. On the day his plans, slowly and solemnly matured, finally burst forth, they will explode with the certain success of the unexpected.

"It's this Monck, Sire, of whom you may never have heard, whose name you may not even know, who stands against your brother Charles II. Charles, believe me, knows that name well, though he doubtless didn't mention it to you. When you say Monck, you say a marvel of depth and tenacity, the only two things against which spirit and ardor are no use. Sire, I was ardent when I was young, and I always had my wits. I can boast about them, since I'm criticized for them. I got pretty far with those two qualities, the son of a fisherman in Piscina who became prime minister to the King of France, and in that capacity, if Your Majesty will recognize it, I've rendered a few services to Your Majesty's throne. Well, Sire! If I'd encountered Monck along my way instead of Monsieur de Beaufort, Monsieur de Retz, or Monsieur le Prince,[49] I'd have been lost. Keep your distance, Sire, or you'll fall into the clutches of this political soldier. Monck's helmet, Sire, is an iron coffer in which he locks away his thoughts, and no one has the key to it. I wear only a biretta of velvet,[50] Sire, so to him I bow and defer."

"What do you think Monck wants, then?"

"Heh! If I knew that, Sire, I wouldn't tell you to be wary of him, because then I'd be stronger than he is. But with Monck, I'm afraid to even guess—to even guess, do you understand? For if I think I've guessed what he wants, I'll stop thinking, and despite myself, I'll follow my guess. Since that man came to power over there, I'm like those damned souls in Dante whose necks have been twisted by Satan so they walk forward but look backward:

I march toward Madrid but look back toward London. To guess, with this devil of a man, is to fool yourself, and if you fool yourself, you're lost. God forbid I should try to guess what he wants; I limit myself to spying on what he does, and that's going far enough. Now, I believe—you understand the scope of the word *believe*?—I *believe* that Monck, though he doesn't want to commit himself to anything, is nonetheless eager to succeed Cromwell. Your Charles II has already sent ten envoys with proposals to him, and he's contented himself with chasing them away, saying nothing more than, 'Begone, or I'll have you hanged.' He's as silent as a sepulcher, that man!

"Right now, Monck supports the Rump Parliament, but this support doesn't fool me: Monck just wants to avoid being assassinated. An assassination would foil him before his goal can be reached, and his goal *must* be reached; or so I believe. Again, don't believe that just because I say I believe it, Sire—I only do that out of habit. I think Monck just supports the Parliament until the time comes to dismiss it. You've been sent to ask for swords, but those swords are to fight against Monck. God forbid we ever fight against Monck, Sire, for Monck will defeat us, and I could never console myself for being beaten by Monck. That victory would be something that Monck would have been planning for a decade. By God! Sire, out of friendship for you, if not out of consideration for himself, let Charles II retire and keep a low profile. Your Majesty can give him one of your châteaux and a little income. But no! That infamous treaty we were just talking about prohibits Your Majesty from even giving him a château!"

"How's that?"

"Yes, Your Majesty is committed to denying hospitality to King Charles, to deny him France itself. That's why you must make your royal brother understand that he can't stay with us, we can't allow him to compromise us, or I myself . . ."

"Enough, Monsieur!" said Louis XIV, rising. "To refuse me a million is your prerogative; those millions are yours to manage. To refuse me two hundred gentlemen is likewise your right, for you are prime minister, and you have, in the eyes of France, the responsibility for peace and war. But to presume to prevent me, the king, from granting hospitality to the grandson of Henri IV, to my cousin, my childhood companion! That's where your power ends and my will begins."

"Sire," said Mazarin, delighted to get off so cheaply, the more so because that's why he'd fought so hard in the first place, "I will always bow before the will of my king. My king can keep the King of England near at hand or in one of his châteaux; you can inform Monsieur Mazarin of it, just don't tell the prime minister."

"Good night, Monsieur," said Louis XIV. "I leave in despair."

"But convinced, which is all that I need, Sire," replied Mazarin.

The king made no response, but withdrew thoughtfully, convinced, not of all that Mazarin had told him, but on the contrary of something he was careful not to mention, which was of the necessity to make a serious study of his place in the affairs of Europe, because those matters seemed complex and obscure to him.

Louis found the King of England sitting in the same chair where he'd left him. On seeing him, the English prince rose, but saw at first glance the discouraging expression on his cousin's face. He spoke first, to help Louis in the painful confession he had to make. "No matter what," he said, "I will never forget the kindness and friendship you've shown me."

"*Hélas*," replied Louis XIV mournfully. "Only empty friendship, Brother."

Charles II went very pale, drew a cold hand across his forehead, and was staggered by momentary dizziness. "I understand," he said at last. "No hope!"

Louis took Charles II by the hand. "Wait, Brother," he said, "don't do anything rash, all might change. It's only reckless acts that ruin a cause. I beg of you, add just one more year's trial to your time of suffering. There's no more reason to take drastic action now than at any other time, neither occasion nor opportunity. Stay near me, Brother, I'll give you one of my houses for a residence, and together we'll keep an eye on events and prepare for what may come; Brother, take courage!"

Charles II withdrew his hand from the king's and stood tall before him. "With all my heart, I thank you, Sire," he said. "But I have pleaded for aid from the greatest king in the world without result, and now I must seek a miracle from God."

And he went out before Louis could say anything more, his head high but hands shaking, with an expression of weary sadness on his face, and a distant gaze that, finding nothing to rest upon in the world of men, seemed to look beyond into unknown lands.

The officer of the musketeers, seeing him pass like a phantom, bowed nearly to the ground before him. He then took a torch, called two of his troopers, and went down the deserted stairs with the unhappy king, holding in his left hand his hat, its plume brushing the steps.

At the gate, the officer asked the king which direction he was going so he could send the musketeers as escort. "Monsieur, you who once knew my father," replied Charles II quietly, "did you ever pray for him, perchance? If so, remember me in your prayers now. Where I go I travel alone, and I beg you to give me neither company nor escort any further."

The officer bowed and sent his musketeers back inside. But he remained for a moment under the portico to watch Charles II walk away until he disappeared into the shadows of the street. "To him, as before to his father," he murmured, "as Athos would say, and with good reason: 'Hail to His Fallen Majesty!'"

Then, climbing the stairs, "How wretched his service is!" he murmured at every step. "What a pitiful master I serve! To go on with this life is intolerable. It's time I acted for myself! No more giving my all for nothing!" he continued. "The master may yet rise and achieve, but the servant is done. *Mordioux!* I'll put it off no longer. Come, you two," he said, entering the antechamber. "Why are you waiting around here? Put out your torches and return to your posts. Oh, you were watching out for me? Keeping an eye on me, my men? You geese! I'm no Duc de Guise, and they won't assassinate me in the narrow hall. Besides," he added to himself, "someone would have to decide to do that, and no one makes decisions since Cardinal Richelieu died. Ah, now there was a man, back in the day! No, it's decided: tomorrow I hang up my hat for good!"

Then, after a thought, he said, "No, not yet! I have one last great challenge before me, but this one, I swear, will be the last, *mordioux!*"

He had scarcely finished when a voice came from the king's chamber. "Monsieur le Lieutenant!" it called.

"I'm here," he replied.

"The king would like to speak to you."

"Come now," said the lieutenant. "Perhaps this is the challenge I was thinking of." And he went in to see the king.

XII

The King and
the Lieutenant

When the king saw the officer come in, he dismissed his valet and his attending gentleman. "Who is on duty tomorrow, Monsieur?" he asked.

The lieutenant bowed with military precision and replied, "I am, Sire."

"What, you again?"

"Always me."

"How can that be, Monsieur?"

"Sire, the musketeers, when traveling, assume all the duties of guarding Your Majesty's household, that is to say, yourself, the queen mother, and Monsieur le Cardinal, who borrows from the king the best part of the royal guard, or at least the most numerous."

"But in between watches?"

"There is no in-between, Sire, just twenty or thirty men of your hundred and twenty who are off duty to rest. At the Louvre it's different, and if we were at the Louvre, I'd rely on my adjutant; but when traveling, Sire, anything can happen, and I prefer to manage things myself."

"So, you're on duty every day?"

"And every night, yes, Sire."

"Monsieur, we can't have that. You must find time to rest."

"Perhaps, Sire, but I'd rather not."

"You'd . . . rather not?" said the king, nonplused by this unusual response.

"I'm saying, Sire, that I'd rather not expose myself to being at fault. If the devil wanted to play a trick on me, Sire, you'll understand that since he knows the man he's dealing with, he'd do it at a moment when I was absent. My duty, and the peace of my conscience, comes before all."

"But that way of life, Monsieur—it will kill you."

"Oh, Sire! I've followed this way of life for thirty-five years and I'm the healthiest man in France and Navarre. Besides, Sire, don't worry about me, I beg you; it's unexpected and I'm not used to it."

The king cut short the conversation with a new question. "Then, you'll be here tomorrow morning?" he asked.

"Like now, like always, yes, Sire."

The king paced back and forth across the room. It was easy to see that he was burning with the need to speak, but some fear restrained him. The lieutenant, erect, immobile, his hat in his hand, his fist on his hip, watched this activity, while grumbling into his mustache, "He hasn't got a half-pistole's worth of resolution in him, upon my honor! I'd wager he won't speak on his own."

The king continued to pace, occasionally glancing toward the lieutenant.

"He's the spit and image of his father," the officer told himself. "He's simultaneously proud, ambitious, and timid. Plague take such a master!"

Louis stopped. "Lieutenant?" he said.

"Right here, Sire."

"This evening, down in the hall, why did you cry out, 'The king's service, His Majesty's Musketeers?'"

"I was obeying your orders, Sire."

"Me?"

"Yourself."

"But I didn't say a word, Monsieur."

"Sire, an order may be given by a sign, by a gesture, or by a look, as clearly as by speech. A servant who had only ears would be but half a servant."

"Your eyes are pretty sharp, then, Monsieur."

"Why do you say that, Sire?"

"Because they see what isn't there."

"My eyes are indeed sharp, Sire, though they've served their master a long time. But when there's something to be seen, they rarely miss the opportunity. Tonight they saw Your Majesty blushing with the effort not to yawn; that Your Majesty looked with eloquent supplication first at His Eminence, and then at Her Majesty the queen mother, and finally at the door that led out of the hall; and they saw all that so well, they practically read the words on Your Majesty's lips that said, 'Who will get me out of here?'"

"Monsieur!"

"Or words to that effect, Sire. Thus, I didn't hesitate; that look was for me, and as good as an order, so I cried, 'His Majesty's Musketeers!' And I was right, Sire, as Your Majesty proved on the spot."

The king turned away to conceal a smile, and then, after a few seconds, turned his gaze back on that countenance so intelligent, so bold and firm, that it looked like the dynamic and proud profile of an eagle facing the sun.[51] "Well done," he said after a short silence, during which he tried, and failed, to stare his officer into dropping his gaze.

But seeing him say nothing more, the officer turned on his heels and took three steps toward the door, murmuring, "He won't speak, *mordioux!* He won't speak."

"Thank you, Monsieur," the king said then.

"Really, that was the only thing missing," continued the lieutenant to himself, "to be thanked for doing my duty as if I might have failed to do it." And he marched to the door in a military jingle of spurs.

But when he arrived on the threshold, he sensed the king's desire calling him back and he turned. "Has Your Majesty told me everything?"

He asked this in a tone impossible to describe, but which, without seeming to actually solicit a confidence, was so persuasively frank that the king replied at once, "Approach me, Monsieur."

"Here, now!" murmured the officer. "It's coming at last."

"Listen to me."

"Every word, Sire."

"You'll mount your horse tomorrow at four in the morning, Monsieur, and you'll have one saddled for me."

"From Your Majesty's stable?"

"No, from the musketeers."

"Very good, Sire. Is that all?"

"Then you will accompany me."

"Alone?"

"Alone."

"Will I come to get Your Majesty, or shall I await him?"

"You'll await me."

"Where shall I do that, Sire?"

"At the park's back gate."

The lieutenant bowed, understanding that the king had said all that he would at that time.

In fact, the king then dismissed him with a friendly gesture. The officer left the king's chamber and returned philosophically to his armchair, where, instead of falling asleep, as one might expect at such an advanced hour of the night, he began to think more deeply than he ever had.

The result of these reflections was less sad than previously. "Come, he's started at last," he said. "Love drives him, and he moves, he moves! This king is nothing in his Court, but he may amount to something as a man. Anyway, we'll see come morning . . . But, oh!" he said suddenly, sitting up very straight. "Now there's an idea, a gigantic idea, *mordioux!* And maybe that idea will make my fortune!"

With this exclamation, the officer rose and paced the broad antechamber, hands in the pockets of his coat. The candle guttered furiously in the path of a cool breeze that entered through the slightly opened window and crossed the room diagonally, projecting a reddish flickering glow, sometimes bright, sometimes diminished, and casting on the wall a great shadow of the lieutenant, drawn in silhouette like a figure from Callot,[52] with the plumed felt hat and the sword at his belt.

"Of course," he murmured, "unless I'm very much mistaken, Mazarin is laying a trap for the young lover; Mazarin set up a time and place for a rendezvous this evening as smoothly as if he were Monsieur Dangeau himself. I heard it all clearly enough: 'Tomorrow morning,' he said, 'they'll be passing the bridge from Blois.' God's death! That's clear enough—especially to a lover! And that explains his embarrassment, his hesitation, and this order: 'Monsieur my Lieutenant of Musketeers, a horse tomorrow, at four in the morning.' Which is as clear as if he'd said, 'Monsieur my Lieutenant of Musketeers, tomorrow at four in the morning, on the bridge from Blois, do you hear?'

"And thus, I'm in possession of a state secret, insignificant though I am. And how did I get it? Because I have sharp eyes, as I just told His Majesty. They say he loves this little Italian doll to distraction! They even say he cast himself at his mother's feet for permission to marry her. Moreover, they say the queen consulted the Holy See of Rome to find out if such a marriage, made against her will, would be valid. Oh, to be twenty-five again! If only those I once had by my side were with me once more! I'd pit Mazarin against the queen mother, France against Spain, and set up a new queen all on my own! But now? Bah!"

And the lieutenant snapped his fingers in disdain. "This miserable Italian, this coward, this peasant who dared refuse a million in gold to the King of England, how quickly would he give me a thousand pistoles if I brought him this news? No, *mordioux!* I'm being childish. I must be drunk! Him, Mazarin, give something to someone? Ha ha ha!"

With an effort, the officer swallowed his laughter. "To sleep," he said. "To sleep, and without delay. This night's work has dulled my edge, and I'll see things more clearly on the morrow."

And having made himself this recommendation, he wrapped himself in his cloak, and sniffed in disdain at his royal neighbor. Five minutes later, he was sleeping with his hands clenched and his lips slightly apart, from which escaped, not his state secret, but a sonorous snore that echoed from the vault of the majestic antechamber.

XIII

Marie de Mancini

The first rays of the sun were barely topping the great trees of the park and gilding the high wind-vanes of the château when the young king, already awake for over two hours, burning with the insomnia of love, opened his shutters to the dawn, and cast a curious glance across the courtyards of the sleeping palace.

He saw that it was the appointed hour; the big clock above the courtyard showed a quarter past four. He didn't call his valet de chambre, still deeply asleep on the other side of the room, but dressed himself. The sound awoke the valet, who awakened quite frightened, afraid he'd overslept and missed his duty, but Louis sent him back to bed, warning him to remain silent. Then he went down the staircase to the courtyard, passed out through a side gate, and saw along the wall of the park a rider who was holding a spare horse by the bridle.

This rider was unrecognizable under his cloak and broad hat. As to the horse, saddled like that of a wealthy bourgeois, it showed nothing remarkable to even the most inquisitive eye. Louis went and took the horse's bridle; without leaving his saddle, the officer bent down and held the king's stirrup as he mounted, then asked in a low voice for orders from His Majesty. "Follow me," replied Louis XIV.

The officer put his horse into a trot behind that of his master, and they rode down toward the bridge. When they were on the other side of the Loire, the king said, "Monsieur, be so good as to ride on until you see a carriage, and then return to warn me; I'll wait here."

"Would Your Majesty deign to give me some details, so I'll recognize the right carriage when I see it?"

"The carriage will bear two ladies and will probably be followed by servants."

"Sire, I don't wish to make a mistake; is there some other sign by which I'd recognize this carriage?"

"It will probably display the arms of Monsieur le Cardinal."

"Very good, Sire," replied the officer, now completely clear on the object of his quest. He spurred his horse into a trot in the direction indicated by the king. But he'd gone scarcely five hundred paces before he saw a carriage drawn by four matched mules coming over the crest of a rise. Behind that carriage came another. At a glance he knew that these were the vehicles he was looking for. He turned on the spot, rode back to the king, and said, "Sire, here come the carriages. The first, in fact, contains two ladies and their maids, while the second carries footmen, supplies, and luggage."

"Ah, very good," replied the king in a voice full of emotion. "Go, please, and tell these ladies that a cavalier of the Court wishes to pay them his private respects."

The officer went off at a gallop. "God's death!" he said as he rode. "Here's a new and honorable position! I complained of being insignificant, and now I'm the confidant of the king. It's enough to make a musketeer burst with pride!"

He approached the carriage and delivered his message with wit and gallantry. There were indeed two ladies in the coach, one a great beauty, though perhaps over-slender, and a second, less favored by nature but lively and graceful, her face alight with willful intelligence. Her keen and piercing eyes, in particular, spoke more eloquently than all the amorous phrases current in that time of gallantry. The officer addressed himself to this second lady without hesitation, though as we've said, the first was perhaps more beautiful. "Mesdames," he said, "I'm the Lieutenant of the Musketeers, here to announce that a cavalier who wishes to pay you his respects awaits you on the road just ahead."

At these words, whose effects he awaited with curiosity, the dark-eyed lady gave a gasp of joy, leaned out the door, and, seeing the rider approaching, extended her arms, calling, "Ah! My dear Sire!" And her eyes brimmed with tears.

The coachman abruptly reined in the mules, the maids tumbled to the carriage floor, and the prettier lady bowed humbly, while her mouth curved in the most ironic smile ever sketched on feminine lips by jealousy.

"Marie! Dear Marie!" said the king, taking the hands of the dark-eyed lady between his own. And then, opening the carriage's heavy door himself, he drew her out with such ardor that she was in his arms before touching the ground. The lieutenant, taking a position on the other side of the carriage, watched and listened without being noticed.

The king offered his arm to Mademoiselle de Mancini and gestured to the coachmen and servants to continue on their way. It was almost six in the morning; the road was still fresh and pleasant; the tall trees lining the highway, with flowers just bursting from their buds, were bedizened with dewdrops that coated their branches with liquid diamonds. The grasses clustered at the foot of the hedges, and the sparrows, who had returned only a few days before, swooped in their graceful curves between sky and water; a breeze perfumed by the flowering forest whispered along the road and wrinkled the surface of the river. All these beauties of the morning, the aromas of the plants, the scent of the earth rising toward the sky, intoxicated the two lovers, walking side by side, leaning against each other, hand in hand, eyes seeking eyes, neither daring to speak, they had so much to say to each other.

The officer saw that the abandoned horse was wandering here and there, distracting Mademoiselle de Mancini, and used this as an excuse to approach and take charge of the royal mount. Then, walking nearby but between the horses, he observed the lovers' every word and gesture.

It was Mademoiselle de Mancini who spoke first. "Ah, my dear Sire!" she said. "So, you're not abandoning me, then?"

"No," the king replied, "as you can see, Marie."

"Everyone told me that once we were separated, you'd think no more of me!"

"Dear Marie, is it only today that you've realized we're surrounded by people eager to deceive us?"

"But, Sire, this journey, this alliance with Spain? They're marrying you off!"

Louis lowered his head. At the same time the officer saw the sun glint from Marie de Mancini's eyes, flashing like daggers drawn from their sheaths. "And you've done nothing on behalf of our love?" asked the young woman after a moment of silence.

"Ah, Mademoiselle! How can you believe that? I threw myself at my mother's feet, I begged, I pleaded. I said that my entire happiness depended on you. I even threatened . . ."

"Well?" Marie asked eagerly.

"Well! The queen mother wrote to the See of Rome, and they told her that an unapproved marriage between us would be invalid and would be nullified by the Holy Father. Finally, seeing there was no hope for us, I asked at least for a delay of my marriage with the infanta."

"That doesn't seem to have kept you from traveling to meet her."

"What would you have? All my prayers, my pleadings, and my tears, have been dismissed, negated by reasons of state."

"And so?"

"So, what, then? What would you have me do, Mademoiselle, with the will of all the powerful leagued against me?"

This time Marie lowered her head. "Then I must say goodbye, and forever," she said. "You know they're exiling me, almost burying me alive. More than that, you know they're planning to marry me off too!"

Louis turned pale and clutched at his heart.

"If it were only a matter of my life, persecuted as I was, I would have yielded—but I thought your life was at stake as well, my dear Sire, so I fought for your future."

"Oh, yes! My love, my treasure," murmured the king, more gallantly, perhaps, than passionately.

"The cardinal would have given in," said Marie, "if you'd gone to him, if you'd insisted. For the cardinal to call the King of France his nephew! Think of it, Sire! He'd risk anything for that, even a war; the cardinal, assured of his sole rule under the double pretext that he'd raised the king and had given him his niece, oh, the cardinal would have fought everybody, overcome all obstacles! Oh, Sire! I can answer for that. I'm a woman, and I see clearly where love is concerned."

These words produced a singular impression on the king. Instead of inflaming his passion, they cooled it. He stopped their progress and said, suddenly, "There's nothing more I can say, Mademoiselle. Everything has failed."

"Except your own will in the matter, dear Sire, isn't that so?"

"Alas!" said the king, blushing. "Do I even have a will of my own?"

"Oh!" cried Mademoiselle de Mancini, as if struck a physical blow. "The king has no will but that which politics dictates, no will but reasons of state."

"It's not will you lack, but love!" cried Marie. "If you loved me, Sire, you'd find the will."

And pronouncing these words, Marie raised her eyes to meet those of her lover, whom she saw more pallid and crushed than an exile who is about to leave his native land forever. "Accuse me of anything," murmured the king, "but don't say I don't love you."

A long silence followed these words, which the king had spoken with an undeniable sincerity.

"I can't bear to think, Sire," continued Marie, making a final effort, "that tomorrow, or the day after, I'll never see you again. I can't bear to think that I'll spend the rest of my days away from Paris, that the lips of an old man, a stranger, will kiss the hand you hold in yours; no, truly, I can't bear to think this, Sire, without my poor heart breaking in despair."

And indeed, Marie de Mancini burst into tears. For his part, the king brought his handkerchief to his lips and stifled a sob. "See," she said, "the carriages have stopped; my sister is waiting, and the time is now. What you decide here will bind us for life! Oh, Sire—do you want me to lose you? Is what you want, Louis, that the one to whom you said, 'I love you,' should belong to someone other than her king, her master, and her beloved? Oh, have courage, Louis! Just say the word, a single phrase, just say, 'I want you!' And all my life will be yours, all my heart will be yours forever."

The king said nothing.

Marie then looked at him as Dido looked at Aeneas in the Elysian Fields, with fierce disdain. "Goodbye, then," she said. "Goodbye to life. Goodbye to love. Goodbye to heaven!"

And she turned to leave, but the king restrained her, seizing her hand, which he carried to his lips. Then, despair prevailing over the resolution that he seemed to have taken internally, he let fall on that beautiful hand a burning tear of regret that made Marie shudder, as though it really had burned her.

She saw the king's wet eyes, his pale brow, his trembling lips, and she exclaimed in a tone impossible to describe, "Oh, Sire! You're the king, so you may weep, but still I must go!"

The king's only reply was to hide his face in his handkerchief.

The horses shied as something like a muffled roar came from the officer who held them.

And then Mademoiselle de Mancini, indignation incarnate, left the king and hastened back to her carriage, calling to the coachman, "Drive, and quickly!"

The coachman obeyed, whipping up the mules, and the heavy carriage squealed on its straining axles, while the King of France, alone, cast down, annihilated, dared not turn to watch it go.

XIV

In Which the King and the Lieutenant Exchange Proofs of Memory

The king, looking like every lover since time began, stood staring blankly at the horizon over which his mistress's carriage had disappeared. When he'd turned away and looked back again a dozen times and had at last succeeded in restoring some calm to his mind and his heart, he remembered that he wasn't alone. The officer was still holding their horses by the bridles and hadn't yet lost all hope of seeing the king's resolve return: *He could still mount up and go after the carriage,* he thought. *We've lost nothing but a little time.*

But the imagination of the lieutenant of Musketeers was more optimistic than the reality, an indulgence the king was careful to avoid. He contented himself with approaching the officer and saying, in a sad voice, "Come, we're done here. To horse."

The king slowly mounted, in weariness and sorrow, and the officer did the same. The king spurred on, and the lieutenant followed.

At the bridge, Louis turned one last time. The officer, patient as a god who has eternity before and after him, still hoped for a return of willpower. But to no avail. Louis rode up the street that led to the château and entered the gate as seven o'clock sounded. Once the king had returned to his chamber, and the musketeer had seen, as he saw everything, a corner of the curtain twitch in the cardinal's window, he uttered a great sigh, like a man freed from heavy shackles, and said quietly to himself, "Now then, old soldier, it's finally over!"

After a few minutes of silence, the king called his attending gentleman. "I'm not at home to anyone until two o'clock," he said. "Do you understand, Monsieur?"

"Sire," replied the gentleman, "someone has already asked to see you."

"Who?"

"Your Lieutenant of Musketeers."

"The one who accompanied me?"

"Yes, Sire."

"Ah!" said the king. "Very well, show him in."

The officer entered. The king gestured to dismiss his gentleman and his valet. Louis watched until they'd closed the door behind them, and when the tapestry had fallen back into place, he said, "Your presence reminds me, Monsieur, that I'd forgotten to warn you to maintain absolute discretion about this morning's events."

"Oh, Sire! Why should Your Majesty bother to give me such a warning? It seems he doesn't know me."

"Yes, Monsieur, that's true. I know that you're discreet, but as I hadn't been specific . . ."

The officer bowed. "Your Majesty has nothing more to tell me?" he asked.

"No, Monsieur. You may withdraw."

"May I request permission not to do so until I've spoken with the king, Sire?"

"What do you have to say to me? Explain yourself, Monsieur."

"Sire, it's a matter of little importance to you but of great importance to me. Forgive me for bringing it up, but if it wasn't urgent and necessary I wouldn't bother, I'd just disappear, silent and meek as always."

"Disappear? What are you talking about?"

"To be brief, Sire," said the officer, "I come to ask for my discharge from Your Majesty's service."

The king started, but the officer was as stolid as a statue.

"Your discharge from me, Monsieur?" said the king. "And for how long, if you please?"

"For good, Sire."

"You would quit my service, Monsieur?" said Louis, unable to conceal his surprise.

"I'm afraid so, Sire."

"Impossible."

"And yet there it is, Sire. I'm getting old; I've been in harness for thirty-five years, and my shoulders are stooping. It's time to give way to younger men. I'm not suited to this new reign, I still have one foot in the old one. Everything nowadays is strange to me, it takes me by surprise and makes me dizzy. In short, I have the honor to ask Your Majesty for my discharge."

"Monsieur," said the king, looking at the officer, who was wearing his soldier's buffcoat with an ease that would have been the envy of a younger man, "you've got more strength and stamina than I have."

"Oh!" shrugged the officer, smiling in false modesty. "Your Majesty says that because I have a pretty good eye, my mustache is still black, I stand straight and sit my horse well, but Sire, that's all vanity, mere illusion, smoke and mirrors! I may look young, but inside I'm old, and within six months I'm sure I'll be a broken down, gouty invalid. And so, Sire . . ."

"Monsieur," interrupted the king, "don't you remember what you told me yesterday? You stood right there and told me you were the healthiest man in France, a stranger to fatigue who could stand at your post night and day. Did you say that, or didn't you? Recall your words, Monsieur."

The officer sighed. "Sire," he said, "old age is vain, and old men must be forgiven for boasting beyond their abilities. I may very well have said that, Sire, but the fact is that I'm exhausted and ask to be retired."

"Monsieur," said the king, with a majestic gesture toward the officer, "you're not giving me your real reasons. You want to leave my service, I see that, but you're hiding your true motives."

"Sire, believe me . . ."

"I believe what I see, Monsieur, and what I see is an energetic and vigorous man, sharp and quick-minded, possibly the best soldier in France, a man who can in no way persuade me that he's in need of a change."

"Ah, Sire!" said the lieutenant, with an edge of bitterness. "Such praise! Truly, Your Majesty confounds me. Energetic, vigorous, sharp, and quick, the best soldier in the army! Your Majesty exaggerates what merit I have to the point where I hardly recognize myself. If I were vain enough to believe even half of Your Majesty's words, I'd think I was a vital, even indispensable man. I'd say that such a servant, endowed with such shining qualities, must be a treasure beyond price. However, I must say, Sire, that for all my life until today, I've been appreciated, in my opinion, at well below my value. So, I repeat, Your Majesty must be exaggerating."

The king frowned, for he felt the officer's bitter speech verged on insolence. "Come, Monsieur," he said, "let's get to the point. If you're dissatisfied with my service, say so. No evasions, now—answer me boldly and frankly. I want to hear you."

The officer, who had been turning his hat in his hands in agitation, looked up at these words. "Oh, Sire!" he said. "That puts me more at ease. Since the question is put so frankly, I'll respond with the same frankness. To speak the truth is a good thing, because it relieves the burden on one's heart, and because it happens so rarely. I will therefore tell my king the truth, while begging him to excuse the bluntness of an old soldier."

Louis now looked at his officer with unconcealed anxiety and made an agitated gesture. "Well, then, speak," he said, "for I'm impatient to hear these truths you have to tell me."

The officer tossed his hat on a table, and his expression, always martial and intelligent, took on a strange new character of solemnity and even grandeur. "Sire," he said, "I resign the service of the king because I'm dissatisfied. The valet, at his work, can respectfully approach his master as I do, give him a report on his labors, turn in his tools, account for any funds expended, and say, 'Master, my day is done, please pay me and send me on my way.'"

"Monsieur!" cried the king, purple with anger.

"Oh, Sire," replied the officer, bowing and bending his knee, "never was a servant more respectful than I am now before Your Majesty; only, you ordered me to tell the truth. Now that I've begun, it must all come out, even if you command me to silence."

And such resolution was displayed in the lines on the officer's face that Louis XIV had no need to urge him to continue, he continued on his own, while the king regarded him with curiosity mixed with admiration.

"Sire, for nearly thirty-five years, as I said, I've served the royal house of France. Few people have worn out as many swords in this service as I have, Sire, and they were good swords too. At first, I was a child, ignorant of anything but courage, but the king your father thought he saw in me a man. I was a man, Sire, when Cardinal Richelieu, who never doubted it, thought he saw in me an enemy. Sire, you could read the story of that battle between the ant and the lion, from first to last, in your family's secret archives. If you ever feel so inclined, Sire, you should do so; the story is worth the trouble, if I dare say so myself. You'll read how the lion, harassed, worn out, panting, finally called for quarter, and to do him justice, he gave as well as he got.

"Oh, those were brave times, Sire, of glorious battles, like an epic of Tasso or Ariosto![53] The heroic works of that age, which no one now would believe, were to us a daily routine. For five years running I was a hero every day, or so some worthy folk have told me, and believe me, Sire, five years of heroism is no small thing! But I believe what I was told by those worthy folk, for they knew whereof they spoke; they were Messieurs de Richelieu, de Buckingham, de Beaufort, and de Retz,[54] the latter a past master of street fighting! As did King Louis XIII, and even the queen, your august mother, who said to me one day, 'Thank you,' though I dare not think of the service I had the honor to render her. Excuse me, Sire, for speaking so boldly, but what I've had the honor to recount to Your Majesty is, as I said, history."

The king gnawed at his lip and threw himself angrily into an armchair.

"I've upset Your Majesty," said the lieutenant. "Well, Sire, that's how the truth is! It's a harsh bedfellow, bristling with iron, hurtful to those who hear it, and sometimes to those who speak it."

"No, Monsieur," the king said. "I invited you to speak, so speak."

"After the service of the king and the cardinal, Sire, came the service of the regency. I fought well in the unrest of the Fronde, though perhaps less well than formerly. But people were growing smaller, and my opponents were lesser men than before. Nevertheless, I led Your Majesty's Musketeers on some dangerous missions in my time with the company.

"They were good times while they lasted! I was Monsieur de Mazarin's favorite: lieutenant, here! Lieutenant, there! Lieutenant, to the right! Lieutenant, to the left! There was hardly a conflict in France in which your humble servant wasn't involved—but soon France wasn't enough for Monsieur le Cardinal, and he sent me to England as an envoy to Monsieur Cromwell. Now there was a man of stone and iron, let me tell you, Sire. I had the honor to get to know him, and to take his measure. A great deal had been promised me if I accomplished that mission, and as I exceeded all expectations, I was generously rewarded: I was promoted to Captain of the Musketeers,[55] that is to say, the most envied military rank at Court, which gives precedence over even the Marshals of France; and that's only fair, for when you say Captain of Musketeers, you say the flower of chivalry and foremost of the brave!"

"Captain, Monsieur?" said the king. "Surely you mean lieutenant."

"Not at all, Sire, I make no such mistake; Your Majesty may rely on me in that regard. Monsieur de Mazarin gave me the promotion."

"Well, then?"

"Well, Monsieur de Mazarin, as you know better than anyone, rarely gives anything away, and what he gives he sometimes takes back. He revoked the rank once peace was made and he no longer needed me. I don't say I was worthy to fill the shoes of Monsieur de Tréville,[56] of illustrious memory, but still, they promised it to me, they'd given it to me, and they should have left it with me."

"Is that why you're dissatisfied, Monsieur? Well, I'll look into it! I love justice, and your claim, though made with military brusqueness, doesn't displease me."

"No, Sire!" said the officer. "Your Majesty has misunderstood me; I no longer press any such claim."

"Don't overdo the modesty, Monsieur. I will look into your affair, and later . . ."

"Oh, Sire, Sire! That word, *later*. For thirty years I've been dining on the bounty of that word, which I've heard spoken by all the high and mighty, and which now I hear from your mouth. *Later!* Meanwhile, I've taken twenty wounds and have reached the age of fifty-four without a louis in my pocket and without ever having found a master who would protect me—me, who has protected so many masters! As of today, that's changed, Sire, and when I'm told *later*, my reply is *now*. That's the change I ask for, Sire. And it might as well be granted me, as it will cost no one anything."

"I didn't expect to hear such language, Monsieur, especially from one who is accustomed to dealing with the *grands*. You forget you're speaking to a king, to a gentleman whose word, I should think, must be accounted as good as your own. When I say *later*, I'm speaking of a certainty."

"I don't doubt it, Sire, but here is the gist of the terrible truth I have to tell you: even if I saw on the table in front of me the baton of a marshal, the Sword of the Constable, and the Crown of Poland, instead of *later*, I swear to you, Sire, I would still say *now*. Please excuse me, Sire—I'm from the country of your grandfather, Henri IV, and there we don't say much, but when we do, we say it all."

"I am just coming into my reign. That future doesn't appeal to you, Monsieur?" said Louis haughtily.

"It seems everything is forgotten," the officer said with nobility. "The master has forgotten the servant, and now the servant is accused of forgetting the master. I live in unhappy times, Sire! I see youth ruled by discouragement and fear, timid and exploited, when it ought to be rich and powerful. Last night, for example, I opened the door of the King of France to admit the King of England, whose father, humble though I am, I very nearly saved, if God hadn't been against me, for the Lord had inspired his enemy

Cromwell. I opened, as I said, that door, to the palace of one brother to another, and I see—alas, Sire, this is a blow to my heart! I see the king's minister turn away the exile and humiliate his master into condemning to misery another king, his equal. I witness my prince, who is young, handsome, and brave, who has courage in his heart and fire in his eyes, I see him tremble before a priest who laughs from behind the curtain of his ministry, where he lies on his bed counting all the gold in France, which he then hides away in secret vaults.

"Yes, I can see it in your expression, Sire: I'm bold to the point of madness. But what would you have? I'm an old soldier, and I say here, to you, my King, things I would cram down the throat of anyone else who dared to say them in front of me. But you commanded me to open the depths of my heart to you, Sire, and I place at Your Majesty's feet all the bitter gall I've amassed over thirty years of service, just as I would spill every drop of my blood for Your Majesty if you ordered me to do so."

The king, without saying a word, wiped away the drops of cold sweat trickling from his temples. The moments of silence that followed this vehement outburst seemed like centuries of suffering to both of them.

"Monsieur," the king said at last, "you spoke the word *forgotten*, the only word I will admit to hearing, and the one to which I'll reply. Others may have been forgetful, but not me, and the proof is that I remember one day during the riots, when the people were furious, and like an angry and roaring sea, they invaded the Palais Royal. On that day, while I pretended to be sleeping, one man, with a naked sword, hid behind my curtained bed to watch over my life, ready to risk his own for me, as he'd already twenty times risked it for my family. Was not this gentleman, whose name I asked—was he not called Monsieur d'Artagnan?* Tell me, Monsieur."

"Your Majesty has a good memory," replied the officer coldly.

"You see, then, Monsieur," continued the king, "if I have such a good memory of my childhood, how much better it must be since I've reached the age of reason."

"Your Majesty has been richly endowed by God," said the officer in the same tone.

"Come, Monsieur d'Artagnan," continued Louis in desperate appeal, "can't you be as patient as I am? Can't you do as I do? Come, now."

"And what is it you're doing, Sire?"

"I'm waiting."

"Your Majesty can wait because he's young, but I, Sire, have no more time to wait. Old age knocks at my door, and death is beyond him, peering into the depths of my house. Your Majesty is at the beginning of life, and full of hope for fortune to come, but I'm at the other end of the horizon, Sire, so far from Your Majesty that I don't have time enough to wait for him to reach me."

Louis took a turn around the room, continually wiping away that cold sweat that would have put his doctors into a fright. "Very well, Monsieur," said Louis XIV curtly. "You desire your discharge? You shall have it. You offer me your resignation from the rank of Lieutenant of the King's Musketeers?"

"I place it humbly at Your Majesty's feet, Sire."

"Fine. I will arrange your pension."

"I shall have a thousand obligations to Your Majesty."

"Monsieur," said the king, making an effort at self-control, "I think you'll be losing a good master."

"I am sure of that, Sire."

"And where will you find another like him?"

"Oh, Sire! I know well that Your Majesty is one of a kind, so I am resolved to never serve another king on this earth and will have no master other than myself."

"You mean it?"

"Your Majesty, I swear it."

"I'll hold you to your word, Monsieur."

D'Artagnan bowed.

"And you know I have a good memory," continued the king.

"Yes, Sire, and yet I wish Your Majesty's memory of this last hour should dim and forget the miseries that I brought before his eyes. His Majesty is so far above the poor and the lowly, that I hope . . ."

"My Majesty, Monsieur, will shine like the sun, which sees everyone, great and small, rich and poor, giving luster to some, warmth to others, and life to all. Adieu, Monsieur d'Artagnan, adieu. You are free."

And the king, choking off a hoarse sob, hurried away into the next chamber.

D'Artagnan took his hat from the table where he'd tossed it and went out.

XV

The Exile

D'Artagnan had scarcely gone down the stairs before the king called in his gentleman of the day. "I have a task for you, Monsieur," he said.

"I am at Your Majesty's command."

"Wait, then."

And the young king wrote the following letter, which cost him more than one sigh, though at times his eyes flashed with triumph.

> *Monsieur le Cardinal,*
>
> *Thanks to your wise counsel, and most particularly to your firm persistence, I've been able to conquer a weakness unworthy of a king. You have too skillfully arranged my future for me to allow an ungrateful impulse to destroy all your work. I have come to understand that I was wrong to want to deviate from the road you've paved for my life. Beyond doubt, it would have been a tragedy for France and for my family for me to allow a misunderstanding between me and my minister.*
>
> *That is certainly what would have happened if I'd made your niece my wife. I understand that now, and henceforth will do nothing to oppose the achievement of my destiny. I'm ready to marry the Infanta Marie-Thérèse.* You can proceed with arranging the conference of negotiation.*
>
> *Your affectionate,*
> *LOUIS*

The king read over his letter, and then sealed it himself. "Take this letter to Monsieur le Cardinal," he said.

The gentleman went out. At the door of Mazarin's suite, he met Bernouin, who was awaiting him anxiously.

"Well?" asked the minister's confidential valet.

"A letter for His Eminence, Monsieur," said the gentleman.

"A letter! Ah! We've been expecting one, after that little trip this morning."

"Oh? You knew that His Majesty . . ."

"In our capacity as prime minister, it's the duty of our office to know everything. His Majesty begs and pleads, I presume?"

"I don't know about that, but he sighed quite a bit while writing it."

"Yes, yes, we know what that means. We sigh from happiness as well as from sorrow, Monsieur."

"Maybe so, but the king didn't look very happy when he came back, Monsieur."

"You must not have looked closely. Besides, you saw only His Majesty when he returned, with just his guard lieutenant. But I held His Eminence's telescope for him and looked through it once he got tired. The lovers both cried, I'm sure of it."

"And you think they cried from happiness?"

"No, from love, and they swore a thousand tender oaths that the king intends to fulfill. This letter is the beginning of that fulfillment."

"And what does His Eminence think of this love, which, by the way, is no secret to anyone?"

Climbing the stairs, Bernouin took the arm of Louis's messenger and said, in an undertone, "Confidentially, His Eminence is counting on its success. I know it means we'll have war with Spain, but bah! The nobility love a good war. The cardinal, moreover, will dower his niece royally, and more than royally. Money will flow, there will be festivals and fireworks, and everyone will be satisfied."

"Well," replied the gentleman, "it seems to me this is a pretty light letter to contain all that."

"Friend," said Bernouin, "I'm sure of what I say; Monsieur d'Artagnan told me everything."

"Really! And what did he say?"

"I approached him to ask if he had any news for the cardinal, without showing our hand, of course, for Monsieur d'Artagnan is a very sharp player. 'My dear Monsieur Bernouin,' he replied, 'the king is madly in love with Mademoiselle de Mancini, and that's all I have to say.' 'Indeed,' I said, 'do you think he's reached the point of opposing His Eminence's plans for him?' 'Ah, don't ask me that; I think the king is capable of anything. He has a soul of iron, and when he wants something, he wants it. If he's resolved in his mind to marry Mademoiselle de Mancini, he'll marry her.' And with that he left me, went to the stables, took a horse that he'd saddled himself, jumped astride and rode off as if the devil were after him."

"What do you think?"

"I think Monsieur Lieutenant knew more than he wanted to say."

"Then, in your opinion, Monsieur d'Artagnan . . ."

"Has gone, in all probability, after the exiles, to do whatever he can to help the king's love affair to success."

And speaking thus, the two confidants arrived at the door to His Eminence's study. His Eminence had shaken the gout and was pacing anxiously in his chamber, listening at the doors and peering out the windows.

Bernouin came in, followed by the gentleman whom the king had ordered to deliver his letter into His Eminence's hands. Mazarin took the letter, but before opening it he composed his features into a bland smile, a useful mask to conceal his emotions, whatever they might be. That way, no matter what impression the letter made upon him, that impression couldn't be read on his face.

"Very good!" he said, after reading the letter over twice. "Excellent, Monsieur. Inform the king that I thank him for his obedience to the queen mother's wishes, and that I will do everything I can to enact his will."

The gentleman went out. As soon as the door closed behind him, the cardinal, who wore no masks for Bernouin, dropped the expression that had cloaked his countenance and said, in his darkest tone, "Call Monsieur de Brienne."

The secretary arrived five minutes later. "Monsieur," Mazarin told him, "I've just done a great service for the monarchy, the greatest I've ever rendered. You will bear this letter, which is proof of it, to Her Majesty the queen mother, and when she's returned it to you, you will file it in Box B, which contains similar documents related to my service."

Brienne went out, and as this momentous letter had already been opened, he didn't fail to read it on his way. It goes without saying that Bernouin, who followed at his elbow, also read it over his shoulder. Thereafter the news spread through the château so quickly that Mazarin had reason to fear it might reach the queen's ears before Monsieur de Brienne handed her Louis's letter. Shortly thereafter all the orders were given for departure, and Monsieur de Condé, after attending the king's pretense of a morning *lever*,[57] inscribed on his tablets the city of Poitiers as the next destination of Their Majesties.

And thus was unraveled in a few minutes an intrigue that had been the secret fascination of half the diplomats of Europe. It had, however, nothing very clear as an immediate result other than the poor Lieutenant of Musketeers' loss of his post and his income—though it's true that in exchange he had won his freedom.

We shall soon see how Monsieur d'Artagnan took advantage of this. For the moment, we hope the reader will be so kind as to allow us to return to the Inn of The Médicis, and a window that had just opened there at the very moment when the orders were given up at the château for the king's departure. This window opened out from one of the rooms of Charles II. The unhappy prince had spent the night in bitter musing, his head in his hands and his elbows on a table, while Parry, old and weary, slept slumped in a corner, exhausted in mind and body.

It was a strange destiny for that faithful servant, now witnessing a second generation suffering a frightful series of misfortunes like those that had burdened the first. When Charles II considered this new defeat he'd just suffered, when he fully comprehended the dreadful isolation that awaited him now that this last hope had failed him, he was seized by a sort of dizziness and had fallen back into an armchair. Then God took pity on the unfortunate prince and sent to him sleep, the innocent brother of death.

He didn't awaken until half past six, when the sun was already shining into his room, and Parry, afraid to move lest he wake the prince, was looking with profound sadness at the young man, whose eyes were still red from the day before, and whose cheeks were pale from suffering and privation. Finally, the sound of some heavy wagons rumbling down toward the Loire had awakened Charles. He rose, looked around like a man at a loss for where he was, saw Parry, took his hand between his own, and told him to go and settle their account with Master Cropole.

Master Cropole, when totaling the bill with Parry, acquitted himself, it must be said, like an honest man. He made only his usual complaint, that the two travelers had eaten nothing, which was doubly embarrassing for his kitchen and because he had to charge them for something they hadn't consumed but was nonetheless wasted. Parry couldn't argue with this, and paid.

"I hope," said the king, "that it wasn't the same with our horses. I didn't see their food listed on the bill, and it would be a shame for travelers like us to get down the road and find our horses collapsing from hunger."

Master Cropole, hearing this, assumed an air of majesty and replied that the feeding troughs of The Médicis were no less hospitable than its kitchen.

The king mounted his horse, as did his servant, and the two took the road to Paris, encountering almost no one on the way, in the streets or outskirts of the town. The blow was most severe for the prince, as this was a new exile. Unfortunate people cling to their slightest hopes, as the fortunate do to their bounties, and when forced to leave the places where hope has tempted their hearts, they feel the deadly grief of the banished when they embark on their ships of deportation. A heart already wounded many times over suffers at every new sting, and good becomes no more than the brief absence of ill, a mere cessation of pain. In such misfortunes God seems to offer hope as a torment, like the drop of water the rich sinners in Hell asked of Lazarus.

For a moment, when he'd been welcomed by his brother Louis, hope for Charles II had been more than just a fleeting joy. Then reality had intervened, and the blow of Mazarin's refusal had revealed that hope to be nothing more than a dream. Louis XIV's promise had been nothing more than a mockery, a farce—like Charles's crown, like his scepter, like his so-called friends, like everything promised in his royal infancy and lost in his proscribed youth. Mockery! All promises were mockery for Charles II, all but the cold, dark repose promised by death.

Such were the thoughts of this unhappy prince as, slumped in the saddle, almost dropping the reins, he rode into the gentle warm sunlight of May, which in his somber misanthropy the exile saw only as the final insult to his grief.

XVI

"Remember!"

About half an hour after the two travelers left Blois, a rider rapidly approached them, raising his hat as he hurried past. The king paid little attention to the young man, who was in his early twenties, and who turned in the saddle to give a friendly wave back along the road toward a man standing in front of a gate, beyond which was a handsome house of red brick and white stone with a slate roof, off to the left of the road the prince was following.

The man by the gate was tall and spare, with the white hair of the elderly, and responded to the young man's wave with gestures of farewell as tender as that of a father toward a son. The young man finally disappeared around a turn behind the tall trees that lined the road, and the old man was turning toward the house, when the two travelers, arriving in front of the gate, attracted his attention. The king, as we said, was riding with head bowed, arms loose, almost allowing the horse to choose his own way, while Parry, just behind him, had removed his hat to enjoy the warmth of the sun, and was looking left and right as they rode along. His eyes met those of the old man leaning against the gate, who suddenly gasped and took a step toward the two travelers, as if struck by an unexpected sight. From Parry, his eyes turned to the king, where his gaze paused for a moment. This scrutiny, brief though it was, caused an immediate change to come over the old man, for scarcely had he recognized the youngest of the two travelers—we say recognized, for only positive recognition could explain his behavior—scarcely had he recognized the youngest of the two travelers when he clasped his hands together in surprise, then raised his hat and bowed so low he was almost kneeling.

Distracted though the king was by his dark reflections, this nonetheless caught his attention. He stopped his horse, turned to Parry and said, "Lord above, Parry, who is this man who salutes me thus? Do you suppose, by any chance, that he knows me?"

Parry, pale and agitated, had already turned his horse toward the gate. "Oh, Sire!" he said suddenly, stopping five or six paces from the old man. "Sire, I'm stunned and amazed, for I think I know this good man. Yes, it's he, himself! Would Your Majesty permit me to speak with him?"

"Of course."

"Is it really you, Monsieur Grimaud?" asked Parry.

"Yes, it's me," said the tall old man, straightening up but retaining his attitude of respect.

"I was right, Sire," said Parry. "This man is the servant of the Comte de La Fère, that worthy gentlemen whom I've spoken of so often with Your Majesty that the memory of him must be engraved on both your mind and your heart."

"He who assisted the king my father in his final moments?" asked Charles. And the king visibly shuddered at the memory.

"Exactly, Sire."

"Alas!" said Charles. Then, addressing Grimaud, whose bright, intelligent eyes seemed to encourage him to speak, he said, "Your master, Monsieur le Comte de La Fère, does he live nearby?"

"There," replied Grimaud, pointing to the red and white house beyond the gate.

"And is the Comte de La Fère home at present?"

"Around back, under the chestnut trees."

"Parry," said the king, "I don't want to miss this unexpected chance to thank the gentleman who's shown our house such generosity and devotion. Please hold my horse, *mon ami*."

And tossing his bridle to Grimaud, the king went alone toward Athos's house, like an equal to meet an equal. Charles, informed by the laconic Grimaud of where the count would be found, went around the house to the left and then straight to a tree-lined lane. It was easy to find; the tops of those tall trees, already covered with blossoms, towered above their neighbors.

Stepping into the pattern of light and shadow cast by the variegated foliage above, the young prince saw a gentleman strolling with his arms behind his back, apparently plunged into a deep reverie. Without any doubt but that this was the gentleman so often described to him, Charles II marched right up to him without hesitation. At the sound of his footsteps the Comte de La Fère turned, and seeing a stranger of elegant and noble aspect approaching him, he drew his hat from his head and waited. A few paces short of him Charles II stopped, took his own hat in his hand, and in response to the count's mute interrogation, said, "Monsieur le Comte, I have come because I have a duty to perform. I have for a long time wished to express a deep gratitude to you. I am Charles II, son of Charles Stuart, who reigned over England and died on the scaffold."

At this illustrious name, Athos shivered with frisson, and at the sight of the young prince standing before him and holding out his hand, two tears momentarily stood in his beautiful eyes. He bowed respectfully, but the prince took his hand and said, "See how unfortunate I am, Monsieur le Comte. It's only by chance that I find myself here. Alas! I ought to have people around me whom I love and honor, but I'm reduced to honoring their services in my heart and holding their names in my memory. If it wasn't for your servant, who recognized mine as we rode by your gate, I would have passed your house as if it were that of a stranger."

"All too true," said Athos, answering with his voice to the first part of the prince's speech, and with a bow to the second. "Indeed, Your Majesty has seen some dark days."

"And alas, there may be worse yet to come!" replied Charles.

"We must have hope, Sire!"

"Count, Count!" said Charles, shaking his head. "I hoped until last night, like a good Christian, I swear it."

Athos looked at the king as if to ask him to continue. "Oh, the story is easily told!" said Charles II. "Exiled, despoiled, and scorned, I resolved, despite my reluctance, to tempt fortune one more time. Is it not written on high that, for our family, all good and ill eternally derive from France?

You know something about that, Monsieur, you who were one of those Frenchmen whom my unhappy father found at the foot of his scaffold on the day of his death, as he'd found them at his right hand on the day of battle."

"Sire," said Athos modestly, "I wasn't alone, and my companions and I did, under the circumstances, only what our honor as gentlemen compelled us to do, that's all. But Your Majesty was about to do me the honor to tell me . . ."

"Of course. I was under the protection—pardon my hesitation, Count, but for a Stuart, as I know you understand, it's difficult to say that word—under the protection of my cousin the Stadtholder of Holland, but he wouldn't undertake to do more than that without the intervention, or at least the authorization, of France. So, I came to ask for the support of the King of France, but he refused me."

"The king refused you, Sire!"

"Oh, not him! I must be fair to my younger brother Louis. It was Monsieur de Mazarin."

Athos bit his lips.

"You think perhaps I should have expected such a refusal," said the king, seeing the count's expression.

"That was indeed my thought, Sire," the count replied respectfully. "I know that Italian of old."

"I'd resolved to push this thing to its end and know once and for all the outcome of my destiny; I told my brother Louis that, to compromise neither France nor Holland, I'd pursue my throne personally, and just needed two hundred gentlemen, if he'd give them to me, or a million in gold, if he'd lend it to me."

"Well, Sire?"

"Well, Monsieur! I'm now experiencing something strange, the grim satisfaction of despair. There is in some souls, and now I find that I'm one of them, a sort of serenity in the realization that all is lost and it's time, at last, to give in."

"Oh!" said Athos. "I hope that Your Majesty has not yet arrived at that extremity."

"To say that to me, Monsieur le Comte, to try to revive hope in my heart, shows that you don't understand what I've told you. I came to Blois, Count, to beg of my brother Louis the alms of a million that I needed to resolve my troubles, and my brother Louis has refused me. So, you see that all is lost."

"Would Your Majesty permit me to voice a contrary opinion?"

"Count, do you think me so ill-informed that I don't understand my own situation?"

"Sire, I have always noted that it's when things seem darkest that there come the greatest turns of fortune."

"Thank you, Count, and it is indeed a thing of beauty to encounter hearts like yours with enough confidence in God and in monarchy not to despair of royal fortune, no matter how low it falls. Unfortunately, your words, dear Count, are like those remedies they call 'sovereign,' which might heal curable wounds, but have no power over death. Thanks for your perseverance in attempting to console me, and for your past devotions, but I know what to expect.

"Nothing will save me now. You see, my friend, I'm so convinced of it that I'm taking the road to final exile with ancient Parry, and will go savor my poignant sorrow in the hermitage Holland has offered me. There, believe me, Count, all will soon come to an ending and death will quickly find me, the way it's summoned by a soul that tires of its body and aspires only to heaven!"

"Your Majesty has a mother, a sister, and brothers; he is the head of a family and should ask a long life of God rather than a quick death. Your Majesty may be exiled, even hunted, but you have the right on your side, and should aspire to the dangers of combat and affairs of state rather than the repose of heaven."

"Count," said Charles II with a smile of indescribable sadness, "have you ever heard of a king who's reconquered his realm with no more than a single servant the age of Parry and the three hundred crowns he carries in his purse?"

"No, Sire. But I've heard, more than once, of a dethroned king who's regained his realm with a firm will, perseverance, some friends, and a million in gold carefully deployed."

"But didn't you hear what I said? I asked for that million from my brother Louis and was refused."

"Sire," said Athos, "will Your Majesty grant me a few more minutes and listen closely to what I have to tell him?"

Charles II looked searchingly at Athos. "Willingly, Monsieur," he said.

"I hope Your Majesty will allow me to lead the way," the count said, going toward the house.

And he led the king into his study and gave him a chair. "Sire," he said, "Your Majesty has just informed me that, given the state of affairs in England, a million would suffice to reconquer his realm, isn't that so?"

"Enough to attempt it, at least, and to die like a king if it failed."

"Well, Sire! Will Your Majesty, as promised, deign to listen to what I have to say?"

Charles nodded his head in assent. Athos went to the door, looked out to make sure no one was near, closed and locked it, and returned. "Sire," he said, "Your Majesty knows well that I assisted the most noble and unfortunate Charles I when his executioners brought him from St. James to Whitehall."

"Yes, indeed, I recall and will always remember it."

"Sire, it's a mournful story for a son to hear, especially when he's already heard it countless times, but I must repeat it to Your Majesty without leaving out a single detail."

"Speak, Monsieur."

"When the king your father mounted the scaffold, or rather passed from his room onto the scaffold built outside his window, everything had been prepared for his escape. The executioner had been abducted, a hole had been excavated beneath the floor of his apartment, and I myself was concealed below the planks when I suddenly heard them creak above my head."

"Parry has informed me of all these details, Monsieur."

Athos bowed and continued, "Then I will tell you what he could not, Sire, for the following passed only between God, your father, and me, and has been shared with no one, not even my dearest friends. 'Step away,' the august victim said to the masked executioner, 'but only for a moment, for I know I belong to you, but strike only at my signal. I want to be free to utter my final prayer.'"

"Your pardon," said Charles II, his features pale, "but you, Count, who know so many details of that fatal event, even some, as you said just now, that you've never before revealed—do you know the name of that infernal executioner, of that coward who hid his face so he could assassinate a king with impunity?"

Athos also paled slightly. "His name?" he said. "Yes, I know it, but I will not speak it."

"And what has become of him? No one in England knows his fate."

"He is dead."

"But he didn't die in bed, not a calm and gentle death, the death of an honest man?"

"He died a violent death on a terrible night, caught between the wrath of men and the gales of God. His body was pierced to the heart by a dagger and sank into the depths of the ocean. May God forgive his murderer!"[58]

"Very well, then," said King Charles II, who saw that the count wished to say no more.

"The King of England, after having, as I said, spoken to the masked executioner, added, 'Don't strike me, understand, until I extend my arms and say, *Remember!*'"

"In fact," said Charles in a hollow voice, "I know that was the final word spoken by my unhappy father. But for what purpose, and to whom?"

"To the French gentleman hidden just beneath the scaffold."

"To you, Monsieur?"

"Yes, Sire, and every word he said, through those planks covered in black fabric, still resounds in my ears. The king got down on one knee. 'Comte de La Fère,' he said, 'can you hear me?' 'Yes, Sire,' I replied. Then the king bent down closer."

Charles II, heart beating with grief like a hammer, also leaned toward Athos to catch every word that escaped the count's lips. His head bent till it touched Athos's head.

"As I said," continued the count, "the king leaned closer. 'Comte de La Fère,' he said, 'you were unable to save me. It wasn't meant to be. Now, having spoken to men, and having spoken to God, though I commit a sacrilege, I say my final words to you. On behalf of a cause that I held sacred, I have lost the throne of my fathers and imperiled my children's inheritance.'"

Charles II hid his face between his hands, and a burning tear escaped from between his slender white fingers.

"'A million in gold still remains,' continued the king. 'I buried it in the dungeon beneath the abbey keep in Newcastle just before I left that city.'"

Charles raised his head with an expression mixing sadness and joy that would have brought tears to the eyes of anyone who knew of his terrible trials. "A million!" he murmured. "Oh, Count!"

"'Only you know of this money's existence. Use it when the time is right for the greatest benefit to my eldest son. And now, Comte de La Fère, give me your final farewell.' 'Adieu, Sire, adieu!' I whispered."

Charles II rose and went to lean his burning forehead against the cool glass of the window.

"It was then," continued Athos, "that the king spoke the word *Remember!*— addressed to me. And as you see, Sire, I have remembered."

The king couldn't resist a flood of emotion. Athos saw his shoulders convulsively shaking, heard sobs escaping from deep in his chest. But Athos was silent, overwhelmed by the bitter memories he'd cascaded onto that royal head. Charles II, with a violent effort, left the window, swallowed his tears, and returned to his seat near the count. "Sire," Athos said, "I thought till today that it was not yet time to employ this final resource, but I have kept my eyes fixed on England and I felt the time was approaching. Tomorrow I had planned to begin seeking Your Majesty's whereabouts and then go to him. Since he has come to me, it's clear that God intended us to find each other."

"Monsieur," said Charles, in a voice still choked with emotion, "you are to me as an angel sent by God, a savior sent from beyond the grave by my father himself. But believe me, for ten years civil war has ravaged my country, slaughtering men and plowing up the ground. We're as unlikely to find gold still buried in the earth as we are to find love in the hearts of my subjects."

"Sire, the place where His Majesty buried his million is well known to me, and I'm sure no one has disturbed it. Has Newcastle Abbey been demolished, torn down stone by stone? That's what it would take."

"No, the abbey still stands, but at the moment General Monck occupies Newcastle and is encamped there. The only place where I can still find aid, my last resource, is in the hands of my enemies."

"General Monck, Sire, can't have discovered the treasure of which I speak."

"Yes, but must I go through Monck to recover this treasure? You can see, Count, that I must yield to destiny, as it strikes me down every time I get up. How could I do it with no servants but Parry, whom Monck has already chased off once? No, no, Count, we must accept this final blow."

"But where Your Majesty cannot go, what Parry cannot do, don't you think that I might succeed?"

"You, Count! You would go?"

"If it pleases Your Majesty, yes, Sire," said Athos, saluting the king, "I will go."

"But you're happy and settled here, Count!"

"I am never happy, Sire, when I have a duty unfulfilled, and the king your father charged me with the supreme duty to watch over your fortune and employ it when the time came. Your Majesty has but to give me the sign and I will go with him."

"Ah, Monsieur!" said the king, forgetting all royal etiquette and throwing his arms around Athos's neck. "You prove to me there's still a God in heaven, a God who sometimes sends his messengers to we who suffer on this earth."

Athos, deeply moved by the young man's emotional display, thanked him with profound respect and then went to the window. "Grimaud!" he called. "Our horses."

"What? You'd go right away?" said the king. "Truly, Monsieur, you're a man of wonder."

"Sire!" said Athos. "I can think of nothing more urgent than Your Majesty's service. Besides," he added with a smile, "it's a habit developed while in the service of the queen your aunt and the king your uncle. How could I do otherwise in the service of Your Majesty now?"

"What a man this is," murmured the king. Then, after a moment's reflection, "But no, Count, I can't expose you to such dangers. I have no way to reward such services."

"Bah!" said Athos, laughing. "Your Majesty must be jesting, as he has a million in gold! If only I had even half that sum, I'd already have raised a regiment. But, thanks be to God, I still have a few rolls of coins and some family jewelry, which Your Majesty, I hope, will deign to let his devoted servant share with him."

"No, but I'll share it with a friend—on the condition that my friend allows me to repay him later and share with him thereafter."

"Sire," said Athos, opening a coffer and drawing out gold and gems, "here's more than we need. Fortunately, there are four of us in case we encounter thieves."

Joy brought a rosy flush to the pale cheeks of Charles II. He saw two horses being led up to the portico by Grimaud, who was already booted for the road.

At the gate, the count said to a servant, "Blaisois, give this letter to the Vicomte de Bragelonne. For everyone else, we've gone to Paris. I entrust the house to you, Blaisois." His servant bowed, embraced Grimaud, and shut the gate behind them.

XVII

In Which Aramis Is Sought
but Only Bazin Is Found

Two hours had scarcely passed since the departure of the master of the house, whom Blaisois had watched until he'd disappeared on the road toward Paris, when a cavalier mounted on a sturdy piebald stopped in front of the gate and called, *"Holà!"* to the stable boys. They, with the gardeners, were gathered in a circle around Blaisois who, having been left in charge, was giving the estate's servants their orders.

The accent of this *Holà!* sounded familiar to Blaisois, who turned to look and then cried, "Monsieur d'Artagnan! . . . You there, hurry, run and open the gate!"

A swarm of eight lively lads ran to the gate and quickly dragged it open, bowing and scraping, for everyone knew the welcome their master always gave this visitor even if the valet's remarks hadn't spurred them on.

"Ah!" said Monsieur d'Artagnan with a pleasant smile, balancing on one stirrup before dropping to the ground. "And where is my dear count?"

"Your luck is out, Monsieur," said Blaisois, "and so is that of our master the count, for what will he say when he finds that he's missed you? Monsieur le Comte, by a stroke of fate, departed less than two hours ago."

D'Artagnan didn't seem very concerned. "All right, Blaisois," he said. "Since you speak the purest French of anyone, you can give me a lesson in grammar and proper speech while I await your master's return."

"That's impossible, Monsieur; it would be far too long a wait," said Blaisois.

"You don't expect him back today?"

"Nor tomorrow, Monsieur, nor the day after that. Monsieur le Comte has gone on a journey."

"A journey!" said d'Artagnan. "Nonsense! Admit you're telling me a fable."

"Monsieur, it's the absolute truth. Monsieur le Comte did me the honor of placing the house in my care, and he added in that voice of his, so full of authority and affection, 'Tell anyone who asks that I've gone to Paris.'"

"Well, then!" said d'Artagnan. "If he's off to Paris, that's all I needed to know. You should have told me that right away, you clown. You say he has a two-hour lead?"

"Yes, Monsieur."

"I'll catch up with him in no time. Is he alone?"

"No, Monsieur."

"Who's with him?"

"A gentleman I don't know, an old man, and Monsieur Grimaud."

"They won't ride as fast as I do . . . I'm off!"

"Monsieur, if you will only listen to me for a moment," said Blaisois, putting a hand to the horse's reins.

"All right, but be quick and don't make a speech out of it."

"Well, Monsieur! I believe this mention of Paris was nothing but a decoy."

"Oh ho!" said d'Artagnan. "A decoy, eh?"

"Indeed, Monsieur. I would swear that Monsieur le Comte's destination isn't Paris."

"Why do you think that?"

"Why? Because Monsieur Grimaud knows where our master is headed, and he promised me that, the next time he went to Paris, he'd take some money along for delivery to my wife."

"Oh, so you have a wife?"

"I have one, a local girl, but Monsieur thought her a chatterbox, so I sent her to live in Paris. Sometimes that's inconvenient, but at other times it's quite pleasant."

"I understand, but to the point: you don't think the count has gone to Paris?"

"No, Monsieur, for then Grimaud would have broken his word, which is quite impossible."

"That *is* impossible," repeated d'Artagnan, suddenly thoughtful, because he was quite convinced. "Well done, good Blaisois, and thank you."

Blaisois bowed.

"Now, see here, you know I'm not just curious, I have genuine business to conduct with your master. So, think, if you can, of anything he might have said. A single word, even a syllable, you understand, could put me on the trail."

"Upon my word, Monsieur, I heard nothing. I'm completely ignorant of Monsieur le Comte's destination. And I never eavesdrop at doors, as such things just aren't done in this house, it's quite forbidden."

"*Dame*, that is going to make it difficult," said d'Artagnan. "But you must, at least, know when he's planning to return?"

"No more, Monsieur, than I know where he's gone."

"Come, Blaisois, are you holding out on me?"

"Monsieur doubts my sincerity! Oh, Monsieur, I'm stricken with grief!"

"The devil take his golden tongue! A fool with a loose word would be worth a dozen of him," muttered d'Artagnan. Then, aloud, "Farewell, then!"

"Monsieur, please depart knowing I tender you all my respects."

"Pompous ass," d'Artagnan said to himself. "He's insufferable!" He gave the house a final glance, turned his horse and rode off with the nonchalance of a man who hasn't a worry in the world.

But once he was around the wall and out of sight, he took a deep breath and said, "Could Athos actually be at home? No, all those idlers loitering around Blaisois would have been hard at work if their master was around. Athos, on a journey? It's incomprehensible."

He shook his head. "Ah, bah! This is all damned mysterious. But, anyway, he's not the man I need right now. That man's in Melun, in a certain presbytery I know of. And that's forty-five leagues from here, which means four days. On, then—the weather is fine, and I'm free to go where I will! Never mind the distance."

Then he put his horse into a trot, on the road toward Paris. On the fourth day he arrived in Melun, as predicted.

D'Artagnan rarely paused to ask for directions or other common information unless he was seriously off course, preferring to rely on his own wits and perceptions, his thirty years of experience, and his habit of reading the faces of both men and their houses. At Melun, d'Artagnan quickly found his presbytery, a charming old building with plastered red brick walls, vines climbing up to the gutters, and a stone cross atop the gable of the roof. From the ground floor of this house came a noise, or rather a clamor of voices, like the cheeping of chicks when the chattering brood has just hatched. The deepest of these voices was reciting the alphabet in fat, fruity tones, pausing to correct his followers and lecture them on their mistakes.

D'Artagnan recognized this voice, and as the ground floor window was open, he leaned down over his horse and called out under the vines that grew above the window, "Bazin! Bonjour, my dear Bazin!"[59]

A short, fat man, with a flat face, a skull crowned with gray hair cut in an imitation tonsure, and an old black velvet cap, rose when he heard d'Artagnan. Though instead of *rose*, it would be more accurate to say *leapt up*. Bazin jumped to his feet, upending his little school chair, which the children scrambled to grab in a scrum that resembled the Greeks trying to wrest the body of Patroclus from the Trojans. Bazin not only jumped, he also dropped his chalk board and stick.

"You!" he said. "*You*, Monsieur d'Artagnan?"

"Yes, me. Where is Aramis . . . I mean the Chevalier d'Herblay . . . or do I mean the Vicar General?"[60]

"Why, Monsieur," Bazin said with dignity, "*Monseigneur* is at his diocese."

"You say what?" said d'Artagnan.

Bazin repeated his statement.

"*Ah ça!* So, Aramis has a diocese?"

"Yes, Monsieur. Why not?"

"He's a bishop, then?"

"Where have you been keeping yourself?" said Bazin cheekily. "How did you not know that?"

"My dear Bazin, we men of the sword, being pagans, know very well when a man is made a colonel or a marshal of France, but devil take me if I'd know if he were promoted to bishop, archbishop, or even pope! We don't hear such news until everyone else is already over it."

"Hush! Such talk!" said Bazin, glaring. "You'll ruin these children, whom I've tried so hard to teach proper behavior."

In fact, the children seemed quite taken with d'Artagnan, admiring his horse, his long sword, his spurs, and martial air. They particularly admired his commanding voice, and all began swearing, "Devil take me! Devil take me!" amid gales of laughter, which amused the old musketeer, but made the pedagogue lose his head.

"There!" he said. "You see? Shush, you brats! Whenever you show up, Monsieur d'Artagnan, all my best efforts are undone! Disorder rides in with you, and Babel is revived! Good God, you rascals, *shush!*" And the worthy Bazin rained blows right and left that didn't silence the students, but certainly changed the nature of their cries. "At least," he panted, "you won't lead anyone astray this time."

"Is that what you think?" said d'Artagnan, with a smile that made Bazin's shoulders shudder.

"Oh, yes he could," Bazin muttered.

"Where is your master's new diocese?"

"Monseigneur René is Bishop of Vannes."

"Who appointed him?"

"Who but the Superintendent of Finances, our neighbor?"

"What! Monsieur Fouquet?"*

"Exactly."

"Aramis is in favor with him?"

"Monseigneur preaches every Sunday in the superintendent's chapel at Vaux, and then they go hunting together."

"Ah!"

"And Monseigneur often composed his homilies, or rather, his sermons, with the advice of Monsieur le Surintendant."

"Oh? And does he preach in verse, our worthy bishop?"

"Monsieur, do not mock at sacred matters, for the love of God!"

"Settle down, Bazin! Then Aramis is at Vannes?"

"At Vannes, in Brittany."

"Now I think, Bazin, that you're bearing false witness."

"No, just look, Monsieur, the apartments in the presbytery are empty."

"He's right," d'Artagnan said to himself, as a glance told him the place had the air of an empty house.

"But Monseigneur must have written to inform you of his promotion."

"When did this happen?"

"A month ago."

"Oh, that's no time at all! Aramis must not have needed me for anything yet. But see here, Bazin, why didn't you go with your master?"

"I can't, Monsieur, I have my duties here."

"Your lessons?"

"And my little penitents."

"What, you confess them? Have you been ordained a priest?"

"I'm going to be. It's my calling!"

"When do you take orders?"

"Oh," Bazin said complacently, "now that monseigneur is a bishop, I'll have my orders in no time, or at least my dispensations." And he rubbed his hands together.

Deluded or not, he certainly believes it, d'Artagnan thought. "Some dinner, Bazin."

"At once, Monsieur."

"A chicken, some soup, and a bottle of wine."

"It's Saturday, a day of fasting," said Bazin.

"I have a dispensation," said d'Artagnan.

Bazin looked at him skeptically.

"Don't look at me like that, you cockroach!" said the musketeer. "If you, the servant, are counting on receiving dispensations, then I, the bishop's comrade, am certainly entitled to some myself, so don't tell my stomach it can't have meat. Now be good to me, Bazin, or by God, I'll complain to the king, and then you'll never confess anyone. You know very well that the nomination of bishops is the king's prerogative, and the king's on my side, so I'll have my way."

Bazin smiled smugly. "You may have the king, but we have the Superintendent of Finances," he said.

"Are you mocking the king?"

Bazin said nothing, but his smile was eloquent.

"My supper," said d'Artagnan. "It's going on seven o'clock."

Bazin turned and ordered the eldest of his students to go warn the cook. Meanwhile d'Artagnan was looking over the presbytery. "Huh," he said. "I doubt Monseigneur finds this worthy of his new grandeur."

"Oh, we have the Château de Vaux," said Bazin.

"How's that compared to the Louvre?" d'Artagnan replied archly.

"It's rather better," replied Bazin, with the greatest complacence.

"Is it?" said d'Artagnan. He might have prolonged the discussion to assert the superiority of the Louvre, but the lieutenant noticed that his horse was still tied to the door handle. "The devil!" he said. "Have my horse attended to! Your master the bishop hasn't its equal anywhere in his stables."

Bazin looked askance at his horse and said, "Monsieur le Surintendant has given us two pair from his stables, any one of which is worth four of yours."

D'Artagnan flushed, and his hand twitched as he considered where to bring it down on Bazin's head. But the impulse passed, he reflected a moment, and contented himself with muttering, "The devil! I was right to leave the king's service." He added aloud, "Tell me, worthy Bazin, how many musketeers serve Monsieur le Surintendant?"

"With his wealth, he could hire every musketeer in the realm," replied Bazin, setting down his chalkboard and chasing the children away with his stick.

"The devil!" d'Artagnan repeated.

Just then it was announced that his supper was served and he followed the cook into the dining room, where his meal awaited him.

D'Artagnan sat at the table and boldly attacked his chicken. "It looks to me," said d'Artagnan, gnawing at the tough flesh of his poultry, a fowl they'd apparently forgotten to fatten, "like I made a mistake in not seeking to serve this new master. It seems this Superintendent of Finances is a mighty lord indeed. Really, we know very little at Court, blinded as we are by the rays of the royal sun. It prevents us from seeing the light of other stars, which are different suns just a bit farther away."

Since d'Artagnan, from pleasure and purpose, liked to get people to talk about things that might interest him, he did his best to bandy words with Master Bazin, but it was a waste of effort. Other than continual and hyperbolic praise of Monsieur le Surintendant, Bazin, who was on his guard, would say little. He replied to d'Artagnan's sallies with bland platitudes that did nothing to satisfy his curiosity, and as soon as he'd finished eating the lieutenant went off to bed in a bad temper.

D'Artagnan was shown by Bazin to a rather mediocre room that contained a decidedly bad bed, but d'Artagnan could sleep anywhere. He'd been told that Aramis had gone off with the keys to his private apartment, which didn't surprise him, as Aramis was a careful and orderly man, and moreover usually had plenty to hide in his private rooms. He had therefore attacked the bad bed as boldly as he had the tough chicken, and since he had an ability to sleep as healthy as his appetite, he took no more time to drop off than it had taken him to strip his chicken's bones.

As he was no longer in anyone else's service, d'Artagnan had promised himself that he would sleep as long and deeply as he liked, but despite the good faith in which he'd made that vow, and no matter how badly he wished to stick to it, he was awakened in the middle of the night by a great clatter of passing carriages and mounted servants. A sudden flare of lights set the walls of his room aglow, and he jumped out of bed in his nightshirt and ran to the window. *Is it the king going by?* he thought, rubbing his eyes. *A commotion like this can only belong to royalty.*

"Long live Monsieur le Surintendant!" called, or rather acclaimed a voice from the ground floor that he recognized as that of Bazin, who was waving a handkerchief in one hand and holding high a candelabra in the other. D'Artagnan saw something like a brilliant human form lean out and bow from the window of the principal carriage, while loud bursts of laughter, no doubt evoked by the comical figure of Bazin, echoed from the same carriage, leaving a hearty wake of joy in the train of the passing procession.

"I should have known it wasn't the king," said d'Artagnan. "No one laughs so loudly when the king passes by. Hey! Bazin!" he cried to his neighbor, who was leaning three-quarters of the way out his window so he could watch the carriages drive off. "Hey! Who was that?"

"That," said Bazin smugly, "was Monsieur Fouquet."

"And who were all those people?"

"That was Monsieur Fouquet's court."

"Oh ho!" said d'Artagnan. "Now what would Monsieur de Mazarin think of that?" And he went thoughtfully back to bed, wondering how it was that Aramis always seemed to be in favor with the great powers of the realm. "Is he luckier than I am, or just smarter? Bah!" This was the word with which d'Artagnan, having grown wise, now concluded every internal monologue. Formerly he had said, *"Mordioux!"* which was a spur to action, but now that he was older, he said a philosophical, "Bah!" and that reminded him to rein in his passions.

XVIII

In Which d'Artagnan Seeks Porthos
but Finds Only Mousqueton

Once d'Artagnan was convinced that the "Vicar General" d'Herblay was really absent, and that his friend was nowhere to be found in Melun or environs, he rode away from Bazin without regret, casting a sour look over the magnificent Château de Vaux as he passed, which was even then beginning to shine with the splendor that would be its ruin. Then, setting his jaw in defiance and determination, he pricked up his horse and said, "Come, come, there's still Pierrefonds, where I'll find the finest of fellows with the deepest of pockets. And funds are all I need, since I already have a plan."

We'll spare our readers the mundane events of d'Artagnan's travels, which, going by way of Nanteuil-le-Haudouin and Crépy, reached Pierrefonds on the morning of the third day. From a distance, he saw the old castle of King Louis XII, a domain of the Crown looked after by an old concierge. It was one of those marvelous fortified manors of the Middle Ages surrounded by walls twenty feet thick and a hundred feet tall.

D'Artagnan surveyed those walls, measured the towers with his eyes, and then rode down into the valley beyond. In the distance loomed Porthos's château, situated on the banks of a broad pond and in front of a magnificent forest. It was Pierrefonds, the same estate we've already had the honor to describe to our readers elsewhere, so we'll just content ourselves here with naming it.

After the beautiful trees, with the May sun gilding the green hillsides sloping away toward Compiègne, the first thing d'Artagnan saw was a sort of rolling wooden box drawn by two lackeys and pushed by two others. Within this rolling box was some huge green and gold thing being pushed and pulled through the park's smiling glades. From a distance, this thing was unidentifiable; when he got closer, it appeared to be a great barrel wrapped in gold-trimmed green fabric; and then at last he could make out that it was a man, or rather a man-sized wobble toy, whose wide lower half expanded to fill the rolling box. This man, in fact, was Mousqueton,[61] but a Mousqueton grown immense, with gray hair and a face as red as Punchinello's.

"By God!" cried d'Artagnan. "It's that dear Monsieur Mousqueton!"

"What?" cried the fat man. "Oh, what happiness! What joy! It's Monsieur d'Artagnan! Stop, you rascals!"

These last words were addressed to the lackeys pushing and pulling him. The vehicle came to a halt and the four lackeys, with military precision, doffed their braided hats and lined up behind the box.

"Oh, Monsieur d'Artagnan!" said Mousqueton. "I'd embrace you on my knees, but I've become sadly immobile, as you see."

"*Dame,* dear Mousqueton, age strikes us all."

"No, Monsieur, it isn't age, it's infirmity and affliction."

"Infirm, Mousqueton? You?" said d'Artagnan, looking him over as he took a turn around the box. "Are you crazy, old friend? You're as strong as a three-hundred-year-old oak tree, thank God!"

"Ah, but my legs, Monsieur, my legs!" said the faithful servant.

"What about your legs?"

"They don't want to carry me anymore."

"What ingrates! And you've always fed them so well, Mousqueton."

"Yes, they have nothing to complain about in that regard," said Mousqueton with a sigh. "I've always given my body everything it asked for; I'm not selfish." And Mousqueton sighed anew.

Does Mousqueton sigh this way because he wishes he, too, were a baron? thought d'Artagnan.

"My God, Monsieur!" said Mousqueton, recovering from his sad reverie. "How glad monseigneur will be that you've thought of him."

"Good old Porthos!" said d'Artagnan. "I'm eager to embrace him."

"Oh!" said Mousqueton, clearly moved. "I'll be sure to tell him that when I write to him, Monsieur."

"What?" cried d'Artagnan. "Why write to him?"

"Because I must. This very day, without delay."

"Isn't he here?"

"*Mais non*, Monsieur."

"Is he nearby? Has he gone far?"

"I wish I knew, Monsieur," said Mousqueton.

"God's death!" cried the musketeer, stamping his foot. "Must I lose every hand? But Porthos is such a homebody!"

"No one more so than monseigneur. However . . ."

"However, what?"

"When a friend beckons . . ."

"A friend?"

"But yes! The worthy Monsieur d'Herblay."

"It was Aramis who called for Porthos?"

"This was how it happened, Monsieur d'Artagnan. Monsieur d'Herblay wrote to monseigneur . . ."

"He did?"

"Indeed, Monsieur, a letter so urgent it knocked everything for a loop!"

"Tell me about that, dear friend," said d'Artagnan, "but first, send these fellows out of earshot."

Mousqueton thundered, "Begone, rascals!" so powerfully that without the words, the breath alone would have been enough to blow the four lackeys away.

D'Artagnan sat down on the shaft of Mousqueton's chariot and opened his ears. "Monsieur," said Mousqueton, "monseigneur received a letter from Bishop d'Herblay eight or nine days ago; it was on our day of rustic diversions, which makes it the Wednesday before last."

"What's that?" said d'Artagnan. "The day of rustic diversions?"

"Yes, Monsieur; we have so many diversions out here in the country that it overwhelmed us, so we were forced to organize them into a schedule."

"Now there I recognize the style of Porthos! Such a thing would never have occurred to me. Though it's true I've never been overwhelmed by too many diversions."

"Well, we were," said Mousqueton.

"So, how did you organize them?" asked d'Artagnan.

"That's rather complicated, Monsieur."

"No matter, we have plenty of time, and you speak so well, dear Mousqueton, that it's a pleasure to listen to you."

"It's quite true," said Mousqueton, gratified at having his virtues recognized, "that I've learned a lot in my time with monseigneur."

"I await the schedule of diversions, Mousqueton, and with impatience, for I want to know if I've come on a good day."

"Alas, Monsieur d'Artagnan," said Mousqueton sadly, "but since monseigneur's departure, the diversions have been suspended."

"Well, then, Mousqueton, tell me how it used to be."

"What day should I start with?"

"*Pardieu,* what do I care? Start with Sunday, that's the Lord's day."

"With Sunday, Monsieur?"

"Yes."

"Sunday is devoted to religion: monseigneur goes to Mass, offers the blessed bread, hears sermons and has discussions with our household almoner. This isn't very diverting, but we're expecting a Carmelite from Paris to take over our almonry, an eloquent speaker, or so we've heard. Hopefully that will wake us up because our current chaplain puts us to sleep. So that's Sunday, religious diversions. On Monday, worldly diversions."

"Oh ho!" said d'Artagnan. "And what do you place in that category, Mousqueton? Let's hear about the worldly diversions!"

"Monsieur, on Monday we socialize; we receive and pay visits, we play the lute and dance, we make rhymes, and burn a little incense in honor of the ladies."

"*Peste!* That *is* the height of gallantry," said the musketeer, summoning all the strength in his jaw muscles to keep from smiling.

"On Tuesday, diversions of learning."

"Oh, good!" said d'Artagnan. "Such as? Give us some details, my dear Mousqueton."

"Monseigneur has bought a globe that I'll show you; it fills the whole tower room, except for a gallery he had built around the top, and has a small sun and moon hanging from strings and brass wires. It rotates and is very beautiful. Monseigneur points out distant seas and countries to me; we have no plans to go to them, but it's very interesting."

"Interesting—yes, that's the word," repeated d'Artagnan. "And on Wednesday?"

"Rustic diversions, as I've already had the honor to tell you, Monsieur le Chevalier. We review monseigneur's sheep and goats, and we have the shepherdesses play pipes and dance with torches, as is described in a book in monseigneur's library called *Bergeries.* I think the author died just last month."

"Monsieur Racan,[62] maybe?" said d'Artagnan.

"That's right, Monsieur Racan. But that's not all: we go fishing in the little canal and then we dine wearing crowns of flowers. And that's Wednesday."

"Plague take me, Wednesday doesn't sound bad at all," said d'Artagnan. "And Thursday? What diversions are left for poor Thursday?"

"Plenty, Monsieur," said Mousqueton, smiling. "Thursday we have Olympic diversions. Ah, Monsieur, it's superb! We have all monseigneur's young vassals come and race, wrestle, and throw the discus. Nobody throws the discus like monseigneur, and when he delivers a punch, oh, what a shame!"

"A shame? Really?"

"Yes, Monsieur—I'm afraid we had to give up punching with the cestus. He broke too many heads, jaws, and ribs. It's a lovely sport, but nobody wanted to play anymore."

"So, his wrist . . ."

"Is as strong as ever, Monsieur! These days monseigneur is a little weaker in the legs, as he himself admits, but his strength has all gone into his arms, so that . . ."

"So that he's still strong enough to knock out an ox."

"Better than that, Monsieur, he knocks down walls. Recently, after having dined with one of his farmers—he's so popular with his people—after dinner as a joke he punched the wall, the wall collapsed, the roof fell in, and three men and an old woman were crushed."

"Good lord, Mousqueton! And your master?"

"Oh, monseigneur just got a few scratches on his head. We bathed his wounds in some wine the nuns gave us. But there was nothing wrong with his hand."

"Nothing?"

"Nothing, Monsieur."

"Devil take the Olympic diversions! They must cost him dearly, because the poor widows and orphans . . ."

"They get their pensions, Monsieur. A tenth of monseigneur's fortune has gone that way."

"Let's move on to Friday," said d'Artagnan.

"Friday's diversions are noble and warlike. We hunt, we make weapons, we train falcons and tame horses. Then, Saturday is for intellectual pursuits: we test our wits, we admire monseigneur's pictures and statues, we even write a little and draw up plans—and then we fire monseigneur's cannon."

"You draw plans and then fire cannons . . ."

"Yes, Monsieur."

"Truly, *mon ami*," said d'Artagnan, "Monsieur du Vallon possesses the most subtle and flexible mind I know. There's only one kind of diversion he's overlooked, it seems to me."

"What's that, Monsieur?" asked Mousqueton anxiously.

"The fleshly diversions."

Mousqueton blushed. "What do you mean by that, Monsieur?" he said, looking down in embarrassment.

"I mean the delights of the table, of good wine and an evening spent emptying the bottle."

"Oh, Monsieur, those diversions don't count because we pursue them every day."

"My brave Mousqueton," replied d'Artagnan, "forgive me, but I've been so absorbed in your account of diversions, I forgot the main point of our

conversation, which was to learn what our Vicar General d'Herblay had
written to your master."

"That's true, Monsieur, we got distracted by the diversions," said
Mousqueton. "Well, Monsieur, I'll tell you the whole thing."

"I'm listening, my dear Mousqueton."

"Wednesday . . ."

"The day of rustic diversions?"

"Yes. A letter came, and I brought it to him with my own hands, for I
recognized the writing."

"Well?"

"Monseigneur read it and cried, 'Quick, my horses! My arms!'"

"My God!" said d'Artagnan. "It must have been a duel!"

"No, Monsieur, it contained just these words: 'Dear Porthos, depart now
if you want to get here before the Equinox. I await you.'"

"*Mordioux!*" said d'Artagnan thoughtfully. "That does sound urgent."

"That's what I thought. Anyway," continued Mousqueton, "monseigneur
left the same day, with his steward, hoping to arrive in time."

"And did he arrive in time?"

"I hope so. Monseigneur, who can be excitable, as you know, Monsieur,
kept saying, 'Thunder of God! Who is this Equinox? No matter, he'll have
to have some mighty fine horses to arrive before I do!'"

"So, do you think Porthos got there first?" asked d'Artagnan.

"I'm sure of it. This Equinox, no matter how rich he is, can't have horses
to compare to monseigneur's!"

D'Artagnan suppressed the urge to laugh because the brevity of Aramis's
letter provoked some serious thought. He followed Mousqueton, or rather
Mousqueton's chariot, up to the château, where they sat him down to a
sumptuous meal and he was honored like a king, but he could get nothing
more out of Mousqueton but worry and tears.

D'Artagnan, after a night spent on an excellent bed, continued to ponder
Aramis's letter, wondering what the approach of the equinox had to do with
Porthos's affairs, but came to no conclusion, unless it had something to do

with some love affair of the amorous bishop in which, for some reason, the day had to be equal in length to the night.

Shortly thereafter, d'Artagnan left Pierrefonds as he had left Melun and as he'd left the château of the Comte de La Fère, with a touch of that melancholy that was the darkest of d'Artagnan's moods. Riding head bowed, eyes unfocused, legs hanging limp at his horse's sides, he said to himself, in that vague reverie that sometimes amounts to true eloquence, "No friends, no future, no nothing! With the loss of my old comrades goes the last of my strength! Old age creeps up on us, cold and inexorable, wrapping in its funereal crepe all that was brilliant and capable in youth, then throws that burden over its shoulder and carries it to the bottomless abyss of death." A shudder shook the Gascon to his heart, usually so stalwart and brave against life's misfortunes, and for a few moments the clouds looked black to him and the earth seemed nothing but cemetery dirt about to be shoveled on a grave.

"Where am I going?" he said to himself. "What do I think I'm doing? Alone . . . all alone, without family, without friends . . ."

"Bah!" he suddenly cried. And he put his spurs into his horse, who'd found nothing to be sad about in the abundant oats of Pierrefonds, and took advantage of this permission to let himself out and show his good humor by galloping for a full league. "To Paris!" d'Artagnan said to himself. And the next day he arrived in Paris. His travels had taken him ten days.

XIX

In Which d'Artagnan Brings
His Business to Paris

The lieutenant dismounted in front of a shop in the Rue des Lombards at the sign of the Golden Pestle. A good-looking man wearing a white apron and stroking his gray mustache with a plump hand gave a cry of joy at the sight of the piebald horse and its rider. "Monsieur le Chevalier!" he said. "It's you!"

"Bonjour, Planchet!"[63] replied d'Artagnan, stooping slightly to enter the shop.

"Quick, someone," cried Planchet, "take Monsieur d'Artagnan's horse, make up his room, prepare his supper!"

"Thanks, Planchet! Hello, my children," said d'Artagnan to the hurrying shop boys.

"Will you just give me a moment to send off this order of coffee, molasses, and raisins?" said Planchet. "It's going to the kitchens of Monsieur le Surintendant."

"Send it, send it."

"It won't take but a moment, and then we'll have supper."

"Arrange for us to dine in private," said d'Artagnan. "I want to talk with you."

Planchet gave his old master a wary look.

"Oh, don't worry! It's nothing disagreeable," said d'Artagnan.

"Good! All the better!" And Planchet breathed freely again, as d'Artagnan sat himself down on a basket of corks and absorbed the ambience. The shop was well stocked and pervaded with an aroma of ginger, cinnamon, and cracked pepper that made d'Artagnan sneeze.

The shop boys, happy to be in the presence of a warrior as renowned as a Lieutenant of Musketeers who personally served the king, worked with conspicuous diligence while serving their customers with a snotty disdain that more than one took notice of.

Planchet counted the day's money and closed his ledgers while making polite asides to his old master. He had with his customers the brusque manner and high-handed familiarity of the successful merchant who serves everyone on an equal footing. D'Artagnan observed these nuances with a pleasure we shall analyze later. He watched as night came on, and finally Planchet led him up to a room on the first floor, where, among the crates and bales, a very well-furnished table was set for two guests.

D'Artagnan took advantage of a moment of respite to consider the appearance of Planchet, whom he hadn't seen for a year. The intelligent Planchet might be a little softer in the middle, but his wits were still sharp. His shining eyes still gazed keenly out of their sunken orbits, and fat, which softens all the features of the human face, had yet to swallow his prominent cheekbones, indicators of shrewdness and avarice, or his pointed chin, which showed finesse and perseverance. Planchet reigned in his dining room with as much majesty as in his shop. He offered his old master a meal that was frugal, but entirely Parisian: a roast chicken from the baker's oven, with vegetables, salad, and dessert from the shop itself. D'Artagnan was pleased when the grocer drew from his private stock a bottle of that Anjou wine that, throughout d'Artagnan's life, had always been his favorite drink.

"Formerly, Monsieur," said Planchet, with a smile brimming with good nature, "I was the one who drank your wine, so it's only fitting that now you drink mine."

"And with God's grace, friend Planchet, I'll continue to drink it for a while to come, I hope, for now at last I'm free."

"Free! You've gone on leave, Monsieur?"

"Forever!"

"You've quit the service?" said Planchet, stupefied.

"Yes, I've retired."

"And the king?" cried Planchet, who couldn't imagine how the king could manage without d'Artagnan.

"The king will have to try his luck with others. . . . But now that we've eaten, and you're in an expansive mood, it encourages me to share secrets, so open your ears."

"They're open." And Planchet, with a laugh that was honest rather than knowing, uncorked another bottle of the white wine.

"No, let me keep my wits about me," said d'Artagnan.

"What, you, to lose your head, Monsieur . . . ?"

"Well, now that my head is my own, I intend to take good care of it. First, let's talk about finances; how are we doing for money?"

"Quite well, Monsieur. The twenty thousand livres I had from you are invested in my business, which earns nine percent; I give you seven, with two remaining for me."

"And you're happy with that?"

"Delighted. Are you bringing me more?"

"Better than that . . . but do you need more?"

"Oh, not at all. I can get credit from anyone now. I'm expanding my business."

"That was your plan."

"I play the banker a bit. I buy the goods of my peers when they're over-extended and lend money to those who are struggling to pay debts."

"Without usury?"[64]

"Oh, Monsieur! In just the last week I've had two encounters on the boulevard[65] over the word you just pronounced."

"What!"

"It was a straight loan, you understand—the borrower gave me a deposit of brown sugar as security on condition I could sell it if he didn't repay me by a certain date. I lent him a thousand livres; when he didn't repay me, I sold the sugar for thirteen hundred livres. When he heard that, he demanded three hundred livres. I refused, pretending I'd sold the sugar for only nine hundred. He called me a usurer. I asked him to repeat that word at night on the boulevard. He's a former guardsman, so he came, and I passed your old sword through his left thigh."

"*Tudieu!* You're some kind of a banker, you are!" said d'Artagnan.

"Above thirteen percent, I fight," replied Planchet. "Those are my principles."

"Take only twelve," said d'Artagnan, "and call the rest premium and brokerage fees."

"That's good advice, Monsieur. Now, your business?"

"Ah, Planchet! It's a long story, and hard to explain."

"Tell me anyway."

D'Artagnan scratched at his mustache like a man unsure of where to start and how much he dared say.

"Is it an investment?" asked Planchet.

"In a way."

"With a decent return?"

"A beautiful return: four hundred percent, Planchet."

Planchet smacked the table so hard the bottles jumped and clattered. "Good God! Is it possible?"

"It will probably be higher," said d'Artagnan coolly, "but I'd rather be conservative."

"The devil!" said Planchet, leaning closer. "That . . . Monsieur, that's incredible. How much can we put in?"

"Twenty thousand livres each, Planchet."

"That's your entire stake, Monsieur. For how long?"

"For one month."

"And that gets us?"

"A profit of fifty thousand livres each."

"It's monstrous . . . ! To win a pot like that, there must be fighting involved."

"I do believe there will be a fair amount of fighting," said d'Artagnan, just as coolly. "But this time, Planchet, it's just the two of us, and I'll risk the fighting."

"Monsieur, I won't let you risk it alone."

"Planchet, it's out of the question. You'd have to leave your business."

"The affair isn't in Paris, then?"

"No."

"Ah! Abroad?"

"In England."

"A country wide open for trade, indeed," said Planchet. "A country I know well. Just out of curiosity, Monsieur, what sort of affair is this?"

"Planchet, it's a restoration."

"Of monuments?"

"Yes, or *a* monument. We're going to restore Whitehall."

"That *does* sound important. And you think in a month . . . ?"

"I can manage it."

"That's your specialty, Monsieur, and once you get going . . ."

"Yes, I know my business—but I'll consult with you and listen to what you have to say."

"That's quite an honor . . . but I don't know much about these monuments."

"Planchet, you're quite wrong, and are as able an architect as I am."

"Thank you."

"I had, I confess, been tempted to offer the partnership to my old comrades, but none of them were home. Which is a shame, because I know no one more daring or skillful."

"*Ah ça!* So, you think there will be opposition and the business will have competition?"

"Oh, yes, Planchet, I do."

"I'm keen to hear the details, Monsieur."

"Very well, then, Planchet: lock all the doors."

"Yes, Monsieur." And Planchet locked them up tight.

"Good. Now, come over here."

Planchet obeyed.

"And open the window, so the sound of passersby and wagons will drown out what we have to say."

Planchet opened the window as he'd been ordered, and the clamor of the street engulfed the room: voices calling, wheels clattering, dogs barking, it was just as deafening as d'Artagnan had hoped. He took a sip of the white wine, leaned forward and said, "Planchet, I have a plan."

"Ah, Monsieur! That's just like you," replied the grocer, trembling in anticipation.

XX

Of the Company Formed in the Rue des Lombards under the Sign of the Golden Pestle to Execute d'Artagnan's Plan

After a moment of silence, during which d'Artagnan seemed to gather a great many thoughts, he said, "Of course, you know all about His Majesty Charles I, King of England?"

"Alas, yes, Monsieur! You left France to go help him, and despite that help he fell and almost took you down with him."

"Exactly. I see you still have a good memory, Planchet."

"*Peste*, Monsieur! What would be astounding is if I'd forgotten any part of that story. When you've heard Grimaud, who, as you know, speaks but rarely, tell the tale of the beheading of King Charles, of how you sailed through the night in a gunpowder-mined sloop, and beheld that awful Monsieur Mordaunt tossing in the sea with a golden-handled dagger buried in his chest, you're not likely to forget it."

"But there are people who forget such things, Planchet."

"Yes, those who never saw them, or heard Grimaud tell of them."

"Well! Since you remember all that, I need remind you of only one thing, that King Charles had a son."

"Not to correct you, Monsieur, but he had two," said Planchet. "I saw the second, the Duke of York, here in Paris one day when he was on his way to the Palais Royal, and was told he was the second son of King Charles I. As to the eldest, I have the honor to know his name, but I've never seen him."

"Quite so, Planchet, and it's him we must speak of, that eldest son once known as the Prince of Wales, and now called Charles II, King of England."

"A king without a kingdom, Monsieur," replied Planchet sententiously.

"Yes, Planchet, a most unfortunate prince, less happy than the lowest beggar in the most miserable quarter of Paris."

Planchet made a gesture full of that bland compassion accorded to distant strangers one never expects to meet. Besides, he didn't hear anything in this sentimental eulogy that seemed to bear on his main interest, Monsieur d'Artagnan's plan of business.

D'Artagnan, from his habit of observing humanity, understood Planchet's thoughts. "We're coming to it," he said. "This former Prince of Wales, a king without a kingdom, as you so aptly put it, Planchet, caught my attention. I watched him beg the assistance of Mazarin, who is a low skinflint, and the help of King Louis, who is a child, and it seemed to me, who knows a thing or two, that in the intelligent gaze of this exiled king, in his essential nobility, a nobility that rises above all his suffering, I saw the stuff that makes a man, and the heart that makes a king."

Planchet tacitly approved of all this, but in his eyes at least, it didn't cast any light on d'Artagnan's plan. The latter continued, "That's what I told myself, and it started me thinking. Now listen closely, Planchet, because we're coming to the point."

"I'm listening."

"Kings are not so thick on the ground that you can easily find one when you need one. Now, this king without a kingdom is in my opinion a rare resource, a precious seed that might burgeon and bloom if a capable hand, discreet and vigorous, sowed it well and truly, in the right soil, climate, and time."

Planchet nodded mechanically, showing that he didn't yet understand.

"Poor little king seed! That's what I said to myself, and I was actually moved, Planchet, which makes me think that perhaps I'm being moved to folly. That's why I wanted to consult with you, my friend."

Planchet blushed with pleasure and pride.

"Poor little king seed, I said! I'll be the one who picks you up and plants you in good soil."

"Good God!" said Planchet, looking searchingly at his old master, as if beginning to doubt his reason.

"What's that?" asked d'Artagnan. "Are you all right?"

"Me? Fine, Monsieur."

"You said, 'Good God!'"

"I did?"

"I'm sure of it. Are you starting to understand?"

"I confess, Monsieur d'Artagnan, that I'm a little afraid . . ."

"To understand?"

"Yes."

"To understand that I want to restore his throne to King Charles II, who has no throne? Is that it?"

Planchet almost leapt from his chair. "*Ohé!*" he cried, frightened. "So that's what you mean by a *restoration!*"

"Yes, Planchet. Isn't that the right word for it?"

"No doubt, no doubt. But have you thought about this?"

"About what?"

"About what's going on over there?"

"Where?"

"In England."

"And what's going on there, Planchet?"

"First of all, Monsieur, I beg your pardon for presuming to worry about these things, which are not my concern, but since you're proposing a business venture to me . . . you are proposing I join a venture, aren't you?"

"A superb one, Planchet."

"Then since you're proposing a joint venture, I have the right to discuss it."

"Discuss away, Planchet; from discourse comes wisdom."

"Well! Since I have Monsieur's permission, I'll tell him that in the first place, there's the Parliament."

"Very well. And after that?"

"After that, the army."

"Good. And then?"

"And then, the entire nation!"

"Is that everything?"

". . . The entire nation, which consented to the fall and execution of the last king, father of this one, and stands by that consent."

"Planchet, my friend," said d'Artagnan, "your reasons stink like old cheese. The nation? That nation is fed up with these trumped-up gentlemen who grant themselves barbaric titles while singing psalms. When it comes to singing, my dear Planchet, I've noticed that nations prefer drinking songs to plainchant. Remember the Fronde, and the songs we sang in those days? Say hey! Good times, eh?"

"Not so much; I was nearly hanged."

"But *were* you hanged?"

"No."

"And didn't you found your fortune while singing those songs?"

"Well . . . yes."

"So, you can have nothing to say against them."

"All right! Then I return to the Parliament and the army."

"And I say that I'll borrow twenty thousand livres from Monsieur Planchet, and put in twenty thousand livres of my own, and with this forty thousand I'll raise my own army."

Planchet clasped his hands in woe, for he really thought d'Artagnan had lost his mind. "An army! Oh, Monsieur," he said, with a gentle smile, for fear of pushing the madman into a rage. "A . . . large army?"

"About forty men," said d'Artagnan.

"Forty men against forty thousand isn't going to do it. Now, you alone are worth a thousand men, Monsieur d'Artagnan, I know that well, but how will you find thirty-nine others who are worth as much as you? Even if you find them, how would you pay them?"

"Not bad, Planchet. *Diable,* you speak like a courtier."

"No, Monsieur, I say what I think, and what I think is that at the first pitched battle you fight with your forty men, I'm afraid . . ."

"So, I won't fight any pitched battles," said the Gascon, laughing. "From Antiquity on, we have plenty of examples of tactical retreats and strategic marches that achieve their goals by avoiding the enemy rather than meeting him. You should know that, Planchet, you who commanded Parisians on the day they were to fight musketeers, and maneuvered to avoid them so skillfully that you never left the Place Royale."[66]

Planchet laughed. "For a fact," he replied, "if your forty men stay hidden with any skill, they may hope never to have to fight. But then, how do you propose to achieve your goal?"

"I'll tell you. Here, then, is how I propose to speedily restore His Majesty Charles II to his throne."

"Great!" said Planchet, all attention. "But first, it seems to me we're forgetting something."

"What?"

"We've dismissed the nation, because they prefer drinking songs to psalms, and the army, because we won't fight them. But there's still the Parliament, which doesn't sing at all."

"And which also doesn't fight. How you, Planchet, an intelligent man, can worry about a bunch of debaters who call themselves Rumps and Barebones is beyond me! I'm not worried about the Parliament, Planchet."

"All right, since Monsieur isn't worried about them, we'll move on."

"Yes, and now we're coming to the crux. Do you remember Cromwell, Planchet?"

"I certainly heard a lot about him, Monsieur."

"He was a tough old soldier."

"With a big appetite on top of it."

"What do you mean?"

"He swallowed England at a single gulp."

"Well, Planchet! What if, the day after he swallowed England, someone had swallowed Monsieur Cromwell?"

"Oh, Monsieur! It's one of the first axioms of mathematics that the container must be larger than the contained."

"Quite so! And that, right there, is our venture."

"But Monsieur Cromwell is dead, and his container is the tomb."

"My dear Planchet, I'm pleased to see that you've become not only a mathematician, but also a philosopher."

"Monsieur, in my grocery, I use a lot of newspaper as wrapping, and I learn from it."

"Bravo! Then you're aware, since you learned not only mathematics and philosophy but also a little history, that the previous Cromwell, who was so great, was followed by another who was much smaller."

"Yes, the one called Richard—who did as you did, Monsieur d'Artagnan, and resigned his position."

"Good, very good! After the great one, who died, and the small one, who resigned, there has come a third. This one is called Monsieur Monck: he's a skillful general in that he's never fought a battle, a capable diplomat because he never says anything, and before greeting someone in the morning, he thinks about it for twelve hours and then says good evening, which people call miraculous, saying he's always right."

"Indeed, that's impressive," said Planchet, "but I know of another politician quite like him."

"Monsieur de Mazarin, am I right?"

"Himself."

"You're right, Planchet; except Monsieur de Mazarin doesn't aspire to the Throne of France, and that changes everything, you see. Well! This Monsieur Monck, who already has England roasted on a plate and opens his mouth to swallow it, this Monsieur Monck, who tells the envoys of Charles II and Charles II himself, '*Nescio vos* . . .'"

"I don't speak English," said Planchet.

"Yes, leave that to me," said d'Artagnan. "'*Nescio vos*' means 'I know you not.' This Monsieur Monck, the most important man in England, once he's swallowed her . . ."

"Well?" asked Planchet.

"Well, my friend! I go over there with my forty men, and I'll pack him up, carry him off, and bring him to France, where I see two bright possibilities."

"Ooh, I see one!" cried Planchet, carried away by enthusiasm. "We'll put him in a cage and folks will pay money to see him."

"Well, Planchet, that's a third possibility that hadn't occurred to me, I must say."

"Do you think it's a good one?"

"Yes, certainly—but I think mine are better."

"Let's hear yours, then."

"Number one is to hold him for ransom."

"For how much?"

"*Peste!* A fellow like that must be worth a hundred thousand crowns."

"Oh, yes!"

"So, my first idea is to ransom him for a hundred thousand crowns."

"And the other . . . ?"

"The other, which is even better, is to give him to King Charles, who, no longer having a general of the army to fear, and a diplomat to argue with, will restore himself, and once restored, will pay me the hundred thousand crowns in question. That's the venture I propose; what do you say to that, Planchet?"

"It's magnificent, Monsieur!" said Planchet, trembling with emotion. "And how did this wonderful idea come to you?"

"It came to me one morning on the banks of the Loire, when King Louis XIV, our beloved monarch, wept over the hand of Mademoiselle de Mancini."

"Monsieur, I grant you that your idea is sublime. But . . ."

"Ah! There's always a *but.*"

"Permit me! But it's a bit like the skin of the bear the fools tried to sell, you know, before they'd caught the bear. Now, taking Monsieur Monck means a fight."

"No doubt; that's why I'm raising my army."

"Yes, yes, I understand that, *parbleu!* A surprise attack. Oh, you'll succeed at that, Monsieur, because no one's your equal at that sort of thing."

"I have a knack for it, that's true," said d'Artagnan, with a proud simplicity. "You understand that if I had for this business my dear Athos, my brave

Porthos, and my wily Aramis, it would be as good as done. But they're all lost and scattered, and it seems no one knows where to find them, so I'll do it on my own. Now, do you find this venture a good one, at a decent return on investment?"

"All too good."

"What do you mean?"

"It's just too good to come true."

"It can't fail, Planchet, and the proof is that I undertake it myself. There'll be a fine profit for you and a notable feat for me. They'll say, 'Such was the old age of Monsieur d'Artagnan,' Planchet, and I'll have a place in tales and maybe even history."

"Oh, Monsieur!" cried Planchet. "When I think that it's here, in my home, among my brown sugar, prunes, and cinnamon, that this colossal project was born, it makes my shop seem almost like a palace."

"Take care, Planchet, take care: if the least word of this gets out, it's the Bastille for both of us. Take care, my friend, for it's a conspiracy we're plotting here, and Monsieur Monck is an ally of Monsieur de Mazarin."

"Monsieur, when one has had the honor of calling you master, one knows no fear, and when one has the privilege of being your partner, he's a silent one."

"Very well, that's more your worry than mine, for in a week I'll be in England."

"Then go, Monsieur, go, and the sooner the better."

"So, the money is available?"

"It will be tomorrow, I'll get it for you personally. Would you prefer gold or silver?"

"Gold is more portable and convenient. But how shall we memorialize this? Let's see."

"*Mon Dieu*, nothing could be simpler: you'll just write me a receipt."

"No, that's *too* simple," said d'Artagnan. "We must do this thing properly."

"Usually I'd agree, but since it's you, Monsieur d'Artagnan . . ."

"And what if I'm killed over there, slain by a musket ball, or poisoned by their beer?"

"Monsieur, please believe that if that happened, I would be so upset by your death that I wouldn't care about money."

"Thank you, Planchet, but the problem remains. We shall, like two attorneys' clerks,[67] draw up an agreement, a sort of treaty that could be called a deed of partnership."

"Willingly, Monsieur."

"I know writing is hard work, but we'll give it a try."

Planchet went and got a pen, ink, and paper. D'Artagnan took the pen, dipped it in the ink, and wrote:

Between Messire d'Artagnan, former Lieutenant of the King's Musketeers, resident at the Hôtel de la Chevrette, Rue Tiquetonne,
And Sieur Planchet, Grocer, resident at the Sign of the Golden Pestle, Rue des Lombards,
It is agreed that:
A company with a capital of forty thousand livres is formed around an idea brought by Monsieur d'Artagnan. Sieur Planchet, who knows of this idea and approves of it in all respects, will pay twenty thousand livres into the hands of Monsieur d'Artagnan. He demands no repayment nor interest before Monsieur d'Artagnan returns from a trip to England.
For his part, Monsieur d'Artagnan undertakes to contribute twenty thousand livres, which he will add to the twenty thousand already invested by Sieur Planchet. He will expend the forty thousand livres as he sees fit, committing himself to a goal as set forth below.
The day that Monsieur d'Artagnan has by some means restored His Majesty King Charles II to the Throne of England, he will pay into the hands of Sieur Planchet a sum of . . .

Seeing d'Artagnan pause, Planchet said naïvely, "The sum of one hundred fifty thousand livres."

"Hang it! No," said d'Artagnan, "the division can't be by halves, that wouldn't be right."

"However, Monsieur, we each put half in," said Planchet timidly.

"Yes, but listen to the full clause, Planchet, and if it doesn't sound equitable in every respect, well! We'll strike it out."

And d'Artagnan wrote:

However, as Monsieur d'Artagnan brings to the venture, besides his capital of twenty thousand livres, his idea, his efforts, and moreover risks his life, which he prefers not to lose, Monsieur d'Artagnan will keep, out of three hundred thousand livres, two hundred thousand for himself, making his share two-thirds.

"Very good," said Planchet.

"So, that sounds right?"

"Perfectly right, Monsieur."

"And you'll be content with a hundred thousand livres?"

"*Peste!* I should think so. A hundred thousand livres for twenty thousand!"

"And within one month, you understand."

"What, one month?"

"Yes, I'm asking for only one month."

"Monsieur," said Planchet generously, "I'll give you six weeks."

"*Merci,*" replied the musketeer politely.

After which, the two partners reread the agreement.

"It's perfect, Monsieur," said Planchet, "and the late Monsieur Coquenard, the first husband of Madame la Baronne du Vallon,[68] could have done no better."

"You think so? Well, then! Let's sign it."

And they added their signatures.

"This way," said d'Artagnan, "I'll be under no obligations to anyone."

"But I'll be under obligation to you," said Planchet.

"Not at all, because no matter how much I prefer not to, if I lose my life over there, Planchet, you lose your whole investment. *Peste,* that reminds me of the most important clause of all, which I'll add: 'In the event that Monsieur d'Artagnan is deceased in this venture, repayment is considered made, and Sieur Planchet forgives the ghost of Monsieur d'Artagnan the twenty thousand livres he loaned to the company.'"

This final clause made Planchet frown in fear and doubt, but when he saw in his partner that eye so brilliant, that hand so steady, that spine so firm and supple, he took courage and without hesitation added his initials to the clause. D'Artagnan did the same. And thus was drawn up the first deed of partnership, a form of agreement that may occasionally have been abused since then.

"And now, dear master" said Planchet, pouring a last glass of Anjou wine for d'Artagnan, "let's get some sleep."

"No," d'Artagnan replied, "the hardest task is still ahead of me, for I have to think things through."

"Bah!" said Planchet. "I have such confidence in you, Monsieur d'Artagnan, that I wouldn't trade my option on a hundred thousand livres for ninety thousand in cash."

"And, devil take me!" said d'Artagnan. "I think you're right."

Upon which d'Artagnan took a candle, went up to his room, and went to bed.

XXI

In Which d'Artagnan Prepares to Travel on the Behalf of Planchet and Co.

D'Artagnan thought so well over night that by morning his plan was fully formed. "There!" he said, sitting up on his bed, putting his elbow on his knee and his chin in his hand. "I'll seek out forty men, sure and solid, recruiting people who are somewhat compromised but with the habit of discipline. I'll promise each one five hundred livres for a month, if they survive, and nothing if they don't, or half for their dependents. As for food and lodging, that's on the English, who have cattle in the pasture, bacon in the smoke-house, chickens in the coop, and barley in the barn. I'll offer my troop to General Monck and he'll sign us up. I'll get into his confidence and abuse it at the first opportunity."

But d'Artagnan paused there, shook his head, and interrupted himself. "No," he said, "If I did that, I'd never be able to tell Athos about it. It's too dishonorable. I can't resort to violence after committing myself to him," he continued. "With my forty men, I'll have to fight a guerilla action. Yes, but what if I run up against, not forty thousand English as Planchet said, but even as few as four hundred? I'll be beaten, especially since, out of my forty, at least ten will get themselves killed out of stupidity.

"No, in fact, it would be impossible to find forty dependable men; there just aren't that many. I'll have to be satisfied with thirty. With ten fewer men I can justify avoiding an encounter, and if one happens anyway, I'll have thirty good soldiers rather than forty fools. Plus, I save five thousand livres, or an eighth of my capital, which is all to the good. So, then: thirty men. I'll divide the troop into three squads, we'll separate, make our way through the country, and meet at a rendezvous point. That way, ten by ten, we'll raise no alarms, cause no suspicion, and pass unnoticed. Yes, thirty, that's the number, all right. Three tens; three, the divine number! And then, when we're reunited, we'll still be a pretty imposing company. But, oh! I'm an idiot!" continued d'Artagnan. "I'll need thirty horses. It's a disaster; how the devil did I forget about horses? You can't undertake a campaign like this without horses. Well, it has to be done; I can buy the horses once we're across, and besides, there's nothing wrong with English horses.

"But also, plague take it, three squads mean three commanders, and that's another problem. Of the three, I'm one, of course, but hiring the other two will cost almost as much as the rest put together. No, I definitely must have no more than one lieutenant.

"Based on that, I'll reduce my troop to twenty men. That isn't very many, just twenty men, but if I was determined to avoid encounters with thirty men, I'll be even more so with twenty. Twenty is a manageable number, and besides, it reduces the number of horses I'll need by ten, which is a bonus. And then, with a good lieutenant . . .

"*Mordioux!* See where you get with patience and calculation? I started out with forty men, and now I'm going to do the same job with twenty. Ten thousand livres saved at one stroke, and with better results. The critical point now is the finding of this lieutenant. So, I'll find him, and then . . . but it won't be that easy. I need someone brave and experienced, another me.

"Yes, but a lieutenant would have to share my secret, a secret that's worth a million, and as I'm paying my man only ten thousand livres, or fifteen hundred at best, he'll sell that secret to Monck. No lieutenants, *mordioux!* Besides, even if the lieutenant was as mute as a disciple of Pythagoras, he'd be sure to have in his squad a favorite soldier whom he'd make his sergeant, and this sergeant would find out his secret even supposing the lieutenant is honest.

"And the sergeant, cheaper and less honest, will sell the whole thing for fifty thousand livres. Come, come, it's impossible! Decidedly, the lieutenant is impossible. But then we're done with fractions, because I can't divide my troop in two and be in two places at once, without another me who ... but why have two squads when I have only one captain? What's the point of weakening the troop by sending one squad left and the other right? A single troop, *mordioux!* But a band of twenty men riding cross country looks suspicious to everyone; if a troop of twenty riders is spotted, a company will be sent after them, they'll demand the password, we won't know it, and Monsieur d'Artagnan and his men will be shot like rabbits. I'll reduce my troop to ten men; I'll act simply and with a unified force; I'll have no choice but to be prudent, which is already halfway to success in the kind of affair I'm undertaking. A larger troop would have tempted me into some reckless folly. Ten horses can be brought from here or bought over there. An excellent idea! I'm happier already. No suspicions, no passwords, no encounters. A mere ten men, why, they're just taken for drovers or clerks. Ten men leading ten horses loaded with merchandise will be overlooked, or even well received, no matter where they go.

"Ten men traveling on behalf of the house of Planchet and Co., France. Nothing more need be said. These ten men, dressed like laborers, might carry hunting knives, carbines behind their saddles, even pistols in their holsters. They don't look suspicious because their business is open and aboveboard. Oh, they might look a bit like smugglers, but so what? Smuggling's not a hanging offense like polygamy. The worst that can happen to us is that they confiscate our goods.

"Confiscated goods? No big deal. Come, come, this plan is superb. Just ten men, ten men I'll handpick, ten men who will be as good as forty, and cost me a quarter as much. And for greater security, I won't speak a word about our goal, I'll just say, 'My friends, there's a blow to strike.' Satan himself would have to get up extra early to play a trick on us. And fifteen thousand livres saved out of twenty—it's just superb!"

Thus, comforted by his industrious calculations, d'Artagnan fixed his plan in place and resolved to make no further changes. He already had in mind, on a list furnished by his inexhaustible memory, ten veteran adventurers mistreated by fortune or harried by the law. Therefore, d'Artagnan got up and went right to work, telling Planchet not to expect him at breakfast and maybe not dinner.

A day and a half spent haunting certain Parisian dives reaped him his harvest, a collection of swashbucklers all individually recruited without the knowledge of the others, so that within thirty hours he had a charming crew of ugly customers, most of them speaking a French less pure than the English they were about to attempt. They were former guardsmen for the most part, men whom d'Artagnan had taken the measure of in various encounters, and whom drunkenness, unlucky sword-wounds, unexpected windfalls at gambling, or thinning of the ranks by Monsieur de Mazarin had forced to seek darkness and solitude, the two great consolations of souls misunderstood and mistreated. They wore on their faces and their outfits the marks of their suffering; some of them were scarred, and all of their clothes were threadbare.

D'Artagnan relieved the most urgent miseries of his brothers in arms with an early distribution of a few of the company's gold crowns; then, having made sure these crowns were employed in the physical rehabilitation of his troopers, he assigned his recruits a rendezvous in northern France, between Berghes and Saint-Omer. They were to meet at the end of six days, and d'Artagnan was sufficiently well acquainted with the goodwill and dependability of these men that he was certain none of them would fail to be waiting.

These orders given, and the rendezvous appointed, d'Artagnan went to make his farewell to Planchet, who was waiting to hear news of his little army. D'Artagnan didn't think it was wise to inform Planchet about his reduction in personnel, as he thought it might diminish his partner's confidence in the venture. Planchet was delighted to hear that the army had been raised, and that he was now a sort of little king with a shop for a throne room, from which he was funding troops to wage war against perfidious Albion,[69] that enemy of all true French hearts.

Planchet happily counted out twenty thousand livres worth of fine double-louis[70] to d'Artagnan on his own account and an equal stack from the fund belonging to d'Artagnan. The Gascon poured the money into two equal purses, and then, weighing them in his hands, he said, "This much money is quite an encumbrance, don't you think, Planchet? It must weigh thirty pounds."

"Bah! To your horse it will be no more than a feather."

D'Artagnan shook his head. "I know what I'm talking about, Planchet. A horse carrying an extra thirty pounds above the weight of his rider and baggage no longer swims a river so easily, nor leaps lightly over a wall or ditch—and if the horse fails, the rider fails. Though of course, you wouldn't know that, Planchet, as you always served in the infantry."

"Then what should we do, Monsieur?" said Planchet, genuinely embarrassed.

"Listen," said d'Artagnan, "I'll pay my army upon their return to Paris. Keep my half of twenty thousand livres for me, which you can put to use during that time."

"What about my half of the money?" said Planchet.

"I'll carry that with me."

"Your confidence does me honor," said Planchet, "but what if you don't come back?"

"I suppose that's possible, though it isn't likely. However, Planchet, in case I don't come back, give me a pen so I can write out my will."

D'Artagnan took a pen and paper and wrote on a single sheet:

I, d'Artagnan, am in possession of twenty thousand livres saved sou by sou for thirty-three years in the service of His Majesty the King of France. I leave five thousand to Athos, five thousand to Porthos, and five thousand to Aramis, to be given, in my name and theirs, to my young friend Raoul, Vicomte de Bragelonne. I leave the final

five thousand to Planchet, that he may distribute the other fifteen
thousand to my friends without regret.

    To that end, I sign this present document,

D'ARTAGNAN

Planchet appeared quite curious to know what d'Artagnan had written. "Here," the musketeer said to him, "read it."

At the final lines, tears sprang from Planchet's eyes. "You think I wouldn't give them your money without this? Take it back—I don't want your five thousand livres."

D'Artagnan smiled. "Accept it, Planchet, accept it, and then you'll lose only fifteen thousand livres instead of twenty. And you won't be tempted to ignore the signature of your master and friend in order not to lose everything."

How well d'Artagnan knew the hearts of men—especially grocers! Those who called Don Quixote crazy because he went to conquer an empire with no help but Sancho, his squire, and who called Sancho mad because he followed that master, would certainly not hesitate to pass the same judgment on d'Artagnan and Planchet. However, the first had one of the subtlest minds to be found among the razor-sharp wits of the Court of France. As to the second, he had rightly acquired the reputation of being one of the smartest grocers in the Rue des Lombards—and therefore all of Paris, and thus all of France.

Now, if one considers these two men from the point of view of other men, and the means by which they intended to put a king on his throne compared to other means, those of average mind, an average that's by no means high, would recoil from the mad arrogance of the lieutenant and the folly of his partner. Fortunately, d'Artagnan wasn't the sort of man to take his opinions from those around him, especially opinions about himself. He had adopted as his motto, "Do the right thing and let others talk." Planchet, for his part, had as his slogan, "Do it and say nothing." And that was how these two flattered themselves that they were right and everyone else was wrong. (Such is the way of geniuses.)

D'Artagnan set out on his journey, and at first he had the most beautiful weather possible, without a cloud in the sky and without a cloud on his spirit, joyful and strong, calm and resolved, and consequently brimming with that fluid energy that powers the human machine when shocks jolt it into action, something that future centuries will probably isolate and reproduce mechanically. As in previous adventures, he went back up the road to Boulogne, now for the fifth time. He could almost, on the way, pick out the footprints of his former travels and recognize the marks of his fist on the doors of roadside inns. His memory, sharp and ever present, brought back the days of his youth, which, thirty years later, hadn't weakened his steel wrist nor discouraged his brave heart.

What a rich nature was that of this man! He had every passion, every fault, every weakness, and an intellectual spirit of contradiction that turned all these vices into virtues. D'Artagnan, thanks to his restless imagination, started at every shadow, and then, ashamed of that fear, marched bravely into the gloom and confronted it, if he found the danger was real. He reacted to everything with emotion, which brought him enjoyment. He delighted in the company of others but was never bored with his own, and if one could have eavesdropped on him when he was alone, he'd have been heard laughing at the jokes he made for himself, or the imaginary mind games he played where one would expect only boredom.

D'Artagnan was perhaps less cheerful than he would have been if he expected to find his good friends at Calais instead of his ten rogues, but melancholy didn't afflict him more than once a day, so he had only five visits from that dark deity before sighting the sea at Boulogne, and those visits were brief. Then, once d'Artagnan was nearing the theater of action, every feeling but that of confidence disappeared, to be seen no more.

From Boulogne, he followed the coast to Calais. For Calais was the site of the rendezvous, and in Calais he'd told each of his recruits to await him at the Grand Monarch Inn, where prices were moderate, where sailors took their meals, and where men of the sword, if they kept the blades in their leather scabbards, would find lodging, food, wine, and the other sweet things of life for thirty sous a day.

He arrived at Calais at half past four in the evening. D'Artagnan intended to surprise his recruits in a relaxed state and take stock of them, to judge whether they'd be good and dependable companions.

XXII

D'Artagnan Travels for the House of Planchet and Co.

The Grand Monarch Inn was located on a small street that ran parallel to the docks without overlooking the harbor itself; a few alleys, like rungs between the parallel sides of a ladder, connected the dockside to the parallel street. By these alleys, one could cut through quickly from the harbor to the street or from the street to the harbor.

D'Artagnan arrived at the harbor, turned up one of these alleys, and came out right in front of the Grand Monarch Inn. The moment was well chosen and reminiscent of his arrival at the Inn of the Jolly Miller in Meung.[71] Some sailors who'd been playing at dice had quarreled and were exchanging furious threats. The host, the hostess, and two pot boys anxiously watched these angry gamblers and the circle of sailors surrounding them, bristling with knives and axes and seemingly ready for war.

However, though grumbling, the two quarrelers returned to their game.

Two other men were sitting on a stone bench near the door, while four tables placed near the far wall of the common room were occupied by eight more. The two men on the bench and the eight at the tables took no part in either the game or the quarrel. In these cold and indifferent spectators d'Artagnan recognized his ten recruits.

The quarrel revived and intensified. Like the sea, every passion has a tide that rises and falls. At the height of his fury one sailor turned over the table, scattering the money that had been on it. Instantly, the inn's staff and guests all pounced on the rolling coins, gathering what they could and slipping away while all the sailors tore into each other.

Only the two men on the bench and the eight farther inside kept out of the fray, and though they didn't seem to know each other or be coordinating their actions, all seemed determined to remain impassive despite the angry cries and clink of coins. The sole activity was from the two at the nearest table, who used their feet to firmly repel any fighters who rolled up to them. Two others, while staying out of the fracas, did draw their fists from their pockets, while another pair, to avoid a wave of combatants, took to their tabletop, like people surprised by a flood.

"Come, now," said d'Artagnan to himself, who had missed nothing we've just recounted, "here's a pretty troop: circumspect, calm, unruffled by noise, but with a ready defense—*peste!* I could hardly ask for better."

Suddenly his attention was drawn to the middle of the common room. The two sailors who'd been pushed away by the feet of the men at the nearest table were reconciled by their shared outrage at this insult. One of them, half-drunk with anger and completely drunk on beer, started threatening the smaller of the two men at the table, asking him by what right he could put his feet on sailors, who were creatures of God and not dogs. And to make his inquiry more pointed, he shook his fist under the nose of d'Artagnan's recruit. The recruit turned pale from what might have been either anger or fear, and the sailor, concluding it must be fear, raised his fist with the evident intention of bringing it down on the stranger's head. However, though the threatened man scarcely seemed to move, he struck the sailor in the stomach so hard that the man reeled away across the room, crying out in pain.

Immediately, rallied by esprit de corps, the comrades of the injured man fell as one on his conqueror. This latter, maintaining the sangfroid he'd previously shown, and without making the mistake of drawing his weapons, picked up a heavy beer stein and knocked down his first two or three assailants. Then, as he was about to be overwhelmed by numbers, the seven other silent men within, who'd previously stood aside, suddenly decided that this was their battle and rushed to his aid.

Meanwhile, the two abstainers at the door turned toward the mêlée with frowns that seemed to indicate their intention to hit the sailors from behind if they didn't stand down. The host, his potboys, and two bystanders had gotten embroiled in the fracas and were being soundly beaten. The Paris recruits, however, were striking like Cyclopes, placing their blows with a tactical skill it was a pleasure to behold. Finally, forced to retreat in the face of superior numbers, they entrenched themselves behind the largest table, which four of them upended. Then the two from the doorway finally waded in swinging wooden benches, which like the arms of siege engines laid out eight sailors in four blows.

The floor was strewn with fallen men and the dusty air resounded with cries of pain as d'Artagnan, satisfied with this demonstration, marched into the room naked sword in hand, striking down with the pommel on every sailor's head that raised itself. Standing in the middle of the room, he shouted, *"Holà!"* which brought the fight to a sudden end. The wounded sailors surged away from the center of the room to its edges, leaving d'Artagnan alone on the field and in sole possession.

"What's all this about?" he demanded of all and sundry in the majestic tone of Neptune pronouncing the *Quos ego.*[72]

Immediately, at the first sound of his voice (to continue the Virgilian metaphor), d'Artagnan's recruits, who recognized their lord and master, dropped their aggressive attitudes and put down their tankards and trestles. The sailors, for their part, seeing the long sword, strong arm, and martial air of a man who appeared accustomed to command, picked up their wounded and their cracked mugs and went on their way.

The Parisians straightened themselves and saluted their leader while d'Artagnan was being regaled with thanks and congratulations by the Grand Monarch's innkeeper. He accepted these plaudits like a man who knew he deserved them and announced that, while the host was preparing his supper, he would go for a walk along the harbor. Immediately each of the recruits, who understood the summons, took his hat, straightened his buffcoat, and followed d'Artagnan. But d'Artagnan, strolling along like a tourist, never paused for a moment and made straight for the dunes. Meanwhile the ten men, surprised at finding themselves walking among a pack of strangers, all looked askance at one another.

It was only when they were among the deepest dunes that d'Artagnan, smiling at seeing them so worried, turned and said, with a reassuring gesture, "There, there, Messieurs! Don't be so suspicious of each other, for you're going to be comrades, and must get along together."

Then their hesitation disappeared, the men breathed easily again, and began looking over their new companions with some satisfaction. After this mutual appraisal they turned back to their leader, who had long experience of dealing with men of this caliber and regaled them with the following improvised speech, delivered with typical Gascon energy: "Messieurs, you all know who I am. I've engaged you, knowing you to be brave and ready to join a glorious expedition. Regard working for me just as if you were working for the king—but I warn you now that if you behave like that in public, I'll crack your heads with whatever happens to be convenient. You're well aware, Messieurs, that state secrets are like lethal poison: as long as the poison is in its bottle and the bottle is corked, it's harmless—but once it's out of the bottle, it kills. Now, come closer, and I'll share with you as much of the secret as I may."

Curious, the men gathered around him. "Come near," continued d'Artagnan, "so close that not the birds over our heads, the rabbits in the dunes, nor the fishes in the waves can hear us. We're going to investigate and report to Monsieur le Surintendant des Finances as to how much English smuggling is harming French trade. I intend to go everywhere and see everything. We shall be poor Picard fishermen thrown up on the coast by a squall. It goes without saying that we'll sell fish just as if we were real fishermen.

"Of course, someone might guess who we really are and confront us, in which case we must be able to defend ourselves. That's why I chose you, men of spirit and courage. But we'll keep our heads down and stay out of trouble, confident because we're backed by a powerful patron who can protect us from anything. Only one thing worries me, but I'll explain it in hopes you can put it to rest. I don't want to have to bring along a stupid crew of actual fishermen, who'd be a real nuisance, but if there were, among you, some who'd followed the sea . . ."

"Oh, no problem there!" said one of d'Artagnan's recruits. "I was a prisoner of the pirates of Tunis[73] for three years and can navigate like an admiral."

"See there?" said d'Artagnan. "Luck is on our side!"

The air of pleased surprise with which d'Artagnan said this was feigned, however, for he knew quite well that this "prisoner of the pirates" was himself an old corsair and had engaged him with that background in mind. But d'Artagnan never said more than he had to say, preferring to leave people in doubt. He therefore appeared to take the man's explanation at face value, accepting the result without worrying about the cause.

"And I, as it happens," said a second man, "have an uncle who's a foreman in the port at La Rochelle. As a child, I played on boats every day, and can handle rowing and sailing as well as any sailor of the Ponant."[74]

This man lied only a little more than his fellow, having spent six years rowing in His Majesty's galleys at La Ciotat. Two others were more honest, confessing that they'd spent a couple of years as soldiers on prison ships. Thus, of the ten men of war in d'Artagnan's troop, four also qualified as sailors, so he was armed for both land and sea, a detail that would have made Planchet swell with pride had he known of it.

Then it was just a matter of issuing the general orders, which d'Artagnan did with precision. He commanded his men to make for The Hague, half following the coast to Breskens, the others taking the road to Antwerp. The rendezvous was set for a fortnight hence by calculating travel time to the central square of The Hague. D'Artagnan advised his men to pair up however they liked and travel by twos. He himself chose two of the least disreputable figures, a couple of former guardsmen he'd known previously whose only faults were that they were gamblers and drunkards. These men weren't entirely lost to civilization, and with clean clothes and good habits, their hearts would be steady again. D'Artagnan, to avoid jealousy among the men, made all the others go on ahead. He kept his two favorites back, gave them clothes from his own supply, and set off with them.

It was to this pair, whom he seemed to honor with his complete confidence, that d'Artagnan made a false confession intended to guarantee the success of the expedition. He explained to them that it wasn't a question of how much English smuggling harmed French trade, but rather how much

English trade could be harmed by French smuggling. The men appeared convinced by this, as indeed they were.

D'Artagnan was certain, of course, that at the first carousal with the others, these two, once drink had loosened their tongues, would divulge his false confession to the entire band. He thought this gambit couldn't fail.

Two weeks after their meeting in Calais, the entire company was reassembled in The Hague. Then d'Artagnan saw that all of them, showing remarkable intelligence, had already assumed the guise of sailors who'd been recently washed up from the sea. D'Artagnan found them quarters in a dive on Newkerkestreet while he lodged comfortably on the Grand Canal.

He learned that the King of England had returned to his ally William II of Nassau, Stadtholder of Holland,[75] and moreover that the rejection by King Louis XIV had put a chill on the welcome he'd felt before. Consequently, Charles had been lodged in a small house in the village of Scheveningen, in the dunes on the seaside, about a league outside The Hague. There, it was said, the unfortunate exile consoled himself for his banishment by gazing, with that melancholy particular to the princes of his race, out into the immensity of the North Sea, which separated him from England as it had formerly separated Mary Stuart from France. There, beyond the beautiful grove of Scheveningen, where golden heather grows on the dunes of fine sand, Charles II also vegetated, less happy than the heather because he, self-aware, lived a life of the mind, and went from despair to hope and back again.

D'Artagnan made the short trip to Scheveningen to confirm for himself what was reported about the prince. And in fact, he saw Charles II, pensive and alone, come out of a small door facing the woods and roam along the shore at sunset, without even attracting the notice of the fishermen who, returning in the evening, grounded their boats, like the Greeks of the islands, high on the sand of the beach.

D'Artagnan recognized the king, saw him staring somberly over the immense expanse of the waters, absorbing on his pale face the red rays of the sun already bisected by the horizon. Then Charles II returned to the house alone, slowly and sadly, amusing himself by making the sand creak beneath his footsteps.

That same evening, d'Artagnan rented for a thousand livres a fishing boat, a dogger worth four thousand. He paid the thousand down and left the other three thousand as a deposit with the harbor burgomaster. After that he secretly embarked his six soldiers, unseen in the dark, and at three in the morning, at high tide, he boarded openly with his four sailors and set out, relying on the skill of his former galley slave as if he were the foremost pilot of the port.

XXIII

In Which the Author Is Forced, Despite Himself, to Recount a Little History

While kings and men were thus occupied with England, which thought to govern itself—and which, to be fair, had never been governed so poorly—a man upon whom God had rested his gaze and laid his finger, a man destined to write his name in glowing letters in the book of history, worked on while presenting to the world a face both bold and mysterious. He was headed somewhere but no one could guess his destination, though England, France, and all Europe watched him march with a firm step and head held high.

Monck had just declared his allegiance to the liberation of the Rump Parliament, that representative body that General Lambert,[76] in imitation of Cromwell, whose lieutenant he'd been, had locked up so closely, to force it to submit to his will, that no member had been able to break the blockade to escape, and only one, Peter Wentworth, had been able to get in.

Lambert and Monck: everything was summed up in these two men, one of whom represented military despotism and the other republicanism. These two men were the sole political survivors of the revolution in which Charles I had lost his crown and then his head. Lambert made no secret of his intentions: he sought to establish a military government and place himself at its head.

Monck, known to be a staunch republican, was said by some to be in favor of supporting and retaining the Rump Parliament, the visible (though degenerate) representation of the republic; others said that Monck, adroit and ambitious, merely wanted to use this parliament, which he seemed to protect, as a stepping-stone to the throne that Cromwell had made vacant but had never assumed himself.

Thus, Lambert, by persecuting the Parliament, and Monck, by declaring in favor of it, had declared themselves one another's enemies. Monck and Lambert, therefore, had raised armies for themselves, Monck in Scotland, attracting the Presbyterians and the royalists, that is, the malcontents, and Lambert in London, which always strongly opposed the most visible power—in this case, the Parliament.

Monck had raised an army, pacified Scotland, and found there an asylum; from there he watched and was watched in turn. But Monck knew that the day had not yet come, that day marked by the Lord for a great change, and so his sword stayed in its sheath. Unassailable in his wild and mountainous Scotland, general and absolute king of an army of eleven thousand veterans whom he had more than once led to victory, informed of affairs in London as well as, or even better than Lambert, who was garrisoned in the city, this was the position of Monck when, a hundred leagues from London, he declared for the Parliament.

Lambert, on the other hand, occupied the capital. That was the center of all his operations, and there he gathered around himself all his friends, as well as the discontented of the lower classes, eternally inclined to favor the enemies of constituted power. It was in London, then, that Lambert heard of Monck's declaration of support for Parliament from beyond the Scottish frontier. He decided there was no time to lose, for the Tweed was not so far from the Thames that an army couldn't leap from one to the other, especially if it was well commanded. He also knew that once it entered England, Monck's army would increase like a rolling snowball, a growing globe of fortune that would be, for one so ambitious, a stepping-stone to elevate him to his goal. Lambert therefore gathered his army, formidable both for its quality and its size, and moved to meet Monck, who, like a careful navigator sailing through reefs, was advancing in short marches, nose to the wind, listening to every sound and sniffing the breeze blowing from London.

The two armies arrived in close proximity at Newcastle. Lambert, the first to arrive, occupied the city itself; Monck, always circumspect, halted outside and established his headquarters at Coldstream, on the Tweed.[77]

The sight of Lambert's troops spread joy through the ranks of Monck's, while on the contrary the sight of Monck threw Lambert's army into disarray. One might have thought that these intrepid warriors, who'd made so much noise in the streets of London, had set off in the hope of avoiding an encounter and instead found themselves facing an army, one that followed not just a banner, but a cause and a principle. It seemed to have occurred to these once-fearless battalions that maybe they weren't as good citizens as Monck's men, who supported the Parliament, while Lambert supported nothing but himself.

As to Monck, if any thoughts occurred to him they must have been sad—or so says History, that modest lady who, it's said, never lies—because the story she recounts is that on the day of Monck's arrival in Coldstream not a sheep could be found in the entire town. If Monck had commanded an English army, that would have been enough to cause the entire army to desert. But the Scots, unlike the English, don't require meat on a daily basis; the Scots, a poor and sober race, can survive on a little barley crushed between two stones, mixed with some cold water and cooked on a flat rock.

The Scots, having been issued their barley, didn't care then if there were no sheep to be found in Coldstream. However, Monck, unused to barley cakes, was hungry, and his staff officers, as hungry as he was, looked anxiously right and left to see where their supper would come from. Monck called for reports, but his scouts, on arriving in the town, had found it deserted, its pantries empty, and as for butchers and bakers, there were none to be found in Coldstream. No one could find a single loaf of bread for the general's table.

As report succeeded report, each one less encouraging than the last, Monck, seeing the fear and dismay on the faces around him, announced that he wasn't the least bit hungry—and in any event, they were bound to eat the following day as Lambert seemed likely to give battle, and if he lost they'd have his provisions, while if he won they'd be relieved of the problem of being hungry.

This didn't seem to console very many of them, but that didn't appear to bother Monck, who though of mild demeanor was beneath it as rigid as a rock. So, everyone had to be satisfied with that, or at least appear to be. Monck, just as hungry as his soldiers, but pretending not to care about the absence of sheep, cut a half-inch of tobacco from the plug of a sergeant on his staff and began to chew it, assuring his lieutenants that hunger was an illusion, and besides, no one can feel hungry if he has something to chew on. This jest mollified some of those who hadn't been reassured by the proximity of Lambert's provisions; the discontented dispersed, the guard took up its routine, and night patrols commenced, while the general continued chewing his frugal meal in the open door of his tent.

Between his camp and that of his enemy was an old abbey, of which there are almost no signs today, but which was standing at the time and was known as Newcastle Abbey.[78] It was built on a broad meadow between the fields and the river, a marshy plain watered by springs and flooded in heavy rain. However, in the midst of this marshland of tall grass, rushes, and reeds, was some higher ground formerly occupied by the vegetable gardens, park, paddocks, and outbuildings that radiated from the abbey, like one of those big sea stars with a round body and legs splaying out all around its circumference.

The vegetable garden, one of the abbey's long legs, extended almost to Monck's camp. Unfortunately, as we've said, it was early June, and the garden, long abandoned, had little to offer. Monck had set a guard on the spot to prevent surprise attacks; the campfires of the enemy forces were visible beyond the abbey, but between the abbey and these fires stretched the Tweed, unrolling like a luminous serpent beneath the shade of some great green oaks. Monck was well acquainted with this position, as Newcastle and its environs had served as his headquarters more than once. He knew that by day his enemy could probably throw scouts into the ruins and provoke a skirmish, but that at night they'd be careful not to risk it. He was safe enough. Thus, his soldiers were able to see him, after he'd had what he'd laughably called his supper of chewing tobacco, sitting like Napoleon on the eve of Austerlitz on his folding chair, half under the light of his lamp and half under the glow of the moon that was beginning to climb to the zenith.

It was about nine-thirty at night. Suddenly Monck was drawn from his half-sleep, real or feigned, by a troop of soldiers who, approaching with joyous cries, kicked his tent poles and thrummed its ropes to awaken him. There was no need for such a commotion; the general opened his eyes and asked, "Well, my children, what's going on?"

"General," answered several voices, "you shall eat at last."

"I have eaten, Gentlemen," he calmly replied, "and was quietly digesting, as you see. But come in and tell me your news."

"It's good news, General."

"Oh? Has Lambert announced that he'll fight us tomorrow?"

"No, but we've captured a dogger carrying fish to his camp at Newcastle."

"Then you've done wrong, my friends. These London gentlemen are delicate and must have their fish course. You'll put them into a bad mood and then tomorrow they'll be ruthless. It would be improper, I think, not to send Lambert this boat full of fish, unless . . ." The general thought for a moment. "Tell me, if you please" he continued, "just who are these fishermen?"

"Picard sailors who fish along the coasts of France and Holland and were blown to ours by a gale."

"Do any of them speak our language?"

"Their captain has a few words of English."

The general's suspicions were aroused by this report. "Very well," he said. "I'd like to see these men; bring them to me."

An officer immediately went off to fetch them.

"How many are there?" continued Monck. "And what sort of boat is it?"

"There are ten or twelve of them, General, manning a sort of dogger, as they call it, that looked Dutch-built to us."

"And you say they were carrying fish to Lambert's camp?"

"Yes, General. They seem to have made a pretty good catch."

"We'll see about that," said Monck. At that moment the officer returned, bringing with him the fishermen's captain, a man about fifty to fifty-five years old, but good-looking. He was of medium height and wore a jerkin of coarse wool with a hat pulled down over his eyes. A cutlass hung from his belt, and he walked with the hesitation of a sailor who, on a rocking deck, was never sure where his foot would come down, placing his feet solidly and deliberately.

Monck looked him over for a long minute, while the fisherman smiled back at him with that expression, half cunning and half foolish, common to the French peasant. "Do you speak English?" Monck asked him in excellent French.

"A bit, and that badly, Milord," replied the fisherman. This answer came less with the lively and terse accent of the folk of the mouth of the Loire than with the slight drawl of the counties of southwest France.

"But you do speak it," continued Monck, to hear more of his accent.

"Oh! We seafarers speak a little of every language," replied the fisherman.

"So, you're a fishing sailor?"

"Today, at least, I'm a fisherman, Milord, and a fine fisherman too! I took a barbel that must weigh thirty pounds, and over fifty mullets. I also have a bucket full of little whitings that will be perfect for frying."

"You sound to me like one who's fished more often in the Bay of Biscay than in the Channel," said Monck, smiling.

"Indeed, I come from the South; does that keep me from being a good fisherman, Milord?"

"Not at all, and I'd like to buy your catch. But first tell me honestly, where were you taking it?"

"Milord, in all honesty I was making for Newcastle, following the coast, when a large party of horsemen, coming up in the opposite direction, signaled me to turn my boat toward Your Honor's camp or suffer a volley of musketry. Since I wasn't armed for war," added the fishermen, smiling, "I thought it best to obey."

"And why were you going to Lambert's camp and not to mine?"

"Milord, I'll be frank, if Your Lordship gives me permission."

"I'll permit it, and if necessary even order it."

"Well, Milord! I was going to Lambert's camp because those city gentlemen pay well, while your Scots—Puritans, Presbyterians, Covenanters, whatever you call them—don't eat very much and don't pay anything."

Monck shrugged, though he couldn't keep from smiling at the same time. "And why, coming from the South, are you fishing along our shores?"

"Because I was stupid enough to get married in Picardy."

"Maybe so, but Picardy isn't England."

"Milord, the man launches his boat to sea, but God and the wind move the boat where they please."

"You didn't intend to approach our coast?"

"Not at all."

"What was your intended route?"

"We were returning from Ostend, chasing the mackerel, when a strong southerly wind took us, and seeing it was useless to fight it, we rode it out. Then it was necessary, so as not to lose our catch, to make for the nearest English port, which happened to be Newcastle. We were told that was lucky because there were many people camped there, both inside and outside the city, gentlemen both wealthy and hungry, so we headed for Newcastle."

"And your crew, where are they?"

"Oh, my crew, they stayed on board; they're simple, uneducated sailors."

"While you . . . ?" said Monck.

"Oh, me!" said the captain, laughing. "I used to sail with my father, trading, and I know how to say *penny, crown, pistole, louis* and *double-louis* in every language of Europe, so my crew listens to me like an oracle and obeys me like an admiral."

"Then, you're the one who decided Lambert would be the better customer?"

"Yes, of course. And to be frank, Milord, was I wrong?"

"That's what you're going to find out."

"In any case, Milord, if there was a mistake, I'm the one responsible, and you mustn't blame my crew for it."

He definitely has his wits about him, thought Monck. Then, after a few moments of silence while he considered the fisherman more closely, the general asked, "You come from Ostend, isn't that what you told me?"

"Yes, Milord, straightaway."

"Then you must have heard what they're saying on the coast, as I've no doubt they're interested in French and Dutch affairs. What do they say about the King of England?"

"Ah, Milord!" said the fisherman, with an expression of honest pleasure. "You're in luck, because you couldn't find a better person to ask about that than me. Listen to this, Milord: after putting in at Ostend to sell the few mackerel we'd taken, I saw the ex-king walking along the dunes waiting for the horses that were to take him to The Hague. He's a tall, pale man, with black hair and a rather severe look. He seemed unwell, and I think the air of Holland might not be good for him."

Monck listened closely to the fisherman's rapid and colorful speech, which, though in a language not his own, still managed to get his ideas across clearly. The fisherman spoke a strange mélange of English, French, and some unknown words that were probably Gascon. Fortunately, his eyes spoke for him, and were so eloquent that one could miss a word from his mouth but still get the meaning from his expression.

The general seemed increasingly satisfied with his interrogation. "You must have heard that this ex-king, as you call him, was traveling to The Hague for some purpose."

"Oh, yes!" said the fisherman. "Indeed, I did."

"What was this purpose?"

"What else?" said the fisherman. "Isn't he consumed with the idea of returning to England?"

"So they say," said Monck thoughtfully.

"Not to mention," said the fisherman, "that the stadtholder . . . you know, Milord? William II?"

"Well?"

"He intends to aid him with all his power."

"Ah! You heard that?"

"No, but I believe it."

"So, you follow politics, then?" asked Monck.

"Oh, Milord, you know how it is! We sailors, who are used to studying the air and the water, that is, the two most changeable things in the world, are rarely mistaken about what else we must travel through."

"Come," said Monck, changing the subject, "I hear you're able to feed us well."

"I'll do my best, Milord."

"How much are you charging for your fish?"

"I'm not such a fool as to set a price, Milord."

"Why's that?"

"Because my fish are yours."

"By what right?"

"By the right of might."

"But I intend to pay you."

"That's very generous of you, Milord."

"As much as it's worth too."

"I'd never ask that much."

"What do you ask, then?"

"Just to be able to leave."

"To go where? To General Lambert's camp?"

"What!" cried the fisherman. "Why would I go to Newcastle if I no longer have any fish?"

"In any event, listen to me."

"I'm listening."

"I have some advice."

"Really? Milord wants to pay me, and give me advice to boot? Milord overwhelms me."

Monck looked closely at the fisherman, whom he seemed to suspect of sarcasm. "Yes, I want to pay you, *and* offer you some advice, because the two things are connected. If you go, then, to General Lambert's camp . . ."

The fisherman shrugged, as if to say, *I won't argue.*

Monck continued, "Don't go by way of the marsh. You'll be carrying money, and in the marsh you might encounter some Scottish ambushers I've posted there. They're hard folk and won't understand the language you speak, though it seems to me to be made of three languages. They might take what I will have given you, and then, when you're back in your country, you'll say that General Monck has two hands, one Scottish and one English, and that he takes back with the Scottish hand what he gave with the English."

"Oh, General, I'll go wherever you say, never fear," said the fisherman, with an anxiety too sincere to be feigned. "But if we're staying, I just want to stay near here."

"I believe you," said Monck, with the hint of a smile. "But I don't have room for you in my tent."

"I'd never presume so far, Milord, and only ask Your Lordship to point out where we should go. Anywhere will do, for a night is soon passed."

"Then I'll have you escorted back to your boat."

"As Your Lordship pleases. Only, if Your Lordship included a carpenter in that escort, I'd be grateful."

"Why is that?"

"Because the gentlemen of your army, Milord, in drawing my boat up the river by a horse-drawn cable, dragged it along the rocky shore, and now I have two feet of water in my hold."

"All the more reason for you to spend the night on your boat, it seems to me."

"Milord, I am at your service," said the fisherman. "We'll unload our baskets wherever you say, you'll pay me whatever you like, and you'll send me on my way when it suits you to do so. You see how easy I am to get along with."

"Come, now, you're not such a bad fellow," said Monck, whose scrutiny hadn't detected a single shade of duplicity in the fisherman's eye. "Hey! Digby!"

An aide-de-camp appeared.

"You will escort this worthy lad and his crew to the row of tents by the canteen, in front of the marsh; that way they'll be within reach of their boat but won't have to sleep on the water tonight. What is it, Spithead?" he asked a newcomer who came in suddenly. This Spithead was the sergeant from whom Monck had borrowed the tobacco for his supper.

"Milord," he said, in English, of course, "a French gentleman has just presented himself at the guard post and is asking to speak with Your Honor."

Though this report was made in English, the fisherman responded with a slight start, which Monck, occupied with the sergeant, failed to notice. "And who is this gentleman?" asked Monck.

"He told me, Milord," replied Spithead, "but these French names are so devilish hard for a Scot to say that it didn't stick with me. However, this gentleman, from what the guards told me, is the same one who presented himself yesterday when Your Honor declined to receive him."

"True enough; I was holding a staff meeting."

"What would Milord care to do about this gentleman?"

"Have him brought to me."

"Should we take any precautions?"

"Such as?"

"Such as blindfolding him, for example."

"To what end? He can only see what I want him to see, which is that I'm surrounded by eleven thousand brave men who ask nothing better than to cut their throats for the honor of the Parliament of England and Scotland."

"And this man, Milord?" said Spithead, pointing at the fisherman, who during this conversation had stood silently with a blank expression, like a man who sees but doesn't understand.

"Ah, right," said Monck. Then, turning to the fish merchant, he said, "Farewell, my good man; I've selected your lodgings. Digby, take him away. Don't worry, we'll send you your money presently."

"Thank you, Milord," said the fisherman, who bowed and left with Digby. About a hundred paces from the tent they came upon his crew, who were whispering volubly among themselves, betraying some anxiety, but he made a gesture that seemed to reassure them. "Hoy, you lot," he said, "come along. His Lordship General Monck has the generosity to pay for our fish and the goodness to offer us hospitality for the night."

The fishermen fell in behind their captain, and, escorted by Digby, the little troop marched toward the canteen, where they'd been assigned their lodgings.

As they walked through the gloom, the fishermen passed the guard who was escorting the French gentleman to General Monck. This gentleman was on horseback and wrapped in a large cloak, so the captain couldn't get a good look at him, despite his curiosity. As for the gentleman, unaware that he was passing fellow countrymen, he paid no attention to the little troop.

The aide-de-camp installed his guests in a reasonably clean tent, dislodging an Irish cook-wife who went off with her six children to sleep wherever she could. A large fire was burning in front of this tent, casting its flickering light over the open pools in the marsh, which were rippled by a cool breeze. Once the crew was settled, the aide-de-camp wished the sailors a good evening, pointing out that the swaying masts of their boat were visible from the tent door, proof that it was still afloat. This sight seemed to please the fishermen's captain.

XXIV

The Treasure

The French gentleman whom Spithead had announced to Monck, and who, enveloped in his cloak, had passed near the fisherman after he'd left the general's tent five minutes before, passed through a series of guard posts without so much as glancing around him to avoid appearing too inquisitive. As ordered, he was escorted to the general's tent. The gentleman was left alone in the sort of canvas antechamber at the tent's entrance, where he awaited Monck, who was not long in appearing once he'd heard his man's report. He paused at the gap in the canvas door to study the face of this man who'd requested an interview. The soldier who'd accompanied the French gentleman must have reported that he'd behaved with discretion, for the first impression the foreigner received from his reception by the general was more favorable than he might have expected from such a suspicious man.

Nevertheless, as was his usual custom when meeting a stranger, Monck surveyed the man with a penetrating gaze, which, for his part, the foreigner tolerated without showing embarrassment or anxiety. After a few moments, the general indicated with a nod and a gesture that he was ready to listen.

"Milord," said the gentleman in excellent English, "I've requested an interview with Your Honor on a matter of consequence."

"Monsieur," replied Monck in French, "you speak our language well for a son of the continent. I beg your pardon, because perhaps the question is indiscreet, but do you speak French with the same purity?"

"It's not surprising, Milord, that I speak English fluently, as I lived in England during my youth and since then have visited it twice." These words were spoken in a French so pure that it not only revealed the speaker as a Frenchman, but a native of the region of Tours.

"And where in England did you live, Monsieur?"

"In my youth, in London, Milord. After that, in 1635, I took a pleasure trip to Scotland, and in 1648 I resided for a time in Newcastle, specifically in that abbey whose gardens are occupied by your army."

"Your pardon, Monsieur, but you understand why I must ask such questions, do you not?"

"I'd be astonished if you didn't, Milord."

"Now, Monsieur, how may I serve, and what do you ask of me?"

"Well, Milord—but first, are we alone?"

"Completely so, Monsieur, except for the guard outside at his post." And saying this, Monck lifted aside the tent door, showing the gentleman the sentry ten paces beyond, where he could be summoned at a single word.

"In that case, Milord," said the gentleman, in a tone as calm as if he were speaking with an old friend, "I'm determined to speak with Your Honor because I know you to be an honest man. Moreover, what I'm about to say will prove the esteem in which I hold you."

Monck, astonished at the tone that claimed between the French gentleman and himself at least equality, raised his piercing gaze to the stranger's face, and with the merest trace of irony in his voice, though his expression never changed, he said, "Thank you, Monsieur—but first, who are you, if you please?"

"I already gave my name to your sergeant, Milord."

"Your pardon, Monsieur, but he's Scottish, and found your name difficult to retain."

"I'm called the Comte de La Fère, Monsieur," said Athos with a bow.

"The Comte de La Fère?" said Monck, searching his memory. "Pardon me, Monsieur, but it seems to me this is the first time I've heard that name. Do you fill an office at the Court of France?"

"No. I am a simple gentleman."

"Of what rank?"

"King Charles I made me a Knight of the Garter, and Queen Anne of Austria gave me the Cordon du Saint-Esprit. Those are my only dignities, Monsieur."

"The Garter! And the Saint-Esprit! You're a knight of both orders, Monsieur?"

"Yes."

"And on what occasions were such favors granted to you?"

"For services rendered to Their Majesties."

Monck looked with astonishment at this man, who appeared so simple and yet at the same time so grand; then, as if he'd renounced the intention to penetrate the mystery of this simplicity and grandeur, since the stranger didn't seem disposed to give him any information than what he'd already conveyed, he said, "So, it was you who presented yourself at the guard post yesterday?"

"And who was sent away; yes, Milord."

"Many commanders, Monsieur, wouldn't let any outsider enter their camp, especially on the eve of a probable battle; but I'm not like my colleagues, and I prefer to leave no loose ends behind me. To me, all advice has value; every danger was sent by God as a warning or test, and I weigh it in my hand and respond with the energy it deserves. Thus, you were turned away yesterday only because I was taking counsel of my staff. Today I am free, so speak."

"Milord, it was quite proper for you to receive me, as my business doesn't concern the battle you're about to have with General Lambert, nor with your camp, and the proof is that I turned my head as I passed through your men and closed my eyes so I couldn't count your tents. No, what I have to say to you, Milord, is on my own account."

"Speak, then, Monsieur," said Monck.

"Just now," continued Athos, "I had the honor to tell Your Lordship that I once resided in Newcastle; this was at the time when King Charles I was turned over to Cromwell by the Scots."

"I know," said Monck coldly.

"At that moment I had a large sum of gold, and on the eve of the battle, perhaps due to some presentiment as to what would happen the next day, I hid it in the main cellar of Newcastle Abbey, beneath that tower the top of which you can see by the moon's silvery light.

"My treasure was buried there, and I came to beg Your Honor to allow me to retrieve it before, perhaps, if the battle turned that way, a mine or some other engine of war might destroy the building and scatter my gold, exposing it to the soldiers."

Monck was a judge of men, and he saw in this one a model of energy, reason, and discretion. He could only attribute to magnanimous discernment the confidence the French gentleman showed in him, and he showed himself profoundly touched by it. "Monsieur," he said, "you have divined my character well. But is the sum worth taking the risk? Can you even believe it's still there?"

"It's there, Milord, I have no doubt of it."

"That answers one question, but what of the other? I asked if the sum was so great that it's worth exposing yourself in this way."

"It is that great, Milord, for it's a million in gold that I packed into two barrels."

"A million!" Monck cried, and this time it was Athos who looked at him so long and searchingly that his distrust returned. *Here*, Monck thought, *is a man who's setting a trap for me . . .* Aloud, he said, "So, Monsieur, you would like to retrieve this sum, as I understand it?"

"If you please, Milord."

"Today?"

"This very evening, because of the circumstances that I explained to you."

"But, Monsieur," objected Monck, "General Lambert is as near to that abbey as I am. Why didn't you address yourself to him?"

"Because, Milord, when one acts on matters of importance, one must trust one's instincts over all. And General Lambert doesn't inspire in me the confidence that you do."

"So be it, Monsieur. I'll help you retrieve your money, assuming it's still there, which it may not be. Since 1648 a dozen years have passed and many things have happened."

Monck offered this excuse to see if the French gentleman would grasp at it, but Athos didn't deviate. "I assure you, Milord," he said firmly, "that

I'm convinced those two barrels are still there and have changed neither position nor possessor."

This answer removed one suspicion from Monck but suggested another. What if this Frenchman was some agent sent to lead the protector of Parliament astray? The gold might be only a decoy, a lure meant to excite the general's avarice. A treasure like that couldn't really exist. It was up to Monck to expose the gentleman's ruse and turn the tables on his enemies, adding another triumph to his name.

Once Monck had decided what he had to do, "Monsieur," he said to Athos, "no doubt you will do me the honor of sharing my supper this evening."

"Yes, Milord," replied Athos with a bow, "for you do me an honor that is in accord with my esteem for you."

"It's all the more gracious of you to accept this offer under the circumstances, which are that my cooks are few and poorly trained and my foragers have returned this evening with empty hands. In fact, if it wasn't for a fisherman of your own country who strayed into my camp, tonight General Monck would have no supper at all. I have fresh fish, however, thanks to this sailor."

"Milord, it is principally for the honor of spending a bit more time with you that I accept."

After this exchange of civilities, which had done nothing to quell Monck's suspicions, the supper, or what stood in for one, was served before them on a wooden folding table. Monck invited the Comte de La Fère to seat himself at the table and sat down across from him. The single platter, stacked with boiled fish, that was offered to the illustrious guests, promised more to hungry stomachs than to sophisticated palates.

While supping—that is, eating fish and washing it down with bad ale—Monck had Athos tell him of the concluding events of the Fronde, the reconciliation of Monsieur de Condé with the king, and the probable marriage of His Majesty to the Infanta Maria Teresa. But he avoided any allusion to the current political situation that united, or rather disunited,

England, France, and Holland, and Athos did the same. During this conversation Monck became convinced of one thing, confirming his first impression, which was that he was dealing with a man of great distinction.

This man was no assassin, and Monck couldn't imagine him as a spy. But he showed enough resolve and finesse that he might be a conspirator. When they rose from the table, Monck asked, "You really believe in your treasure, Monsieur?"

"Yes, Milord."

"Seriously?"

"Quite seriously."

"And you're sure you can find where it was buried?"

"At a single glance."

"Well, Monsieur!" said Monck. "Out of curiosity, I will go with you. In fact, you need me or one of my lieutenants as your escort, or you wouldn't be allowed to move freely through the camp."

"General, I wouldn't allow you to trouble yourself with this if I didn't need your company—but as I recognize that your company is not only honorable but necessary, I accept."

"Do you think we ought to take any soldiers with us?" Monck asked Athos.

"No point to it, I think, General, unless you believe they're needed. Two men and a horse will suffice to carry the barrels to the sloop that brought me here."

"But surely you must dig, through earth, brick, and stone, and you don't intend to do that yourself, do you?"

"General, there's no need to pry or dig. The treasure is hidden beneath the abbey's burial vault, under a stone that's drawn up by a big iron ring. Beneath that, it's four steps down into a crypt. The barrels are there, placed end to end and covered with plaster to form the shape of a bier. The right stone has a certain inscription on it, and since this is a delicate matter that depends on trust, I'll share the secret with Your Honor. The inscription reads, *Hic jacet venerabilis Petrus Guillelmus Scott, Canon. Honorab.*

Conventus Novi Castelli. Obiit quarta et decima die. Feb. ann. Dom., MCCVIII. Requiescat in pace."

Monck didn't miss a word of this. He was astonished by either the amazing duplicity of this man and the superior manner in which he played his role, or at the candid good faith in which he presented his request in a situation where a million in gold could be lost at the stroke of a dagger, in the middle of an army that would regard the theft as rightful restitution.

"All right," he said, "I'll accompany you, and the adventure is so intriguing I'll carry your torch personally." And saying this, he buckled on a short sword and thrust a pistol into his belt, in the act of which his doublet opened enough to reveal beneath it the rings of a mail coat intended to turn an assassin's blade. He took a Scottish dirk in his left hand, and said to Athos, "Are you ready, Monsieur? I am."

Athos, on the other hand, removed his dagger and put it on the table, unbuckled his sword belt, which he placed next to the dagger, and, unbuttoning his doublet while affecting to look for his handkerchief, revealed nothing beneath it but a fine cambric shirt and no other arms or armor.

This is indeed a singular man, thought Monck. *He's unarmed. Has he laid an ambush down there?*

"General," said Athos, as if he'd guessed Monck's thoughts, "you said we should go alone, which would usually be right, but a high commander should never expose himself to such risk. It's night, and the marsh might conceal hidden dangers; bring someone with you."

"You're right," said Monck. And raising his voice, he called, "Digby!"

His aide-de-camp appeared.

"Fifty men armed with sword and musket," Monck said, looking at Athos.

"Not enough, if there's real danger," said Athos, "and far too many if there isn't."

"I'll go alone," Monck said. "Digby, I don't need anyone after all. Let's go, Monsieur."

XXV

The Marsh

In going from the camp to the Tweed, Athos and Monck crossed the same ground Digby had crossed bringing the fishermen from the Tweed to the camp. The aspect of the place, and the appearance of the changes wrought upon it by the actions of men, made a deep impression on the imagination of a man as sensitive as Athos. Athos saw only desolation, while Monck looked only at Athos as he looked around at heaven and earth, and sought, and thought, and sighed.

Digby, to whom the general's last order, and particularly the tone in which it was given, seemed unusual, had followed the two, staying about twenty paces behind. But the expression of the general, upon turning around and seeing that his final orders hadn't been executed, was such that the aide-de-camp realized he was out of line and returned to his tent. He supposed that the general wanted to make one of those incognito inspections of the camp that a veteran commander never fails to make on the eve of a battle, and then tried to explain to himself the presence of Athos, as a subordinate tries to figure out everything mysterious done by his superior. Digby decided that Athos must be a sort of spy who was reporting important information to the general.

At the end of ten minutes' walk between the tents and supply posts, which were thickest near headquarters, Monck arrived at a pathway that split into three directions. The branch on the left led to the river, the middle branch to Newcastle Abbey, while the path to the right crossed the outer lines of Monck's camp, that is, the lines closest to Lambert's army.

Across the river was an advance post of Monck's army, one hundred and fifty Scots who were keeping an eye on the enemy. They had swum across the Tweed, and if attacked were to swim back, giving the alarm, but as there was no bridge at this spot, and Lambert's soldiers seemed less eager to enter the water than Monck's, he wasn't much worried about that flank.

This side of the river, about five hundred paces from the old abbey, the fishermen were lodged in a busy anthill of small tents put up by the soldiers of the local clans to house their wives and children. This haphazard bivouac was visible by the glow of the half-moon, which gleamed from stacked musket barrels and highlighted every white piece of linen and canvas.

Monck arrived with Athos at this spot, a dark landscape lit only by the moon and a dying fire at the little crossroads of three paths. There Monck stopped and said to his companion, "Monsieur, do you know your way?"

"General, if I'm not mistaken, the middle road leads straight to the abbey."

"That's the way; but we're going to need a light to go down into the vaults." Monck turned around. "Ah ha! Digby followed us anyway, it appears. All the better; he can get us what we need."

"Yes, General, a man has been shadowing us for quite a while."

"Digby!" cried Monck. "Digby! Come here, please."

But, instead of obeying, the shadow started as if in surprise and then withdrew instead of advancing, crouching and making off to the left toward the riverbank and the little camp where the fishermen were lodged.

"It seems it wasn't Digby," said Monck.

The pair observed the shadow as it disappeared, but it wasn't strange to see someone moving around at eleven o'clock at night in a camp of ten to twelve thousand men, and Athos and Monck weren't alarmed by this apparition.

"Well, we're going to need some kind of light, a lantern or a torch, so we can see where we're putting our feet, so let's find one," said Monck.

"General, any soldier we meet can light our way."

"No," said Monck, thinking he saw a way to determine if there was any complicity between the Comte de La Fère and the fishermen. "No, I'd rather have one of those French sailors who came in tonight to sell me their fish. They leave in the morning and they'll take the secret with them. If the rumor spread through the Scottish army that there were treasures hidden in Newcastle Abbey, my Highlanders will think there's a million under every flagstone and they won't leave one brick standing on another."

"As you wish, General," replied Athos in a tone so natural it was clear that, soldier or sailor, it was all the same to him, and he had no preference.

Monck took the left causeway, beyond which the man he'd mistaken for Digby had disappeared, and encountered a patrol that, going around the bivouac, was returning toward headquarters. The soldiers stopped him and his companion, Monck gave the password, and they continued on their way.

Another soldier, awakened by the exchange, rose draped in plaid to see what was going on. "Ask him where the fishermen are," said Monck to Athos. "If I speak to him, he'll recognize me."

Athos approached the soldier, who pointed out the right tent. Monck and Athos went toward it. It seemed to the general that as they approached a shadow like the one they'd seen before slipped into the tent, but when he looked within he realized he must have been mistaken, for everyone there was asleep, lying pell-mell with legs and arms across each other. Athos, thinking he might be suspected of colluding with these other Frenchmen, stayed outside.

"*Holà!*" said Monck in French. "Wake up in there." Two or three sleepers sat up. "I need a man to light my way," continued Monck.

Everyone stirred at that, some rising and standing. The captain had risen first. "Your Honor can count on us," he said, in an accent that made Athos start. "Where do you want to go?"

"You'll find out. A lantern, who has one? Quickly, now!"

"Yes, Your Honor. Would Your Honor like me to accompany him?"

"You or whoever, I don't care, so long as someone lights my way."

Strange, thought Athos. *What a distinctive voice that fisherman has.*

"A light, there," cried the captain. "Move it!" Then, whispering to one of his nearby companions, "Take the lantern, Menneville," he said, "and be ready for anything."

One of the fishermen struck flint to steel, ignited a piece of tinder, and with this match lit a lantern. The whole tent was instantly illuminated. "Are you ready, Monsieur?" said Monck to Athos, who had turned so his face wasn't exposed to the light.

"Yes, General," Athos replied.

"Ah! That French gentleman," whispered the fishermen's captain. "*Peste!* It's a good thing I thought to give you the job, Menneville, as he might recognize me. Light their way!"

This was spoken at the far end of the tent, and so low that Monck didn't hear a syllable; in any event, he was talking with Athos. Menneville was gathering what he needed while listening to his chief's orders.

"Well?" said Monck.

"Be right there, General," said the fisherman.

Monck, Athos, and the fisherman left the tent. *Impossible,* thought Athos. *What could I have been thinking?*

"Go ahead, and take the middle path," said Monck to the sailor. "Stretch those legs!"

They hadn't gone twenty paces before the same shadow once more emerged from the tent, and, crawling along parallel to the causeway, behind a fence of hanging nets, kept a curious eye on the general's progress.

All three disappeared into a rising mist. They were walking toward Newcastle Abbey, whose white stones appeared out of the gloom like sepulchers. After standing for a few seconds under the portico, they went through the gate. The door had been splintered by axes. Inside, a squad of four men was sleeping soundly in a corner of the court, so certain were they that there was no chance of attack on this flank.

"The presence of these men doesn't bother you?" said Monck to Athos.

"On the contrary, Monsieur, they can help us roll out the barrels, if Your Honor will permit it."

"Very well."

These sentries, asleep though they were, awoke when they heard their visitors advancing through the brambles and grass that grew in the outer court. Monck gave the password and they went into the abbey's interior, led by the man with the lantern. Monck came last, watching Athos's every movement, his naked dirk in his sleeve, ready to plunge it to the hilt into the French gentleman at the first sign of betrayal. But Athos unhesitatingly marched on through the halls and corridors with a sure step.

Not a single door or window was intact. The doors had been burned, some while still on their hinges, where they stood blackened by the fire but only partly consumed, the flames having burned out before they could devour the great oak slabs held together by iron hasps and nails. As for the windows, every inch of glass had been broken out, and night birds, frightened by the lantern light, fled out through the gaping frames. Meanwhile above great bats began to circle the intruders, the lantern light casting their shadows fitfully against the naked walls. Thinking about it, Monck found this spectacle reassuring, as the presence of the animals meant there were no men lurking deeper in the abbey.

After traversing many rubble-strewn chambers and tearing down more than one vine that had grown across a doorway, Athos arrived at the great hall under the central tower, with its chapel built over the vaults below. There he stopped. "Here we are, General," he said.

"Have you found the right slab?"

"Yes."

"Indeed, I see this flagstone has a ring, but it's mortared down flat."

"We need a lever."

"That's easily gotten." Looking around, Athos and Monck spotted an ash sapling three inches in diameter growing up in a corner, toward a window now filled by its branches. "Do you have a knife?" Monck asked the fisherman.

"Yes, Monsieur."

"Hack down this tree, then."

The fisherman drew a cutlass and obeyed, though not without notching its blade. When the trunk was stripped, it served as a lever, and the three men opened the crypt. "Wait there," said Monck to the fisherman, pointing to a corner of the chapel. "We have black powder to dig up, and your lantern would be dangerous."

The man recoiled in fear and retreated to the spot assigned to him, while Monck and Athos turned back to the crypt, where luckily a beam of moonlight fell directly on the stone that the Comte de La Fère had come so far to find.

"There it is," said Athos, showing the general the slab with its Latin inscription.

"Indeed," said Monck. Then, offering the Frenchman one final opportunity to give up his pretense, he said, "Have you noticed, lining the chapel, the number of broken statues?"

"Milord, you have no doubt heard of the religious practice of the Scots whereby they erect statues of the deceased to protect the valuable objects they had in life. Some soldiers no doubt thought those statues might conceal treasure beneath them, so they overthrew the statues and cracked open their pedestals. But the tomb of the venerable canon before us was never distinguished by a monument, protected instead by your Puritans' superstitious fear of sacrilege; not an inch of this tomb has been chipped."

"That's true," said Monck.

Athos took up his makeshift lever.

"Do you want any help?" asked Monck.

"Thank you, Milord, but I don't want Your Honor to put your hand to work on any labor that you might not wish to take responsibility for later, once you knew the consequences."

Monck raised his head. "What do you mean by that, Monsieur?" he asked.

"What I mean is . . . wait, that man."

"Right," said Monck. "I understand what you fear, so let's put him to the test."

Monck turned toward the fisherman, whose silhouette was outlined by the light of his lantern. "*Come here, friend,*" he ordered the man in English.

The fisherman didn't budge.

"It's fine," he continued, "he doesn't understand English. Speak in English, if you please, Monsieur."

"Milord," replied Athos, "I have known men who, under certain circumstances, are able to pretend not to answer a question posed in a language they supposedly don't understand. The fisherman may be more cunning than we think. Please dismiss him, Milord."

No doubt about it, thought Monck, *he wants me alone in this vault with him. No matter, let's see this to the end; he's only one man, and I should be a match for him.*

"My friend," Monck said in French to the fisherman, "wait for us outside the entrance, and make sure no one comes in to disturb us."

The fisherman moved to obey.

"Leave your lantern," said Monck. "It will just reveal your location and might attract a stray musket shot."

The fisherman seemed to appreciate this advice, set down his lantern, and disappeared under the arch of the entrance.

Monck went and took up the lantern, which he brought down into the crypt. "So!" he said. "There's a fortune hidden in this tomb?"

"Yes, Milord, and in five minutes you will cease to doubt it."

And saying this, Athos used the ash lever to strike a violent blow on the surface of the plaster, which cracked and split. He inserted the lever into the crack and pried up whole slabs of plaster, which split and fell aside. Then the Comte de La Fère resorted to his hands, tearing off hunks of mortar with a strength one would never have suspected in such delicate fingers.

"Milord," said Athos, "this is the concealing masonry of which I told Your Honor."

"Yes, but I don't yet see any barrels," said Monck.

"If I had a dagger," said Athos, looking around, "you'd see them sooner. Unfortunately, I forgot mine in Your Honor's tent."

"I'd offer you mine," said Monck, "but the blade isn't strong enough for what you have in mind."

Athos seemed to hunt around for an object that would serve the purpose he desired. Monck watched every movement of his hands, every expression of his eyes. "Why don't you ask that fisherman for his blade?" said Monck. "He has a cutlass."

"Ah, quite so!" said Athos. "The one he used to cut down that tree." He went to the staircase. "My friend," he called to the fisherman, "toss me your cutlass, if you please, I need it."

The weapon clanged down the steps.

"Take it," said Monck. "It looks to me like a solid enough instrument, and a firm hand could make good use of it."

Athos seemed to accord to Monck's words only the natural and simple meaning in which they were couched. He also didn't notice, or didn't seem to notice, that when he returned toward Monck, Monck stepped back, putting his left hand on the butt of his pistol; the right hand already held his dirk. Athos set to work, turning his back toward Monck and putting his life in his hands. He made a few sharp and adroit blows on the connecting plaster that separated it into two parts, and Monck could then see two barrels placed end to end encased in a chalky shell.

"Milord," said Athos, "you see that my presentiments are proven true."

"Yes, Monsieur," said Monck, "and I have every reason to believe you're satisfied, do I not?"

"Entirely. The loss of this money would have been a terrible blow to me, but I was certain that God, who protects the good cause, would not have allowed us to lose the gold that could let us triumph."

"Upon my honor, you're as mysterious in your words as in your actions, Monsieur," said Monck. "Just now, I didn't understand what you meant when you said that I might not want to be responsible for the task you just accomplished."

"I had good reason to say that, Milord."

"And now you speak of the good cause. What do you mean by those words, *the good cause?* At present we're fighting for five or six causes here in England, which doesn't keep anyone from regarding their own, not only as good, but as the best. Which is yours, Monsieur? Speak frankly, and then we'll see if on this point, to which you attach such great importance, we are of the same opinion."

Athos gave Monck one of those penetrating looks as if probing for deception; then, removing his hat, he began to speak in a solemn voice, while his listener, hand to his face, allowed his long, nervous fingers to ply his mustache and beard, while his vague and melancholy gaze wandered aimlessly around the crypt.

XXVI

Heart and Mind

"Milord," said the Comte de La Fère, "you are a noble Englishman and man of integrity, and you speak with a noble Frenchman who is a man of heart. The gold contained in these two barrels, when I told you it was mine, that was wrong; it's the first deliberate lie I've ever told, though it's true it was only temporary. This gold belongs to King Charles II, exiled from his country, driven from his palace, orphaned at the same time of his father and his throne, and deprived of everything, even the sad consolation of kissing on his knees that stone on which the hands of his murderers inscribed the simple epitaph that cries out for eternal vengeance against them, 'Here lies King Charles I.'"

Monck paled slightly, and an imperceptible shiver rippled his skin and bristled his mustache.

"I," continued Athos, "the Comte de La Fère, the sole and final remaining loyalist of that poor abandoned prince, have offered to come find the man upon whom the fate of royalty in England today depends. I came and stood in this man's gaze, placed myself naked and unarmed in his hands, and now I say to him, 'Milord, here is the last resource of a prince whom God made your master, as his birth made him your king, but upon you and you alone depend his life and his future. Will you use this money to console England for the evils she's suffered under anarchy—that is to say, will you help, or at least not hinder King Charles II in doing it?'

"Here you are the master, you are the king, the all-powerful master and king, because sometimes chance defeats the work of time and God. I am here alone with you, Milord; if the thought of sharing power alarms you, if my complicity disturbs you, you are armed, Milord, and here is a grave already dug. If, on the other hand, the enthusiasm of your cause elevates you, if you are what you seem to be, if your hand, in what it undertakes, obeys your mind, and your mind follows your heart, here is the means of destroying forever the cause of your enemy, Charles Stuart. Kill therefore the man who stands before you, for that man won't return to the one who sent him without that fortune that Charles I, his father, confided to him, kill him and keep the gold that might be used to carry on the civil war. Alas, Milord, that is the fatal situation of that unhappy prince, that he must either corrupt or kill; for everything resists him, all are against him, yet he is marked with the divine seal of royalty, and to be true to his blood, he must retake the throne or die trying on the sacred soil of his fatherland.

"Milord, you have heard what I have to say. To anyone other than the illustrious man whom I address, I would have said, 'Milord, you are poor; Milord, the king offers you this million as down payment on a great bargain: take it and serve Charles II as I have served Charles I, and I am sure that God, who listens to us, who sees us, who reads in your heart what is hidden from all human eyes, I am sure that God will grant you a happy eternal life after death.' But to General Monck, to the illustrious man whose measure I believe I have taken, I say, 'Milord, there is a brilliant place for you in the history of nations and kings, an immortal and imperishable glory. With no motive but the good of your country and the interest of justice, you can become the prime supporter of your king. Many others have been conquerors or usurpers; you, Milord, will be satisfied to be the most virtuous, honest, and worthy of men; you will have held a crown in your hand and instead of fitting it to your brow, you will have placed it on the head for whom it was made. Oh, Milord! Act thus, and you will bequeath to posterity the most glorious name a mortal can bear."

Athos stopped. During the whole time the noble gentleman was speaking, Monck hadn't given the slightest sign of approval or disapproval. Despite this earnest speech, his eyes had scarcely shown even a glint of intelligence. The Comte de La Fère looked at him sadly, and seeing that dull visage, felt discouragement enter his heart.

Finally, Monck stirred, and breaking the silence, said in a soft and solemn voice, "Monsieur, I am going to use your own words to answer you. To anyone other than you, I would respond with expulsion, imprisonment, or worse. Because in fact, you tempt me and at the same time force my hand. But you are one of those men, Monsieur, to whom one can't refuse the attention and consideration they deserve. You're a brave gentleman, Monsieur, for I know one when I see one. You mentioned a fortune that the late king set aside for his son; are you not one of those Frenchmen who, as I've heard, attempted to rescue Charles from Whitehall?"

"Yes, Milord, in fact I was under the scaffold during his execution, where I, having been unable to redeem him, received on my forehead the blood of the martyred king. At the same time, I heard the last word of Charles I, for it was to me that he said, 'Remember!' And in saying 'Remember,' Milord, he was referring to the gold now at your feet."

"I have heard a great deal about you, Monsieur," said Monck, "but I'm glad I had the opportunity to meet you for myself and not to judge you at second hand. I will give you explanations I've shared with no one else, so you'll appreciate the distinction I make between you and those who've been sent to me before."

Athos bowed, eager to absorb the words about to fall from Monck's mouth, as rare and precious as drops of dew in the desert.

"You speak to me of King Charles II," said Monck. "But tell me, I pray you, Monsieur, what does that shadow of a king mean to me? I have grown old in war and in politics, two things that, today, are so closely bound together that every man of the sword must fight for his rights and ambition on his own behalf, rather than blindly follow the orders of an officer, as in ordinary wars. For myself, I desire nothing, but I fear everything—for on the outcome of today's war depends the freedom of England, and perhaps of every Englishman. Why, given the situation of free action I've made for myself, should I shackle myself to a stranger? For that's all that Charles is to me.

"Insofar as Charles has fought battles here and lost them, he's a bad general; inasmuch as he's failed in every negotiation, he's a bad diplomat; and since he bemoans his misery in all the courts of Europe, he shows a character weak and cowardly. Nothing of nobility, nothing of leadership, nothing of strength has he shown, this genius who aspires to govern one of the greatest realms of the Earth.

"So, I know this Charles only by his weaknesses; and you want me, a man of good sense, to go and freely enslave myself to this creature who is my inferior militarily, politically, and personally? No, Monsieur. Once some great and noble action has taught me to appreciate this Charles, I may recognize his rights to a throne that we removed from his father, because he lacked all those virtues that so far are also lacked by the son. But when it comes to rights, I recognize only my own; the revolution made me a general, and if I desire it, my sword will make me the Protector. Let Charles show us what he's made of, let him present himself fairly, let him enter the competition that is open to genius, and most of all let him remember that he comes of a race of which we will ask more than of any other. Monsieur, we need speak no more of this; as for me, I neither refuse nor accept. I watch, and I wait."

Athos knew that Monck was so well informed about everything relating to Charles II that there was no point to further argument—this was neither the time nor place for it. "Milord," he said, "it's only left for me to thank you."

"For what, Monsieur? Because you judged my character well and were proven right? Is that worthy of thanks? That gold you take to King Charles will serve to test him for me; once I see what he does with it, that may give me a new opinion."

"Isn't Your Honor concerned he might compromise himself by allowing such a sum to reach the hands of his enemy?"

"My enemy, you say? Why, Monsieur, I don't have any enemies. I am in service to Parliament, which orders me to fight General Lambert and King Charles—their enemies, not mine—and so I fight them. If the Parliament, on the contrary, ordered me to fly my flag in the port of London, to assemble my soldiers on the riverbank to receive King Charles II . . ."

"You would obey?" Athos gasped.

"Forgive me," said Monck, smiling. "Here I am, with a head of gray hair, about to speak childish nonsense. Where is my mind?"

"So, you wouldn't obey?" said Athos.

"I didn't say that either, Monsieur. The good of my country comes before everything else. God, who had a reason for giving me strength, probably wanted me to use that strength for the good of all; at least I think so, for he also made me perceptive. If the Parliament ordered me to do that, I . . . would consider."

Athos frowned. "I see, then," he said, "that Your Honor definitely isn't disposed to favor King Charles II."

"Always you question me, Monsieur le Comte. Now it's my turn, if you please."

"Do so, Monsieur, and may God inspire you to reply as honestly as I shall!"

"When you have brought this million back to your prince, what will you advise him to do?"

Athos fixed Monck with a look both proud and resolute. "Milord," he said, "while others might advise using that million as a lever in negotiations, I'd tell the king to raise two regiments with it, bring them into Scotland, which you have just pacified, and give the people those freedoms that the revolution had promised but has not delivered. I would advise him to command this little army in person—and it would grow, believe me—and then to die, flag in hand and sword in its sheath, saying, 'Englishmen! Here is the third of my race whom you'd kill: beware of the justice of God!'"

Monck lowered his head and thought for a moment. "If he succeeded," he said, "which is unlikely, though not impossible, for everything is possible in this world, what would you counsel then?"

"To think that by the will of God he had lost his crown, but by the goodwill of men he regained it."

An ironic smile touched Monck's lips. "Unfortunately, Monsieur," he said, "kings rarely listen to good advice."

"Ah, but Milord, Charles II is no king," replied Athos, smiling in his turn, albeit with a different expression than Monck's.

"Come, let's end this, Monsieur le Comte. We've said enough, haven't we?" Athos bowed.

"I'll give the order to have you and your two barrels taken wherever you like. Where are you staying, Monsieur?"

"In a little village at the mouth of the river, Your Honor."

"I know this village; it's composed of no more than five or six houses, is it not?"

"That's it; I've taken the largest, which I'm sharing with a couple of fishnet knotters. It's their boat that brought me here."

"But you have a vessel of your own, Monsieur?"

"Mine is anchored a quarter of a mile offshore, where it awaits me."

"But you don't intend to leave immediately?"

"Milord, I hope to try one more time to convince Your Honor."

"You won't succeed," replied Monck, "but it's important for you to leave Newcastle without your passage raising the least suspicion toward either of us. My officers think that Lambert will attack me tomorrow. I, on the contrary, think he won't make a move; in my eyes it seems impossible. Lambert commands an army without a common cause, and that's no army at all. I have told my soldiers to consider my authority subordinate to a superior authority, so that after me, around me, or above me, they still have something to follow. The result is that, if I die, my army won't be immediately demoralized, and even if, for example, I decided to leave the camp for a while, as I sometimes do, there wouldn't be in my troops the least shadow of anxiety or disorder. Today I am the great magnet that draws together all the natural and sympathetic forces of the English. All this scattered iron that's sent against me, I will draw it together.

"At this moment Lambert's command consists of eighteen thousand deserters—though I didn't share that number with my officers, as you can

well imagine. Nothing is more useful to an army than the feeling of imminent battle; everyone is careful, everyone is alert. I tell you this so you can
rest assured that you can stay nearby safely. A week from now, there will
be a new situation, either from battle or negotiation. At that time, because
you've judged me to be an honest man, and confided to me your secret—and
I must thank you for your confidence—I'll either visit you or send for
you. I sincerely ask you not to leave until we've spoken again."

"I so swear, General!" cried Athos, so transported by joy that, despite
his natural reserve, he couldn't suppress a sparkle in his eye.

Monck spotted this flash, and immediately stifled one of those mute
smiles that passed across his lips when he saw that someone believed they'd
divined what he was thinking.

"So, Milord," said Athos, "a week will be the extent of our delay?"

"One week, yes, Monsieur."

"And during this week, what shall I do?"

"If there's a battle, keep out of it, I pray you. I know you French are curious about these kinds of amusements, and you'd like to assess our manner of
fighting, but you'd just catch a stray bullet. Our Scots are terrible marksmen,
and I'd hate to see a worthy gentleman like you return wounded to France.
I don't want to have to be responsible for sending your million on to your
prince for you, for that would look like I was paying the pretender to wage
war on the Parliament, and with some justification. Go then, Monsieur, stay
low, and keep to what's agreed between us."

"Ah, Milord!" said Athos. "What joy it would be to be the first to penetrate to that noble heart that beats beneath your cloak."

"So, you believe that I keep secrets," said Monck, without changing
the half-wry expression on his face. "Why, Monsieur, what secrets do you
think could be kept in the hollow head of a soldier? But it's getting late, and
our lantern is burning down; time to call our man. *Holà!*" cried Monck in
French, approaching the foot of the stairs. "*Holà!* Fisherman!"

The fisherman, numbed by the night's chill, replied in a hoarse voice
asking what was wanted.

"Go to the sentry post," said Monck, "and order the sergeant there, on the behalf of General Monck, to come here at once."

This was an easy commission to fulfill, for the sergeant, intrigued by the presence of the general in this deserted abbey, had slowly followed, coming little by little until he was only a few steps from the fisherman. Thus, the general's order reached him directly and he hurried to comply.

"Get a horse and two men," said Monck.

"A horse and two men?" repeated the sergeant.

"Yes," Monck replied. "Can you get a packhorse with two paniers?"

"Sure, no more than a hundred paces from here in the Scottish camp."

"Good."

"What do I do with the horse, General?"

"Look here."

The sergeant came down the three or four steps that separated him from Monck and appeared in the vault. "Do you see, there by that gentleman?" Monck said to him.

"Yes, General."

"You see those two barrels?"

"Yes, Sir."

"These two barrels contain, one of them powder, the other musket balls. I want you to have these barrels taken to the little village at the mouth of the river, which I intend to garrison with two hundred muskets. You understand that this mission is secret, because this is a flanking movement that could decide the battle."

"Oh! Yes, General," murmured the sergeant.

"Good! So, tie these two barrels on the horse, and then you and the two men are to escort this gentleman, who is my friend, to his house. But, you understand, without attracting attention."

"I'd go through the marsh if I only knew a way," said the sergeant.

"I know one," said Athos. "It's narrow but it's solid, as it's laid over piles. If we're careful, we can manage it."

"Do what this cavalier tells you to," said Monck.

"Whoa! These barrels are heavy," said the sergeant, trying to lift one.

"About four hundred pounds each, if they contain what they should, eh, Monsieur?"

"More or less," said Athos.

The sergeant went to find the two men and the horse. Monck, left alone with Athos, seemed inclined to make only small talk, while distractedly examining the vault. Then, hearing the hooves of the horse, he said, "I'll leave you with your men, Monsieur, and return to the camp. You should be safe."

"I can count on seeing you again, Milord?" asked Athos.

"So I've said, Monsieur, and it will be my great pleasure." Monck held out his hand to Athos.

"Oh, Milord, if only you would!" murmured Athos.

"Hush, Monsieur!" said Monck. "We agreed to say no more about it."

And, saluting Athos, he went up, passing the men on the stairs who were coming down. He'd gone no more than twenty paces outside the abbey when he heard a long, low whistle. Monck cocked an ear but, seeing nothing, continued on his way. Then he remembered the fisherman and looked around for him, but the fisherman had disappeared. However, if he'd looked a bit more closely, he'd have seen his man bent over double, slipping like a snake along the stones and losing himself in the mist, skimming along the surface of the marsh. And if he could have seen through the mist, he'd have seen something else that would have attracted his attention, which was that the masts of the fishermen's boat showed it had moved closer in to the river bank.

But Monck saw nothing and, thinking he had nothing to fear, took the deserted causeway that led to the camp. It was as he did so that the disappearance of the fisherman struck him as strange, and he began to have serious suspicions. He had just placed at Athos's orders the only soldiers who were near enough to protect him, and he had nearly a mile to cross to return to camp.

The fog rose and thickened, so that one could barely distinguish objects at a distance of ten paces. Monck thought he heard a sound like the beat of an oar echoing from the swamp on his right. "Who's there?" he shouted.

But no one answered. Then he cocked his pistol, took his dirk in hand, and hurried on without another word. Calling for help, when there was no urgent reason to do so, seemed to him to be beneath him.

XXVII

The Next Day

It was seven in the morning: the first light of day glanced from the pools in the marsh, the sun reflected in them like a crimson ball, when Athos, getting up and opening his bedroom window, which looked out on the riverbank, saw not fifteen paces away the sergeant and men who'd escorted him the day before, and who, after leaving the barrels at his house, had returned to the camp by the causeway.

Why, having returned to camp, had the men come back again? That was the question that suddenly occupied Athos's mind.

The sergeant, head up and alert, seemed to have been waiting for the moment the gentleman would appear to question him. Athos, surprised to find before him those he'd seen departing the day before, was unable to conceal his astonishment.

"There's no reason for surprise, Sir," said the sergeant. "Yesterday the general ordered me to watch over your safety, and I'm obeying that order."

"The general is in camp?" asked Athos.

"Doubtless, Sir, since you left him yesterday going there."

"Very well! Wait a moment and I'll go there to give an account of your loyal service, and to recover my sword, which I left yesterday on the table."

"That suits us perfectly," said the sergeant, "for we were going to ask you to do that."

Athos thought he noticed a sardonic edge to the sergeant's expression, but the adventure in the vault might have excited the man's curiosity, in which case it was no surprise to read on his face the ideas disturbing his mind. Athos shut all the doors firmly and gave the keys to Grimaud, who had taken up residence in the shed over the locked door to the cellar where the barrels were stored.

The sergeant escorted the Comte de La Fère to the gates of the camp. There, a new guard squad awaited and took over for the four men who'd accompanied Athos thus far. This new guard was commanded by Aide-de-Camp Digby, who, during their walk, regarded Athos with such baleful looks that the Frenchman wondered what he'd done to deserve them, when the day before he'd been so perfectly respectful.

He continued on his way toward headquarters while keeping to himself his observations about his escort and situation. Inside the general's tent, where he'd been taken the day before, he found three superior officers, Monck's lieutenant commander and two colonels. Athos saw that his sword was still on the general's table, where he'd left it the day before.

None of these officers had seen Athos before, and therefore didn't know him. Monck's lieutenant commander asked, indicating Athos, if this was the gentleman with whom Monck had left the tent.

"Yes, Your Honor," said the sergeant, "the very same."

"I never denied it," said Athos haughtily. "And now, it seems to me, Gentlemen, it's my turn to ask you the point of all these questions, especially the tone in which they're asked."

"Monsieur," said the lieutenant commander, "if we address these questions to you, it's because we have the right to do so, and if we do so in such a tone, it's because that tone, believe me, is appropriate to the situation."

"Gentlemen," said Athos, "you don't know me, but I must tell you that I recognize no one here as my equal except General Monck. Where is he? Let me be taken before him, and if he has any questions to ask me, I'll answer them, and to his satisfaction, I hope. I repeat, Gentlemen: where is the general?"

"God's death! You'd know better than we where he is," said the lieutenant. "Me?"

"That's right, you."

"Sir, I don't understand you," said Athos.

"You *will* understand me—but first of all, for God's sake, Monsieur, keep your voice down. Now, what did you talk about with the general yesterday?"

Athos smiled disdainfully.

"We don't want your smiles," said one of the colonels angrily, "we want answers."

"And I, Gentlemen, declare that you'll get no response unless it's in the presence of the general."

"But you're well aware that you're asking the impossible," said the same colonel.

"That's the second time you've responded strangely to my request," said Athos. "Is the general gone?"

Athos's question was asked in such obvious good faith, and with such an air of naïve surprise, that the three officers exchanged glances. The lieutenant commander spoke by tacit agreement of the two other officers. "Monsieur," he said, "the general left you yesterday on the outskirts of the abbey?"

"Yes, Sir."

"And you went . . . ?"

"It's not for me to answer that, it's up to those who escorted me. They're your soldiers, question them."

"But if it pleases us to question you?"

"Then it will please me to answer you, Sir, that I don't know anyone here, I know only the general, and it's to him that I'll respond."

"Perhaps, Monsieur, but we are in charge, we're set up as a council of war, and when you stand before judges, you must answer them."

To this the face of Athos expressed only surprise and disdain, rather than the fear the officers expected their threat to evoke. "Scottish or Englishmen to judge me, a subject of the King of France—me, here under the safeguard and protection of British honor!" said Athos, shrugging his shoulders. "It's madness, Gentlemen."

The officers looked at him. "Then, Monsieur," said the leader, "you pretend not to know where the general is?"

"As to that, Sir, I already said so."

"Yes, but that answer just isn't believable."

"It's nonetheless true, Sir. People of my rank don't usually lie. I'm a gentleman, as I told you, and when I wear at my side the sword that, through an excess of delicacy, I left last night on that table where it still is today, no one, believe me, tells me anything I deem unworthy to hear. However, today I'm disarmed; if you claim to be my judges, then judge me. But if you're merely executioners, then kill me."

"Oh, really, Monsieur," said the lieutenant in a more courteous voice, struck by Athos's grandeur and self-possession.

"Sir, I came here to speak confidentially with your general on matters of importance. He received me with no ordinary welcome, as your soldiers can convincingly report. If your general gave me such a welcome, it's because he knew I was worthy of his esteem. So, don't suppose I'm going to reveal my secrets to you, let alone his."

"But those barrels, what do they contain?"

"Haven't you asked your soldiers that? What did they tell you?"

"That they contained powder and shot."

"And where did they get that information? They must have told you."

"From the general; but we're not fools."

"Take care, Sir, for it's not me you're calling a liar, it's your commander."

The officers looked at each other again. Athos continued, "In front of your soldiers, the general asked me to wait a week for him, that in one week he'd have an answer for what I'd asked him. Should I have left? No, I'm here and I wait."

"He told you to wait for a week!" said the lieutenant.

"He said that, Sir, though he knew I had a sloop at anchor outside the river mouth and could have embarked on it yesterday and sailed away. Now, if I'm still here, it's solely to conform to the general's wishes. His Honor

advised me not to leave until he'd given me a final audience at the end of a
week. So, I tell you again, I'm waiting."

The lieutenant commander turned to the other two officers and said, in
a low voice, "If that gentleman is right, there's reason to hope. The general
has sometimes conducted negotiations so secret he thought it unwise to
warn even us. If so, then the outside limit of his absence will be a week."

Then, turning to Athos, "Monsieur," he said, "your statement is of the
gravest importance; will you repeat it under oath?"

"Sir," replied Athos, "I have always lived in a world in which my word
is regarded as a sacred oath already."

"However, this time, Monsieur, the circumstances are more serious than
any in which you've previously found yourself. This involves the security
of an entire army. Consider: the general has disappeared, so we must search
for him. Was the disappearance natural? Was some crime committed?
Should we pursue our investigations, no matter what, or should we wait
patiently? At this point, Monsieur, everything depends on what you have
to say to us."

"Asked in that way, Sir, I don't hesitate to reply," said Athos. "Yes, I had
come to speak confidentially with General Monck to ask him for a response
relating to certain interests. Yes, the general, being unable, no doubt, to
provide an answer in advance of the expected battle, asked me to wait a
week longer in the house where I was lodging, promising me that in a week
he would see me again. Yes, all of the foregoing is true, as I swear by God,
who is the absolute master of my life and yours."

Athos pronounced these words with such solemnity and majesty that
the three officers were nearly convinced. However, one of the colonels made
a final attempt: "Monsieur," he said, "though we're now persuaded of the
truth of what you say, there's still a strange mystery in all this. The general
is too prudent a man to abandon his army on the eve of battle without giving
at least one of us a warning. As for me, I admit I can't help but believe that
some strange event is behind his disappearance. Yesterday, some foreign
fishermen came to sell us their fish, and were lodged with the Scots near

the road used by the general to go to the abbey with monsieur and then to return. It was one of those fishermen who lit the general's way with a lantern. In the morning, boat and fishermen had both disappeared, carried away on the midnight tide."

"I don't see anything unnatural in that," said the lieutenant. "After all, those people weren't prisoners."

"No, but I repeat, it was one of them who lighted the way of the general and monsieur to the abbey vault, and Digby assured us that the general was suspicious of them. Now, who can prove these fishermen weren't colluding with monsieur here, and that once the blow was struck, monsieur, who is certainly brave, didn't stay to reassure us by his presence and turn aside an investigation?"

This argument made an impression on the other two officers.

"Sir," said Athos, "permit me to say that your reasoning, plausible though it sounds, falls apart where it concerns me. I stayed behind, you say, to allay your suspicions. But on the contrary, Gentlemen, I can have suspicions as well as you have, and I say it's impossible for the general, on the eve of a battle, to go off without saying anything to anyone. Yes, there is some strange event involved in this, and rather than remain idle and waiting, you must exhibit all possible activity and vigilance. I am your prisoner, Gentlemen, on parole or otherwise. My honor is engaged in learning what has become of General Monck, so much so that if you said, 'Depart!' I'd say, 'No, I remain.' And if you asked for my opinion, I'd say, 'Yes, the general is the victim of some plot or conspiracy, for if he were going to leave the camp, he'd have told me so. Seek, search everywhere, by land and by sea; the general hasn't left, at least not of his own free will.'"

The lieutenant commander shared a significant look with the other officers. "No, Monsieur," he said, "now you go too far. The general is unlikely to be a victim in these events, and in all likelihood he's directed them. General Monck has done this kind of thing before. It would be a mistake for us to be alarmed; no doubt his absence will be short-lived, so we should be careful to avoid doing something out of fear to announce his absence, because if we demoralize his army that, to the general, would be the true crime. The general is giving us proof of his confidence in us, and to be worthy of his esteem we must wreath the whole affair in profound silence. We're going to safeguard monsieur, not out of distrust because he's committed a crime, but to better ensure the secret of the general's absence by keeping him with us, so until further notice monsieur will live here at headquarters."

"Gentlemen," said Athos, "you forget that the general entrusted me with a charge over which I must keep watch. Give me whatever guard you please, shackle me if you must, but use my house as my prison. Otherwise I swear the general, on his return, will reproach you for it, on my faith as a gentleman."

The officers consulted with one another for a moment, and then the lieutenant commander said, "So be it, Monsieur; return to your house."

They gave Athos a guard of fifty men who surrounded his house, not losing sight of him for a moment. The secret was kept, but hours passed, and then days, without the return of the general or any word of him.

XXVIII

Contraband Merchandise

Two days after the events just related, while General Monck was expected to return to the camp at any instant—but did not—a small Dutch dogger, with a ten-man crew, dropped anchor offshore from Scheveningen, almost within cannon-shot of the port. It was the darkest hour of the night and the tide was rising in the gloom, an excellent time to disembark passengers and unload merchandise.

The harbor of Scheveningen, which curved in a broad crescent, was shallow and moreover unsafe; almost nothing anchored there but large Flemish hoys or local Dutch fishing boats, which the sailors drew up on the sand on rollers, as Virgil says the ancients did in the Mediterranean. When the tide is rising it isn't safe to bring a vessel too close to shore, for if the wind is stiff its prow can be driven into the sand, and the sand of that coast is spongy: what it takes in it doesn't give up so easily. This was probably why a longboat detached from the dogger as soon as it dropped anchor and came in with eight of its sailors, who surrounded a long oblong object, some sort of basket or box.

The shore was deserted; the few fishermen who lived in the dunes were in bed. The sole watchman who guarded the coast—a coast very poorly guarded, since disembarking from large vessels was impossible—was imitating the sleeping fishermen as far as possible, though he had to sleep in his sentry box instead of a bed. The only sound to be heard was the whistling of the night breeze as it hissed through the heather on the dunes. But the approaching sailors must have been suspicious men, for the apparent solitude didn't satisfy them, and their boat, barely visible as a dark blot on the ocean, slipped in without sound, eschewing the noisy use of oars, until the tide drove it onto the sand.

The moment he felt the keel strike a single man jumped out of the longboat, after giving a brief order in a voice that indicated the habit of command. As a consequence of this order, several muskets immediately showed themselves by the faint light from the sea, that mirror of the sky, and the oblong bundle previously mentioned, which doubtless contained some form of contraband, was carried ashore with infinite care.

Immediately, the man who'd landed first ran diagonally past the village of Scheveningen, heading for the nearest grove of the wood. There he sought that house that we saw once before through the trees, and which we know was the temporary, and very humble, dwelling of he who was called by courtesy the King of England.

Everyone was asleep there as elsewhere; only a big dog, of the breed the fishmongers of Scheveningen harness to their little carts to carry their fish into The Hague, began a wild barking as soon as he heard the stranger's footsteps outside the windows. But this reception, instead of frightening the newcomer, seemed on the contrary to delight him, for his voice might not have been enough to awaken the inhabitants of the house, but with the dog's assistance his voice was hardly needed. The stranger therefore waited until the repeated barking had had its probable effect, and then ventured to call out. At that sound the mastiff began to roar with greater violence, and soon another voice was heard within, quieting the watchdog. Once the dog had settled down, a voice, weak, broken, and polite, said, "Wh-what do you want?"

"To call on His Majesty King Charles II," said the stranger.

"What do you want with him?"

"I want to speak with him."

"Who are you?"

"Ah, *mordioux!* Too many questions. I don't like talking through doors."

"Just tell me your name."

"I don't like to announce my name in the open air. Look, it's not like I'm going to eat your dog—I just hope to God he doesn't eat me."

"You bring news, maybe, Monsieur?" replied the voice, patient and hesitant like that of an old man.

"In fact, I do bring news, and news you'd never expect! So, open up, won't you?"

"Monsieur," continued the old man, "on your soul and conscience, do you believe your news is worth waking the king for?"

"For the love of God! My dear Monsieur, you won't be sorry, I swear to you, for putting him to the trouble. I'm worth my weight in gold, word of honor!"

"Monsieur, I simply cannot open this door until you tell me your name."

"Must I, then?"

"That's my master's order, Monsieur."

"All right! My name is . . . but I warn you, my name won't tell you anything."

"Nevertheless, tell me anyway."

"Well! I'm the Chevalier d'Artagnan."

The voice gave a happy gasp. "My God!" said the old man on the other side of the door. "Monsieur d'Artagnan! What joy! I thought I recognized that voice."

"Well!" said d'Artagnan to himself. "They know my voice here. How flattering!"

"Oh, yes, we know it!" said the old man, throwing open the locks. "And here's the proof."

And with these words he admitted d'Artagnan who, by the light of the lantern in the old man's hand, recognized the stubborn guardian. "God's death!" he cried. "It's Parry! I should have known."

"Parry, yes, my dear Monsieur d'Artagnan, it is I. What joy to see you again!"

"Well said: what joy!" said d'Artagnan, squeezing the old man's hands. "Çà! Now you'll warn the king, won't you?"

"But the king is asleep, my dear Monsieur."

"God's death! Awaken him and he won't scold you for disturbing him, I promise you."

"Do you come on behalf of the count?"

"Which count?"

"The Comte de La Fère."

"On the behalf of Athos? My faith, no—I come on behalf of me. Let's go to the king, Parry! I need to see the king!"

Parry didn't feel a duty to resist any longer; he'd known d'Artagnan a long time and knew that, Gascon though he was, his words never promised more than they could deliver. He led the way across a courtyard and a small garden, soothed the dog, who seriously wanted a taste of musketeer, and knocked on the shutter of a small chamber on the ground floor of a rear pavilion. Immediately a small dog within began imitating the big dog in the courtyard.

"Poor king!" d'Artagnan said to himself. "These are his bodyguards. Though it's true they're not the worst sentries I've seen."

"What is it?" asked the king from within the chamber.

"Sire, it's the Chevalier d'Artagnan, who's brought news."

No more noise from within, just the door quickly opened. Bright light flooded the corridor and the garden, for the king had been working by lamplight. Papers were scattered across his desk where he had begun the draft of a letter that, by its many erasures, showed the difficulty he was having in writing it.

"Come in, Monsieur le Chevalier," he said. But upon turning he saw only a fisherman, and asked, "What were you talking about, Parry, and where is the Chevalier d'Artagnan?"

"He is before you, Sire," said d'Artagnan.

"In such an outfit?"

"Yes. Look closely at me, Sire; don't you recognize the man you saw at Blois in the antechambers of King Louis XIV?"

"I do, Monsieur, and I recall that I had much to thank you for."

D'Artagnan bowed. "It was my duty to behave as I did, once I knew I was dealing with Your Majesty."

"You bring me news, you say?"

"Yes, Sire."

"On the behalf of the King of France, no doubt?"

"*Ma foi*, no, Sire," replied d'Artagnan. "Your Majesty must have seen that the King of France is occupied only with his own majesty."

Charles rolled his eyes and sighed.

"No, Sire," continued d'Artagnan, "I bring news that I've made myself. However, I dare to hope that Your Majesty will hear this news with some favor."

"Speak, Monsieur."

"If I'm not mistaken, Sire, Your Majesty spoke forcefully at Blois about the frustration of his affairs in England."

Charles flushed. "Monsieur," he said, "I spoke of that only to the King of France."

"No, Your Majesty is mistaken," said the musketeer coolly. "When kings are in trouble, they also speak to me. In fact, that's the only time they speak to me; once the sun shines again, they speak to me no more. But I have for Your Majesty, not only the greatest respect, but also absolute devotion—and when that comes from a d'Artagnan, Sire, it means something. Now, when I heard Your Majesty complain of the turns of fate, I found him noble, generous, and ill-served by fortune."

"In truth," said Charles, astonished, "I'm not sure which is greater, your respect or your liberties."

"You can decide that later, Sire," said d'Artagnan. "So, Your Majesty complained to his brother Louis XIV of the difficulties he was having in returning to England and regaining his throne without men or money."

Charles shrugged in a manner that betrayed some impatience.

"And the principal obstacle he found blocking his way," continued d'Artagnan, "was a certain general commanding the armies of Parliament and who was acting like another Cromwell. Isn't that what Your Majesty said?"

"Yes; but I repeat to you, Monsieur, these words were spoken for the king alone."

"And you will find, Sire, that you're glad they also fell into the ears of his Lieutenant of Musketeers. This man who was frustrating Your Majesty was called General Monck, I think. Did I hear his name rightly, Sire?"

"Yes, Monsieur—but once more, what is the point of these questions?"

"Oh, I'm well aware, Sire, that etiquette doesn't permit us to question kings. I hope that later Your Majesty will forgive me this discourtesy. Your Majesty added that if only he could come face to face to confer with him, then by force or persuasion he would remove this stubborn obstacle, the only real barrier he found in his path."

"That's all true, Monsieur; my destiny, my future, my obscurity or my glory depend on that man. But what did you gather from that?"

"Just one thing: that if this General Monck is as troublesome as you say, it would be worthwhile to rid Your Majesty of him or make him your ally."

"Monsieur, since you listened to my conversation with my royal brother, you know that a king who has neither men nor money has no way of dealing with a man like Monck."

"Yes, Sire, I know that was your opinion—but fortunately for Your Majesty, it wasn't mine."

"What are you saying?"

"That with neither an army nor a million, I've done what Your Majesty thought could be done only with a million or an army."

"What! What do you mean? What have you done?"

"What have I done? Well, Sire! I went across to get this man who was so frustrating Your Majesty."

"To England?"

"Exactly, Sire."

"You went to England to get General Monck?"

"Did I do something wrong, by chance?"

"Really, Monsieur, you must be mad!"

"Not in the least, Sire."

"You've taken Monck prisoner?"

"Yes, Sire."

"From where?"

"From the middle of his camp."

The king gaped and blinked.

"And having plucked him from the causeway at Newcastle," said d'Artagnan simply, "I've brought him to Your Majesty."

"You've brought him to me!" cried the king indignantly, thinking this was a hoax.

"Yes, Sire," replied d'Artagnan without changing his tone. "I've brought him to you. He's just beyond, in a big box pierced with holes so he can breathe."

"Good Lord!"

"Oh, don't worry, Sire, we've taken good care of him. He arrives in good condition and perfect health. Is it Your Majesty's pleasure to meet and confer with him, or shall I dump him in the Channel?"

"Good Lord!" repeated Charles. "Good Lord! Monsieur, is this true? You're not insulting me with some low jest? You've pulled off such a bold and brilliant feat? Impossible!"

"Would Your Majesty permit me to open the window?" said d'Artagnan, opening it. The king didn't even have time to say yes. D'Artagnan gave a long, high-pitched whistle, which he repeated three times into the silence of the night.

"There!" he said. "They'll bring him to Your Majesty."

XXIX

In Which d'Artagnan Begins to Fear the
Investment of Planchet and Co. Might Be Lost

The king couldn't contain his surprise, looking back and forth from the smiling musketeer to the dark window opened onto the night. Before he could arrange his thoughts, six of d'Artagnan's men—for two had remained to guard the boat—brought to the house, where Parry received them, that oblong object that contained at that moment the destinies of England.

Before leaving Calais, d'Artagnan had had a carpenter in that town make a sort of special coffin, large and deep enough for a man to turn easily around in it. The bottom and the sides were densely padded, forming a bed soft enough that the roll of the waves didn't turn the box into a punishment cage. The little grating that d'Artagnan had mentioned to the king was like the visor of a helmet, installed at the height of a seated man's face. It had a solid shutter so that at the slightest cry it could stifle the sound, and even, if need be, smother the one who cried out.

D'Artagnan was well acquainted with the character of his crew, as well as that of his prisoner, and during the crossing had been afraid of only two things: that the general would prefer death to this strange bondage and get smothered in trying to cry out, or that his crew would allow themselves to be tempted by the prisoner's offers and put d'Artagnan in the box in place of Monck. Therefore, d'Artagnan had spent the last two days and nights next to the trunk alone with the general, offering him wine and food which were refused, and repeatedly trying to reassure him about the eventual outcome of his singular captivity. Two pistols and his sword on the nearby table were his precautions against interference from outside.

Once they arrived at Scheveningen, he stopped worrying. His men dreaded trouble with the authorities ashore, and he had enlisted as his second-in-command the man we've seen answer to the name Menneville, who acted as his lieutenant. The latter, being less vulgar a spirit than the others, had more at stake than they because he had more of a conscience. He believed he had a future in the service of d'Artagnan and would have been cut to pieces rather than violate his leader's orders. Therefore, it was to him that, once ashore, d'Artagnan had confided the box, and the life, of the general. It was also to him that d'Artagnan had given the order to bring the box when he heard the triple whistle.

We've seen that the lieutenant obeyed. Once the trunk was in the king's house, d'Artagnan dismissed his men with a gracious smile, saying, "Messieurs, you've rendered a great service to His Majesty King Charles II, who within six weeks will be King of England. Your reward will be doubled; return to wait for me at the boat." They departed with such joyful whoops and cries that they even frightened the big watchdog.

D'Artagnan had had the trunk brought into the king's antechamber. He closed the outer doors of this chamber with great care, after which he opened the trunk, saying to the general, *"Mon Général,* I have a thousand pardons to ask of you; my methods were unworthy of a man such as you, I'm well aware, but I had to have you take me for a fishing boat captain. And transportation in England can be so awkward. But here, General," continued d'Artagnan, "you are free to get up and walk again."

That said, he cut the bonds that tied the general's arms and legs. The latter got up, and then sat down with the expression of a man who expects imminent death.

D'Artagnan then opened the door to Charles's study and said to him, "Sire, here is your enemy, General Monck; I had taken a personal vow that I would bring him to you. It is done, and now it's up to you. Monsieur Monck," he added, turning to the prisoner, "you are before His Majesty King Charles II, Sovereign Lord of England and Scotland."

Monck raised his coldly stoic gaze to the young prince, and replied, "I recognize no King of England and Scotland; I don't even know anyone here who is worthy to bear the title of gentleman, for it was in the name of King Charles II that an agent, whom I took for an honest man, came to take me in an infamous trap. I fell into this trap, the more fool me—but now you, the plotter," he said to the king, "and you, the executioner," he said to d'Artagnan, "hear every word I have to say to you: you have my body, and you can kill me, if you have the nerve to do it, but you'll never have my mind or my soul. And now don't ask me for another word, because from this moment forward I will not open my mouth even to shout. I have spoken."

He pronounced these words with the fierce and invincible resolution of the most diehard Puritan. D'Artagnan saw that his prisoner was a man who knew the value of every word and who fixed that value by the tone with which he pronounced them. "The fact is," he whispered to the king, "that the general is just that implacable; he didn't take a mouthful of bread or a drop of wine for two days. But from this moment it's Your Majesty who decides his fate, and I wash my hands of him, as Pilate said."

Monck, standing pale and resigned, waited with eyes glowering and arms crossed. D'Artagnan turned to him and said, "You must understand that your speech, lovely as it was, is no use to anyone, not even you. His Majesty wanted to speak to you, but you refused him an interview; now that you're here face to face, brought by a force independent of your own will, why would you force us to take measures that are ignoble and unworthy? Speak, devil take you! If only to say no."

Monck didn't open his lips; Monck didn't blink an eye; Monck just stroked his mustache with an air that announced he wasn't at all mollified. Meanwhile, Charles II was deep in thought. He was facing Monck for the first time, the man he'd wanted so long to see, and with that profound gaze that God gives to eagles and to kings, he had sounded the depths of his heart.

He recognized Monck was sincere in his determination to die before he'd speak, entirely consistent with so grave and distinguished a man who had been humiliated so cruelly. Charles II suddenly made one of those fateful decisions upon which an ordinary man bets his life, a general his career, and a king his realm. "Sir," he said to Monck, "in certain respects, you are entirely justified. I don't ask you to answer me, but I do ask you to listen."

There was a moment of silence during which the king gazed at Monck, who remained impassive.

"Just now you directed a painful reproach to me, Sir," continued the king. "You said that one of my agents went to Newcastle to set a trap for you, and as an aside I must have it understood that that can't be said of Monsieur d'Artagnan here, whom I sincerely thank for his generous, even heroic devotion."

D'Artagnan bowed respectfully. Monck just stroked his mustache.

"But Monsieur d'Artagnan—and please note, Mister Monck, that I don't say this to excuse myself—Monsieur d'Artagnan went to England on his own initiative, without avarice, without orders, without hope, like the true gentleman he is, to render a service to an unfortunate king, and to add one more glorious exploit to the illustrious history of a life already full of them."

D'Artagnan, somewhat abashed, flushed and coughed a little. Monck didn't budge.

"I see you don't believe that, Mister Monck," said the king. "That's understandable; such acts of devotion are so rare it's reasonable to doubt them."

"Monsieur would be badly mistaken not to believe you, Sire," said d'Artagnan anxiously, "for what Your Majesty has said is utterly true, so true that I now see that by going to bring back the general, I was completely in the wrong. And in truth, if that's the case, I'm in despair."

"Monsieur d'Artagnan," said the king, taking the musketeer's hand, "you have obliged me as much as if you'd actually helped my cause, for you have revealed to me an unknown friend to whom I'll be forever grateful and will always love."

And the king shook his hand warmly. "Plus," he continued, bowing to Monck, "you've introduced me to an enemy whom I now know to esteem at his proper value."

The Puritan's eyes flashed, but only once, before his expression resumed its dark impassivity.

"So, Monsieur d'Artagnan," continued Charles, "here is what's been interrupted: the Comte de La Fère, whom you know, I believe, had gone to Newcastle . . ."

"Athos?" cried d'Artagnan.

"Yes, I believe that's his nom de guerre. The Comte de La Fère had gone to Newcastle in hopes of arranging a conference with me or my representative when you somewhat violently abbreviated the negotiation."

"*Mordioux!*" replied d'Artagnan. "That must have been him I saw coming into the camp the same night I entered with my fishermen . . ."

A barely perceptible furrowing of Monck's brow told d'Artagnan he was right.

"Yes," he murmured, "I thought his figure and his voice seemed familiar. The devil! Oh, Sire, forgive me! I believed I'd steered my ship so carefully."

"There's nothing wrong, Monsieur," said the king, "except the general accuses me of having laid a trap for him, which I did not. No, General, these are not the means I planned to use with you, as you'll soon see. Meanwhile, when I give you my word as a gentleman, Sir, you can take it, believe me. Now, Monsieur d'Artagnan, listen."

"On my knees, Sire!"

"You are mine, are you not?"

"As Your Majesty has seen. Too much so!"

"Good. From a man like you, one word is enough—and the acts count even more. General, please follow me. Come with us, Monsieur d'Artagnan."

D'Artagnan, surprised, was quick to obey. Charles II went out, Monck followed him, and d'Artagnan followed Monck. Charles took the path by which d'Artagnan had come to him; soon the fresh sea air struck the faces of the three night walkers, and, fifty paces beyond a little gate that Charles opened, they found themselves atop a low dune, facing the ocean that, having stopped its advance, pawed at the shore like a restless monster. Charles II, pensive, walked with his head down and his hand under his cloak.

Monck followed him, his arms ready and his eyes alert.

D'Artagnan came last, his fist on the pommel of his sword.

"Where is the boat that brought you, Messieurs?" Charles said to the musketeer.

"Over there, Sire; I have seven men and an officer who await me at that small boat next to that little fire."

"Ah, yes! That boat drawn up on the sand, I see it. But you certainly didn't come from Newcastle in a longboat?"

"No, Sire, I have a hired dogger that's at anchor about a cannon shot from the dunes. It was in that dogger that we made the trip."

"Sir," said the king to Monck, "you are free."

Monck, despite himself, let out a murmur of surprise. The king nodded and continued, "We're going to wake up a fisherman from this village who will put his boat to sea this very night to take you back to wherever you would go. Monsieur d'Artagnan, here, will escort Your Honor. I place Monsieur d'Artagnan under the safeguard of your integrity, General Monck."

Monck muttered another syllable of surprise, and d'Artagnan let out a deep sigh. The king, without seeming to notice, knocked on the gate of a pine-wood fence that surrounded the first shack at the edge of the dunes. "Hey! Keyser!" he cried. "Wake up!"

"Who's calling me?" asked the fisherman.

"It's me, Charles, the king."

"Ah, Milord!" said Keyser, appearing at the door wrapped in the sail in which he slept like a hammock. "What can I do for you?"

"Captain Keyser," said Charles, "set sail at once. Here is a traveler who hires your boat and will pay you well; oblige him."

And the king stepped back a few paces to allow Monck to speak freely with the fisherman.

"I wish to go over to England," said Monck, who spoke enough Dutch to be able to make himself understood.

"This very moment, if you want," said the fisherman.

"How long before we can go?" said Monck.

"Not half an hour, Your Honor. My eldest son is already up and readying the boat, since we sail with the tide at three in the morning."

"Well! Is it settled?" asked Charles, approaching again.

"Yes, Sire, all but the price," said the fisherman.

"That's my affair," said Charles. "This gentleman is my friend."

At that word, Monck shivered all over and looked at Charles.

"Good, Milord," replied Keyser. And just then they heard his eldest son signaling from the shore with a blast on a bull's horn.

"And now, Gentlemen, on your way," said the king.

"Sire," said d'Artagnan, "may it please Your Majesty to give me just a few minutes? I have hired men I'm leaving behind and must notify them."

"Whistle for them," said Charles, smiling.

D'Artagnan whistled loudly, and while Keyser went to warn his son, Menneville and four men came up at a run.

"Here's payment as promised," said d'Artagnan, showing them a purse containing twenty-five hundred livres in gold. "Wait for me in Calais at the place you know of."

And d'Artagnan, uttering a deep sigh, dropped the purse into Menneville's hands.

"What, are you leaving us?" the men said anxiously.

"For a short time," said d'Artagnan, "or a long one, who knows? But with these twenty-five hundred livres and the two thousand five hundred you've already received, you've been paid according to our agreement. So, go happily, my children."

"What about the dogger?"

"Don't worry about it. It's back in port."

"But our things are still aboard."

"Go get them and then be on your way."

"Yes, Commander."

D'Artagnan returned to Monck and said, "Sir, I await your orders, for it seems we're going together, unless my company is disagreeable to you."

"On the contrary, Monsieur," said Monck.

"Let's go, Milords! We're ready!" Keyser's son called.

Charles saluted the general with nobility and dignity, and told him, "You will forgive me for the violence and inconvenience you've suffered once you're convinced I didn't cause them."

Monck bowed deeply but said nothing. Charles spoke a final word to d'Artagnan, but aloud rather than privately, saying, "Thank you for your services. They'll be repaid by the Lord God, who reserves for me alone, I hope, all trials and pain."

Monck followed Keyser and his son and went aboard with them. D'Artagnan came last, murmuring, "Ah, my poor Planchet! I'm afraid we've made a bad investment."

XXX

The Stock of Planchet and Co. Rebounds

During the passage, Monck spoke to d'Artagnan only when absolutely necessary. When the Frenchman hesitated to join him at supper, a poor meal of salt fish, biscuits, and gin, Monck called to him and said, "To table, Monsieur!"

That was all. D'Artagnan, precisely because he was himself extremely concise when engaged in important affairs, didn't think this curtness augured a favorable result for his situation. As he had plenty of time to himself, he used it in racking his brain to try to figure out how Athos had met Charles II, how they had conspired on his mission to England, and how he'd gotten into Monck's camp. The poor Lieutenant of Musketeers pulled a hair from his mustache every time he thought that Athos must have been the cavalier who'd accompanied Monck to the abbey on the night of the abduction.

Finally, after a crossing of two days and two nights, the skipper landed at the spot designated by Monck, who'd given all the orders during the passage. It was at the village at the mouth of the river where Athos had taken lodgings. The day was fading; the beautiful sun, like a buckler of red steel, was dipping its lower edge into the sea's blue horizon. The fishing boat was making its way up the river, which was wide enough at its mouth, but Monck, in his impatience, ordered it to the shore, and Keyser landed him, along with d'Artagnan, on the muddy river bank among the reeds. D'Artagnan, resigned to obedience, followed his master Monck like a chained bear, but the position was humiliating, and he grumbled under his breath that the service of kings, even the best of them, was a bitter calling.

Monck set a quick pace. One might almost say he wouldn't really be certain he was back in England until he'd reached the few houses of sailors and fishermen scattered around the little quay of this humble harbor.

Suddenly d'Artagnan shouted, "Look! God love me, there's a house afire!"

Monck looked up. There was indeed a house beginning to be devoured by fire. It had begun at a little shack attached to its side, and flames were beginning to lick at the roof. The cool evening breeze was feeding it. The two travelers quickened their pace, hearing shouts and seeing, as they approached, a troop of soldiers waving their arms and surrounding the burning house. This was no doubt what had kept them from noticing the approach of the fishing boat.

Monck stopped short for a moment, and for the first time expressed his thoughts in words. "Hmm!" he said. "What if they're not my soldiers, but Lambert's?"

These words contained both concern and a reproach that d'Artagnan understood perfectly. In fact, during the general's absence, Lambert might have brought to battle, defeated, and dispersed the parliamentary troops, occupying the terrain once held by Monck's army, bereft of their greatest asset. To this possibility, passing from Monck's thoughts to his own, d'Artagnan reasoned, *There are two ways this could go: if Monck is right and only Lambert's men are left in this area, I should be well received, since it's to me they owe their victory; or nothing has changed and Monck, delighted to find his army still camped in the same place, will go easy on me.*

While thinking this through, the two travelers continued their advance and soon found themselves in a small crowd of sailors, who watched the burning of the house with dismay but dared not say anything, intimidated as they were by the soldiers. Monck addressed one of these sailors, asking, "What's going on?"

"Sir," the man replied, not recognizing Monck as a senior officer under the thick cloak that enveloped him, "this house is inhabited by a foreigner, and the soldiers became suspicious of him. They wanted to enter his house under the pretext of escorting him to the camp, but he, despite their numbers, threatened any man who crossed his threshold with death, and the first man who risked it, the Frenchman laid out with a pistol shot."

"Ah, so he's a Frenchman?" said d'Artagnan, rubbing his hands. "Good!"

"What do you mean, *good?*" asked the fisherman.

"No, I meant he *should* . . . not, or something. Gah, this language!"

"He shouldn't have, all right. It made the other soldiers as angry as lions, and they fired at least a hundred musket shots at the house, but the Frenchman was safe behind the wall, and anyone who approached the door was shot by his lackey, and can he shoot! Those who tried the window met the pistol of his master. Now seven men are down—count them!"

"Ah, my brave compatriot!" muttered d'Artagnan. "Just wait till I join you, and together we'll deal with this rabble!"

"A moment, Monsieur," said Monck. "Wait."

"For long?"

"No, just long enough for me to ask a question." Then, turning back to the sailor, "My friend," he asked, with an emotion that despite himself he couldn't quite suppress, "tell me whose soldiers these are, if you would?"

"And whose soldiers would they be but those of that madman Monck?"

"So, there hasn't been a battle yet?"

"Why would there be? What's the point? Lambert's army is melting away like snow in April. Most are coming over to Monck, both officers and soldiers. In another week Lambert won't have more than fifty men."

The fisherman was interrupted by a fresh volley of shots aimed at the house, and by a pistol fired in reply, which felled the most reckless of the attackers. The fury of the soldiers was at its height. The flames were still rising, and a plume of fire and smoke swirled above the house top.

D'Artagnan could no longer contain himself. "*Mordioux!*" he said and looked accusingly at Monck. "You call yourself a general, but you let your soldiers burn down houses and assassinate people while you watch happily, warming your hands at the fire! What kind of a man are you?"

"Patience, Monsieur, patience," said Monck, smiling.

"Patience! Until this brave gentleman is roasted, is that it?" And d'Artagnan leapt forward.

"Stay here, Monsieur," said Monck imperiously. And he himself advanced toward the house.

An officer stepped up and called out to the besieged, "The house is on fire, you'll be ashes inside an hour! Here, there's still time—tell us what you did with General Monck, and we'll let you come out safely. Answer me, or by Saint Patrick . . . !"

The besieged didn't answer; no doubt he was reloading his pistol.

"We sent for reinforcements," the officer continued. "In a quarter of an hour there will be a hundred men around this house."

"I'll answer you when everyone has withdrawn," said the Frenchman. "I will come out freely and go to the camp myself, or I'll die right here!"

"A thousand thunders!" cried d'Artagnan. "That's Athos's voice! Ah, you rabble!"

And d'Artagnan's sword flashed from its scabbard. Monck paused and gestured to him to stop. Then he said, in a resounding voice, "Halt! What are you doing here? Digby, what's this fire? Why all this commotion?"

"The general!" Digby gasped, his sword dropping.

"The general!" repeated the soldiers.

"Well? Is that so amazing?" said Monck in a calm voice. Then, into the resulting silence, he said, "Come, who set this fire?"

The soldiers lowered their heads.

"What! I ask and am not answered?" said Monck. "What! I find fault, and no one repairs it? That fire is still burning, I think."

Immediately twenty men rushed forward, gathering buckets, jars, and pails, extinguishing the fire with the same ardor they'd shown in setting it.

But ahead of them, first and foremost, d'Artagnan ran up to the house with a ladder, shouting, "Athos! It's me, d'Artagnan! Don't kill me, old friend."

And moments later he was holding the count in his arms.

Grimaud, meanwhile, dismantled the ground floor fortifications while maintaining his air of calm. He started once upon hearing d'Artagnan's voice, but otherwise, having opened the door, he stood serenely on the threshold, arms crossed.

When the fire was out, the soldiers were unsure what to do next, Digby most of all. "Forgive us, General," he said. "What we did was out of love for Your Honor, whom we thought lost."

"You're mad, Gentlemen. Lost! Does a man like me get lost? Can I not leave when necessary at will, even without warning? Do you take me for some minor town burgess? Is a gentleman who's my friend and guest to be besieged, threatened, and burned on suspicion? What does this word mean, *suspicion?* God damn me, I should shoot everyone this brave gentleman left alive myself!"

"General," said Digby piteously, "we were twenty-eight, and now eight of us are fallen."

"I authorize the Comte de La Fère to send the remaining twenty to join those eight," said Monck, extending a hand toward Athos. "Oh, just send them back to camp," said Monck, with a gesture of dismissal. "Mister Digby, place yourself under arrest for one month."

"But, General . . ."

"That will teach you, Sir, to act on your own without my orders."

"I was acting at the orders of the lieutenant commander."

"The lieutenant commander had no authority to give such an order, and he'll stand to arrest in your place if I find he ordered that this gentleman be burned."

"He didn't order that, General, he ordered us to bring him to camp, but the count wouldn't go with us."

"I didn't want anyone to plunder my house," said Athos, with a significant look at Monck.

"And quite right too. The rest of you, to camp, I say!"

The soldiers marched off with their heads down.

"Now that we're alone," said Monck to Athos, "Tell me, Monsieur, why you persisted in staying here, when you have a sloop . . ."

"I was waiting for you, General," said Athos. "Didn't Your Honor ask me to wait a week for another audience?"

An agonized look from d'Artagnan made it clear to Monck that these two men, so brave and honest, hadn't connived at his abduction. This just confirmed what he already knew. "Monsieur," he said to d'Artagnan, "you were entirely right. Just give me a moment to chat with the Comte de La Fère."

D'Artagnan took advantage of the respite to go and greet Grimaud.

Monck asked Athos to lead him to his living chamber. The room was still full of smoke and debris. More than fifty musket balls had passed through the window and peppered the walls. Monck found a table, an inkwell, and writing materials; he took pen and paper, wrote a single line, signed it, folded the sheet, sealed it with the signet on his ring, and handed the letter to Athos, saying, "Monsieur, if you would, take this letter to King Charles II, going at once if there's nothing to keep you here."

"And the barrels?" said Athos.

"The fishermen who brought me will help you get them aboard. Be gone, if possible, within the hour."

"Yes, General," said Athos.

"Monsieur d'Artagnan!" called Monck out the window. D'Artagnan rushed in. "Embrace your friend and say farewell, Monsieur, for he's returning to Holland."

"To Holland!" said d'Artagnan. "And I?"

"You're at liberty to go with him, Monsieur, but I'd prefer you to stay," said Monck. "Will you refuse me?"

"Oh, no, General! I'm at your service." D'Artagnan embraced Athos and said a brief goodbye.

Monck watched them both closely. Then he personally oversaw the preparations for departure, the loading of the barrels, the embarkation of Athos, and finally, taking the bemused d'Artagnan by the arm, led him toward Newcastle. Following Monck, d'Artagnan said to himself, "Well, well—it seems to me that shares in the firm of Planchet and Company are on the rise."

XXXI

Monck Reveals Himself

D'Artagnan, though he flattered himself that things were going well, didn't really have a firm grasp of the situation. He had a lot to think about: Athos's association with the king, his friend's journey to England, and the unexpected results of the collision of his own plot with the mission of the Comte de La Fère.

Best just to set it aside. He'd committed an indiscretion, and though he'd done what he set out to do, d'Artagnan found himself with none of the rewards of success. At least, with everything lost, there was nothing more to risk.

D'Artagnan followed Monck through the camp to headquarters. The general's return had produced a remarkable effect, for everyone had thought him lost. But Monck, with his austere expression and upright bearing, seemed to question why his eager lieutenants and delighted soldiers should be so happy.

To the lieutenant commander who hurried to meet him, and explained how anxious his sudden departure made them, he said, "Why is that? Am I obliged to report to you?"

"But, Your Honor, the sheep without the shepherd will tremble."

"Tremble!" replied Monck in his calm and resonant voice. "What a word! God damn me, Sir! If my sheep don't have teeth and claws, I give up being their shepherd. You trembled, Sir?"

"For you, General."

"Mind your own concerns and not mine. I may not have the wits that God gave Oliver Cromwell, but I have what He gave to me, and I'm satisfied with them, few as they may be."

The officer had no reply, and thus Monck silenced all his people, who were convinced that he'd been on an important mission or had been testing them—which showed how little they understood this patient and scrupulous genius. Monck, if he still had the faith of his allies the Puritans, must have given thanks to his patron saint for getting him out of d'Artagnan's box.

Meanwhile, our musketeer was telling himself, *"Mon Dieu!* Monsieur Monck must have less pride than I have, for I declare, if someone had locked me in a trunk with a grate across its mouth and carried me like a boxed-in veal-calf across the sea, I would hold such a grudge for my time in the trunk, and such animosity for the one who locked me in, that if I saw as much as the shadow of a smile cross the face that man, or thought I saw him mocking my posture while in the box, *mordioux!* I'm afraid I'd carve my dagger across his throat in memory of the grate, and put him into a real coffin in memory of the fake casket he'd kept me in for two days."

And d'Artagnan was honest in saying this, for our Gascon did have a rather thin skin.

Fortunately, Monck was thinking about other things. He didn't say a word about the past to his former conqueror, instead inviting him to be a close observer of his work. Monck took him along when he went on reconnaissance to achieve one of his goals, the rehabilitation of d'Artagnan's spirit. The latter behaved like the most flattering courtier, admiring Monck's troop dispositions and the organization of his camp, and joking about the ramparts ringing Lambert's camp, saying that he'd built a camp large enough to house twenty thousand men when in the end an acre would be enough for the corporal and fifty guards who would be left loyal to him.

Monck, as soon as he'd arrived, had accepted the proposal for a parley that Lambert had made the day before, which Monck's lieutenants had refused on the pretext that Monck was unwell. This parley was neither long nor interesting: Lambert demanded the fealty of his rival, and Monck declared he owed fealty to no one but the majority party.

Lambert then asked if it wouldn't be easier to end the quarrel by an alliance rather than a battle. Monck asked for a week in which to consider. Lambert could scarcely refuse, even though he'd come north with the stated intent of devouring Monck's army. After this interview Lambert's people grew impatient, as nothing had been decided upon, neither a treaty nor a battle. The rebel army began, as d'Artagnan had foreseen, to prefer the good cause over the bad, and the Parliament, "rump" though it was, over the empty pomposities of General Lambert.

They began to recall the good food they'd had in London, the profusion of ale and sherry that the burghers of the City had lavished on their friends, the soldiers; they bit with disgust into the black bread of war, and tasted the brackish water of the Tweed, too salty for the glass, too bland for the pot, and they said to themselves, "Wouldn't we be better off on the other side? Aren't they preparing roasts in London for Monck?" From then on, the only news from Lambert's army was of desertion. The soldiers found that this war conflicted with their principles, which, like discipline, is the motivation that gives a force its purpose. Monck defended the Parliament, and Lambert attacked it. Monck had no more respect for the Parliament than Lambert did, but its name was embroidered on his flags, leaving nothing for the opposition to write on theirs but *Rebellion*, which sounded bad in the ears of the Puritans. They went from Lambert to Monck like humble sinners from Baal to God.

Monck figured that at a thousand desertions a day, Lambert could hold out for twenty days. But like a snowball gathering speed and mass as it rolls downhill, the desertion accelerated, so that a hundred left the first day, three hundred the second, and a thousand the third, at which point Monck thought they'd reached the anticipated rate. But a thousand desertions soon became two thousand, and then four thousand. By the end of the week, Lambert, feeling like he no longer had the means to accept a battle if it was offered, made the wise decision to escape in the night to return to London, hoping to head off Monck and arrive where he could consolidate his power with the remnants of the military party.

But Monck, unconcerned and showing no haste, marched toward London as a conqueror, increasing his army by absorbing lesser parties as he passed. He went into camp at Barnet, about four leagues from the city, praised by the Parliament, who thought they saw in him a protector, and watched by the people, who waited to see him commit himself before they judged him. D'Artagnan himself couldn't tell from his tactics what to think. He watched, and he admired.

Monck couldn't enter London before committing himself without getting embroiled in a prolongation of the civil war. He bided his time for some weeks.

Suddenly, when no one expected it, Monck struck, driving the remnants of the military party out of London, installing himself in the City among the burghers by order of the Parliament; and then, when the burghers began to cry out against Monck, just when even the soldiers began to question their commander, Monck, sensing that the majority was ready for it, declared that the Rump Parliament must resign, step aside, and yield its place to a government that was more than just a joke. Monck made this declaration backed by fifty thousand swords, joined by the end of the day by five hundred thousand citizens of London, who acclaimed the move with shouts of joy.

And then, just when the people, after their triumphal celebrations and parties in the street, were looking for a leader they could pledge to follow, word went out that a vessel had left The Hague bearing Charles II and his fortune. "Gentlemen," said Monck to his officers, "I go to welcome the legitimate king. Whoever loves me will follow me!"

A roar of acclamation followed these words, which d'Artagnan couldn't hear without a shiver of pleasure. "*Mordioux!*" he said to Monck. "You are bold, Sir."

"You'll go with me, won't you?" said Monck.

"Lord, yes, General! But, tell me, if you would, what was in the letter you wrote for Athos—I mean, the Comte de La Fère—on the day we arrived?"

"I have no more secrets from you," replied Monck. "I wrote these words: 'Sire, I expect Your Majesty at Dover in six weeks.'"

"Ah!" said d'Artagnan. "Rather than bold, instead I say 'well played.' It was a fine stroke!"

"You know something of such matters," Monck replied. It was the only reference he ever made to his trip to Holland.

XXXII

How Athos and d'Artagnan Met
Once More at the Hartshorn Inn

The King of England made his entrance with great pomp at Dover, and then again at London. He had brought his mother and sister and summoned his brothers. England had for so long been left to herself, that is, to tyranny, anarchy, and unreason, that the return of King Charles II, whom the English knew only as the son of a man they'd beheaded, was celebrated throughout the three kingdoms. The warm reception and general acclamation that welcomed his return struck the young king so strongly that he said into the ear of James of York, his younger brother, "In truth, James, it seems we were mistaken to be so long absent from a country where we're so well loved."

The royal procession was magnificent. Beautiful weather framed the solemnities. Charles had regained all his youth, all his good humor, and seemed transfigured; all hearts seemed to smile on him like the sun. Among this noisy crowd of courtiers and admirers, who didn't seem to remember that they'd conducted the new king's father to his scaffold at Whitehall, was a man in the uniform of a Lieutenant of Musketeers, looking on with a smile on his thin, clever lips, sometimes at the people shouting their blessings, sometimes on the prince borne on this tide of emotion and who saluted above all the women who tossed bouquets beneath his horse's feet.

"It's a fine thing to be a king!" said this man, lost in his contemplation, so absorbed that he stopped in the middle of the street, letting the crowd and procession pass by and around him. "Here indeed is a prince bedecked with gold and diamonds like a Solomon, covered with flowers like a spring meadow, on his way to plunge his hands into the immense treasury that his faithful subjects, formerly so unfaithful, have filled with cartloads of gold, in coins and ingots. They've thrown enough flowers at him to bury him twice, though if he'd appeared here less than two months ago, they'd have thrown bullets and musket balls rather than bouquets. Decidedly, it's something to be born of a certain rank, no offense to the lowborn who say they're not worse for being born low."

The procession went marching on, with the king and his adulation beginning to move off toward the palace, though this didn't mean our officer wasn't being considerably jostled. "*Mordioux!*" continued the philosopher. "So many people treading on my feet with so little regard, or rather none at all, since they're English and I'm French. If one asked these people, 'Who is Monsieur d'Artagnan?' they'd reply, '*Nescio vos*'—I don't know you. But tell them, 'There goes the king, and there goes General Monck,' and they'd shout, '*Vive le roi! Vive* General Monck!' until their lungs wore out. However," he continued, regarding the crowd with that look so keen and so proud, "consider, good people, what your King Charles has done, and what General Monck has done, and then think of what that wretched foreigner called Monsieur d'Artagnan has done. Of course, you can't think about it because it's unknown, but what does that matter? That doesn't keep Charles II from being a great king, though he was exiled for twelve years, nor Mister Monck from being a great general, though he took a trip to Holland in a box. So, since one must acknowledge that one is a great king and the other is a great commander, I say *Hurrah for King Charles II! Hurrah for General Monck!*"

And his voice mingled with the voices of thousands of spectators, rising above them for a moment, and to show his true devotion, he even waved his hat in the air. But he was stopped by a hand on his arm in the middle of this show of loyalism (which is what in 1660 they called what we now call *royalism*).

"Athos!" d'Artagnan cried. "You, here?" And the two friends embraced.

"You are here! And being here," continued the musketeer, "why aren't you in the midst of that crowd of courtiers, my dear Count? What! You, the hero of the day, not riding at the left side of His restored Majesty, as

General Monck rides on his right? Really, I can understand the character of neither you nor of the prince who owes you so much."

"Always mocking, my dear d'Artagnan," said Athos. "Will you never correct this unseemly fault?"

"But seriously, why aren't you part of the procession?"

"I'm not part of the procession because I don't wish to be."

"And why don't you wish to be?"

"Because I'm neither envoy, ambassador, nor representative of the King of France, and it doesn't suit me to associate myself so closely with another king whom God didn't make my master."

"*Mordioux!* You were pretty close to the king his father."

"That's another thing, my friend; he was on his way to death."

"And yet what you did for this one . . ."

"I did because it was what I had to do. But I deplore all ostentation, as you know. May King Charles II, who no longer needs me, leave me to retire back into the shadows. That's all I ask of him."

D'Artagnan sighed.

"What would you have?" Athos said to him. "Anyway, my friend, it looks to me like this joyous return of the king to London saddens you, though you did at least as much for His Majesty as I did."

"Could it be," replied d'Artagnan, with his Gascon laugh, "that I did a great deal for His Majesty without his being aware of it?"

"Oh, but the king knows it well, my friend!" said Athos.

"He knows it!" said the musketeer bitterly. "By my faith! You'd never suspect it, and up to a moment ago I almost forgot it myself."

"But he, my friend, will not forget—I'll answer for it."

"You tell me that to console me a little, Athos."

"For what?"

"*Mordioux!* For all the expenses I've had. I've ruined myself, friend, for the restoration of this young prince who just cantered by, riding on his bay horse."

"The king doesn't know you've ruined yourself, *mon ami*, but he's aware that he owes you a great deal."

"Does that get me anywhere, Athos? Tell me! To be fair, I must say you performed your mission nobly and well. But I, who seemingly almost wrecked it, was the one who really made it succeed. Follow my thinking on this: you might not have been able to convince General Monck by persuasion or diplomacy, but my rude means of conducting the dear general to our prince gave Charles the opportunity to be generous, a generosity inspired solely by my blessed blunder, and Charles sees himself repaid for it by this restoration engineered by Monck."

"All that, dear friend, is undeniably true," Athos replied.

"Well! As undeniably true as that is, it's just as true that I, though beloved of General Monck, who calls me his dear captain all day long, though I'm neither his dear nor his captain, and though appreciated by the king, though he's already forgotten my name—it's just as true, I say, that when I return to my native country, I'll be cursed by the soldiers whom I'd led to hope for a big payoff, and cursed by my brave Planchet, from whom I borrowed much of his fortune."

"How's that? What the devil does Planchet have to do with all this?"

"Why, everything, old friend! Here's the king, splendid, smiling, and adored, there's General Monck who thinks he's brought him back, you who believe you supported him, I who think I nudged them all together, the citizens who feel they've reconquered him, the king himself who thinks he's negotiated his restoration, but none of this is true: in reality, Charles II, King of England, Scotland, and Ireland, was replaced on his throne by a French grocer of the Rue des Lombards named Planchet. And such is grandeur! 'Vanity,' says Scripture, 'all is vanity!'"

Athos couldn't help but laugh at his friend's joke. "Dear d'Artagnan!" he said, taking his hand affectionately. "Have you turned philosopher? Wasn't it enough for you to have saved my life by your timely arrival with Monck when those damned parliamentarians wanted to broil me alive?"

"Well, you know," said d'Artagnan, "you just about deserved to be broiled, my dear Count."

"What? For protecting King Charles's million?"

"What million?"

"Ah, right! You never knew about that. But you mustn't be angry with me about it, my friend, for it wasn't my secret. That word *Remember* that King Charles pronounced on the scaffold . . ."

"The word that means *Souviens-toi*?"

"Exactly. That word meant *remember* that I have a million in gold buried in the vaults of Newcastle Abbey, and that million belongs to my son."

"Ah, very nice! Now I understand. But what I also understand, and it's frightful, is that every time he thinks of me, His Majesty Charles II will say, 'There was a certain man who nearly made me lose my crown. Fortunately, I was generous, noble, and clever enough to save the day.' That's what he'll say of me, that young gentleman who came to the Château de Blois in a shabby black doublet, hat in his hand, to ask me if I'd admit him to see the King of France."

"D'Artagnan, d'Artagnan, you're wrong," said Athos, placing a hand on the musketeer's shoulder.

"I'm in the right."

"No, because you don't know the future."

D'Artagnan looked his friend right between the eyes and began to laugh. "In truth, my dear Athos, you talk just like Cardinal Mazarin."

Athos flinched.

"Sorry!" continued d'Artagnan, laughing. "Pardon me if I offended you. But the future! Ha ha ha! Such pretty words that promise so much, words spoken from lips that have nothing else to offer! *Mordioux!* After having met so many who promise, when will I meet someone who delivers? But never mind that," continued d'Artagnan. "What are you doing here, dear Athos? Are you the king's treasurer?"

"What! The king's treasurer?"

"Yes, if the king has a million, he must need a treasurer. The King of France, who hasn't a copper, has a Surintendant des Finances, Monsieur Fouquet. Though it's true that there it's Fouquet who has the millions."

"Oh, that million is long spent," laughed Athos in his turn.

"I see, it's become satin, gemstones, velvet, and plumes of all kinds and of every color. All these princes and princesses were in urgent need of tailors and couturiers. Do you remember, Athos, what we spent to equip ourselves for the La Rochelle campaign, for clothes and horses? Two or three thousand livres each, by my faith! But a king is greater than we are and needs a million to outfit himself. But Athos, if you're not treasurer, at least tell me you're in well at Court?"

"Faith of a gentleman, I wouldn't know," replied Athos simply.

"Come now! You don't know?"

"No, I haven't seen the king since Dover."

"So, he's forgotten you as well. God's death! That's appalling."

"His Majesty has had many affairs to attend to!"

"Oh, right!" said d'Artagnan, with one of those sarcastic expressions unique to him. "It's almost enough to make me admire Monsignor Mazarini. Really, Athos? The king hasn't seen you?"

"No."

"And you're not furious?"

"Me? Why? Do you imagine, old friend, that I did what I did for the king? That young man, I scarcely know him. I defended his father, who represented a sacred principle to me, and I allowed myself to be drawn to the son out of sympathy for that same principle. Besides, he's a worthy knight and a noble individual, like his father, whom you remember."

"That's true, he was a fine, brave man, who had a sad life but made a good death."

"Well, then, my dear d'Artagnan, understand this: to that king, that man of heart, that noble soul-mate, if I dare call him so, I swore at the supreme hour to faithfully preserve the secret of the fortune that was to help his son when the time was right; and that young man came to me, he told me of his misfortune, not knowing me for anything but a living memory of his father. And I accomplished for Charles II what I had promised to Charles I, that's all. What matter to me whether he's grateful or not? I did this service for myself, to fulfill my obligation and responsibility, not for him."

"I've always said," replied d'Artagnan with a sigh, "that selflessness is the finest thing in the world."

"As to that, dear friend," said Athos, "aren't you in the same position I am? As I understood it, you allowed yourself to be moved by that young man's misfortunes; you were more selfless than I, for I had a duty to fulfill, while you owed absolutely nothing to the martyr's son. You didn't have to repay the price of that precious drop of blood that fell on my brow beneath the scaffold. You acted solely from the heart, that noble and good heart you hide under your apparent skepticism and sarcastic irony. Perhaps it did cost a servant's fortune, and your own, you benevolent miser, and maybe no one knows of that sacrifice. No matter! Of course, you want to return Planchet's money, I understand that, for it isn't proper for a gentleman to borrow from his inferior without repaying him capital and interest. Well, then! If necessary, I'll sell La Fère or a small farm or two. You'll pay Planchet, and I'll still have enough grain in my barns for the two of us and Raoul. That way, my friend, you'll have no debts to anyone but yourself, and if I know you, it will be more than a little to be able to tell yourself, 'I made a king.' Am I right?"

"Ah, Athos!" murmured d'Artagnan thoughtfully. "I've told you more than once, on the day you take up preaching, I'll go to the sermon—and the day you tell me there really is a hell, *mordioux!* I'll fear the inferno and the pitchforks. You're better than I am, or rather better than anyone is, while I have only one virtue, that of not being jealous. But as to faults, *damn-me,* as the English say, if I don't have all the rest."

"I know of no one the equal of d'Artagnan," Athos replied, "but though we went slowly, we've still arrived at where I've taken lodgings. Won't you come in, my friend?"

"Eh? But isn't this the Hartshorn Inn?" said d'Artagnan.

"I confess, old friend, that I chose it deliberately. I like old acquaintances, and I like returning to the place where you found me collapsed from fatigue, in the depths of despair, on that night of January 30th."

"After I'd discovered the lair of that masked executioner? Yes, that was a terrible day!"

"Come in, then," said Athos, interrupting him.

They entered the former common room. The inn in general, and its common room in particular, had undergone great changes; the musketeers' former host,[79] who had become wealthy, at least for an innkeeper, had closed up the tavern and turned this chamber into a warehouse of colonial merchandise. As for the rest of the house, he rented the rooms out to foreigners.

It was with an indescribable emotion that d'Artagnan recognized all the furnishings in Athos's room on the first floor: the woodwork, the tapestries, and even the framed map that Porthos had studied so lovingly in his spare time. "Eleven years ago!" he said. "*Mordioux!* It seems like a century."

"And to me but a day," said Athos. "Imagine the joy I feel, my friend, in seeing you here, pressing your hand, tossing aside my sword and dagger, knowing I won't need them, and pouring us glasses of sherry without fearing poison. Oh, this joy could only be greater if our two friends were here, sitting at the corners of the table, with Raoul, my beloved Raoul, on the threshold regarding us with his eyes, so brilliant and so sweet!"

"Yes, it's true," said d'Artagnan, moved, "especially the first part of your thought. It's sweet to smile where we so legitimately shivered, thinking from one moment to the next that Monsieur Mordaunt might appear on the landing."

At that moment the door opened, and d'Artagnan, brave as he was, made a frightened start. But Athos understood and said, smiling, "It's our host, come to bring me some correspondence."

"Yes, Milord," said the hotelier, "I do have a letter for Your Honor."

"Thank you," said Athos, taking the letter without looking at it. "Tell me, my dear host, do you recognize monsieur, here?"

The old man raised his head and looked attentively at d'Artagnan. "No," he said.

"He's one of those friends of mine I mentioned to you," said Athos, "who stayed with me here eleven years ago."

"Oh!" said the old man. "I've had so many strangers lodge with me!"

"But we were here on the date of January 30th, 1649," added Athos, hoping to jog the host's memory.

"It's possible," he replied, smiling blandly, "but that was long ago!" He bowed and went out.

"Oh, thanks," said d'Artagnan. "Perform brilliant exploits, instigate revolutions, inscribe your name in brass and stone with the point of your sword, but you'll find nothing harder and less penetrable than the skull of an old landlord—he doesn't recognize me! Well, I'd certainly have recognized him."

Athos, smiling, opened the letter. "Ah!" he said. "It's from Parry."

"Oh ho!" said d'Artagnan. "Read it, my friend, it must be news."

Athos shook his head, and read:

Monsieur le Comte,

The king much regretted not seeing you beside him today at his entrance; His Majesty commands me to say so, and to recall him to your memory. His Majesty expects you this evening at the palace of Saint James between nine and eleven o'clock.

I am, with respect, Your Honor's most humble and obedient servant,

Parry

"You see, my dear d'Artagnan," said Athos, "we mustn't despair of the hearts of kings."

"You're right, and I shall despair no more," said d'Artagnan.

"Oh, my dear, dear friend," said Athos, who hadn't failed to catch the note of bitterness in d'Artagnan's reply, "please pardon me. I didn't mean to hurt my closest comrade, even unintentionally."

"You're quite mad, Athos, and the proof is I'm going to escort you all the way to the palace door. I need a walk, anyway."

"And you'll come in with me, my friend, for I want to tell His Majesty . . ."

"Not at all!" said d'Artagnan, with pride untainted by jealousy. "The only thing worse than begging for oneself is having others beg for you. *Çà!* Let's go, my friend, it's a charming night for a walk. I want, in passing, to show you the home of General Monck, who's lodging me with him; my faith, it's a lovely house! Being a general in England pays better than being a marshal in France, it seems."

Athos allowed himself to be carried away, saddened though he was by d'Artagnan's attempts to be cheerful. The whole city was in the streets; the two friends were met at every corner by enthusiasts who demanded they shout, "Long live good King Charles!" D'Artagnan replied with a grunt, and Athos with a smile. They made their way thus toward Monck's house, which was on the route to the Saint James's Palace.

Athos and d'Artagnan spoke very little on their way because if they had spoken they would have had too much to say. Athos thought that if he spoke he would be too joyful, which might hurt d'Artagnan, while the latter feared to express bitterness that might cause Athos discomfort. It was a strange silence that hovered between contentment and discontent.

D'Artagnan yielded first to the itch to speak, saying, "Do you remember, Athos, that passage in the *Memoirs of d'Aubigné*[80] in which that devoted servant, a Gascon like me, and poor like me, and I was almost going to say brave like me, recounts the stinginess of Henri IV? My father always told me, I remember, that d'Aubigné was a liar. And yet, take a look at all the princes descended from the Great Henri!"

"Come now, d'Artagnan," said Athos, "the kings of France, misers? You're mad, my friend."

"Oh, you never see others' faults, you're too perfect. But in reality, Henri IV was stingy, as was his son, Louis XIII. We know something about that, don't we? Gaston took that vice to extremes, and everyone around him hated him for it. Henriette, poor woman, had no choice but to be frugal, when she had nothing to eat some days and nothing to burn for heat in the winters, and that's the example she gave to her son Charles II, grandson of the great Henri IV, and as miserly as his mother and his grandfather. Come, isn't that a family tree of the tight-fisted?"

"D'Artagnan," said Athos, "how can you be so harsh on that race of eagles called the Bourbons?"

"And I forgot the finest example, that other grandson of the Béarnaise, Louis XIV, my ex-master. I believe we can fairly call him miserly since he wouldn't lend a million to his brother Charles! Oh, I see I'm starting to annoy you, but fortunately we've arrived at my house, or rather the house of my friend Monck."

"Dear d'Artagnan, I'm not annoyed, just saddened. It's cruel, in fact, to see a man of your merit unrewarded by the position that his services should have brought him. It seems to me that your name, old friend, ought to rank up there with the greatest names of war and diplomacy, as worthy of fortune and honor as Luynes, Bellegarde, and Bassompierre.[81] You are right, my friend, a hundred times over."

D'Artagnan sighed, and led his friend under the portico of Monck's house at the edge of town, saying, "Allow me to stop in and leave my purse here, for if, in the crowd, these clever London crooks, who are light-fingered even by Parisian standards, rob me of the rest of my poor crowns, I won't have enough to buy passage back to France. And I'm eager to get back to France and will be delighted to see it again, now that all my old prejudices against England have been reconfirmed, with new ones added."

Athos said nothing. "I'll just be a moment," d'Artagnan said to him. "I know you're in a hurry to get on to receive your reward, but believe me, I'm no less eager than you to enjoy it, albeit from a distance. Wait for me."

D'Artagnan was halfway across the vestibule when a man, half footman and half soldier, who served Monck in the capacities of both doorman and guard, stopped our musketeer and said, in English, "Excuse me, Milord d'Artagnan!"

"Well, what is it?" replied the latter. "Is the general ready to dismiss me? All that was missing was for me to be sent away!"

These words, spoken in French, made no impression on the guard, as he spoke only English mixed with Scots. But Athos was sad because it was beginning to look like d'Artagnan was right.

The Englishman gave a letter to d'Artagnan. "From the general," he said.

"Well, there it is: my dismissal," said the Gascon. "Should I read it, Athos?"

"You must be mistaken," said Athos, "or the only honest people left are you and me."

D'Artagnan shrugged his shoulders and tore open the letter, while the Englishman held up a lantern to help him read it.

"Well! What does it say?" said Athos, seeing the reader's expression change.

"Here, read it yourself," said the musketeer.

Athos took the paper and read:

Monsieur d'Artagnan, the king very much regretted that you didn't come to Saint Paul with his cortège. His Majesty says he missed you, and I missed you as well, dear Captain. There is only one way to repair this: His Majesty expects me at nine o'clock at the palace of Saint James; will you join me there? His Most Gracious Majesty appoints that hour for the audience he grants you.

The letter was signed *Monck.*

XXXIII

The Audience

"Well?" said Athos in a voice of gentle reproach, when he'd read Monck's letter to d'Artagnan.

"Well!" said d'Artagnan, red with pleasure and a little shame at having been so quick to accuse the king and Monck. "It's a very polite gesture . . . and amounts to nothing, of course . . . but it is polite, nonetheless."

"I found it hard to believe the young prince would be ungrateful," said Athos.

"The fact is that his present is still very near his past," replied d'Artagnan. "After all, everything prior to this indicated I was right."

"I admit it, dear friend, I admit it. Ah! Now we'll see your well-earned recompense. You can't believe how happy this makes me."

"So, then," said d'Artagnan, "Charles II receives General Monck at nine o'clock, and will receive me at ten; and a fine audience it is, the kind they call at the Louvre the 'bestowal of Court Holy Water.' Let's go, old friend, and place ourselves under the spout."

Athos made no reply, so the two of them went on their way toward Saint James's Palace, which was surrounded by a crowd there to see the silhouettes of the courtiers through the windows, and perhaps a glimpse of the royal personage. Eight o'clock was striking as the two took their places in a gallery full of courtiers and hopeful petitioners. Everyone noticed their modest foreign attire and proud profiles, so noble and full of character.

For their part, Athos and d'Artagnan, having taken the measure of the assemblage at a glance, resumed chatting together. A great noise suddenly came from one end of the gallery. it was General Monck making his entrance, followed by more than twenty officers all hoping for one of his smiles, for the day before he'd been master of England, and they imagined a fine tomorrow for he who'd restored the family Stuart.

"Gentlemen," said Monck, turning toward them, "I pray you, remember that now I am no one. Not long ago I commanded the principal army of the republic, but now that army is the king's, into whose hands I commit, at his order, my power of yesterday."

Dismayed surprise showed on all the officers' faces, and the circle of admirers and supplicants that had ringed Monck a moment before gradually widened and dispersed itself into the general surge of the crowd. Monck simply waited in the antechamber like everyone else. D'Artagnan couldn't keep from remarking upon this to the Comte de La Fère, who frowned.

Suddenly the door to Charles's audience chamber opened and the young king appeared, preceded by two of his household officers. "Good evening, Gentlemen," he said. "Is General Monck here?"

"Here I am, Sire," the old general replied.

Charles strode up to him and took his hands in a friendly grip. "General," the king announced, "I have just signed the patent making you Duke of Albemarle, and my intention is that no one in this kingdom should equal you in power and in fortune, because, except for Montrose,[82] no one has equaled you in loyalty, courage, and talent. Gentlemen, the duke is commander in chief of our armies on land and at sea, and in that capacity, honor him and pay him your respects."

While everyone hastened to gather around the general, who received their congratulations with his usual impassivity, d'Artagnan said to Athos, "To think that this duchy, this command of the armies on land and at sea, all these grandeurs, in short, were contained in a box six feet long by three feet wide!"

"Friend," said Athos, "greater grandeurs than those are enclosed in smaller boxes—forever."

Suddenly Monck noticed the two gentlemen where they stood apart, waiting for the crowd to thin out. He made his way to them through the throng, surprising them in the middle of their philosophical reflections. "You were talking about me," he said with a smile.

"Milord," replied Athos, "we were also talking of God."

Monck thought for a moment and then responded cheerfully, "Gentlemen, let us also speak of the king, if you will; for you have, I believe, an audience with His Majesty."

"At nine o'clock," said Athos.

"Or ten," said d'Artagnan.

"Let's go to his audience chamber right now," Monck replied, making a gesture for his two companions to precede him, to which neither of them would consent.

During this debate, conducted in French, the king had returned to the center of the gallery. "Ah, my Frenchmen!" he said, in that tone of carefree cheer that he was still able to summon despite his many troubles and sorrows. "The Frenchmen, my consolation!"

Athos and d'Artagnan bowed.

"Duke, bring these gentlemen into my chamber," said the king, adding in French, "I am all yours, Messieurs."

And he promptly dismissed his Court so he could attend to *his Frenchmen,* as he called them. "Monsieur d'Artagnan," he said, entering his audience chamber, "I'm pleased to see you again."

"Sire, having the honor to salute Your Majesty in his own palace of Saint James's, my joy could not be greater."

"Monsieur, you have done me a great service, and I owe you a debt of gratitude. Though I don't want to encroach on the rights of our commander in chief, I wish to offer you a post worthy of you near to our person."

"Sire," replied d'Artagnan, "when I left the service of the King of France, I promised my prince it was not to serve another king."

"Come," said Charles, "that displeases me greatly, for I like you, and I'd hoped to do a lot for you."

"Sire . . ."

"Here, now," said Charles with a smile, "is there no way I can persuade you to set that aside? Duke, help me here. What if you were offered—if I offered you—the command of all my musketeers?"

D'Artagnan bowed even lower than before, and said, "I should always regret refusing what Your Gracious Majesty offers me, but a gentleman has only his word, and that word, as I had the honor to tell Your Majesty, is pledged to the King of France."

"Then we'll say no more about it," said the king, turning to Athos—and leaving d'Artagnan plunged into the deepest pit of disappointment.

"Ah! It's just like I said," murmured the musketeer. "Words! Court Holy Water! Kings have the amazing talent of offering what they know can't be accepted and thus appear generous without risk. Fool! Oh, triple fool for hoping even for a moment!"

Meanwhile, Charles took Athos by the hand. "Count," he said, "you've been a second father to me, and the service you've rendered can never be repaid. You were made by my father a Knight of the Garter,[83] an order to which not even the kings of Europe are invited, and by the queen regent you were made a Chevalier du Saint-Esprit,[84] an order no less illustrious. Now I award you the ribbon of the Order of the Golden Fleece[85]—it was sent to me by the King of France who had been given two by the King of Spain, his father-in-law, on the occasion of his recent marriage.[86] But I, in return, have a further service to ask of you."

"Sire!" said Athos, flustered. "The Golden Fleece, for me! When the King of France is the only other person in my country who shares that distinction!"

"I want you to be, in your country and everywhere, the equal of all those whom sovereigns have honored with their favor," said Charles, lifting the chain from around his neck. "And I am certain, Count, that my father smiles on this from the depths of his tomb."

"How strange it is," said d'Artagnan to himself, as his friend received on his knees the eminent order conferred upon him by the king, "how incredible that I always see the rain of prosperity fall on those around me, while not a drop reaches me! If one were the jealous type, it would be enough to make him tear out his hair, word of honor!"

Athos rose, and Charles embraced him tenderly. "General," he said to Monck, then, stopping himself with a smile, "excuse me, I meant to say Duke. And if I made that mistake, it's because *duke* just seems too short to me. I need to find a longer title, one that brings you close enough to the throne that I could say to you, 'My Brother,' as I do to Louis XIV. But I have it! To make you almost my brother, my dear Duke, I name you Viceroy of Ireland and Scotland.[87] That way I won't again call you by too short a title."

The duke took the king's hand, though without apparent joy or enthusiasm, as he did everything. Yet his heart had been stirred by this final favor. Charles, skillfully managing his generosity, had given the duke time to form a wish, though he might not have wished for as much as he was awarded.

"*Mordioux!*" grumbled d'Artagnan. "Here come the rains again. Oh! It's enough to drive one mad." And he turned aside with an air so sad and comically pitiful that the king couldn't restrain a smile.

Monck was preparing to take his leave of Charles. "What's this, my brother?" said the king to the duke. "Are you leaving?"

"If it please Your Majesty, for in truth, I'm very tired. The emotion of the day has been exhausting, and I need my rest."

"But you're not leaving without Monsieur d'Artagnan, I hope!" said the king.

"Why, Sire?" said the old warrior.

"You know perfectly well why," said the king.

Monck looked at Charles with astonishment. "I beg Your Majesty's pardon," he said, "but I don't know what he means."

"I suppose that's possible—but if you've forgotten, I'm sure Monsieur d'Artagnan has not."

Now it was the musketeer's turn to be astonished.

"See here, Duke," said the king, "aren't you lodging with Monsieur d'Artagnan?"

"I have the honor to offer lodging to Monsieur d'Artagnan, yes, Sire."

"And this idea was yours and yours alone?"

"Mine and mine alone, yes, Sire."

Well, of course it had to be that way . . . since the prisoner always lodges with his conqueror."

Monck flushed. "Ah, that's true! I am Monsieur d'Artagnan's prisoner."

"Quite so, Monck, since you have yet to ransom yourself—but don't worry, it was I who took you from Monsieur d'Artagnan, so I will pay your ransom."

D'Artagnan's eyes regained their cheerful sparkle, for the Gascon began to understand. Charles turned toward him. "The general," he said, "isn't wealthy and can't pay you what he's worth. I am certainly richer, but now that he's a duke, and nearly a king, he's worth a sum that perhaps even I couldn't pay. Come, Monsieur d'Artagnan, be lenient: how much do I owe you?"

D'Artagnan, delighted by this turn of events but maintaining his self-possession, said, "Sire, Your Majesty has no cause to be alarmed. When I had the good luck to capture His Grace, Mister Monck was still a general, so only the ransom of a general is due to me. But if the general will give me his sword, I'll consider myself paid, for there is nothing in the world but a general's sword that's worth as much as he is."

"*Odds fish*, as my father used to say," cried Charles II. "That's a gallant speech from a gallant man—don't you agree, Duke?"

"Upon my honor, Sire, I do!" replied the duke. And he drew his sword. "Monsieur," he said to d'Artagnan, "here is that which you asked for. Many have owned better blades, but, modest as mine is, I've never surrendered it to anyone."

D'Artagnan took with pride this sword that had just made a king.

"Here, now!" said Charles II. "What! Is a sword that placed me on the throne to go out of my kingdom rather than be added one day to the crown jewels? No, upon my soul, I think not! Captain d'Artagnan, I'll give you two hundred thousand livres for this sword; if that's not enough, tell me so."

"It isn't enough, Sire," replied d'Artagnan with grave seriousness. "And moreover, I don't want to sell it—but Your Majesty wishes it and that is an order. I obey, then—but the respect in which I hold the illustrious warrior listening to us commands me to estimate his worth at half again that assessment. I therefore ask three hundred thousand livres for the sword, or Your Majesty may have it for nothing."

And, taking it by the point, he presented the sword to the king. Charles II burst out laughing. "Oh, gallant man and happy companion! Isn't it so, Duke? Am I right, Count? Odds fish! How that pleases me. Here, Chevalier d'Artagnan," he said, "take this."

And, going to a table, he wrote a voucher on his treasury for three hundred thousand livres.

D'Artagnan took it, and turning gravely to Monck, he said, "I still asked too little, I know, but believe me, Duke, I would rather die than be ruled by avarice."

The king laughed again like the jolliest Cockney in his kingdom. "You must come back and see me again before you go, Chevalier," he said. "I need to lay by a supply of cheer before my Frenchmen leave me."

"Ah, Sire! Unlike the duke's sword, I'll give you the cheer for free," replied d'Artagnan, whose feet scarcely touched the ground.

"And you, Count," added Charles, turning to Athos, "come back as well, for I have an important message to confide to you. Duke, your hand." Monck shook hands with the king. "Adieu, Messieurs," said Charles, extending a hand to each of the Frenchmen, who touched them to their lips.

"Well, then!" said Athos when they were outside. "Are you satisfied?"

"Hush!" said d'Artagnan, grinning with joy. "I haven't been to see the treasurer yet, and the roof could still fall on my head."

XXXIV

The Embarrassment of Riches

D'Artagnan didn't waste any time: as soon as it was convenient and opportune, he paid a visit to His Majesty's Treasurer. There he had the great satisfaction of exchanging a bit of paper covered with an ugly scrawl for a prodigious quantity of crowns, all newly struck with the image of His Most Gracious Majesty Charles II.

D'Artagnan had long ago learned to master his emotions, but on this occasion he couldn't help expressing a joy the readers may forgive, if they deign to be indulgent toward a man who, since his birth, had never seen so many coins and rolls of coins laid out before him in a pattern truly pleasing to the eye. The treasurer enclosed these rolls in sturdy sacks and sealed each bag with the arms of England, a favor that treasurers do not grant to everybody.

Then, impassive and just as polite as he ought to be to a man honored by the friendship of the king, he said to d'Artagnan, "Take your money, Sir."

Your money. Those words made a thousand strings thrum in d'Artagnan's heart where he'd never felt them before. He had the sacks loaded on a small cart and returned home, thinking deeply. A man who possesses three hundred thousand livres can no longer have an unlined brow; a wrinkle for every hundred thousand livres is the least he can expect.

D'Artagnan locked himself in, refused to open the door to anyone, wouldn't eat, just sat with the lamp burning, a pistol cocked on the table, watching his fortune all night, considering how to keep those lovely crowns, which had passed from the royal coffers to his own, from somehow passing out of his coffers and into the pockets of a thief. The best means the Gascon could devise was to box his treasure up under locks so strong no tool could break them, and so clever no ordinary key could open them.

D'Artagnan remembered that the English are masters of mechanisms of security, and resolved to go the next day to find a mechanic who could sell him a safe. He didn't have to go far: Mister Will Jobson, residing in Piccadilly, listened to his propositions, understood his needs, and promised to construct a lock for him so secure he would be freed from all fear of the future.

"I will make for you a mechanism totally new," he said. "At the first serious attempt to crack your lock, a hidden aperture will open, and a miniature gun will shoot out a lovely copper bullet the weight of a mark, which will discommode your thief while making a resounding report. What do you think?"

"I think it sounds ingenious!" said d'Artagnan. "I particularly like the lovely copper bullet. So, Mister Mechanic, your terms?"

"Two weeks to make it, and fifteen thousand livres payable on delivery," replied the artisan.

D'Artagnan grimaced. Two weeks were enough time for every thief in London to have their way with his fortune, and then he wouldn't need a safe. As for the fifteen thousand livres, it was a high price to pay for what his vigilance could do for nothing. "I'll . . . think about it," he said. "Thank you, Sir."

And he returned home at a run—but no one had disturbed his treasure.

That same day, Athos came to visit his friend and found him so anxious he confessed to being surprised. "What! Here you are rich but not happy?" he said. "You who always wanted wealth . . ."

"My friend, the pleasures we aren't used to are worse than the sorrows we're familiar with. You've always had money; can you give me some advice? When one has money, what does one do with it?"

"That depends."

"What did you do with yours so as not to end up either a miser or a spendthrift? 'For greed withers the heart, and prodigality wastes it'—isn't that how it goes?"

"Even Fabricius[88] couldn't say it better. But, in truth, having money never troubled me."

"Come, do you invest it in annuities?"

"No; you know I have a pretty good country house, and this house comprises the majority of my wealth."

"Yes, so you've said."

"Well, you can be as rich as I am, even richer if you like, by the same means."

"But your income from rent—do you save it?"

"No."

"What would you think of a hidden wall cache?"

"I've never used such a thing."

"Then you have some confidential partner, some reliable businessman who manages your funds and pays a decent interest?"

"Not at all."

"My God! What do you do, then?"

"I spend whatever I have and no more than that, my dear d'Artagnan."

"Well, there! But you're a sort of lesser prince, with fifteen or sixteen thousand livres of revenue to fritter away, plus expenses to keep up appearances."

"But I don't see that you're much less noble than I am, my friend, and your fortune should be quite enough for you."

"Three hundred thousand livres! It should be three times enough."

"Your pardon, but it seems to me you told me . . . or I thought I understood . . . that is, you also have a partner . . ."

"Ah, *mordioux!* That's right!" cried d'Artagnan, coloring. "There's Planchet! I forgot about Planchet, upon my life. Well! There's my three hundred thousand broken into . . . such a shame, it was a nice round figure. But it's true, Athos, I'm not rich at all, really. What a memory you have!"

"Good enough, yes, God be praised."

"The worthy Planchet," groaned d'Artagnan. "His golden dreams come true. What an investment, *peste!* Well, what was said is said."

"How much will you give him?"

"Oh, he's not a bad lad," said d'Artagnan. "I'll do right by him. But I was put to considerable trouble, you see, had expenses, and all that must be taken into account."

"I know you can be trusted, *mon cher,*" said Athos serenely, "and I don't worry about the good Planchet; his interests are better off in your hands than in his. But now that we have no more to do here, we can go whenever you're ready. You just need to take your leave of His Majesty, ask him if he has any orders, and we can see the towers of Notre Dame within a week."

"Frankly, my friend, I'm burning to leave, so I'll go and pay my respects to the king."

"While I'm just going to meet a few people in the city," said Athos, "and then I'm yours."

"Will you lend me Grimaud?"

"With all my heart. What do you need him for?"

"A simple task that won't wear him out—I just need to ask him to sit by this table with my pistols and keep an eye on my coffers of coins."

"Very well," Athos replied imperturbably.

"He won't go off on his own?"

"No more than the pistols would."

"Then I'll go to see His Majesty. Au revoir."

D'Artagnan hastened to Saint James's Palace, where Charles II, who was writing his correspondence, kept him in the antechamber a full hour. As d'Artagnan walked back and forth across the gallery, from the doors to the windows and the windows to the doors, he thought he saw someone with a cloak like Athos's leaving through the outer vestibule, but just as he was about to go see for himself the usher summoned him in to see His Majesty.

Charles II rubbed his hands while receiving our musketeer's thanks. "Chevalier," he said, "you're wrong to think you owe me any gratitude, because I haven't paid even a quarter of the worth of the story of the box in which you encased our brave general . . . or rather the excellent Duke of Albemarle." And the king burst out laughing.

D'Artagnan thought it would be impolite to interrupt His Majesty and looked away modestly.

"By the way," continued Charles, "has my dear Monck really forgiven you?"

"Forgiven me! I certainly hope so, Sire."

"Heh! It must have been a cruel passage. Odds fish! To jug the leading personage of the English Revolution like a herring! I wouldn't trust him if I were in your place, Chevalier."

"But, Sire . . ."

"Yes, I'm well aware that Monck calls you his friend . . . but he has too calculating an eye not to have a sharp memory behind it, and a forehead that tall indicates great pride—you know, *grande supercilium*."

"I really must learn some Latin," d'Artagnan said to himself.

"Here, you must let me arrange your reconciliation," said the king, enchanted with the idea. "I know just how to do it . . ."

D'Artagnan gnawed his mustache. "Would Your Majesty permit me to speak the truth?"

"Speak, Chevalier, speak."

"Well, Sire, you're starting to frighten me! If Your Majesty tries to manage my affairs, as he seems to wish, I'm a doomed man—the duke will have me assassinated."

The king burst out laughing again, which made d'Artagnan genuinely alarmed. "Sire, I beg, promise me you'll let me handle this matter myself. And now, if you have no further need of my services . . ."

"Not yet, Chevalier. You don't really want to leave?" laughed Charles with increasingly disturbing hilarity.

"If Your Majesty has nothing more to ask of me."

Charles grew more serious. "One more thing. Go see my sister, Princess Henrietta.* Does she know you?"

"No, Sire . . . but an old soldier like me won't find favor with a young and cheerful princess."

"And I say to you that I wish my sister to know you. I want her to know that she can count on you at need."

"Sire, everything dear to Your Majesty is sacred to me."

"Quite so . . . Parry! Come here, good Parry."

The side door opened, and Parry came in, his face lighting up when he saw the chevalier.

"What's Rochester* doing?" asked the king.

"He's on the canal with the ladies."

"And Buckingham?"*

"The same."

"Perfect. Bring the chevalier to Villiers—that's the Duke of Buckingham, Chevalier—and ask the duke to introduce Monsieur d'Artagnan to Milady Henrietta."

Parry bowed and smiled at d'Artagnan.

"Chevalier," continued the king, "this is your final audience, and you may take your leave whenever you please."

"Thank you, Sire!"

"But make your peace with Monck."

"Oh! Sire . . ."

"You know that one of my vessels is at your disposal?"

"Sire, you overwhelm me! I couldn't think of putting Your Majesty's officers to such trouble for me."

The king clapped d'Artagnan on the shoulder. "It's not just for you, Chevalier, but also for an ambassador I'm sending to France—one you'll be happy to have for a companion, I think, for you know him."

D'Artagnan looked at the king in surprise.

"It's a certain Comte de La Fère, whom you call Athos," added the king, ending the conversation as he'd begun it, with a burst of laughter. "Adieu, Chevalier, adieu! Love me as I love you."

And with that, making a gesture to Parry to inquire if anyone awaited him in the adjacent study, the king disappeared into that room, leaving the audience chamber to the chevalier, still stunned by this unusual interview.

The old man took him amicably by the arm and led him into the gardens.

XXXV

On the Canal

On the green waters of the canal, bordered by marble stonework that time had marred with black spots and grassy tufts, majestically glided a long, flat barge, blazoned with the arms of England, surmounted by a canopy and hung with long damask curtains that trailed golden fringe into the water. Eight rowers, loosely plying their oars, made her move along the canal with the languid grace of the swans, who, disturbed in their aquatic territory by the barge's wake, glared from a distance as it passed in its splendor and clamor. We say clamor because the barge contained four guitar and lute players, two singers, and several courtiers glittering with gold and precious stones, all showing their white teeth at each other in an effort to please Milady Stuart, granddaughter of Henri IV, daughter of Charles I, and sister of Charles II, who sat on the barge's dais in the place of honor. We know this young princess, having seen her in the Louvre with her mother, bereft of firewood, bereft of bread, kept alive by the Coadjutor and the Parliament of Paris. She'd had, like her brothers, a hard youth, but now she'd suddenly awakened from that long, horrible dream to find herself seated at the foot of a throne, surrounded by courtiers and flatterers. And like Mary Stuart upon leaving her prison, she aspired to life and liberty, and moreover, to power and wealth.

Princess Henrietta had grown up to become a remarkable beauty, and her prominence in the recent restoration had already made that beauty famous. Misfortune had humbled her pride, but prosperity had restored it to her. She glowed with the joy of her youth, like those hothouse flowers that, wilted for a night by the first frost of autumn, recover in the warmth of the next day and bloom more splendidly than ever. George Villiers, second Duke of Buckingham, the son of he who played such a celebrated role in the first volume of this history—Villiers of Buckingham, a handsome cavalier, melancholy with women and merry with men, and Wilmot, Lord Rochester, merry with both sexes, were at that moment standing before Lady Henrietta, vying for the privilege of making her smile.

As for that young and beautiful princess, lying back on a velvet cushion embroidered with gold, trailing a languid hand in the water, she listened nonchalantly to the musicians without really hearing them, and heard every word of the courtiers without appearing to listen to them. For Lady Henrietta, this charming creature who combined the feminine graces of France and England, had never yet loved, and thus was cruel in her coquetry. So, the smile, that naïve favor of young ladies, never lit up her face, and if she raised her eyes, it was to fasten them so directly upon one or the other of the cavaliers that their gallantry, usually so bold, was abashed and made timid.

Meanwhile, the barge slid along, the musicians played frantically, and the courtiers, like the singers, began to run out of breath. It must have seemed all too monotonous to the princess, for she suddenly shook her head impatiently and said, "Come, that's quite enough, Gentlemen. Let's go ashore."

"Ah, Milady, how unfortunate we are," said Buckingham. "Our canal excursion has failed to please Your Highness."

"My mother's waiting for me," replied Lady Henrietta, "and I must tell you candidly, Gentlemen, that I'm bored."

But upon saying that cruel word, the princess tried with a glance at each to console the two young men, who seemed dismayed by such frankness. The looks produced their effects and the two faces brightened—but immediately, as if the royal coquette thought she might have offered too much to mere mortals, she turned her back on her two orators and fell into a reverie that evidently had nothing to do with them. Buckingham bit his lip in anger, for he was truly in love with Lady Henrietta, and as a result took everything seriously. Rochester bit his lip as well, but his mind always dominated his heart, and he was merely suppressing a malicious laugh.

The princess was allowing the eyes she'd turned away from the young men to gaze across the banks to the gardens and lawns when she saw Parry and d'Artagnan approaching in the distance. "Who's coming over there?" she asked.

The two young men instantly spun about. "It's Parry," replied Buckingham, "no one but Parry."

"Beg pardon," said Rochester, "but it seems to me he has a companion."

"Yes, I see," replied the princess languidly, then added more sharply, "but what did you mean by 'no one but Parry,' Milord?"

"I meant, Milady," replied Buckinham, piqued, "that the loyal Parry, the ubiquitous Parry, the wandering Parry, seems to me quite insignificant."

"You are mistaken, Your Grace: Parry, the wandering Parry, as you call him, has always wandered in service to my family, and so to see this old man is always a pleasure for me."

Lady Henrietta followed the usual routine of pretty women when toying with men of passing from capricious to contrary; her gallant had submitted to her caprice and now must suffer her contradiction. Buckingham bowed but said nothing.

"It's true, Milady," said Rochester, bowing in his turn, "that Parry is a model servant—but he's no longer young, Milady, and we laugh only with the lighthearted. Is he lighthearted, this old man?"

"Enough, Milord," said Lady Henrietta drily. "The subject of this conversation irritates me." Then, as if speaking to herself, "It's truly incredible how little regard my brother's friends have for his servants!"

"Ah, Milady!" cried Buckingham. "Your Highness pierces my heart with a dagger forged by your own hands."

"What is the meaning of this speech, Duke? It has the sound of bad poetry."

"It means, Milady, that you yourself, so good, so charming, so sensitive, have laughed sometimes, or at least smiled, at the random maunderings of the ancient Parry, for whom Your Highness today has such a marvelous fondness."

"Well, Milord!" said Lady Henrietta. "If I forgot my manners so far as to do that, it's ill-mannered of you to remind me of it." She made an impatient gesture. "The good Parry wants to speak to me, I think. Lord Rochester, have them put in to the bank, if you please."

Rochester hastened to repeat the princess's command. A few moments later, the barge touched the canal's bank. "Step ashore, Gentlemen," said Lady Henrietta, reaching for the arm offered by Rochester, though Buckingham was nearer to her and had presented his first.

Then Rochester, with an ill-concealed pride that smote the heart of the unhappy Buckingham, escorted the princess across the gangplank the crew had extended from the royal barge to the bank. "Where to, Your Highness?" asked Rochester.

"As you see, Milord, toward that good Parry, who wanders, as Lord Buckingham put it, searching for me with eyes weakened by the tears he's shed for our misfortunes."

"God's wounds, but Your Highness is sad today," said Rochester, "in light of which, our chattering must make us seem like ridiculous fools."

"Speak for yourself, Milord," interrupted Buckingham bitterly. "As for me, I displease Her Highness so much I seem like nothing at all."

Neither Rochester nor the princess replied to this; Lady Henrietta only pressed her cavalier to walk faster. Buckingham was left behind and took advantage of his isolation to take his anger out on his handkerchief, tearing the batiste to pieces with his teeth.

"Parry, good Parry," called the princess in a gentle voice, "come this way. I see you're looking for me, and I'm waiting."

"Indeed, Milady, let's wait," said Rochester, charitably coming to the aid of the duke, who was still behind them. "Even if Parry can't see Your Highness, the man with him would be guide enough for a blind man, for he has sharp, even fiery eyes. His gaze glows like a lantern."

"Lighting a strong face and a martial figure," said the princess, to sting the young nobles. Rochester bowed. "One of those vigorous and manly soldiers one sees only in France," she added, with the persistence of a woman certain of her impunity.

Rochester and Buckingham looked at each other as if to say, *What makes her do that?*

"Milord Buckingham, go see what Parry wants," said Lady Henrietta.

The young man, who regarded this command as a sign of favor, was encouraged and hurried to meet Parry, who, accompanied by d'Artagnan, was slowly making his way toward the trio of nobles. Parry walked slowly due to his age; beside him, d'Artagnan marched slowly but with dignity, ennobled by the consciousness that he was now worth a third of a million.

Eager to follow the desires of the princess, who had sat down upon a marble bench as if fatigued by her brief walk, Buckingham approached Parry, and when he was within a few paces the old man recognized him. "Ah, Milord!" he said, wheezing. "Would Your Grace kindly oblige the king?"

"In what way, Mister Parry?" asked the young man, his usual hauteur tempered by his desire to please the princess.

"Well! His Majesty would like Your Grace to present monsieur, here, to Her Highness Henrietta Stuart."

"And who is monsieur, here?" asked the duke coldly.

D'Artagnan, as we know, was quick to take offense, and the Duke of Buckingham's tone irritated him. He looked the courtier in the eye, and his own eyes flashed beneath a frowning brow—but he mastered himself and said calmly, "Monsieur le Chevalier d'Artagnan, Milord."

"Pardon, Monsieur, but that tells me your name, nothing more."

"Meaning?"

"Meaning I don't know you."

"Then I have the advantage of you, Sir," d'Artagnan replied, "for your family is known to me, particularly the first Duke of Buckingham, your illustrious father."

"My father?" said Buckingham. "Now that you mention it, Monsieur . . . the Chevalier d'Artagnan, you said?"

D'Artagnan bowed. "In person," he said.

"Beg pardon, but aren't you one of those Frenchmen who was involved in some secret intrigue with my father?"

"Precisely, Your Grace—I'm one of those Frenchmen."

"Then, Monsieur, permit me to say that it's strange that my father, during his lifetime, never mentioned your name."

"No, Your Grace, though he heard it at the moment of his death; it was I who sent to him, by way of Queen Anne's valet the warning of the danger he was in. Unfortunately, the warning arrived too late."

"I see, Monsieur," said Buckingham. "I understand now that having hoped to render a service to the father, you come to make a claim upon the son."

"No, Milord—I make no claims upon anyone," d'Artagnan replied coolly. "His Majesty King Charles II, for whom I had the honor to perform some services—I've passed my life in such occupations, Your Grace—King Charles II, who wished to honor me with a favor, asked that I be introduced to Princess Henrietta, his sister, to whom I might have the privilege of being useful in the future. The king happened to know that you were at this moment with Her Highness and sent me with Parry to find you. No mystery and no intrigue. I have nothing else to ask of Your Grace, and if you don't wish to introduce me to Her Highness, I will have to do without you and be so bold as to introduce myself."

"At least, Monsieur," replied Buckingham, wanting to get the last word, "you won't back down from answering some questions about yourself."

"I never back down, Your Grace," said d'Artagnan.

"If you were involved in my father's private affairs, there must be some secret you can reveal that would prove it."

"Those affairs were long ago, well before your time, Your Grace, involving some diamond studs that I received from his hands and returned to France, a matter too private to bandy about now."

"Ah, Monsieur!" said Buckingham eagerly, approaching d'Artagnan and extending his hand. "It is you! You, whom my father sought everywhere, and who has the right to expect so much from us!"

"Expect, Your Grace? In truth, expectations are my forte, and have been all my life."

Meanwhile, the princess, tired of waiting for the stranger to come to her, had risen and was approaching.

"At least, Monsieur," said Buckingham, "you can expect the introduction that you want from me." Then, turning and bowing to Lady Henrietta, the young man said, "Milady, the king your brother desires me to have the honor of presenting to Your Highness Monsieur le Chevalier d'Artagnan."

"So that Your Highness shall have at need a strong defender and a reliable friend," added Parry. D'Artagnan bowed.

"You have something else to add, don't you, Parry?" replied Lady Henrietta, smiling at d'Artagnan while addressing her old servant.

"Yes, Milady," Parry said to her. "The king wishes Your Highness to inscribe that name in her memory so she will remember his worth, for it is to him, as much as to anyone, that His Majesty owes the recovery of his realm."

Buckingham, the princess, and Rochester looked at each other in astonishment.

"That," said d'Artagnan, "refers to another little secret, one that I probably won't boast about to the son of His Majesty King Charles II as I just did to His Grace about his father's diamond studs."

"Your Highness," said Buckingham, "monsieur has just reminded me again of an episode that so excites my curiosity that I would dare to ask her permission to let me take him aside for a moment so I can ask him about it in private."

"Do so, Milord," said the princess, "but do so quickly so that you can return to the sister this friend so devoted to her brother." And she took Rochester's arm while Buckingham took d'Artagnan's.

"Now, tell me, Chevalier," said Buckingham, "all about that affair of the diamond studs, which no one in England knows about, not even the son of its hero."

"Milord, only one person in England had the right to recount that affair, and that was your father. Since he saw fit to keep quiet about it, I must ask you for permission to do the same." And d'Artagnan bowed like a man who clearly intended not to say another word.

"If that's the case, Monsieur, then pardon me for my indiscretion," said Buckingham, "and if, someday, I travel to France . . ." And he turned to glance at the princess, who was paying no attention to him, busy as she was, or seemed to be, in conversation with Rochester.

Buckingham sighed.

"Well?" asked d'Artagnan.

"I was saying that if someday I, too, should travel to France . . ."

"You will, Milord—I'll answer for that," said d'Artagnan, smiling.

"Really? Why?"

"Oh, I have strange powers of prediction . . . and when I predict something, I'm rarely wrong. So, if you come to France . . . ?"

"Well, Monsieur! To you, whom kings take in friendship because you restore them their crowns, I will dare to ask to know a bit more about this great intrigue you shared with my father."

"Milord," replied d'Artagnan, "believe me that I will be honored to speak to you, if you're still happy to remember that you saw me here. And now, if you'll permit me . . ." He turned toward Lady Henrietta. "Milady," he said, "Your Highness is a Daughter of France, and in that capacity I hope to meet her again in Paris. My happiest day will be when Your Highness gives me a command that shows she remembers the recommendations of her august brother."

And he bowed before the young princess, who gave him her hand to kiss with a becoming royal grace.

"Ah, Milady," said Buckingham quietly, "what could I possibly do to obtain from Your Highness the same favor?"

"By Our Lady, Milord," replied Princess Henrietta, "ask Monsieur d'Artagnan, he can tell you."

XXXVI

How d'Artagnan Drew, as if by Fairy Magic, a Country Estate from a Wooden Box

The king's words on the subject of Monck's wounded pride had inspired more than a little anxiety in d'Artagnan. All his life the lieutenant had shown a talent for choosing his enemies, and when he had taken on those who were implacable and invincible it was because he couldn't, under any pretext, do otherwise. But one's point of view can change greatly over the course of a life; it's a magic lantern lensed by a human eye that changes from year to year. One year in which we see things as white and the next year in which we see them as black are separated, on the last day of the year, by a single night.

D'Artagnan, as he was when he left Calais with his ten rogues, was as ready to contend with a Goliath, a Nebuchadnezzar, or Holofernes as he was to spar with a recruit or chat with a barmaid. Then he was like a hawk that, starving, will attack a ram out of blind hunger. But d'Artagnan sated, d'Artagnan rich, d'Artagnan a conqueror, d'Artagnan proud of a difficult triumph, this d'Artagnan had too much to lose not to reckon, tally by tally, the odds of probable disaster.

He was thinking, then, while returning from his royal introduction, of only one thing: how to handle a man as powerful as Monck, a man whom even Charles handled with great care. For, newly restored, the protégé might still need the protector, and if asked would scarcely refuse Monck the small favor of deporting Monsieur d'Artagnan, or throwing him in some dungeon in Middlesex, or arranging a small maritime tragedy in the crossing from Dover to Boulogne. These are the kinds of favors kings do for viceroys without a second thought.

It wasn't even necessary for the king to take an active role in the scenario of Monck's revenge; all he need do was to pardon the Viceroy of Ireland for whatever action he took against d'Artagnan. Nothing more was needed to settle the conscience of the Duke of Albemarle than a *te absolvo* said with a laugh, or the scribbled signature of King Charles at the bottom of a document, and with these two or three words spoken or scrawled, poor d'Artagnan might just as well have never existed.

And as a further circumstance worrisome to one with as much foresight as our musketeer, he was essentially on his own, with only the friendship of Athos as a slight reassurance. Of course, if it was just a matter of sword thrusts, the musketeer could count on his comrade; but in crossing privileges with a king, where the benefit of the doubt might serve to support the position of Monck or of Charles II, d'Artagnan knew Athos well enough to be sure that he'd find his duty most due to the noble survivor and content himself with shedding tears on the tomb of the deceased, composing, if the deceased was his friend, a eulogy of pompous superlatives.

Decidedly, thought the Gascon, reaching the conclusion of those inner reflections we just revealed aloud, *decidedly I must be reconciled with Mister Monck, and with a proof that he holds no grudge. If, God forbid, he remains sullen and unforgiving, I'll give my money to Athos to take to France while I stay in England just long enough to make Monck show his hand; then, at the first hostile sign, I'll decamp, and as I have a keen eye and a light foot, I'll go to ground with Milord de Buckingham, who seems a good devil at heart, and to whom, as recompense for his hospitality, I'll recount the entire history of the diamond studs. At this point it can only compromise an aging queen who need not be ashamed, after being the secret wife of Monsieur de Mazarin,*[89] *of having also been the mistress of a noble lord like the first Buckingham.* "God's death!" he said aloud, "this Monck won't outplay me! And besides, I have an idea."

As we know, a shortage of ideas was never d'Artagnan's problem. During this monologue d'Artagnan had buttoned up his jerkin to his chin, and nothing excited his imagination like this preparation for combat, which the Romans called *accinction.*[90] He was quite wound up by the time he arrived at the house of the new Duke of Albemarle, where he was escorted to the viceroy's presence with a speed that showed he was still regarded as a member of the household.

Monck was in his study. "Milord," said d'Artagnan, wearing a convincing expression of frankness upon his cunning features, "I come to ask Your Grace for advice."

Monck, as buttoned-up morally as his antagonist was physically, replied, "Ask, my friend." And his face presented an expression no less frank than d'Artagnan's.

"Milord, first of all, please promise me secrecy and forbearance."

"I promise you whatever you ask. What is it? Speak!"

"It's just, Milord, that I'm not quite confident of the king."

"Oh, really? And in what way, if you please, my dear Lieutenant?"

"In the way that His Majesty sometimes makes jokes at the expense of his servants—and mockery, Milord, is a weapon that wounds men of the sword like us."

Monck made every effort not to betray his thoughts, but d'Artagnan watched with such close attention that he couldn't miss the almost imperceptible flush on his cheeks.

"But I'm no enemy of such pleasantries, my dear Monsieur d'Artagnan," said Monck with the most natural air in the world. "My soldiers will even tell you that many times in camp I heard with indifference, and even appreciation, the satirical songs Lambert's soldiers sang from their own camp, and which definitely would have scorched the ears of a general more susceptible to mockery than I am."

"Oh, Milord!" said d'Artagnan. "I know that you are completely self-possessed and far above the insecurities of humankind—but there are jokes, and there are jokes. And some of them, I confess, have the ability to irritate me above all expression."

"Of what kind are those, old boy?"

"The kind that foster disrespect for my friends and allies, Milord."

Monck winced ever so slightly, but d'Artagnan noticed it.

"And in what way can the pin that pricks another affect you?" asked Monck. "Tell me that!"

"I'll tell you, Milord: because the pin was intended to prick *you*."

Monck took a step toward d'Artagnan. "Me?" he said.

"Yes, and that's what I don't understand; maybe it's because I don't know him well. How can the king have the heart to mock a man who's served him so much and so well? Why would he amuse himself by setting a gnat like me at the ears of a lion like you?"

"I don't understand what you're telling me," said Monck.

"Very well, consider this! Why didn't the king, who owed me some recompense, reward me like a soldier instead of concocting that ransom story that reflects upon you, Milord?"

"But no," said Monck, laughing, "that doesn't reflect upon me at all, on my oath."

"I know it's not my place to talk, and you know me, Milord, I'm as quiet as the grave, but—don't you get it, Milord?"

"No," Monck said stubbornly.

"If another knew the secret I know . . ."

"Which secret?"

"Why, Milord! The ugly secret of Newcastle."

"Ah! You mean the Comte de La Fère's million?"

"No, Milord—the exploit that involved Your Grace."

"It was a game well played, Chevalier, that's all, and there's nothing more to say about it. You are a man of war, brave and cunning, which shows you combine the qualities of Fabius and Hannibal.[91] You used force, wits, and the resources at hand, and there's nothing to say against that; I should have taken better care to guard myself."

"Thank you, Milord, I expected nothing less from your innate fairness, and if it was just a simple matter of your abduction, *mordioux!* I wouldn't worry—and yet there's the . . ."

"What?"

"The circumstances of that abduction."

"What circumstances?"

"You're well aware, Milord, of what I'm talking about."

"I'm damned if I do!"

"It's that . . . it's hard to say this right out."

"To say what?"

"Well! To speak of that cursed . . . box."

Monck visibly flushed.

"The indignity of the box," continued d'Artagnan, "the wooden coffin, you know?"

"That? Forget about it."

"Made of wooden planks, with air holes and a speaking grate," continued d'Artagnan. "In truth, Milord, the rest of the exploit is fine—but the box, the box! That was a bad joke." Monck squirmed in his chair. "And yet, the fact that I did that," said d'Artagnan, "I, a soldier of fortune, that's understandable, because though it might have been somewhat unworthy, it could be excused by the gravity of the situation. But never mind, I'm circumspect and discreet."

"Oh!" said Monck. "Rest assured that I know you well, Monsieur d'Artagnan, and appreciate your virtues."

D'Artagnan kept a close eye on Monck, detecting all that was passing through the general's mind as he spoke. "But this isn't about me," he said.

"Well, who's it about, then?" asked Monck, beginning to be impatient.

"It's about the king, who's too merry to hold his tongue."

"Well, if he tells all he knows, so what?" said Monck, nervously.

"Milord," replied d'Artagnan, "don't pretend, I beg, with one who speaks as honestly as I do. You have a right to be concerned, no matter how blameless you are. What the devil! It's not proper for a serious man like you, a man who plays with thrones and scepters like an acrobat juggles balls, to be displayed in a box like a curiosity of natural history; if you have enemies—and you're so great, so noble, and so generous that you must have many—and they heard of this, they would make you a laughingstock. A picture circulated of you locked in that box would set half the human race to laughter. Now, it's neither decent nor proper for others to laugh like that at the second personage of the realm."

Monck was beside himself at the idea of being depicted inside the box. The idea of ridicule, as d'Artagnan had wisely foreseen, had gotten to him in a way that neither the hazards of war, the desires of ambition, nor the fear of death could.

Good, thought the Gascon, *he's afraid, and I am saved.*

"Oh, as to the king," said Monck, "don't worry about him, dear Monsieur d'Artagnan—the king won't make fun of Monck, I assure you!" But d'Artagnan saw how his eyes flashed. Monck softened his tone immediately. "The king," he continued, "has too noble a nature, too generous a heart to wish to injure those who mean him good."

"Absolutely!" said d'Artagnan. "I'm entirely of your opinion as regards his heart, but not his head; he means well, but lets his wit carry him away."

"The king's wit won't carry him away from me, I assure you."

"So, you're not at all worried, Milord?"

"On that flank at least I'm unconcerned, yes."

"Got it, I understand, you're unconcerned about the king."

"As I said."

"But you're not as unconcerned about me?"

"I thought I told you that I believe in your loyalty and discretion."

"No doubt, no doubt, but you're overlooking one thing . . ."

"Which is?"

"That I wasn't alone, that I had companions—and such companions!"

"Oh! Yes, I remember them."

"Unfortunately, Milord, they remember you too."

"Well?"

"Well! They're over there at Boulogne, waiting for me."

"And you fear . . . ?"

"Yes, I fear that in my absence . . . *parbleu!* If only I were near them, I could answer for their silence."

"Then I was right to say that the danger, if there was any, would come not from His Majesty, despite his tendency to jest, but from such as your companions, as you say. To be mocked by a king may be tolerated, but by mercenary rabble . . . *Goddamn!*"

"Yes, I understand, that would be unbearable—which is why, Milord, I came to you to say, 'Don't you think I ought to depart for France as soon as possible?'"

"Certainly, if you believe your presence . . ."

"Would impose discipline on those rogues? I'm certain of it, Milord."

"Your presence won't prevent the rumor from spreading if it's already begun."

"Oh, it hasn't yet begun, Milord, I can guarantee that. In any event, you can be sure I'm determined on one thing."

"And that is?"

"To blow the head off the first one to spread such a rumor, and follow with whoever might have heard it. After which, I'll return to England to seek asylum and perhaps employment with Your Grace."

"What, return? Return?"

"Unfortunately, Milord, I know no one here but you, and if I find you again, you may have forgotten me in your new grandeurs."

"Listen, Monsieur d'Artagnan," Monck replied, "you're a charming gentleman, full of wit and courage, and deserve all the rewards the world can offer. Come with me to Scotland and I swear to you, within my viceroyalty you'll find a place that others will envy."

"Ah, Milord, that's impossible right now! At the moment I have a sacred duty to fulfill: I must guard your glory and make sure no mean-spirited jest tarnishes you in the eyes of your peers, and who knows? Perhaps dims the luster of your name in posterity."

"In posterity, Monsieur d'Artagnan?"

"Why, of course! For the sake of posterity all the details of this affair must remain hidden—because, if the ugly story of the wooden box were to spread, everyone would say that you didn't restore the king out of loyalty and your own free will, but because the two of you made a bargain at Scheveningen. Then it would be useless for me to say what had really happened, because people would say I was part of the deal and had gotten my piece of the pie."

Monck frowned darkly. "Glory, honor, integrity," he said, "nothing but empty words!"

"Mist and smoke," d'Artagnan nodded, "through which no one can ever see clearly."

"Well, then! Go to France, my dear Monsieur," said Monck. "Go, and to make England more accessible and receptive to you, accept a gift from me."

What now? thought d'Artagnan.

"On the banks of the Clyde, in a little grove," continued Monck, "I own a house, a *cottage* as we say, and with this house go a hundred acres of land. Accept this from me."

"Oh, Milord . . . !"

"And by Our Lady, there you will have a secure home, that refuge of which you spoke to me just now."

"I'm so very obliged to you, Milord! In truth, I'm unworthy!"

"Not at all, Monsieur," replied Monck with a wry smile, "not at all, it's I who am obliged to you." He shook the musketeer's hand and said, "I'll go have the deed of transfer drawn up right now." And he left.

D'Artagnan watched him leave the room, pensive and even moved. "At last," he said to himself, "I've found a good man. It's sad to feel that it's out of fear that he does this rather than affection, but never mind! I'll just have to make sure the affection continues."

Then, after a moment of further reflection, he said, "But why bother? He's an Englishman!"

And he went out in his turn, a bit dazed by the effort of the contest. "So," he said, "now I'm a landowner. But how the devil will I divide the cottage with Planchet? Unless I give him the land while I keep the house, or I give him the house while I . . . Bah! Mister Monck would never approve of my sharing his house with a grocer! He's far too proud for that. Besides, why mention it at all? I didn't acquire this property with our company's funds, I did it with my own wits, and thus it's entirely mine. Let's go find Athos."

And he made his way toward the lodgings of the Comte de La Fère.

XXXVII

How d'Artagnan Settled the Company's
Liabilities before Reckoning Its Assets

"I'm on a winning streak and no doubt about it," d'Artagnan said to himself. "That star that shines once in the life of every man, even for Job and for Irus,[92] the most unfortunate of the Jews and the poorest of the Greeks, finally shines on me. But I won't be reckless as I take advantage of it, because I'm mature enough to be sensible."

He supped cheerfully that evening with his friend Athos, and though he didn't mention Monck's gift, as they ate he couldn't help asking his friend about sowing, planting, and farm production. Athos replied agreeably, as always. He assumed d'Artagnan was considering becoming a landowner, but more than once he missed his old companion's lively mood and witty sallies. D'Artagnan, preoccupied, took advantage of the greasy remains on his plate to draw figures and make calculations that amounted to pleasantly round sums.

The order, or rather permit, for their embarkation arrived later that evening. While the visa was being handed over to the count, another messenger arrived and gave d'Artagnan a bundle of parchment pages fluttering with all the colorful seals that adorn real estate deeds in England. Athos surprised him skimming through these documents that established the transfer of property. The prudent Monck, or one might say the generous Monck, had converted the gift into a sale with a receipt that acknowledged having been paid the sum of fifteen thousand livres for the transaction.

D'Artagnan had begun reading the deeds before the messenger had even disappeared. Athos watched him and smiled. D'Artagnan, catching one of these smiles over his shoulder, folded up the parchments and thrust them back into their packet.

"Pardon me," said Athos.

"No problem, there are no secrets here, old friend," replied the lieutenant. "I'd just like . . ."

"No, don't tell me anything, I beg. Orders are sacred things, and the person charged with them shouldn't reveal a single word even to his brother or father. Even I, who loves you more tenderly than a brother, a father, or anyone . . ."

"Outside of Raoul?"

"I will love Raoul even more when he is a man, fully formed in all phases of character and behavior . . . in other words, when he's like you, my friend."

"You said that you'd received orders as well; don't you intend to share them with me?"

"No, friend d'Artagnan."

The Gascon sighed. "There was a time," he said, "when you would have laid that order open on the table and said, 'D'Artagnan, read this gibberish to Porthos, Aramis, and myself and tell us what it means.'"

"You're right. We shared the confidence of youth, that generous season when we're ruled by the hot blood of passion!"

"Well, Athos, can I tell you something?"

"Speak, my friend."

"That wonderful time, that generous season, that reign of hot blood, those are all beautiful things beyond doubt, but I wouldn't go back to them. It's just like thinking about your school days—I'm always meeting some fool nostalgic for copying tasks, canings, and crusts of dry bread. It's bizarre, because I never enjoyed that. The old days? No matter how serious and active I was (and you can confirm this, Athos), no matter how simple my everyday clothes, I still would have preferred Porthos's embroidered finery to my threadbare doublet, which was protection from neither the cold winds of winter nor the hot sun of summer. My friend, I can't help but mistrust anyone who says he prefers bad over good. Now, in the good old days, when everything was terrible, every month saw another hole in my coat and my skin, and a gold crown less in my sagging purse; from that awful time of watered wine and constant worry I absolutely regret nothing, nothing, nothing but our friendship. For I still have within me a heart, and by some miracle, that heart wasn't withered by the wind of misery that howled through the holes in my cloak or impaled by the swords of all sorts that made holes in my poor flesh."

"Never regret our friendship," said Athos. "It will die only when we do. Friendship is mainly made up of memories and shared habits, and if you had to make a small satire on mine because I wouldn't reveal my mission to France . . ."

"Me? By heaven, my old and dear friend, if you only knew how little all the world's missions will mean to me from here on out!" And he folded his packet of parchments and shoved it into his travel bag.

Athos rose from the table and called over the host to settle the bill. "As long as I've been your friend," said d'Artagnan, "I've never once paid the bill. Porthos did it often, Aramis occasionally, and you nearly always drew out your purse upon the arrival of dessert. Now that I'm rich, I'd like to see just how heroic it is to pay the bill."

"Go ahead," said Athos, returning his purse to his belt pouch.

The two friends then made their way to the port, not without d'Artagnan frequently looking behind him to check on the transport of his beloved money. Night had spread its thick veil over the muddy waters of the Thames; they could hear the sounds of rolling casks and creaking pullies, the preliminaries to setting sail that had so often quickened the musketeers' hearts when the dangers of the sea were the least of the perils they would face.

This time they were to embark on a large vessel that awaited them at Gravesend, and Charles II, always thoughtful of the little things, had sent one of his river yachts with twelve of his Scots Guards to do honor to the ambassador he was sending to France. By midnight the yacht had seen its passengers onto the larger vessel, and at eight o'clock the next morning that vessel disembarked the ambassador and his friend onto the jetty at Boulogne.

While the count, helped by Grimaud, went to hire some horses for the ride to Paris, d'Artagnan went to the inn where, according to his orders, his little army was to wait for him. These gentlemen were breakfasting on oysters, fish, and spiced eau-de-vie when d'Artagnan entered. They were all in a good mood, and none were yet drunk beyond the ability to reason. They raised a cheer when they saw their commander.

"Here I am," said d'Artagnan. "The campaign is over, and I've come to bring you your promised bonus." Their eyes shone. "I'd wager there's no more than a hundred livres left in the purse of the richest of you!"

"It's true!" they cried in chorus.

"Gentlemen," said d'Artagnan, "these are your final orders. Your mercenary contracts are fulfilled, thanks to that master stroke that made us the master of the England's leading financier. Now I can reveal that the man we had to transport was none other than General Monck's treasurer."

The word *treasurer* was met with obvious approval by his army. D'Artagnan noted that only Menneville's gaze conveyed a certain doubt.

"This treasurer," continued d'Artagnan, "I brought to the neutral territory of Holland, where I persuaded him to sign a certain declaration. Then I took him back to Newcastle, and as he must have been satisfied with our treatment of him, his wooden coffin having been padded so softly and carried so carefully, I asked him for a gratuity for you. Here it is." He dropped a bulging and rather heavy bag onto the tablecloth. All hands reflexively reached for it. "Not so fast, my lambs," said d'Artagnan. "If there are profits, there are also prices."

"Oh?" murmured the assembled rogues.

"We now find ourselves, my friends, in a position that could be dangerous for those who lack brains. To be plain: we stand between the gallows and the Bastille."

"Uh-oh!" gasped the chorus.

"It's not hard to understand. I had to explain the disappearance of his treasurer to General Monck. I waited to do so until the moment of the unexpected restoration of King Charles II, who is one of my friends . . ."

The little army exchanged looks of satisfaction that were smug compared to d'Artagnan's, which was rather proud. "Once the king was restored,

I restored General Monck his man of business—slightly the worse for wear, perhaps, but at least I returned him. Now, General Monck, when he pardoned me, for that was part of the bargain, couldn't refrain from telling me the words I'm about to repeat to you, and which I urge each of you to engrave into your memory: 'Monsieur, that was a good joke, but I don't care much for jokes. If a single word of what you've done ever escapes your lips'—do you hear me, Monsieur Menneville?—'or the lips of your companions, I have in my viceroyalty of Scotland 741 oaken gallows, with hooks of iron and trapdoors greased every week. I would present one of these gallows to each of you, and take note, Monsieur d'Artagnan'—take note as well, Monsieur Menneville—'I would still have seven hundred and thirty gallows left for others. Moreover . . .'"

"Oh!" said the mercenaries. "There's more?"

"One threat more: 'Monsieur d'Artagnan, I am writing to the King of France to report this bargain, with the request that a cell in the Bastille be prepared for each member of your troop who falls into his hands, the lot to be turned back over to me, a request he will certainly comply with.'"

A gasp of fear was heard all around the table.

"Now, now," said d'Artagnan. "The noble Monck had forgotten one thing, which is that he doesn't know any of your names; only I know you, and as you can well believe, I'm not about to betray you. Why would I? And as to you, none of you are foolish enough to betray yourselves, for then the king, to save himself the expense of keeping you in the Bastille, would send you to Scotland to grace one of the 741 gallows. So, there you have it, Messieurs: I have not another word to add to what I've had the honor to tell you. I'm sure I was understood perfectly—was I not, Monsieur Menneville?"

"Perfectly," the latter replied.

"And now, the beautiful crowns!" said d'Artagnan. "Shut the doors."

And he emptied the shiny new gold coins on the table, a few rolling off the edge. Everyone grabbed at the floor. "How pretty!" said d'Artagnan. "Put the loose ones back in the pile so it doesn't throw off my count."

He then doled out fifty gleaming crowns to each of them, receiving nearly as many blessings as coins he allotted.

"Now," he said, "if you could just clean yourselves up a bit and become good and honest citizens . . ."

"But that's so very difficult," said one of the rogues.

"Why would we do that, Captain?" said another.

"Because then I might be able to find you again, and who knows? By then you might need me."

D'Artagnan made a sign to Menneville, who'd been listening to all this coolly and calmly. "Menneville," he said, "come with me. Adieu, *mes Braves!* I needn't warn you to be discreet." Menneville followed him, while the sound of the mercenaries' farewells mingled with the sweet jingle of gold in their pouches.

"Menneville," d'Artagnan said when they were in the street, "you're no fool, so take care not to act like one. You don't impress me as one who fears either the gallows of Monck or the Bastille of His Majesty King Louis XIV, so you will do me the favor to be afraid of me. Now, listen: you say a single word about what you know to anybody, and I'll find you and wring your neck like a chicken's. I already have in my pocket the permission and absolution of our Holy Father the Pope."

"I assure you I know absolutely nothing, Monsieur d'Artagnan, and your every word is to me an article of faith."

"I always knew you had brains," said the musketeer. "Knew it from the first time I met you. These fifty gold crowns I give you as a bonus should show you what I think of you. Take them."

"Thank you, Monsieur d'Artagnan," said Menneville.

"That ought to be enough to enable you to live as an honest man," replied d'Artagnan in a serious tone. "It would be a shame if a mind like yours and the name you no longer dare to use were to disappear into a wasted life. Wipe the slate clean, Menneville, and live for a year as an honest man—you can do it, I just gave you twice the pay of a ranking officer. After a year, come see me, and, *mordioux!* We'll make something of you yet."

Menneville swore, as his comrades had, to be as quiet as the grave. And yet, somebody must have talked eventually, and if it wasn't Menneville or one of the other nine mercenaries, it must have been d'Artagnan, who, as a Gascon, always had a tongue ready to wag. After all, if it wasn't him, who else could it have been? How else could the story of the wooden box bored with breathing-holes have come down to us complete in every detail? Details which, moreover, clear up an unexplained episode in the history of England, left until today out of the accounts of the historians.

XXXVIII

In Which We See that the French Grocer Was Already Well Established in the 17th Century

Once his accounts had been settled and his warnings communicated, d'Artagnan thought of nothing but getting back to Paris as soon as possible. Athos, for his part, was eager to return to the repose of his house. After the fatigues of a journey, whether a man feels well or exhausted, even if the day has been pleasant, he looks forward to its end, for the night will allow him to sleep.

So, from Boulogne to Paris, riding side by side, the two friends, each preoccupied with his own thoughts, encountered nothing interesting enough to relate to the reader: the cavaliers, while considering the future each in his own way, devoted themselves to speed. On the evening of the fourth day after their departure from Boulogne, Athos and d'Artagnan arrived at the gates of Paris.

"Where are you bound for, dear friend?" asked Athos. "I am going straight to my town house."

"And I, straight to my partner."

"Planchet's place?"

"The Golden Pestle? *Mon Dieu,* yes."

"Shall we find a way to meet again?"

"If you stay in Paris, yes, because the city is where I'm staying."

"No. After embracing Raoul, whom I expect to find at my house, I leave immediately for La Fère."

"Well, then! Adieu, my dear and perfect friend."

"Au revoir, rather, because I hope you will come and visit, or even live with me at Blois. You are free, you are rich, I can help you buy, if you like, a property near Cheverny or Bracieux. On one side you'd have the most beautiful woods in the world, backing up on Chambord, while on the other, a lovely marsh. You who love hunting, and who has the soul of a poet, though you won't admit it, will find pheasant, rail, and teal, not to mention long sunsets and such boating that you'll feel like Nimrod and Apollo themselves. While waiting for the sale to close, you'll live at La Fère, and we'll go fly our hawks among the vineyards, as King Louis XIII used to do. It's a suitable life for old soldiers like us."

D'Artagnan took hold of Athos's hands. "Dear Count," he said, "I won't say yes or no. Let me spend the time I need in Paris to order my affairs and little by little get used to the great and growing idea that's shining in my mind. I am rich, as you say, but until I've taken enough time to get used to riches, I'm going to be an insufferable monster, I just know it. Now, at least I've got the sense not to behave like a lackwit in front of a friend like you, Athos. My cloak of wealth is handsome, it's richly embroidered, but it's new, it isn't broken in, and it itches."

Athos smiled. "So be it," he said. "But about this new cloak, dear d'Artagnan, would you like to hear some advice?"

"Indeed, I would!"

"You won't be upset?"

"Speak freely."

"When wealth comes to a person late, that person, to keep from changing, must become either a miser, that is, spend no more than he did before, or a spendthrift, going into debt so quickly that he becomes poor again."

"Hmph. That sounds like sophistry to me, O wise philosopher."

"I don't think so. Will you become a miser, then?"

"No, by God! I've already done that, and more than enough. We must change."

"Then, it's spendthrift?"

"Even less likely, *mordioux!* Debt terrifies me. Creditors remind me of those devils who roast the damned on spits, and as patience isn't my chief virtue, I'm always tempted to send them to hell early."

"You are the wisest man I know and need no advice from anyone. One would be a great fool to think he had anything to teach you. But isn't this Rue Saint-Honoré?"

"Yes, dear Athos."

"And here, on the left, this long, white house is the hôtel where I'm lodging. You'll notice it has only two floors; I occupy the lower, while the other is rented to an officer whose service keeps him far away eight or nine months of the year, so I have the house as much to myself as if I was at home, but without the expense."

"You manage things so well, Athos, in both order and economy! That's what I want to copy. But what can I do? You were born to rank, while I just do the best I can."

"Such flattery! Come, say farewell, dear friend. By the way, give my regards to Planchet; he's a lad of wits, isn't he?"

"And of heart, Athos. Adieu!"

They separated. During this long conversation, d'Artagnan had never for a second lost sight of the packhorse carrying the paniers in which, under a layer of hay, the money sacks were hidden among the other luggage. Nine in the evening was sounding from the belfry of Saint-Merri, and Planchet's shop boys were shuttering the store. Under an awning on the corner of the Rue des Lombards d'Artagnan stopped the postilion[93] who rode the packhorse, and, calling over one of Planchet's lads, told him to watch the horses as well as the postilion. Then he entered the house of the grocer, who'd just finished his supper, and who, on the landing, was anxiously consulting the calendar on which every evening he scratched off the day that had just passed. At that moment when, with a sigh, Planchet drew a line through another day, d'Artagnan kicked firmly at his open side door, the blows setting his iron spurs jingling.

"Good Lord!" cried Planchet. Having taken one look at his partner, the worthy grocer could say no more. D'Artagnan, who couldn't resist the idea of stringing Planchet along, entered with his shoulders slumped and his eyes averted.

My God! thought the grocer, staring at the traveler. *He's destroyed.*

"My dear Monsieur d'Artagnan!" said Planchet, his heart skipping a beat. "You're back! Are you all right?"

"Well enough, Planchet, I suppose," said d'Artagnan with a sigh.

"You aren't wounded, are you?"

"Eh!"

"I see," continued Planchet, more and more alarmed. "The expedition was a rough one?"

"Yes," said d'Artagnan.

A shiver shook Planchet from head to toe.

"I need . . . a drink," said the musketeer, with a pitiful look.

Planchet ran to the sideboard and poured d'Artagnan a large glass of wine. D'Artagnan looked at the bottle. "What wine is this?" he asked.

"Why, it's your favorite, Monsieur," said Planchet, "that good old wine of Anjou that one day nearly cost us so dearly."[94]

"Ah!" replied d'Artagnan with a melancholy smile. "And should I be drinking so expensive a wine, my poor Planchet?"

"Come, dear Master," said Planchet, making a superhuman effort, though his trembling and pallor revealed deep anguish. "I was a soldier, you know, so I'm brave enough to hear it. Don't keep me guessing, Monsieur d'Artagnan. Our money: it's all gone, isn't it?"

D'Artagnan hesitated before answering, a delay that seemed like a century to the poor grocer. Finally, he turned in his chair, head held low, and said slowly, "And if that were so, what would you say to me, my poor friend?"

Planchet, already pale, turned yellow. His eyes twitched, his throat swelled, and he felt as if he was going to swallow his tongue. "Twenty thousand livres!" he murmured. "Twenty . . . thousand . . . !"

D'Artagnan, his head slumping on his neck, his limbs lax, hands drooping, was the very image of discouragement.

Planchet tore a heavy sigh from the very depths of his chest. "Come," he said. "I see how it is. Let's be men. It's over, isn't it? At least, Monsieur, you survived, and that's the important thing."

"No doubt, no doubt. Life is something, I suppose . . . but in the meantime, I'm ruined."

"Cordieu!" said Planchet. "If that's so, Monsieur, there's no need to despair. You can be a grocer with me! I'll make you a partner in my business, we'll share the profits, and when there are no profits, well! We'll share the almonds, raisins, and prunes, and nibble on our last quarter of Dutch cheese."

D'Artagnan could sustain it no longer. "*Mordioux!*" he brightly cried. "You're a brave lad, upon my honor, Planchet! Did you like my little comedy? Look, out there in the street, under that awning—do you see that horse with the paniers?"

"Awning? Horse? Paniers?" said Planchet, his heart sinking at the idea that d'Artagnan had gone mad.

"God's death, yes, those English paniers!" said d'Artagnan, radiant and transfigured.

"Good Lord!" cried Planchet, recoiling before his partner's burning gaze.

"Fool!" laughed d'Artagnan. "You think I'm crazy. *Mordioux!* On the contrary, I've never had a sharper head and a happier heart. To the pack-horse, Planchet—to the paniers!"

"But what paniers, where, for the love of God?"

D'Artagnan pushed Planchet toward the window. "Under the awning over there," he said, "do you see a horse?"

"Yes."

"Do you see how his back bends?"

"Yes, yes."

"Do you see one of your lads talking to the postilion?"

"Yes, yes, yes."

"Well, then! You know that lad's name, since he's one of yours. Call to him."

"Abdon! Abdon!" shouted Planchet from the window.

"Bring the horse," whispered d'Artagnan.

"Bring the horse!" shouted Planchet.

"Now, ten livres for the postilion," said d'Artagnan in the tone used to command a maneuver. "Two lads to bring up the first two bags, two more for the last two, and lively, now! Move It!"

Planchet threw himself down the stairs as if the devil was at his heels. A few moments later the shop boys came up the stairs, bent beneath their burdens. D'Artagnan sent them off to their garrets, shut the door carefully and turned to Planchet, who himself was looking a little wild. "Now," d'Artagnan said, "it's just us." And he spread a large blanket on the floor and emptied onto it the first bag. Planchet did the same with the second, then d'Artagnan, his hand trembling a bit, cut open the third with his knife.

When Planchet heard the thrilling clink of silver and gold, when he saw the shining crowns that glittered like fish swept out of the sea, when he felt his arms plunge up to the elbows into this rising tide of silver and gold coins, the shock hit him all at once, and, as if struck by lightning, he fell down heavily on the enormous heap with a metallic crash. Planchet, overcome by joy, had passed out.

D'Artagnan threw a glass of white wine into his face, which brought Planchet back to life. "Ah! My God! My God!" he repeated as he wiped his mustache and beard. At that time, as now, a grocer wore a cavalier's mustache and a soldier's beard, but bathing in silver and gold, already a rare thing then, is today almost unknown.

"*Mordioux!*" said d'Artagnan. "A hundred thousand livres of this is yours, Monsieur Partner. Count out your share, if you will, and then I'll take mine."

"Oh, the lovely silver, Monsieur d'Artagnan! The beautiful gold!"

"Half an hour ago I confess I was regretting the part that belongs to you," said d'Artagnan, "but now, I regret nothing. You're a fine grocer, Planchet, who keeps good accounts, and good accounts, they say, keep good friends."

"Oh! But first tell me the whole story," said Planchet. "It must be even prettier than the money."

"My faith," replied d'Artagnan, stroking his mustache, "I won't say you're wrong, and if ever a historian demands the whole tale, he'll hear more than he thought he would. Listen, then, Planchet, and I'll tell you."

"And I'll start counting this into stacks," said Planchet. "Please begin, my dear partner."

"It starts like this," said d'Artagnan, drawing a breath.

"And ends like this," said Planchet, picking up his first handful of coins.

XXXIX

Monsieur de Mazarin at His Games

On the evening of the arrival in Paris of our two Frenchmen, in a grand chamber of the Palais Royal,[95] its walls draped in dark velvet that showed off the gilded frames of many handsome paintings, one could see the entire Court arrayed before the sleeping alcove of Monsieur le Cardinal de Mazarin, who was hosting an evening at cards for the king and the queen. Low screens separated three tables placed around the chamber. The king and the two queens were seated at one of these tables; Louis XIV sat across from the young queen, his wife, whom he smiled upon with a genuine expression of happiness. Anne of Austria held the cards against the cardinal, and her daughter-in-law advised her when she wasn't smiling at her husband. Beyond the table, in his bed, lay the cardinal, an emaciated figure, always tired, the Comtesse de Soissons[96] holding his cards for him, which he scanned with a look of calculation and avarice.

The cardinal wore makeup that had been applied by Bernouin, but the rouge glistening on his cheekbones just emphasized the unhealthy pallor of the rest of his face and the sallow yellow flesh of his forehead. Only his eyes glowed brightly, and those feverish eyes, from time to time, attracted worried glances from the king, the queens, and the courtiers. The fact is that Signor Mazarin's gleaming eyes were the inconstant stars in which 17th-century France read its destiny every night and morning.

Monseigneur was neither winning nor losing, so he was neither cheerful nor sour. It was a stagnant state in which Anne of Austria would not have left him, if she could help it, but to engage the invalid's interest through some change of fortune she would have to either win or lose. To win was dangerous, as Mazarin might trade his disinterest for irritation, but to lose she would have had to cheat, and the infanta, who was watching her mother-in-law's game closely, might spot the misplay, and that would be the end of any chance of a good mood from Monsieur de Mazarin.

Taking advantage of this calm, the courtiers were talking among themselves. Mazarin, when he wasn't in an ill temper, was a congenial lord, and he, who never prevented anyone from singing, providing they paid,[97] wasn't tyrant enough to prohibit others' speech, provided they lost.

So, everyone talked. At the first table, the king's younger brother, Philippe, Duc d'Anjou,* admired his handsome face with a mirror-topped box. His favorite, the Chevalier de Lorraine,* though leaning on the prince's chair, was actually listening with secret envy to the Comte de Guiche,* another of Philippe's favorites, who was recounting the juicy details of the various turns of fortune of the royal adventurer Charles II. He told the fabulous tale of his dangerous journey across Scotland, and his terror with the enemy pursuers hot on his trail. He told of nights spent in trees, and days spent in hunger and combat. Gradually, the fate of this unfortunate king had interested the listeners to the point where the game languished, even at the royal table, where the young king, distracted and staring sightlessly at his cards, absorbed without seeming to every detail of the picturesque odyssey described by the Comte de Guiche.

The Comtesse de Soissons interrupted the narrator, saying, "Confess, Count, that you're exaggerating."

"Madame, I repeat like a parrot the stories various Englishmen have told me. I will even admit, to my shame, that I recite an exact copy."

"Charles II would be dead if he'd gone through all that."

Louis XIV raised his proud and intelligent head. "Madame," he said, in a low voice that still harked back to the timid child, "Monsieur le Cardinal will tell you that in my minority, the affairs of France were often unsettled, and if I had been older and obliged to take my sword in my hand, I might have had to do so just to get our evening meal."

"Thank God," replied the cardinal, speaking for the first time, "that Your Majesty exaggerates, and your supper was always prepared perfectly along with that of your servants."

The king blushed.

"Oh!" interrupted Philippe, without ceasing to admire himself. "I remember one time at Melun when nobody had supper except the king. He had two-thirds of a heel of bread, leaving the final third to me."

The whole assembly, seeing Mazarin smile, began to laugh. One flatters kings with the reminder of past distress and the assurance of future fortune.

"The fact is, that the Crown of France has always stayed firmly on the heads of its kings," added Anne of Austria hastily, "and though England's has fallen from their king, every time some chance event shook ours, for there are realm-quakes as well as earthquakes, each time, I say, that rebellion threatened, a timely victory restored us to peace."

"With a few more jewels added to the crown," said Mazarin.

The Comte de Guiche was silent, and the king kept his expression neutral, while Mazarin exchanged a look with Anne of Austria that seemed to thank her for her intervention.

"No matter," said Philippe, smoothing his hair. "My cousin Charles may not be good-looking, but he's very brave and fights like a paladin, and if he continues to fight well, no doubt he'll end up winning a famous battle! Like Rocroi . . ."

"He has no troops," interrupted the Chevalier de Lorraine.

"The King of Holland, his ally, will give him some. I would certainly have given him some if I were the King of France."

Louis XIV turned bright red.

Mazarin affected to watch his game more closely than ever.

"At this moment," continued the Comte de Guiche, "the fate of that unhappy prince is being decided. If he's been deceived by Monck, he's lost. Prison, perhaps even death, will end what exile, war, and privations had begun."

Mazarin frowned.

"Is it certain," said Louis XIV, "that His Majesty Charles II has left The Hague?"

"Quite certain, Your Majesty," replied the young man. "My father[98] received a letter with all the details. It's even known that the king disembarked at Dover; fishermen saw him enter the port. The rest is still a mystery."

"I wish I knew the rest," said Philippe impetuously. "Do you know, Brother?"

Louis XIV blushed again. It was the third time in an hour. "Ask Monsieur le Cardinal," he replied, in a tone that made Mazarin, Queen Anne, and everyone else look at him.

"That means, my son," laughed Anne of Austria to Philippe, "that the king doesn't like us to discuss affairs of state outside the council."

Philippe received this gentle reprimand with good grace and bowed, smiling, first to his brother and then to his mother. But Mazarin saw from the corner of his eye that a group of young nobles was gathering in the corner of the chamber, where the Duc d'Anjou and his favorites the Comte de Guiche and Chevalier de Lorraine, thwarted at discussing affairs aloud, could continue in low voices to say what they wanted. He began to glare at them with suspicion and anxiety in hopes that Anne of Austria would say something to disrupt their conclave, when suddenly Bernouin came in. Sidling up to the bed, he whispered in his master's ear, "Monseigneur, an Envoy from His Majesty the King of England."

Mazarin couldn't conceal a slight reaction, which the king noticed, to the cardinal's annoyance. To avoid appearing indiscreet, not to mention irrelevant, Louis XIV rose, approached His Eminence, and wished him a good night.

The whole assembly rose, with a great noise of chairs pushed back and tables scraping the floor. "Let everyone go, little by little," said Mazarin quietly to Louis XIV, "and give me a few minutes' privacy. I need to address an affair about which I'd like to inform Your Majesty this evening."

"Including the queens?" asked Louis XIV.

"And the Duc d'Anjou," said His Eminence.

And he retired into his alcove, letting the bed curtains fall—but in such a way that he could still see the conspirators in the corner. "Monsieur le

Comte de Guiche!" he called in a quavering voice, while behind the curtain he donned the dressing gown that Bernouin had brought him.

"Here I am, Monseigneur," said the young man, approaching.

"You're a lucky fellow; take my cards and win me a little money from these gentlemen."

"Yes, Monseigneur." The young man sat at the table from which the king had withdrawn to speak with the queens. A serious game began between the count and several wealthy courtiers.

Meanwhile, Phillipe was chatting with the Chevalier de Lorraine, as the swish of the cardinal's silk robe came no more from behind the curtain of the alcove. His Eminence had followed Bernouin into the study adjacent to the bedchamber.

XL

An Affair of State

Upon entering his study, the cardinal found the Comte de La Fère waiting there, admiring a beautiful Raphael hung above a gilded dresser.

His Eminence came in slowly, light and silent as a shadow, hoping to surprise the count's unprepared expression; that was his custom, since he believed that he instantly could read from an envoy's face what direction a conversation would take. But this time, Mazarin's expectations were thwarted, for he could read absolutely nothing from Athos's expression, not even the respect he expected to see on all supplicants' faces.

Athos was dressed in black accented with simple silver embroidery. He wore the Saint-Esprit, the Garter, and the Golden Fleece, three orders of such significance that only a king, or a stage-actor, could wear them all. Mazarin delved for a long moment in his capacious memory trying to remember the name of this man of ice without success. Finally, he said, "I knew that a message would be coming from England."

And he sat down, dismissing Bernouin and Brienne, the latter of whom was preparing, in his capacity as secretary, to take notes.

"On the behalf of His Majesty the King of England, yes, Your Eminence," said Athos.

"You speak French very well, Monsieur, for an Englishman," said Mazarin graciously, still sneaking glances at the Saint-Esprit, the Garter, and the Fleece while trying to place the profile of the messenger.

"I am not English, I am French, Monsieur le Cardinal," replied Athos.

"It's peculiar for the King of England to choose Frenchmen as ambassadors, but I'll take it as a good omen. Your name, Monsieur, if you please?"

"Comte de La Fère," replied Athos, bowing a shade less deferentially than custom and the pride of the all-powerful minister required.

Mazarin twitched his shoulders as if to say, *I do not know that name.*
Athos showed no reaction.

"And you come, Monsieur," continued Mazarin, "to tell me . . ."

"I come on the behalf of His Majesty the King of England to announce
to the King of France . . ."

Mazarin frowned.

"To announce to the King of France," Athos continued impassively,
"the happy restoration of His Majesty Charles II to the throne of his
fathers."

The frosty tone didn't escape the notice of His Canny Eminence. Mazarin
was too familiar with the ways of men not to see, in the cold and almost
haughty politeness of Athos, a measure of hostility that didn't accord with
the ordinary hothouse warmth of discourse at Court.

"You have accreditation, no doubt?" asked Mazarin in a querulous tone.

"Yes . . . Monseigneur."

This word *Monseigneur* came painfully from Athos's lips, almost seeming
to scorch them as it passed.

"In that case, present it."

Athos drew a dispatch from an embroidered velour packet inside his
doublet. The cardinal extended his hand. "Your pardon, Monseigneur," said
Athos, "but the dispatch is for the king."

"Since you are French, Monsieur, you must know the powers of the prime
minister at the Court of France."

"There was a time," replied Athos, "when I took care to respect the
powers of prime ministers—but I since formed, some years ago, the resolution to deal with no one but the king."

"Then, Monsieur," said Mazarin, who was beginning to be annoyed,
"you will deal with neither minister nor king." And Mazarin rose. Athos
returned the dispatch to its packet, bowed gravely, and took a few steps
toward the door.

His sangfroid exasperated Mazarin. "What strange diplomacy is this!"
he cried. "Are we still in the days when Monsieur Cromwell was sending us

cutthroats as envoys?"⁹⁹ You lack only the round helmet on your head and
the Bible at your belt!"

"Monsieur," replied Athos drily, "unlike you I never had the experience
of treating with Monsieur Cromwell, and I only met the envoy you mention
sword in hand; I don't know how he dealt with prime ministers. As to the
King of England, Charles II, I know that when he writes to His Majesty King
Louis XIV, it isn't addressed to His Eminence Cardinal Mazarin; in that
distinction, I don't see any diplomacy."

"Ah ha!" cried Mazarin, lifting his emaciated head and striking his hand
to his brow. "I remember now!"

Athos looked at him, astonished.

"Yes, that's it!" said the cardinal, continuing to stare at his visitor. "Yes, of
course—I recognize you, Monsieur! Ah, *diavolo,* now I needn't wonder . . ."

"Indeed, I was surprised, given Your Eminence's excellent memory, that
Your Eminence didn't recognize me sooner," replied Athos with a smile.

"Always so stiff and recalcitrant, Monsieur . . . Monsieur . . . what did they
call you? Wait a moment . . . the name of a river—Potamos! No, no . . . the
name of an island. Naxos? No, *per Giove,* the name of a mountain—Athos!
That's it! How delightful to see you again, so long as we're not at Rueil,
where you and your damned accomplices made me pay a ransom. Ah, the
Fronde! The cursed Fronde! That stupid chaos! *Ah çà,* Monsieur, why has
your enmity outlasted mine? If anyone had anything to complain about
how that turned out, I don't think it was you, who got away with a whole
skin and the sash of the Saint-Esprit around your neck."

"Monsieur le Cardinal," replied Athos, "please be so kind as to leave me
out of such tale-spinning, I merely have a mission to fulfill. Will you provide
the means of facilitating this mission?"

"I am astonished," said Mazarin, delighted to have recovered his memory
and bristling with malice, "I say, I am astonished, Monsieur . . . Athos . . .
that a Frondeur like you accepted a mission to the great scoundrel Mazarin,
as they used to call me in those times." And Mazarin began to laugh in spite
of a painful cough, which turned the laughter into sobs.

"Monsieur le Cardinal, I have only accepted a mission to the King of France," retorted the count with some asperity, though given the situation he felt he could moderate his hauteur.

"And yet, Monsieur le Frondeur," said Mazarin gleefully, "as to the king, this affair of which you've taken charge . . ."

"With which I was charged, Monseigneur—I don't go running after affairs."

"As you like! I tell you this negotiation must pass through my hands, so let's not waste precious time. Tell me your conditions."

"I have had the honor to assure Your Eminence that only the letter from His Majesty King Charles II contains the essence of his wishes."

"Come! It's ridiculous to be so rigid, Monsieur Athos. One can see you picked up some of the Puritans' habits over there . . . I know your secret message better than you do, and it might be a mistake to have so little regard for a suffering old man who has worked as hard in his life, and campaigned as bravely for his ideas, as you have for yours. So, you don't want to say anything to me? Fine. You don't want my hands to touch your letter? Come with me to my little alcove, where you may speak to the king, and in front of the king. Now, one last question: who gave you the Fleece? I remember how you got the Garter, but as to the Fleece, I have no idea . . ."

"Recently, Monseigneur, Spain, upon the occasion of the marriage of His Majesty Louis XIV, sent to Charles II a blank brevet for the Golden Fleece; Charles II immediately presented it to me, filling in the blank with my name."

Mazarin rose, and, leaning on Bernouin's arm, returned to his alcove, just at the moment when the audiencer in the grand chamber announced, "Monsieur le Prince!"

The Prince de Condé, First Prince of the Blood, the victor of Rocroi, Lens, and Nördlingen, was in fact entering Monseigneur de Mazarin's chambers, followed by his gentlemen, and he'd already saluted the king when the prime minister lifted his curtain.

Athos had time to catch a glimpse of Raoul shaking hands with the Comte de Guiche and exchanged a smile for his respectful bow. He also had time to see the cardinal's radiant face when Mazarin saw before him on the table the enormous pile of gold coins the Comte de Guiche had won by a lucky run with the cards His Eminence had confided to him. Forgetting the ambassador, his embassy, and the prince, for a moment the cardinal's only thoughts were for the gold. "What!" cried the old man. "All this . . . my winnings?"

"Something around fifty thousand crowns, yes, Monseigneur," replied the Comte de Guiche, rising. "Should I allow Your Eminence to resume or shall I continue?"

"Resume? Resume? You're mad! We'd lose all you gained, *peste!*"

"Monseigneur," said the Prince de Condé, bowing.

"Good evening, Monsieur le Prince," said the minister lightly. "It's very good of you to visit a sick friend."

"A friend . . . !" murmured the Comte de La Fère as he considered, stupefied, that word as somehow applied to Mazarin and Condé.

Mazarin guessed the thoughts of the old Frondeur, for he smiled at him in triumph, and immediately said to the king, "Sire, I have the honor to present to Your Majesty Monsieur le Comte de La Fère, ambassador of His Britannic Majesty. An affair of State, Messieurs!" he added, dismissing with a wave of his hand all those who thronged the chamber, and who, with the Prince de Condé at their head, disappeared at a mere gesture from Mazarin.

Raoul, after a final glance at the Comte de La Fère, followed Monsieur de Condé.

Philippe d'Anjou and the queen appeared to be asking each other if they should leave. "It's a family affair," Mazarin said quickly, keeping them in their seats. "Monsieur, here, brings the king a letter from Charles II, now completely restored to the throne, demanding an alliance between Monsieur, the king's brother, and Mademoiselle Henrietta, grand-daughter of Henri IV . . . You might want to give the king your letter of accreditation, Monsieur le Comte."

Athos paused for a moment, stunned. How could the minister know the contents of a letter that had never left his side for a moment? However, always master of himself, he presented his dispatch to the young King Louis XIV, who took it and blushed. A solemn silence reigned throughout the cardinal's chamber while the king read the letter, disturbed only by the clink of gold as Mazarin, with his dry, yellow hands, piled his coins in a coffer.

XLI

The Report

The cardinal's malice hadn't left much for the king to say to the ambassador, but that word *restoration* had struck him. Addressing the count, upon whom he'd had his eyes fixed since he'd entered, he said, "Monsieur, please give us some details of the state of affairs in England. You've just come from that country, you are French, and the orders that decorate your person announce a man of merit who is also a man of quality."

"Monsieur," said the cardinal, turning toward the queen mother, "is the Comte de La Fère, an old servant of Your Majesty."

Anne of Austria was as forgetful as any queen whose life had been a mixture of days both stormy and serene. She glanced at Mazarin, whose wicked smile promised some nasty trick, then she sought, by a look, her own explanation from Athos.

"Monsieur," continued the cardinal, "was one of Tréville's musketeers in the service of the old king. Monsieur is quite familiar with England, where he's traveled for various reasons at various times. He rightly considers himself a subject of the highest merit."

These words evoked all the memories that Anne of Austria most hesitated to reawaken. *England* meant her hatred for Richelieu and her love for Buckingham; *Tréville's musketeers* brought back the odyssey whose terrors and triumphs had agitated a young woman's heart and nearly cast her from a young queen's throne. These words had power, for they rendered mute and attentive all the royal persons who, with various reactions, began to think about the events of those mysterious years that the young hadn't seen and that the old had thought forever buried.

"Speak, Monsieur," said Louis XIV, the first to emerge from wonder, suspicion, and memories.

"Yes, speak," added Mazarin, to whom the malicious prod he'd just given Anne of Austria had restored all his energy and glee.

"Sire," said the count, "a sort of miracle has utterly changed the destiny of King Charles II. Where men could not succeed, God resolved and accomplished."

Mazarin coughed and fidgeted in his bed.

"King Charles II," continued Athos, "left The Hague not as a fugitive nor a victim, but as an absolute king, who, after a voyage away from his kingdom, returns amid universal benedictions."

"A great miracle indeed," said Mazarin, "for if what we heard was true, King Charles II, who returned amid benedictions, went away chased by musket balls."

The king remained impassive. Philippe, younger and more frivolous, couldn't repress a smile that applauded Mazarin for his joke. The king said, "In fact, it seems there was a miracle; but God, though He does much for kings, Monsieur le Comte, nonetheless uses the hands of men to accomplish His plans. To what men does Charles II principally owe his restoration?"

"But," interrupted the cardinal, without concern for the king's pride or feelings, "doesn't Your Majesty know that credit belongs to Monsieur Monck?"

"I know that, of course," replied Louis XIV resolutely, "however, I'm asking Monsieur l'Ambassadeur the causes of this change in Monsieur Monck."

"And Your Majesty's question is to the point," replied Athos, "for, without the miracle that I had the honor to mention, Monsieur Monck would probably have remained an inveterate enemy of King Charles II. God arranged for a strange, bold, and ingenious idea to fall into the mind of a certain man, while a devoted and determined idea entered the mind of another. The combination of these two ideas brought about the change in Monsieur Monck's position, so that from a bitter enemy he became a friend of the fallen king."

"That's just the kind of detail I was asking for," said the king. "What kind of people are these two men you mentioned?"

"Two Frenchmen, Sire."

"In truth, that makes me happy."

"And the two ideas?" interrupted Mazarin. "I'm more curious about ideas than about men."

"Yes," murmured the king.

"The second idea, the devoted, determined, and least important, Sire, was to go dig up a million in gold buried by King Charles I at Newcastle and to use this gold to buy Monck's support."

"Oh ho!" said Mazarin, energized by the word *million*. "But wasn't Newcastle occupied by this selfsame Monck?"

"Yes, Monsieur le Cardinal, which is why the idea had to be determined as well as devoted. It was necessary, if Monsieur Monck refused the negotiator's offers, to restore ownership of this million to King Charles II despite the disloyalty, or rather misplaced loyalty of General Monck. Despite some difficulties, the negotiator was able to work around the general's loyalties and remove the gold."

"It seems to me," said the timid and hopeful king, "that Charles II must not have been aware of this million during his visit to Blois and Paris."

"It seems to me," added the cardinal maliciously, "that His Majesty the King of England was quite aware of the existence of this million but preferred two million to one."

"Sire," Athos replied firmly, "when His Majesty King Charles II was in France, he was so poor he was unable to ride by post, and so hopeless that he several times contemplated death. He was entirely ignorant of the Newcastle million, and if a gentleman, one of Your Majesty's subjects and the appointed ward of the legacy, hadn't revealed the secret to Charles II, that prince would still languish in cruel oblivion."

"Let's return to the strange, bold, and ingenious idea," interrupted Mazarin, who intuitively saw where this was going. "What was that idea about?"

"This: that since Monsieur Monck formed the sole obstacle to the restoration of His Majesty the fallen king, a Frenchman resolved to remove this obstacle."

"Oh ho! Then this Frenchman was a scoundrel," said Mazarin, "and the idea is not so ingenious as to prevent its author from being sent to the Place de Grève[100] by an act of our parliament."

"Your Eminence is mistaken," said Athos drily, "for I didn't say that the Frenchman in question had resolved to assassinate Monck, but to remove him. For French gentlemen, the words of the French language have a precise meaning. Besides, it was an action of warfare, and when kings are served against their enemies, we are not judged by parliament, only by God. So, this French gentleman had the idea to seize the person of Monsieur Monck, and he executed his plan."

The king was thrilled by this exciting story. His Majesty's younger brother pounded the table with this fist, crying, "Ah! How lovely!"

"He carried Monck off?" said the king. "But Monck was in his camp . . ."

"And the gentleman was alone, Sire."

"It's wonderful!" said Philippe.

"Wonderful, indeed!" cried the king.

"Fine! Let the two young lions roar," murmured the cardinal. Then, with an air of contempt he didn't bother to hide, he said, "I was unaware of these details. Can you guarantee their authenticity, Monsieur?"

"All the more easily, Monsieur le Cardinal, since I witnessed them myself."

"You?"

"Yes, Monseigneur."

The king had almost involuntarily drawn nearer to the count, while the Duc d'Anjou pressed Athos on the other side. "After that, Monsieur?" they shouted at the same time.

"Sire, Monsieur Monck, being taken by the Frenchman, was brought to King Charles II in Holland. The king restored Monck's liberty, and the general, in gratitude, gave Charles II in return the throne of England, for which so many valiant people had fought without success."

Philippe clapped enthusiastically. Louis XIV, more thoughtful, turned to the Comte de La Fère and said, "Is it true, all these details?"

"Absolutely true, Sire."

"One of my gentlemen knew the secret of the million and safeguarded it?"

"Yes, Sire."

"The name of this gentleman?"

"It was your humble servant," said Athos simply.

The murmur of admiration that followed swelled Athos's heart. He had reason to be proud, at least. Even Mazarin had raised his arms—and rolled his eyes—toward heaven.

"Monsieur," said the king, "somehow, I will find a way to reward you." Athos began to shake his head. "Oh, not for your honesty! To be paid for that would humiliate you. But I owe you a reward for assisting in the restoration of my brother Charles II."

"Certainly," said Mazarin.

"This triumph in a good cause fills the whole House of France with joy," said Anne of Austria.

"To continue," said Louis XIV, "is it also true that a lone man penetrated the defenses of Monck's camp to carry him off?"

"The man was aided by ten auxiliaries of inferior rank."

"And nothing more?"

"Nothing more."

"Do you know his name?"

"Monsieur d'Artagnan, the former Lieutenant of Your Majesty's Musketeers."

Anne of Austria flushed, Mazarin went yellow with shame, while Louis XIV gasped and broke into a sudden cold sweat. "What men!" he murmured. And, involuntarily, he shot at Mazarin such a glare that it would have terrified him if the minister hadn't had his face turned into his pillow.

"Monsieur," cried the young Duc d'Anjou, laying his fine, white ladylike hand on Athos's arm, "tell that brave man, I beg, that Monsieur, the king's brother, will drink his health tomorrow before a hundred of the finest gentlemen of France!" And having delivered this speech, the young man, noticing that in his enthusiasm he'd disarranged one of his lace cuffs, began to restore it with great care.

"Let us talk business, Sire," interrupted Mazarin, who had neither enthusiasm nor lace cuffs.

"Indeed, Monsieur," replied Louis XIV, and turning to the count, he added, "Proceed with your presentation, Monsieur le Comte."

Athos then commenced to solemnly offer the hand of Princess Henrietta Stuart to that of the young prince, the king's brother. The conference lasted an hour, after which the doors of the chamber were opened to the courtiers, who resumed their places as if nothing had disrupted their evening schedules.

Athos then made his way to Raoul, and father and son shook hands and embraced.

XLII

In Which Monsieur de Mazarin
Becomes Extravagant

While Mazarin was trying to recover from the shock of Athos's revelations, Athos and Raoul exchanged a few words in a corner of the chamber. "Are you back in Paris, then, Raoul?" said the count.

"Yes, Monsieur, since Monsieur le Prince has returned."

"I can't talk with you here, where we're being observed," said Athos, "but I'm going back to my house shortly and will wait to see you there as soon as your service allows." Raoul bowed.

The prince came straight to them. Condé had that penetrating and profound look that distinguishes the more noble species of birds of prey, with several traits that emphasized the resemblance. It's well known that the heir of the illustrious princes of the House of Condé had a low and retreating forehead, beneath which jutted out a long, sharp, aquiline nose, which to the Court's mockers, people pitiless even toward the brilliant, looked more like an eagle's beak than a human nose. In the victor of Rocroi, this penetrating raptor's gaze and imperious expression intimidated those with whom he spoke more than majesty or ordinary good looks would have done. Besides, the flame of ire rose so rapidly to those prominent eyes that in Monsieur le Prince all animation resembled anger. Thanks to this quality, everyone at Court respected the prince, and some, knowing him only by appearance, even feared him.

Now, Louis de Condé advanced on the Comte de La Fère and Raoul with the decided intention of being greeted by one and introduced to the other. No one bowed with more reserved grace than the Comte de La Fère, though he disdained to add to paying his respects all the nuances and flourishes a courtier employs to flatter and to please. Athos knew his personal worth and saluted the prince like a man, with a care and precision that somehow corrected any lack that might offend another's pride.

The prince prepared to speak to Raoul, but Athos forestalled him. "If the Vicomte de Bragelonne wasn't one of the humblest servants of Your Highness, I'd beg to have him pronounce my name before you . . . my Prince."

"I believe I have the honor to speak to Monsieur le Comte de La Fère," Condé immediately said.

"My guardian," added Raoul, blushing.

"One of the most honorable men of the realm," continued the prince, "one of the first gentlemen of France, and one of whom I've heard so much, I've often desired to count him among my friends."

"An honor of which I would be worthy, Monseigneur," replied Athos, "only by my respect and admiration for Your Highness."

"Monsieur de Bragelonne is a fine officer," said the prince, "and it's because, as we see, he's been to a good school. Ah, Monsieur le Comte! In your day, the generals had soldiers . . ."

"That's true, Monseigneur; but today, the soldiers have generals."

This compliment, stated without the accent of flattery, gave a thrill of pleasure to a man whom all Europe regarded as a war hero and who ought to have been sated with praise.

"It's unfortunate for me that you're retired from the service, Monsieur le Comte," replied the prince, "for soon enough the king must pursue a war with Holland or with England, and there will be plenty of opportunities for a man like you who knows England as well as France."

"I think I can tell you, Monseigneur, that I was wise to retire from the service," said Athos with a smile. "France and England will henceforth live as sisters, if I'm to believe my premonitions."

"Your premonitions?"

"Come, Monseigneur, and listen to what's being said at Monsieur le Cardinal's table."

"Among the players?"

"Among the players, quite so, Monseigneur."

In fact, the cardinal had raised himself on one elbow and beckoned to the young brother of the king, who approached him. "Monseigneur," said the cardinal, "I beg you, gather up all these gold crowns."

And he designated the enormous pile of shining yellow coins that the Comte de Guiche had gradually built before him, thanks to a run of luck.

"For me?" cried the Duc d'Anjou.

"These fifty thousand crowns, yes, Monseigneur—they're for you."

"You're giving them to me?"

"That's my intention, Monseigneur," replied the cardinal, voice fading, as if the effort of giving money away had drained all his physical and emotional resources.

"Oh, *mon Dieu!*" murmured Philippe, overwhelmed with joy. "What a happy day!" He began raking coins into his pockets, but when they were filled, more than a third of the gold remained on the table.

"Come here, Chevalier," said Philippe to his favorite, the Chevalier de Lorraine. The favorite came running. "Pocket the rest of this," said the young prince.

This singular scene was regarded by no one nearby as anything more than a touching family moment. The cardinal often assumed the air of a father with the two Sons of France, and the young princes had grown up under his wing, so no one ascribed to pride or presumption, as we would today, this liberality of the prime minister. The courtiers contented themselves with envying the prince, and the king turned his head away.

"I've never had so much money," said the young prince happily, crossing the chamber with his favorite to head for his carriage. "No, never! How heavy it is. It must be a hundred and fifty thousand livres!"

"But why would the cardinal give him so much money?" Monsieur le Prince asked the Comte de La Fère in a whisper. "Is he so very sick, our dear cardinal?"

"Yes, Monseigneur, no doubt he's very ill, as Your Highness can see."

"Ill, yes, but . . . surely not dying? A hundred fifty thousand livres! Oh, that's beyond belief. Come, Count, why is this? Give me a reason."

"Patience a moment, if you will, Monseigneur—here comes the Duc d'Anjou chatting with the Chevalier de Lorraine. I wouldn't be surprised if they spared me the trouble of being indiscreet. Listen to them."

In fact, the chevalier was saying to the prince in a low voice, "Monseigneur, it isn't natural for Monsieur de Mazarin to give money away—careful, you're dropping some coins. Why is the cardinal so generous with you?"

"As I said," Athos murmured in the ear of Monsieur le Prince, "here may be the answer to your question."

"Why is it, Monseigneur?" repeated the chevalier impatiently, while weighing his pockets to calculate the amount that had fallen indirectly to him.

"My dear Chevalier, it's a wedding gift."

"What do you mean, a wedding gift?"

"Why, yes—I'm going to be married!" replied the Duc d'Anjou, without noticing that he was at that moment passing before Monsieur le Prince and Athos, who both bowed deeply.

The chevalier gave Anjou a glare so strange and spiteful that the Comte de La Fère shivered. "You! You, married!" the chevalier repeated. "Oh, that's impossible. How could you be so foolish?"

"Fah, it's not my idea; they're making me do it," replied the Duc d'Anjou. "But come on—we've got money to spend."

Whereupon he disappeared with his companion, laughing and chatting, while all heads bowed at their passage.

Then Monsieur le Prince whispered to Athos, "So, that's the secret?"

"It didn't come from me, Monseigneur."

"He'll marry the sister of Charles II?"

"I think so, yes."

The prince thought for a moment, and then his eye flashed. "In that case," he said slowly, as if talking to himself, "our swords will go back on the wall . . . for a long time!" And he sighed.

All that this sigh contained of ambitions thwarted, of illusions crushed and hopes disappointed, only Athos guessed, for only he had heard the sigh.

The prince immediately took his leave, after which the king departed. Athos, by a sign to Bragelonne, renewed the invitation he'd made at the beginning of the episode.

Little by little the chamber emptied out until only Mazarin remained, alone with the suffering he no longer felt he had to conceal. "Bernouin! Bernouin!" he called in a broken voice.

"What does Monseigneur desire?"

"Guénaud* . . . call for Guénaud," said His Eminence. "It seems to me I'm dying."

Bernouin, alarmed, ran to the study to give an order, and the messenger sent to find the doctor rode so swiftly, he passed the king's carriage in Rue Saint-Honoré.

XLIII

Guénaud

The cardinal's summons was urgent, and Guénaud was quick to obey it. He found his patient sprawled on the bed, his legs swollen and livid and his stomach collapsed. Mazarin had undergone a severe attack of gout. He suffered cruelly and with the impatience of a man who wasn't used to not getting what he wished. At the arrival of Guénaud, he said, "Ah! Now I'm saved!"

Guénaud was a very learned and cautious man who had earned a reputation even before Boileau's satires[101] about him. When he was faced by sickness, even in the person of a king, he treated the patient as a Turk treats a Moor.[102] He didn't reply to Mazarin as the minister expected, with, "The doctor is here now, sickness begone!" On the contrary, after examining the patient he said gravely, "Uh-oh."

"Eh, Guénaud! What kind of tone is that?"

"The tone I take when I see a condition like yours, Monseigneur, which is dangerous."

"The gout? Yes, the gout is awful."

"There are . . . complications, Monseigneur."

Mazarin raised himself on one elbow and questioned him with a look and a gesture. "What are you telling me? Am I more ill than I thought I was?"

"Monseigneur," said Guénaud, sitting down by the bed, "Your Eminence has worked hard in this life, and suffered a great deal."

"But it seems to me I'm not that old. The late Monsieur de Richelieu was only seventeen months younger than I am when he died, and he had a fatal illness. Compared to him, I'm youthful, Guénaud; I'm barely fifty-two."[103]

"Oh, Monseigneur, you're older than that. How long did the Fronde last?"

"Why do you ask that, Guénaud?"

"To make a medical calculation, Monseigneur."

"Well, around ten years, more or less."

"Very well. We must count each year of the Fronde as two years, which makes twenty, and fifty-two plus twenty extra years makes seventy-two. You're really seventy-two years old, Monseigneur, an advanced age." As he said this, he felt the patient's pulse, which conveyed such a negative prognosis that the doctor immediately continued, over the objections of his patient, "Actually, let's call each year of the Fronde three, which puts you at age eighty-two."

Mazarin became deadly pale, and in a thin voice he said, "Are you speaking seriously, Guénaud?"

"Alas! Yes, Monseigneur."

"You took this roundabout way, then, to inform me that I'm extremely ill?"

"*Ma foi,* yes, Monseigneur, and with a man of wits and courage like Your Eminence, a roundabout way still leads to the truth."

The cardinal gasped, and had such trouble catching his breath that it inspired pity even in this pitiless doctor.

"There is illness, and illness," Mazarin replied. "Some may be recovered from."

"That's true, Monseigneur."

"Isn't it?" cried Mazarin, almost with joy. "For in the end, don't we have power and force of will? And genius, *your* genius, Guénaud! What good are science and art if a patient who has access to all of it can't be saved from danger?"

Guénaud started to open his mouth, but Mazarin continued, "Remember that I'm the most faithful of your patients, that I obey you blindly, and consequently . . ."

"I know all that," said Guénaud.

"Then, will I get better?"

"Monseigneur, there is no force of will, no power, no genius, no science that can resist a disease that doubtless comes from God, which he released into the world at Creation with the final power to bring death to men. When a disease is mortal, it kills, and then nothing . . ."

"My disease . . . is mortal?" asked Mazarin.

"Yes, Monseigneur."

His Eminence went limp for a moment, like a man who's been crushed by a falling column. But there was a well-tempered soul, or rather an iron-hard mind, in Monsieur de Mazarin. "Guénaud," he said, reviving a little, "you will allow me to take other opinions. I shall gather all the most learned men of Europe and consult them; I'm willing to try virtually any remedy."

"Surely Monseigneur doesn't suppose that I would presume to make a lone decision on an existence as precious as his. I have already assembled the finest doctors of France and all Europe—there were twelve of them."

"And they said . . . ?"

"They said that Your Eminence has a fatal illness; I have their signed consultations here in my portfolio. If Your Eminence wishes to see the report, he will see the names of all the incurable diseases we discovered. First of all, there is . . ."

"No! No!" cried Mazarin, pushing away the portfolio. "No, Guénaud, I surrender! I surrender!"

This outburst was followed by a profound silence, during which the cardinal regained his senses and recouped his strength. "There's another option," murmured Mazarin. "There are still the charlatans and the mountebanks. In my country, those whom the doctors give up for lost turn to a quack, who out of a hundred might kill ten outright, but still save ninety."

"Over the last month, did Your Eminence not notice that I changed his treatment ten times over?"

"Yes . . . and so?"

"And so, I spent fifty thousand livres to buy—and try—all the secrets of those quacks. The list is exhausted, and so is my purse. You are not healed, and without my care you would be dead."

"It's the end," murmured the cardinal, "the end." He looked darkly around at his accumulated wealth. "I'm going to have to leave it all behind," he sighed. "I'm dead, Guénaud! Dead!"

"Oh, not quite yet, Monseigneur," said the doctor.

Mazarin seized his hand. "How long?" he asked, fixing wide, staring eyes on the doctor's face.

"Monseigneur, we never answer that question."

"To ordinary men, maybe, but to me . . . to me, for whom every minute is a treasure—tell me, Guénaud, tell me!"

"No, no, Monseigneur."

"Answer me, I tell you! Oh, give me another month, and for each of those thirty days I'll pay you a hundred thousand livres."

"Monseigneur," replied Guénaud in a firm voice, "it's God who gives you these days of grace and not I. And God gives to you two more weeks!"

The cardinal sighed deeply and fell back on his pillow, murmuring, "Thank you, Guénaud. Thank you."

The doctor got up to leave, but the moribund man half rose and said, "Silence!" with eyes of flame. And he repeated, "Silence!"

"Monseigneur, I've known this secret for two months, and as you see, I've kept it well."

"Go, then, Guénaud; I'll see to the making of your fortune. Go, but tell Brienne to send me a certain clerk, whose name is Monsieur Colbert."

XLIV

Colbert

Colbert wasn't far away. He'd spent the entire evening in a nearby corridor, chatting with Bernouin and Brienne, and commenting, with the insight of those who haunt the Court, on the news that rippled through the courtiers. And this seems the time to sketch, in a few words, a portrait of one of the most interesting men of his century, and to delineate it as truthfully as contemporary painters might have done. Colbert is a man to whom both the historian and the philosopher have an equal right.

He was thirteen years older than Louis XIV,[104] his future master. Of moderate size, more slender than stout, he had sunken eyes, a downward gaze, and hair black and thick except where it was thinning, which made him take the skullcap early. His expression was severe, even stony, a stiffness that toward his inferiors was pride, and toward his superiors an affectation of worthy virtue. In short, he wore a dour visage at all times, even when looking at himself in a mirror. So much for his exterior.

Professionally, he was admired for his skill and talent with accounts and ledgers, and his ingenuity at harvesting revenue from otherwise barren budgets. It was Colbert who'd come up with the idea of requiring the governors of border posts to feed their garrisons by dunning local sources. That kind of talent had given Cardinal Mazarin the idea of replacing his intendant Joubert, who'd recently died, with Monsieur Colbert, who shaved percentages even more closely.

Colbert had gradually worked his way into the Court despite the liability of low birth, for he was the son of a wine-seller, like his father before him, who had also sold cloth and silk remnants. Colbert, destined by his family for commerce, had first worked for a merchant of Lyons, whom he'd left to come to Paris to study bookkeeping with an auditor at the Châtelet[105] named

Biterne. There he'd learned the art of maintaining financial accounts, and the even more useful art of fudging them.

His severity of manner became his greatest asset, for like Dame Fortune, or like those ladies of antiquity who cared only for their fancies, he seemed principled while actually allowing nothing to stand between him and his goal.

In 1648 Colbert's cousin, the Seigneur de Saint-Pouange, found him a position in the office of Michel Le Tellier, the Secretary of State,[106] who favored him one day by assigning him to bear a message to Cardinal Mazarin. At that time His Eminence was in good health, the stressful years of the Fronde not yet having counted double or triple against his age. He was at Sedan, on internal exile due to a Court intrigue in which Anne of Austria seemed inclined to desert him.

Le Tellier held the threads to this intrigue. He had gotten hold of a letter from Anne of Austria as valuable to him as it was compromising to Mazarin. Using it, he undertook to play that double role he played so often, taking advantage of a conflict by either stoking the adversaries' differences, or by reconciling them. Le Tellier wanted to send Queen Anne's letter to Mazarin, so he would see how far he was exposed and be grateful for the service rendered. But then he wanted it back. To send the letter was easy, but to recover it after lending it was far more difficult.

Le Tellier looked around the office, and seeing the dark and scrawny clerk scribbling away, brows furrowed, he selected him over the most polished gendarme for the task. Colbert was assigned to go to Sedan with the order to share the letter with Mazarin and then bring it back to Le Tellier. He listened to his instructions with scrupulous attention, had them repeated twice, pointedly asked whether recovering the letter was as necessary as sharing it, and was told by Le Tellier, "Even more necessary."

Then he left, traveling like a courier without a care for his health or person. When he reached Mazarin, first he handed to him a note from Le Tellier announcing to the cardinal the sending of the precious letter, and then the letter itself. Mazarin blushed deeply while reading Anne of Austria's letter, gave Colbert a gracious smile, and dismissed him.

"When will I have your response, Monseigneur?" asked the courier humbly.

"Tomorrow."

"Tomorrow morning?"

"Yes, Monsieur."

The clerk made his most deferential bow and turned on his heel. The next morning, he was back again at seven o'clock. Mazarin made him wait until ten. Colbert bided his time patiently in the antechamber, and when his turn came, he went in.

Mazarin handed him a sealed packet, on the envelope of which was written, "To Monsieur Michel Le Tellier, Etc."

Colbert examined this packet with the closest attention, while the cardinal gave him a charming smile and pushed him toward the door. "And the letter from the queen mother, Monseigneur?" asked Colbert.

"It's in the packet with the rest," said Mazarin.

"Ah! Very good," replied Colbert. And, placing his hat between his knees, he began tearing open the packet.

Mazarin uttered a cry. "What are you doing?" he growled.

"Opening the packet, Monseigneur."

"Do you distrust me, you pen pusher? I've never seen such impertinence!"

"Oh, Monseigneur, please don't be angry with me! It's certainly not the word of Your Eminence I distrust, God forbid."

"What, then?"

"It's the thoroughness of your secretaries, Monseigneur. What is a letter? A mere scrap. And can't a scrap be overlooked? And look, Monseigneur, see if I was wrong! Your clerks have overlooked the scrap, for the letter isn't in the packet."

"You're as insolent as you are blind!" cried Mazarin, irritated. "Withdraw and await my summons." And saying these words, he made an Italian gesture of distraction with one hand and whisked the packet away from Colbert with the other, and then went back into his study.

But his anger was soon replaced by thoughtfulness. Mazarin, upon opening the door of his study each morning, found Colbert waiting on a bench, and this dowdy figure humbly but persistently asked for the queen mother's letter.

Eventually, Mazarin ran out of excuses and had to return it. He accompanied this restitution with a severe reprimand, during which Colbert was content to examine, feel, and even smell the paper of the letter, scrutinizing the writing and signature as if he were dealing with the greatest forger in the realm. Mazarin added further rude remarks while Colbert, impassive, having proven to himself the authenticity of the letter, departed as if he were deaf.

It was this conduct that won him the post of the late Joubert, for Mazarin, instead of holding a grudge, admired his tenacity and desired to have it in his own service.

We see from this single story the entire character of Colbert. The events that followed gradually enabled his wit and talent to come to full flower. Colbert wasn't slow to insinuate himself into the cardinal's good graces, and before long he was indispensable. This clerk knew the details of all the cardinal's accounts before His Eminence ever spoke of them. The secrets shared between them were a powerful bond, which is why, when he appeared on the verge of passing into the next world, Mazarin wanted solid advice on how to dispose of the wealth he would leave, so unwillingly, behind him. Thus, after Guénaud's visit the cardinal summoned Colbert, had him sit beside him, and said to him, "Let's have a talk, Monsieur Colbert, and a serious one, because I'm sick and may be about to die."

"Man is mortal," replied Colbert.

"I have never forgotten that, Monsieur Colbert, and have tried to prepare for it. You know that I've amassed a bit of a fortune . . ."

"I know, Monseigneur."

"And how much do you estimate that little fortune comes to, Monsieur Colbert?"

"To forty million five hundred sixty thousand two hundred livres, nine sous, and eight deniers," replied Colbert.

The cardinal sighed deeply and regarded Colbert with admiration, then allowed himself a smile.

"*Known* money," added Colbert in response to this smile.

The cardinal sat bolt upright. "What do you mean by that?" he said.

"I mean," said Colbert, "that besides these forty million five hundred sixty thousand two hundred livres, nine sous, and eight deniers there are thirteen other millions no one knows of."

"*Ouf!*" sighed Mazarin. "What a man this is!"

At that moment Bernouin's head appeared in the doorway. "What is it," asked Mazarin, "and why are you disturbing me?"

"The Theatine father[107] you sent for, Your Eminence's confessor, has arrived, and can't come back again to Monseigneur's until after tomorrow."

Mazarin looked at Colbert, who at once picked up his hat and said, "I'll return another time, Monseigneur."

Mazarin hesitated. "No, no," he said, "I have as much business with you as with him. Besides, you are my temporal confessor, and what I say to one can be heard by the other. Stay, Colbert."

"But, Monseigneur, if there is no privacy of penance, will the confessor agree to it?"

"Don't worry yourself about that. Go back into the alcove."

"I can wait outside, Monseigneur."

"No, no—better that you hear the confession of a man of means."

Colbert bowed and went into the alcove.

"Admit the Theatine father," said Mazarin, closing the curtains.

XLV

Confession of a
Man of Means

The Theatine entered deliberately, showing no astonishment at the noise and disturbance in the household raised by concern for the cardinal's health. "Come, Most Reverend," said Mazarin after a final glance at the curtained alcove. "Come and comfort me."

"Such is my duty, Monseigneur," replied the Theatine.

"Start by sitting comfortably, for I'll begin with a general confession; you'll quickly grant me a good absolution, and I'll feel calm again."

"Monseigneur," said the reverend, "surely you aren't so ill that a general confession is urgent. And it will be very tiring, so take care!"

"Do you suppose it would take long, Reverend?"

"How could it be otherwise when one has lived as complete a life as Your Eminence?"

"Ah, that's true! Yes, the story might be a long one."

"The mercy of God is great," intoned the Theatine.

"Here," said Mazarin, "I'm beginning to alarm myself by thinking of everything I've allowed to pass of which the Lord would disapprove."

"Of course; who would not?" said the Theatine naïvely, turning his narrow face and mole-like features from the light. "Sinners are like that: forgetful before, then scrupulous when it's too late."

"Sinners?" replied Mazarin. "Do you use the term ironically, or to reproach me with the background I've left behind? For as the son of a fisherman,[108] I was certainly a . . . seiner."

"Hmph!" said the Theatine.

"Family pride was my first sin, Reverend, because I allowed it to be said that I'd descended from ancient Consuls of Rome: Geganius Macerinus I,

Macerinus II, and Proculus Macerinus III, all found in the Chronicle of Haolander.[109] For *Macerinus* is temptingly close to *Mazarin*, though Macerinus, as a diminutive, means scrawny. Mazarini is also close to the augmentative, *macer*, which means as thin as Lazarus. Look!" And he showed his arms and legs, emaciated by fever.

"That you are born of a family of fishermen is no shame to you," replied the Theatine, "for indeed, Saint Peter was a fisherman, and you are a Prince of the Church, Monseigneur, as he was its supreme leader. Let's move on, if you please."

"However, I did threaten to put in the Bastille a certain Bounet, a priest of Avignon who wanted to publish a genealogy of the House of Mazarin that was entirely too exaggerated."

"To be believed, you mean?" replied the Theatine.

"Hmph! But if I'd acted on that threat, Reverend, it would have been the vice of pride—another sin."

"His was an abuse of wit, but no one reproaches a person for that sort of crime. Let's move on."

"Mine was an abuse of pride, and I think, Reverend, I should categorize my errors by the mortal sins."

"I like proper categorization."

"I do it by habit. You should know, then, that in 1630—alas! Thirty-one years ago!"

"You were twenty-nine years old, Monseigneur."

"A hot-headed age. I fancied myself a soldier, and at Casale[110] I joined the charge against the arquebusiers, just to show I could ride as well as any cavalier. It's true that I then negotiated the peace between the Spanish and French, which somewhat redeems my sin."

"I don't see the slightest sin in displaying skill at riding," said the Theatine. "It's in perfect taste and does honor to our robes. In my capacity as a Christian, I approve of your halting bloodshed, and as a priest, I'm proud of the bravery of a colleague."

Mazarin bowed his head humbly. "Yes," he said, "but the results!"

"What results?"

"This damned sin of pride gets into everything! Since I'd thrown myself into battle between two armies, smelled the powder and charged lines of soldiers, I began to regard generals with disdain."

"Ah!"

"That's the result: since then, I haven't been able to stand them."

"Well, the fact is," said the Theatine, "that you haven't had many good generals."

"Oh, I certainly had Monsieur le Prince!" cried Mazarin. "And haven't I made him pay?"

"No point in feeling sorry for him, he's had plenty of glory and gain."

"True for Monsieur le Prince, but what of Monsieur de Beaufort, whom I treated so harshly in the dungeons of Vincennes?"[111]

"Yes, but he was a rebel, and the security of the State required you to make that sacrifice. Let's move on."

"I think that's it for pride. There's another category of sin that I hesitate to name . . ."

"Tell me of it, and I'll figure out its category."

"It's a truly great sin, Reverend."

"We'll see, Monseigneur."

"You must have heard tell of . . . certain relations I've had with Her Majesty the queen mother . . . relations that the malicious . . ."

"The malicious, Monseigneur, are fools. Wasn't it necessary, for the good of the State and the best interests of the young king, that you should act as a close adviser to the queen? Move on, move on."

"Believe me, that lifts a terrible burden from me," said Mazarin.

"Trivia and trifles! Find us something serious."

"I've been full of ambition, Reverend . . ."

"That's the price of doing great things, Monseigneur."

"But to covet the tiara of the pope . . ."

"The pope is first among Christians. Why shouldn't you desire that?"

"It's been said in print that, in order to get it, I sold Cambrai to the Spanish."

"You've published pamphlets yourself, so one can't say you've been too harsh on pamphleteers."

"Ah, Reverend, you set my heart free. The rest are mere peccadilloes."

"Tell me."

"There's gambling."

"A worldly pursuit, to be sure, but your position required you to keep a grand house and entertain your guests."

"I loved to win, though."

"No one plays to lose."

"I cheated. A little."

"You took your advantage. Move on."

"That's it, Reverend! I feel no other burden on my conscience. Give me my absolution, and my soul will be ready, when God calls it, to ascend unhindered to his throne."

The Theatine neither moved nor spoke.

"What are you waiting for, Reverend?" said Mazarin.

"The final statement."

"Final statement of what?"

"Of the confession, Monseigneur."

"But I'm finished."

"Oh, no! Your Eminence is mistaken."

"Not that I'm aware of."

"Think hard."

"I've thought as hard as I could."

"Then I'll assist your memory."

"Let's see."

The Theatine coughed several times. "You have not spoken to me of avarice, another mortal sin, nor of the millions," he said.

"What millions, Reverend?"

"Why, *your* millions, Monseigneur."

"*Mon père,* that money belongs to me; why should I speak of it?"

"Because, you see, on that our opinions differ. You say that money is yours, and I think it belongs to others."

Mazarin raised a cold hand to his sweating forehead. "What do you m-mean?" he stammered.

"This: Your Eminence has gained a great deal of wealth in the service of the king . . ."

"Hmph. A great deal? It's not that much."

"In any event, where did this wealth come from?"

"From the State."

"Which means, from the king."

"But what do you conclude from that, Reverend?" said Mazarin, starting to tremble.

"I can reach no conclusion without a list of your revenues. Let's add it up: you have the Bishopric of Metz."

"Yes."

"The Abbacies of Saint-Clément, Saint-Arnoud, and Saint-Vincent, also in Metz."

"Yes."

"You have the Abbey of Saint-Denis, one of the loveliest properties in France."

"Yes, Reverend."

"You have the Abbey of Cluny, a rich living."

"I have that."

"And that of Saint-Médard, at Soissons, with income of a hundred thousand livres."

"I can't deny it."

"Plus, that of Saint-Victor at Marseilles, one of the richest abbeys of the South."

"Yes, *mon Père*."

"Over a million a year. With the income of the cardinalate and the ministry, call it two million."

"But . . ."

"Over ten years, that's twenty million . . . and twenty million at interest that compounds to fifty per cent gives, in ten years, another twenty million."

"For a Theatine father, you're quite an accountant!"

"Since 1644, when Your Eminence granted our order the monastery we occupy near Saint-Germain-des-Prés, I have reckoned the society's accounts."

"And mine as well, I see, Reverend."

"One must know a little bit about everything, Monseigneur."

"Well, then! Your conclusion?"

"I conclude that your baggage is too heavy to carry across the threshold of Paradise."

"So, I'm . . . I'm damned?"

"Unless you make restitution, yes."

Mazarin uttered a pitiful cry. "Restitution! But, good Lord, to whom?"

"To the master of this money—to the king!"

"But it's the king who gave it all to me!"

"Not so! The king signed no such decrees."

Mazarin sighed and groaned. "Absolution," he said. "Absolution!"

"Impossible, Monseigneur. Restitution," replied the Theatine. "Restitution!"

"But you absolved me of the other sins before. Why not this one?"

"Because," replied the reverend, "to absolve you of this sin is a crime for which the king would never absolve *me*, Monseigneur."

Upon which, the confessor stood and, sighing with unease, left the same way he had come.

"Oh, my God," groaned the cardinal. "*Holà!* Come here, Colbert—I'm sick, very sick!"

XLVI

The Bequest

Colbert emerged from behind the curtains. "Did you hear?" said Mazarin.

"Alas! Yes, Monseigneur."

"Is he right? Is that money ill-gotten?"

"A Theatine, Monseigneur, is a bad judge on matters of finance," Colbert replied coldly. "However, it may be that, by his theological lights, Your Eminence has made some mistakes. We often find it so . . . when we die."

"The first mistake is that of dying."

"True, Monseigneur. But on whose behalf does he think you're mistaken? That of the king."

Mazarin shrugged his shoulders. "As if I hadn't saved his State and its finances!"

"That cannot be denied, Monseigneur."

"It can't? Then, I've earned no more than a legitimate salary, despite what my confessor thinks?"

"Beyond all doubt."

"And I can retain for my family, always so needy, the better part of what I've earned!"

"I see no obstacle to that, Monseigneur."

"I was sure, Colbert, that if I consulted you, you'd give me good advice," replied Mazarin with joy.

Colbert made his sour miser's grimace. "Monseigneur," he interrupted, "we must consider whether the Theatine's words are not some sort of snare."

"A snare? Why? The Theatine is an honest man."

"He believed Your Eminence was at death's door, since Your Eminence summoned him for confession. Did I not hear him say to you, 'Distinguish what the king has given you from what you've earned for yourself'? Recall,

Monseigneur, if he said something like that to you, though in the terms of a Theatine father."

"He might have."

"In which case, Monseigneur, I'd say you've been required by the father to . . ."

"To make restitution?" cried Mazarin in alarm.

"I . . . wouldn't disagree."

"To make full restitution! You can't mean it. You talk like the confessor!"

"Restitution of a part—that is to say, His Majesty's part—or else, Monseigneur, there could be trouble. Your Eminence is too able a politician to ignore the fact that at this moment the king doesn't have even a hundred fifty thousand livres in his coffers."

"That is not my business," said Mazarin triumphantly, "but rather that of Monsieur le Surintendant Fouquet, whose accounts you're aware of, as I've shared them with you in recent months."

Colbert pinched his lips at the name of Fouquet. "His Majesty," he said between his teeth, "has no money but that collected by Monsieur Fouquet; your fortune, Monseigneur, would look like food to the starving."

"Yes, but I'm not the king's superintendent of finances, I have my own sources. I'm sure I can find something to help His Majesty, some legacy, but . . . I can't neglect my own family . . ."

"A meager legacy will dishonor and offend the king. Bequeathing a mere part to His Majesty is as much as admitting that what you're keeping wasn't legitimately acquired."

"Monsieur Colbert!"

"I thought Your Eminence did me the honor to ask for my advice."

"Yes, but you're ignorant of the principal details of the issue."

"I'm ignorant of nothing, Monseigneur; for ten years I've reviewed every column of figures calculated in France and have engraved them so deeply on my memory that, from the disbursals of Monsieur Le Tellier, who is reliable, to the secret skimming of Monsieur Fouquet, who is fraudulent, I could recite, line by line, every expenditure from Marseilles to Cherbourg."

"I suppose you'd have me throw all my money into the king's coffers!" cried Mazarin sardonically, from whom the gout then wrenched several painful groans. "Then the king would have nothing to blame me for, but he'd amuse himself at my expense with my millions, and rightly so."

"Your Eminence has misunderstood me. I did not at all mean that the king should spend your money."

"To me it seems clearly otherwise, since you advise me to give it to him."

"Ah!" replied Colbert. "That's because Your Eminence, preoccupied with the problem, completely overlooks the character of His Majesty Louis XIV."

"How so?"

"I believe his character, if I may dare to say so, centers on the sin that Monseigneur confessed just now to the Theatine."

"You may so dare. What sin is that?"

"It is pride. Pardon, Monseigneur, I mean majesty; kings don't show pride, that's a mere human emotion."

"Pride will do—and yes, you're right. So?"

"So, Monseigneur, if I've reasoned correctly, Your Eminence has only to offer all his fortune to the king, and without delay."

"Why is that?" asked Mazarin, intrigued.

"Because the king won't accept the entire amount."

"What? A young man without money who's consumed by ambition?"

"Indeed."

"A young man who wishes me dead."

"Monseigneur . . ."

"To inherit, yes, Colbert—yes, he'd like me dead, so he can inherit. Triple fool that I am not to have seen it! But I'll thwart him."

"You will. Because if the bequest is made in the right form, he'll refuse it."

"Come, now!"

"I'm certain of it. A young man who's accomplished nothing, who yearns for recognition, who burns to be the sole ruler, won't take anything just handed to him—he wants to achieve everything on his own. This prince, Monseigneur, won't be content with the Palais Royal left to him by Richelieu, nor the magnificent Palais Mazarin that you've built, nor the Louvre of his ancestors, nor even with Saint-Germain where he was born. I predict that all that does not come from him, he will scorn."

"And you guarantee that if I give my forty million to the king . . ."

"If the bequest is couched in certain terms, I guarantee he'll refuse it."

"What terms are these?"

"I can write them out if Monseigneur wishes me to."

"But what advantage will I gain from this?"

"An enormous one. No one will be able to accuse Your Eminence of the rampant avarice of which the pamphleteers reproach the most brilliant mind of the century."

"You're right, Colbert, you're right. Go to the king on my behalf and present him my will and testament."

"Your *bequest,* Monseigneur."

"But he might accept it! What if he accepts it?"

"Even then, you'd still have thirteen million for your family, and that's no small sum."

"But then you'd be a fool—or a traitor."

"And I'm neither one nor the other, Monseigneur. You seem very much afraid that the king will accept it, but oh! Be more afraid if he doesn't."

"If he doesn't agree, we must make sure he overlooks the thirteen million I have in reserve. But . . . yes, I will do it. Yes. Ah, but here comes the pain again! Weakness overcomes me—I'm very ill, Colbert; it's near the end."

Colbert trembled. The cardinal was very ill indeed: he was sweating profusely in his bed of pain, and the frightening pallor of his face, streaming with perspiration, was a sight to touch the heart of the most hardened physician. It clearly touched Colbert, for he rushed from the room, calling Bernouin to come to the sick man's aid, and then exited into the corridor.

There, walking back and forth, with a pensive expression that made his vulgar visage almost noble, shoulders hunched, neck extended, lips twitching to his tumbling thoughts, he nerved himself up for a risky endeavor. Meanwhile, no more than ten paces away, just the other side of a wall, his master writhed in anguish with pitiful cries, thinking no longer of the treasures of the earth, nor the joys of paradise, but of the horrors of hell.

While hot towels, topical ointments, and tonics were feverishly administered by Guénaud, who'd been recalled to the cardinal's side, Colbert, holding his big head in both hands to suppress his own fever of ideas, considered the wording of the bequest that he would submit to Mazarin at the first opportunity his illness allowed. The cries at the approach of death from the cardinal, that pillar of the past, seemed to stimulate the genius of this thick-browed thinker who was already turning toward the new sun that would regenerate the future.

Colbert returned to Mazarin when reason also returned to the patient, and persuaded him to dictate a bequest in the following terms:

> As I prepare to appear before God, the master of all men, I pray that the king, who was my master upon earth, will repossess the abundance which his kindness has granted me, and which my family will be happy to see pass into his illustrious hands. The details of my property have been prepared whenever His Majesty requests, or when the last breath passes from the lips of his devoted servant.
>
> Jules, Cardinal de Mazarin

The cardinal sighed as he signed this. Colbert sealed the packet and carried it immediately to the Louvre, where the king had just returned. Then he went home, rubbing his hands together with the satisfaction of a workman on a job well done.

XLVII

How Anne of Austria Gave Louis XIV One Sort of Advice and Monsieur Fouquet Gave Him Another

The news of the cardinal's condition had already spread, and it attracted at least as many people to the Louvre as the news of the marriage of Monsieur, the king's brother, once that had been officially announced.

No sooner had Louis XIV returned home, still pondering the things he'd seen and heard that evening, when the audiencer announced that the same crowd of courtiers who, that morning, had attended his lever, had returned to attend his *coucher*[112]—a favor that, during the reign of the cardinal at Court, had been rarely accorded to the king, who'd seen them flock instead to the cardinal despite the king's displeasure. But with the minister down, as we've seen, with a serious attack of gout, the flock of flatterers flew to the throne. Courtiers have an amazing instinct for sensing events in advance, a supreme science that makes them diplomats divining political difficulties, generals foretelling the outcomes of battles, and doctors diagnosing diseases. Louis XIV, who had learned this lesson from his mother, among others, understood from this turnout that His Eminence Monseigneur Cardinal Mazarin must be very ill indeed.

Anne of Austria had scarcely finished escorting the young queen to her chambers, reclaiming the ceremonial tiara from her brow, when she returned to seek out her son in his study. There, alone, disturbed, and with an unquiet heart, he allowed himself, as if to exercise his will, to indulge in surging waves of terrible anger. His was a royal anger that forced events when it broke out, but which, thanks to his burgeoning self-control, never erupted in more than brief outbursts. In fact, his confidant Saint-Simon[113] later mentioned his astonishment when, fifty years later, he lost his temper at a little lie told by his son the Duc de Maine, and the result was a hail of blows with a cane on a poor lackey who'd pilfered a biscuit.

The young king was thus in the grip of a sad fury and said to himself when he saw his reflection in a mirror, "O King! King in name, but not in fact. O Phantom, rather, vain image that you are! Lifeless statue that has no power beyond provoking a reflexive salute from courtiers, when will you raise your velvet-clad arm and tighten your silken-gloved fist? When will you be able to open your lips to do other than sigh or smile at the stupid immobility of the other statues in the gallery?"

Smacking his forehead with his hand, suddenly desperate for air, he went to the window where he saw some cavaliers below, chatting in animated whispers. These gentlemen were just curious onlookers, eager subjects for whom a king is a wondrous curiosity, like a rhinoceros, crocodile, or serpent.

He struck his forehead again and said, "King of France! Some title! People of France! What a mob of creatures! I've just returned to my royal palace of the Louvre, my horses are still steaming, and I caught the attention of barely twenty people who watched as I passed . . . Twenty? What am I saying? No, not even twenty interested in the King of France, not even ten King's Archers to guard my house—archers, people, guards, everyone is at the Palais Royal. Why, dear God? Don't I, the king, have the right to ask that?"

"Because," said a voice responding to his own, from the study doorway, "the Palais Royal is home to all the money—in other words, all the power—of he who would reign."

Louis turned suddenly; the voice was that of Anne of Austria. The king shuddered, then advanced toward his mother and said, "I hope Your Majesty paid no attention to those vain remarks that just show how the solitude and sorrow of kings can affect even the happiest personality."

"I paid attention to only one thing, my son: that you were complaining."

"Me? Not at all," said Louis XIV. "No, really, you're mistaken, Madame."

"Then what were you doing, Sire?"

"I imagined I was under the eye of my tutor and was developing an argument for debate."

"My son," replied Anne of Austria, shaking her head, "you're wrong to be ashamed of your words, and wrong not to take me into your confidence. The day will come, maybe as soon as tomorrow, when you'll need to remember this axiom: 'Gold is the only power, and those who have that power are the only true kings.'"

"You don't mean to cast blame on those who've gained wealth under my rule, do you?" asked the king.

"No," said Anne of Austria sharply. "No, Sire, those who became wealthy under your rule are rich because you willed it, and I have no envy or complaint against them. They have doubtless served Your Majesty well enough for Your Majesty to permit them to attend to their own recompense. That's not what I hear in your words that reproaches me."

"God forbid, Madame, that I should ever reproach my mother for anything!"

"Besides," continued Anne of Austria, "the Lord doesn't grant riches on this earth forever; the Lord, as a corrective for honors and wealth, gives us suffering and disease, and no one," added Anne of Austria with a painful smile that proved she didn't except herself from this funereal premise, "no one carries their grandeur and wealth into the grave. In that way, the young reap the fruitful harvest sowed by the old."

Louis listened with increasing attention to these words, as Anne of Austria seemed to offer them as some sort of consolation. "Madame," said Louis XIV, looking his mother in the eye, "do you, in fact, have something else you wish to tell me?"

"Absolutely nothing, my son—only, you must have noticed how ill Monsieur le Cardinal was this evening."

Louis looked at his mother, seeking some emotion in her voice, some sadness in her expression. Indeed, Queen Anne's face seemed somewhat altered, but by a suffering of a personal character. Perhaps this change was due to the cancer that was even then gnawing at her breast.[114] The king said, "Indeed, Madame, Monsieur de Mazarin is very ill."

"And it would be a great loss to the realm if His Eminence was called to God. Don't you agree, my son?" asked Anne of Austria.

"Yes, Madame, certainly, a great loss to the realm," said Louis, coloring. "But the danger can't be that great, it seems to me, as Monsieur le Cardinal isn't that old."

The king had just finished speaking when an usher stepped in under the door tapestry and stood with a roll of paper in his hand, waiting for the king to acknowledge him.

"What's that?" asked the king.

"A message from Monsieur de Mazarin," replied the usher.

"Give it to me," said the king. And he took the paper. But just as he was about to unroll it, a great noise arose in the courtyard, the gallery, and the antechambers. "Ah ha!" said Louis XIV, who seemed to recognize this commotion. "Did I say there was only one king in France? I was wrong, there are two."

At that moment the door opened, and Superintendent of Finance Fouquet appeared before Louis XIV. His horses had made the noise in the court-yard, his retainers had made the commotion in the gallery, and it was he the courtiers had loudly welcomed in the antechambers, an uproar that stirred as he passed and continued long after his passage. It was this clamor that Louis XIV regretted not hearing when he came through.

"He's not the king you think he is," Anne of Austria said quietly to her son. "He's just a wealthy man, that's all."

Nonetheless, her bitter feelings gave these words a hateful tone, though Louis's expression, on the contrary, remained calm, not a wrinkle showing on his forehead. He nodded politely to Fouquet and continued to unroll the paper he'd received from the usher. Fouquet saw this movement, and, with a manner both easy and respectful, approached Anne of Austria so as not to interrupt the king. Louis unrolled the paper, but he didn't read it;

he listened to Fouquet compliment his mother on the graceful turn of her hand and arm.

The queen's frown relaxed a bit and she almost smiled. Fouquet noticed that the king, instead of reading, was watching and listening, and he made a half-turn so that, while continuing to speak to Anne of Austria, he was also facing the king.

"Do you know, Monsieur Fouquet," said Louis XIV, "that His Eminence is ill?"

"Yes, Sire, I know that," said Fouquet, "and very ill indeed. I was at my country estate of Vaux when I heard the news and dropped everything to come."

"You left Vaux this evening, Monsieur?"

"An hour and a half ago, yes, Your Majesty," said Fouquet, consulting a watch encrusted with diamonds.

"An hour and a half!" said the king, who had enough control to restrain his anger but not to hide his surprise.

"I understand Your Majesty is skeptical, and rightly so, but I did come that quickly, wonderful as it sounds. I recently received from England three pairs of horses that I was assured were very lively; I had them posted at intervals of four leagues, and I tried them tonight. I rode them in relay from Vaux to the Louvre[115] in an hour and a half, so Your Majesty can see it was money well spent."

The queen mother's smile couldn't conceal her jealousy. Fouquet reacted before she could express it. "Indeed, Madame," he hastened to add, "such horses are made, not for subjects, but for kings, for kings must never defer to their subjects in anything."

Louis raised his head. "However, so far as I know," interrupted Anne of Austria, "you're not a king, are you, Monsieur Fouquet?"

"Which is why, Madame, the horses await only a signal from His Majesty before entering the stables of the Louvre. If I allowed myself to try them, it was only to ensure that I didn't offer the king anything less than a marvel."

The king flushed deep red.

"You know, Monsieur Fouquet," said the queen, "that it isn't the custom at the Court of France for a subject to offer such a present to his king?"

Louis started.

"I had hoped, Madame," said Fouquet anxiously, "that my love for His Majesty, my unending desire to please him, would serve to mitigate my failure of etiquette. It was not a present that I presumed to offer him, but rather a tribute I hoped to pay him."

"Thank you, Monsieur Fouquet," said the king politely. "I appreciate your intention, as I do love good horses, but I'm not wealthy enough to keep them—as you, my Surintendant des Finances, should know better than anyone. I am unable, however much I might like them, to purchase such an expensive set."

The queen mother seemed to be enjoying the minister's awkward position, but Fouquet gave her a haughty glance and replied, "Luxury is the virtue of kings, Sire; it is by luxury that they approach divinity, for by luxury they are elevated above other men. By luxury a king rewards his subjects and honors them. Under the golden sun of this royal luxury grows the luxury of individuals, the source of wealth for the people.[116] His Majesty, by accepting the gift of six such incomparable horses, would pique the vanity of our domestic breeders of Limousin, Perche, and Normandy, and their subsequent efforts to excel would benefit everyone . . . But the king is silent, and therefore I stand convicted."

During this speech Louis XIV, to keep his temper, rolled and unrolled the letter from Mazarin, though without looking at it. His eyes lit upon it at last, and he gasped at its first line.

"What is it, my son?" asked Anne of Austria, drawing nearer.

"Can this be from the cardinal?" said the king, continuing to read. "Yes, it is from him."

"Has his illness grown worse?"

"Read it," said the king, handing the letter to his mother, as if he thought that only by reading it could Anne of Austria believe the paper's astonishing contents.

Anne of Austria read it in her turn, and as she did her eyes sparkled with a joy that Fouquet noticed, though she tried to turn away. "It's a bequest, a regular deed of gift," she said.

"A bequest?" repeated Fouquet.

"Yes," said the king, speaking to his Surintendant des Finances. "Yes, on the eve of death, Monsieur le Cardinal makes me a bequest of all his wealth."

"Forty million!" cried the queen. "Ah, my son! This is a fine gesture on the cardinal's part, one that will contradict a host of vile rumors. Forty million, slowly gathered and then returned in one fell swoop to the royal treasury, the act of a loyal subject and a true Christian."

And after casting a final glance at the note, she returned it to Louis XIV, who was thrilled at the size of the sum mentioned. Fouquet had withdrawn a few steps and was silent. The king approached and handed him the letter. The superintendent gave it a brief, haughty look, then bowed and said, "Yes, Sire, it's a bequest, as I see."

"You must reply, my son," cried Anne of Austria. "You must reply, and right away."

"In what way, Madame?"

"By a visit to the cardinal."

"But it's scarcely an hour since I left His Eminence," said the king.

"Then write, Sire."

"Write!" said the young king with disgust.

"Indeed," replied Anne of Austria. "It seems to me, my son, that a man who makes such a bequest has the right to expect a speedy show of gratitude." And turning to the superintendent, she said, "Don't you agree, Monsieur Fouquet?"

"The bequest is worth the trouble, yes, Madame," replied the superintendent with a hauteur that didn't escape the king's notice.

"Accept it, then, and thank him," insisted Anne of Austria.

"What says Monsieur Fouquet?" asked Louis XIV.

"His Majesty wants to know what I think?"

"Yes."

"Thank him, Sire . . ."

"Ah!" said Anne of Austria.

"But don't accept it," continued Fouquet.

"And why is that?" demanded Anne of Austria.

"You said so yourself, Madame," replied Fouquet. "Because kings must not and cannot receive gifts from their subjects."

The king remained silent in the face of these two very different opinions.

"But . . . forty million!" said Anne of Austria, in the same tone that Marie Antoinette much later said, "You tell me that much!"[117]

"I know," Fouquet said, laughing. "Forty million is a nice round sum, an amount that might tempt even a monarch's conscience."

"But, Monsieur," said Anne of Austria, "instead of dissuading the king from receiving this present, point out to His Majesty, in your official capacity, that these forty million will make his fortune."

"It is precisely, Madame, because this forty million is a subject's fortune that I say to the king, 'Sire, if it's indecent for a king to accept from a subject six horses worth twenty thousand livres, it's that much more dishonorable to owe his fortune to a subject who was less than scrupulous in the collection of that fortune.'"

"It's not your place, Monsieur, to give the king such a lesson," said Anne of Austria, "unless you provide a replacement for the forty million you cause him to lose."

"The king shall have it whenever he wishes," said the Surintendant des Finances, bowing.

"Yes, by squeezing it out of the people," said Anne of Austria.

"And weren't they squeezed, Madame, when they sweated out the forty million offered in this bequest?" Fouquet replied. "In any event, His Majesty asked for my opinion, and he has it. If His Majesty asks for my assistance, it shall be the same."

"Come, come, accept it, my son," said Anne of Austria. "You are above such petty considerations."

"Refuse it, Sire," said Fouquet. "While a king lives, he has no other measure but his conscience, no other judge but his will—but when he is dead, posterity will applaud or accuse."

"Thank you, Mother," replied Louis, bowing respectfully to the queen. "And thank you, Monsieur Fouquet," he said, politely dismissing the superintendent.

"Will you accept it?" Anne of Austria asked again.

"I'll think about it," replied the king, looking at Fouquet.

XLVIII

Agonies

The same night the bequest was sent to the king, the cardinal had himself taken to Vincennes.[118] The king and the Court followed him there. The last glimmers of this torch still cast enough light to outshine, in its radiance, the combined light of the rest of the Court. Moreover, as we saw, the young Louis XIV, a faithful satellite of his minister, still orbited in his gravitation until the final moments. Mazarin's illness, following Guénaud's prediction, had worsened; it was no longer an attack of gout, it was the grip of death. And there was one more thing that afflicted the dying man with an even greater agony: the anxiety of having made that bequest to the king, the gift that, according to Colbert, the king would return unaccepted to the cardinal.

The cardinal had a lot of faith, as we've seen, in the predictions of his financial secretary—but the sum was a great one, and no matter how brilliant Colbert was, from time to time the cardinal had his doubts, thinking that it might have been the Theatine who was mistaken, and there was at least as great a chance that he wouldn't be damned as that Louis XIV would reject his millions.

Moreover, the longer the delay before the bequest was returned, the more Mazarin thought that forty million was enough to risk losing something as hypothetical as a soul. Mazarin, though a cardinal, was first and foremost a prime minister, and in that capacity committed to materialism almost as much as an atheist. Every time the door opened he turned to look, longing to see the return of his unhappy bequest, but he was deceived by hope and lay back down again with a sigh, finding his sorrow all the deeper because for a moment he'd forgotten it.

Anne of Austria, too, had followed the cardinal to Vincennes. Her heart, though age had made it selfish, couldn't refuse to bear this dying man witness to a sadness she owed him in her quality as a wife, according to some, and in her capacity as sovereign, according to others. She had adopted, as it were, the face of mourning in advance, and all the Court followed her example.

Louis, in order not to show on his face what was passing in his soul, confined himself to his apartment with his old governess as his only company. The more he thought that he was approaching the end when all restraint would be lifted from him, the humbler and more patient he became, gathering himself like all strong men who have secret plans, preparing to spring forward more effectively at the decisive moment.

Last rites had been secretly administered to the cardinal, who, faithful to his habits of concealment, fought against the appearance, and even the reality, of his situation, pretending to keep to his bed as if merely afflicted by a passing malady. Guénaud, for his part, maintained absolute discretion, and when questioned, tired of being interrogated, he said nothing except, "His Eminence is still full of youth and strength, but God wills what he wills, and when he decides to take a man, that man will be taken." These words, though spoken with the greatest care and reserve, were really intended for an audience of two: the king and the cardinal.

Mazarin, despite Guénaud's predictions, continued to deceive himself, or rather, to play his part so well that even the most cunning courtiers, when saying he deceived himself, were actually his dupes.

Louis, who hadn't seen the cardinal for two days—his mind fixed on the bequest that also preoccupied the cardinal—didn't know the cardinal's real condition. The son of Louis XIII, following in the footsteps of his father, had been the king so little until then that, while longing for rule, his desire was coupled with the fear of the unknown. As to the bequest, having made up his mind, a resolution he'd shared with no one, he decided to ask Mazarin to receive his visit. It was Anne of Austria, in her constant attendance on the cardinal, who received the king's proposal, and she passed it on to the dying man, who heard it and trembled. Why did Louis XIV wish this audience? Was it to refuse the bequest, as Colbert had predicted? Was it to accept it with gratitude, as Mazarin feared?

Nevertheless, despite his rising anxiety, the dying man didn't hesitate for a moment. "His Majesty will be quite welcome, yes, very welcome indeed," he said, dismissing Colbert with a gesture that he, sitting at the foot of the bed, understood very well. "Madame," continued Mazarin, "would Your Majesty please assure the king of the truth of what I've just said?"

Anne of Austria rose; she, too, was eager to resolve the question of the forty million that was at the forefront of everyone's minds.

After Queen Anne left, Mazarin made a great effort and leaned toward Colbert, saying, "Well, Colbert! Two unhappy days have passed, two mortal days, and, as you see, the bequest has not been returned."

"Patience, Monseigneur," said Colbert.

"Patience! Are you mad, you wretch? You advise me to be patient! In truth, Colbert, you mock me—I'm dying, yet you tell me to be patient!"

"Monseigneur," said Colbert with his usual coolness, "it's impossible that things won't turn out as I said. His Majesty comes to see you so that he can return the bequest personally."

"You think so? Well, I, on the contrary, am quite sure His Majesty is coming to thank me for it."

Anne of Austria returned at that moment; on her way to find her son, she'd encountered another charlatan with a miracle cure, a medicinal powder sure to save the cardinal. Anne brought a sample of this powder, but that wasn't what the cardinal was interested in and he wouldn't even look at it, insisting that life wasn't worth the trouble it took to continue it. But once he'd uttered this maxim of philosophy, his secret, so long concealed, finally burst forth. "That powder, Madame, has no bearing on the situation. I made a small bequest to the king two or three days ago, and until now, out of delicacy no doubt, His Majesty hasn't spoken of it. But the moment has arrived for explanations, and I beg Your Majesty to tell me if the king has any ideas on the matter."

Anne of Austria opened her mouth to reply, but Mazarin stopped her. "The truth, Madame," he said. "In the name of heaven, the truth! Don't flatter a dying man by offering him vain hope." He stopped himself at a look from Colbert that told him he was going too far.

"I know," said Anne of Austria, taking the cardinal's hand. "I know that you have offered, not a small bequest, as you modestly call it, but a generous, a magnificent gift; I know how painful it would be for you if the king . . ."

Mazarin listened, dying as he was, with the intensity of ten living men. "If the king?" he repeated.

"If the king," continued Queen Anne, "didn't heartily accept what you so nobly offer."

Mazarin fell back on his pillow like the tragic clown Pantaloon, with the exaggerated despair of a man who abandons himself to a shipwreck—but he retained enough strength and presence of mind to throw at Colbert one of those looks that exceed the tragedy of ten epic poems.

"It's true, isn't it," added the queen, "that you'd consider the king's refusal a kind of insult?"

Mazarin rolled his head on his pillow without uttering a single syllable. The queen was deceived, or pretended to be deceived, by this behavior. "Therefore, I've given him sound advice," said she, "and though certain others, jealous no doubt of the glory you'll gain by your generosity, tried to persuade the king to refuse the bequest, I took your side and argued so well that I hope you won't have to suffer such a denial."

"Oh!" murmured Mazarin from behind half-closed eyes. "That's a service I won't forget for a single minute during the few hours I have left to live."

"And I must say that it wasn't without difficulty that I rendered it to Your Eminence," added Anne of Austria.

"Ah, *peste,* I believe it. Ohh!"

"*Mon Dieu,* what is it?"

"I'm burning up."

"Are you suffering so badly?"

"Like the damned!"

Colbert wished he could disappear through the floor.

"Then," continued Mazarin, "Your Majesty thinks that the king"—he paused for several seconds—"that the king is coming here to pay me the compliment of accepting?"

"So I think," said the queen.

Mazarin assassinated Colbert with a look like daggers. Just then, the ushers announced the king was approaching through the crowded antechambers. This announcement caused a stir, and Colbert took advantage of it to slip out through a side door.

Anne of Austria arose and awaited her son. Louis XIV appeared in the chamber's doorway, his eyes going straight to the dying man, who no longer took the trouble to even half rise for the monarch from whom he thought he had nothing more to expect.

An usher rolled an armchair next to the bed. Louis saluted his mother, then the cardinal, and sat down. The queen sat down in her turn. The king glanced behind him, and the usher, understanding the look, waved those courtiers who remained in the room out ahead of him.

As the velvet curtains fell across the door, silence fell over the chamber. The king, still childish and timid before he who had been his master since his birth, respected him all the more in the supreme majesty of impending death. He dared not start the conversation, feeling that every word must weigh with significance, not just in this world, but the next.

As for the cardinal, he had only one thing on his mind: his bequest. It was not the pain of his illness that gave him that dejected expression and dull look, it was the expectation of the gratitude that was about to come tumbling from the king's mouth, destroying all hope of restitution.

It was Mazarin who first broke the silence. "Your Majesty," he said, "are you also lodged here at Vincennes?"

Louis nodded.

"It's a gracious favor that you grant to a dying man," continued Mazarin, "and which will make his death that much easier."

"I hope," replied the king, "that I've come to visit, not a dying man, but a patient still able to be cured."

Mazarin made a movement of his head that signified, *Your Majesty is very good, but I know the truth of the matter.* "The final visit, Sire," he said, "the final visit."

"If that were so, Monsieur le Cardinal," said Louis XIV, "then I've come one final time to hear the advice of a guide to whom I owe everything."

Anne of Austria was a woman; she could no longer restrain her tears. Louis showed himself much moved as well, but Mazarin was even more moved than his guests, though for different motives.

Here the silence fell again. The queen dabbed at her cheeks, and Louis regained his resolve. "I said," continued the king, "that I owe a great deal to Your Eminence."

The cardinal's eyes devoured Louis XIV, for he felt the approach of the supreme moment.

"And," continued the king, "the principal object of my visit is to deliver sincere thanks for that final testimony of friendship that you sent me."

The cardinal's cheeks inflated, his lips parted, and the most lamentable sigh he'd ever uttered prepared to issue from this chest. "Sire," he said, "I've impoverished my poor family, and ruined all who depend upon me, which some might call a mistake, but at least no one can say that I refused to sacrifice everything to my king."

Anne of Austria resumed her weeping.

"Dear Monsieur Mazarin," said the king, in a tone more serious than one would have expected given his youth, "I think you misunderstand me."

Mazarin raised himself on one elbow.

"There's no question of ruining your dear family, nor of robbing your dependents. No, that must not be!"

Come, he's going to leave me a bit after all, thought Mazarin. *Let's get as much as we can.*

The king softens enough to be generous, thought the queen. *Just let him not be too generous—this chance at a fortune will never come again.*

"Sire," the cardinal said aloud, "my family is large, and my nieces will be destitute when I'm gone."

"Oh, don't worry about your family," the queen interrupted hastily. "Dear Monsieur Mazarin, we will hold no friends more precious than yours; your nieces will be my children, the sisters of His Majesty, and whenever favors are distributed in France, it will be to those you love."

Rubbish! thought Mazarin, who knew better than anyone what faith to put in the promises of monarchs.

Louis read the dying man's thoughts on his face. "Fear not, dear Monsieur de Mazarin," he said, with a sad and half-ironic smile. "Mesdemoiselles de Mancini will lose their most precious blessing in losing you, but they will nonetheless remain the richest heiresses in France, since you've given me their dowry . . ."

The cardinal held his breath.

". . . and I restore it to them," continued Louis, drawing from his doublet and placing on the cardinal's bed the letter of bequest that, for two days, had been the burning obsession of Mazarin's mind.

"What did I tell you, Monseigneur?" came a whisper from the side door behind the bed.

"Your Majesty returns my bequest!" cried Mazarin, so overcome by joy that he forgot his role of benefactor.

"Your Majesty refuses the forty million!" cried Anne of Austria, so stupefied that she forgot her role of mourner.

"Yes, Monsieur le Cardinal; yes, Madame," replied Louis XIV, tearing up the letter that Mazarin hadn't dared take back. "Yes, I annihilate this act that despoiled an entire family; the wealth acquired by His Eminence in my service is his and not mine."

"But, Sire, consider!" cried Anne of Austria. "Your Majesty doesn't have even ten thousand crowns in his coffers!"

"Madame, I have just committed my first act of royalty, which I hope will worthily inaugurate my reign."

"Ah, Sire, you're right!" said Mazarin. "It's truly grand, truly generous what you've done here!" And he picked up, one after another, the pieces of the bequest scattered on his bedclothes to make sure it was the original and not a copy. Finally, he found the piece bearing his signature and, recognizing it, fell back on his pillows. Anne of Austria, unable to hide her disappointment, raised her eyes and hands to the heavens.

"Ah, Sire!" cried Mazarin. "My God! Sire, you will be blessed by my whole family! *Perbacco!* If any member of my family ever causes you trouble, just frown and I will rise from my grave."

These theatrics didn't produce quite the effect Mazarin had counted upon. Louis had already passed on to considerations of a higher order, while as for Anne of Austria, unable to continue without giving in to the anger she felt at the magnanimity of her son and the hypocrisy of the cardinal, she rose and left the room to find another venue for her spite.

Mazarin understood completely, and, afraid that Louis XIV might rescind his decision, to distract him he began to groan and cry out, like Scapin in a later role, making that sublime jest for which the sad grumbler Boileau dared to criticize Molière.[119] But gradually his cries subsided, and when Anne of Austria left the room they ceased entirely.

"Monsieur le Cardinal," said the king, "do you have any advice to give me?"

"Sire," replied Mazarin, "you are already wisdom itself, prudence incarnate. As for benevolence, let's not speak of it; what you have done exceeds the generosity of all men from antiquity to modern times."

The king remained cool, unmoved by this praise. "So, Monsieur," he said, "you speak only of gratitude. Doesn't your experience, which is far greater than my wisdom, prudence, and generosity, inspire you to give me any counsel that will help me in the future?"

Mazarin thought for a moment. "You came here," he said, "to do a great thing for me and for mine, Sire."

"No need to talk about that," said the king.

"Well!" continued Mazarin. "I do want to give you something in exchange for the forty million that you so royally gave up."

Louis XIV made a gesture that indicated he'd heard enough flattery.

"I wish to give you an opinion," said Mazarin, "a single idea more valuable than all those millions."

"Monsieur le Cardinal!" interrupted Louis XIV.

"Sire, hear my advice."

"I'm listening."

"Come near, Sire, for I'm getting weaker . . . closer, Sire, closer."

The king leaned down over the bed of the dying man.

"Sire," said Mazarin, so quietly that the breath of his words came like a whisper from the tomb into the ears of the young king, "Sire . . . *never have a prime minister.*"

Louis sat up, astonished.

This advice amounted to a confession.

And it was a treasure indeed, this sincere confession from Mazarin. The cardinal's legacy to the young king consisted of no more than these six words—but these six words, as Mazarin had said, were worth millions in gold.

Louis sat stunned for a moment. As for Mazarin, he acted as if he'd said nothing unusual.

The young king finally spoke. "Apart from your family, Monsieur de Mazarin, do you have anyone else to recommend to me?"

A slight drumming sounded from the side door behind the bed. Mazarin understood. "Yes, yes," he said quickly. "Yes, Sire, I recommend to you a wise man, honest and capable."

"His name, Monsieur le Cardinal?"

"His name will be entirely unknown to you, Sire—it's Monsieur Colbert, my financial secretary. Oh, you can trust him," added Mazarin with emphasis. "Everything he's predicted has come to pass, and he has a sharp eye for business and for judging men, one that's never mistaken. He's surprised even me. Sire, I owe you a great deal, but I think I settle the score by giving you Monsieur Colbert."

"All right," said Louis faintly, for as Mazarin had said, the name of Colbert was unknown to him, and he thought the cardinal's enthusiasm might be no more than the delirium of a dying man.

The cardinal had fallen back again on his pillow. "For now, Sire, adieu," murmured Mazarin. "I still have a hard road to travel before I present myself before my new master. Adieu, Sire."

The young king felt tears in his eyes. He leaned over the dying man, already more than half dead . . . and then he hurried away.

XLIX

Enter Colbert

That night was one of anguish for both the dying man and the king.

The dying man awaited his deliverance.

The king awaited his freedom.

Louis never went to bed. An hour after he'd left the cardinal's chamber, he heard that the dying man, recovering a little strength, had had himself dressed, rouged, and combed, and had asked to receive the latest ambassadors. Like Caesar Augustus, he seemed to regard the world as a theater and wanted to play out properly the last act of his comedy.

Anne of Austria didn't visit the cardinal again; she had nothing more to do there. The appearance of propriety was the pretext for her absence. Besides, the cardinal didn't ask for her, as the advice the queen had given her son still irked him.

Toward midnight, while still fully dressed, Mazarin entered his final agony. He had reviewed his will, and as that document was the exact expression of his desires, and he feared someone with another agenda would take advantage of his weakness to get him to change it, he'd given it to Colbert, a most vigilant sentry who posted himself in the corridor outside the cardinal's bedroom.

The king, confining himself to his room, sent his old governess every hour to Mazarin's suite for the latest report on the cardinal's health. After having heard that Mazarin had had himself dressed to receive the ambassadors, Louis next heard that they were beginning the prayers for the dying.

At one o'clock in the morning Guénaud prepared a final potion, his Remedy Heroic. This was a prime example of a period that saw everything as swordplay, an old attitude that, though on its way out, still clung to belief in a "secret thrust" effective even against death. Mazarin, after taking this remedy, was able to breathe easily for almost ten minutes. Immediately he gave orders that the word should be spread of a sudden improvement.

The king, at this news, felt cold sweat break out on his forehead; having glimpsed his liberty, slavery seemed darker and less acceptable than ever. But the next report completely changed the face of things: suddenly Mazarin scarcely breathed at all, and had trouble following the prayers that the Curate of Saint-Nicolas-des-Champs recited before him.

The king began to march back and forth in his chamber, consulting, as he walked, several papers taken from a bureau to which he alone had the key.

A third time the governess returned: Monsieur de Mazarin was making jokes and had ordered the cleaning of his *Flora* by Titian.[120]

Finally, at about half past two in the morning, the king could no longer stand the strain—he hadn't slept for twenty-four hours. Sleep, so powerful at that age, took hold of him for about an hour. But he didn't go to bed, he slept in an armchair.

Around four o'clock the governess entered the room and woke him up. "Well?" the king asked.

"Well, my dear Sire!" said the governess, wringing her hands sadly. "Well! He is dead."

The king rose suddenly, as if a steel spring had brought him to his feet. "Dead!" he cried.

"Alas! Yes."

"For sure?"

"Yes."

"Officially?"

"Yes."

"Has the news been announced?"

"Not yet."

"Then, who told you the cardinal was dead?"

"Monsieur Colbert."

"Monsieur Colbert?"

"Yes."

"And he was sure of what he told you?"

"He'd just come from the bedchamber where he'd spent several minutes holding a mirror up to the cardinal's lips."

"Ah!" said the king. "And what has become of this Monsieur Colbert?"

"He's just left His Eminence's chamber."

"To go where?"

"To follow me."

"So, then he's . . . ?"

"Here, Sire, waiting outside your door for when it pleases you to receive him."

Louis sprang to the door, opened it himself, and saw Colbert standing there and waiting. The king started at the sight of this statue all dressed in black.

Colbert bowed with profound respect and took two steps toward His Majesty.

Louis withdrew into his room, gesturing for Colbert to follow him. Colbert came in. Louis dismissed the governess, who closed the door behind her as she left.

Colbert stood humbly near the door. "What have you come to tell me, Monsieur?" said Louis, troubled by this surprise intruder who seemed to divine his secret thoughts.

"That the cardinal has just passed away, Sire, and that I bring you his final farewell."

The king paused thoughtfully for a moment, looking attentively at Colbert. It was apparent that the cardinal's last words were on his mind. "So, you're Monsieur Colbert?" he asked.

"Yes, Sire."

"His Eminence's loyal servant, as he described you to me?"

"Yes, Sire."

"Guardian of some of his secrets?"

"Of all of them."

"The friends and servants of His Late Eminence will be dear to me, Monsieur, and I'll make sure that you find a place in my own service."

Colbert bowed.

"You're a financial secretary, Monsieur, are you not?"

"Yes, Sire."

"And Monsieur le Cardinal employed you in his accounting?"

"I had that honor, Sire."

"But you didn't do anything for the royal budget, I believe."

"On the contrary, Sire, it was I who gave Monsieur le Cardinal an idea that saved Your Majesty's treasury three hundred thousand livres a year."

"What idea was that, Monsieur?" asked Louis XIV.

"Your Majesty is aware that the Hundred Swiss[121] display silver lace on all their uniform ribbons?"

"Of course."

"Well, Sire! I proposed that their ribbons be made with imitation silver. No one can tell the difference, and three hundred thousand livres can feed a regiment for half a year, or buy ten thousand good muskets, or build a ten-gun flute[122] ready to sail."

"That's true," said Louis XIV, looking more attentively at the character before him. "And, my faith, that's a sensible savings, for it's ridiculous to have soldiers wearing lace like they're lords."

"I'm happy that His Majesty approves," said Colbert.

"And is that the only job you had with the cardinal?" asked the king.

"It was I whom His Eminence charged with examining the accounts of the Superintendent of Finances, Sire."

"Ah!" said Louis XIV, who had been about to dismiss Colbert when he was stopped by these final words. "So, it was you His Eminence charged with auditing Monsieur Fouquet. And what was the result of this audit?"

"It found a deficit, Sire. If Your Majesty will permit me . . . ?"

"Speak, Monsieur Colbert."

"I ought to give Your Majesty some explanations."

"No need, Monsieur; you audited the accounts, so tell me the balance."

"Easily done, Sire. Empty everywhere, money nowhere."

"Take care, Monsieur, you're impugning the management of Monsieur Fouquet, whom everyone says is a capable man."

Colbert flushed, then turned pale, for he felt that from this moment, he was at war with a man whose power was nearly as great as that of the late minister. "Indeed, Sire, a very capable man," Colbert repeated with a bow.

"But if Monsieur Fouquet is a capable man who, despite his capability, lacks funds, whose fault is that?"

"I accuse no one, Sire, I just state the facts."

"Very well; summarize your accounts and present them to me. There's a deficit, you say? But a deficit can be temporary—credit comes back, the funds replenish."

"No, Sire."

"Not this year, perhaps, I understand that, but next year?"

"Next year, Sire, is as exhausted as this year."

"And the year after that?"

"The same."

"What are you telling me, Monsieur Colbert?"

"That the next four years' revenue is expended in advance."

"We'll need a loan, then."

"We'll need three, Sire."

"I'll create offices and sell them, and the price of the posts will be paid into the treasury."

"Impossible, Sire, for post upon post has already been created and sold, most with their requirements left blank so that the purchasers need do nothing to fulfill them—which means Your Majesty can't even force them to resign for noncompliance. Furthermore, Monsieur le Surintendant sold the posts at a one-third discount, so the people are further burdened, and Your Majesty doesn't even profit from it."

The king frowned. "Explain that to me, Monsieur Colbert."

"If Your Majesty can formulate his question more clearly, I shall try to explain what he wishes to know."

"You're right—clarity is what we need."

"Yes, Sire, clarity. God is God above all because he made the light."

"Then, tell me, for example, if Monsieur le Cardinal is dead," asked Louis XIV, "now that I rule as king, what if I want some money?"

"Your Majesty has none."

"How can that be, Monsieur? Can't the superintendent find me any money?" Colbert shook his heavy head.

"Why?" said the king. "Are the State's revenues so completely committed that there's no income at all?"

"At this point, Sire, yes."

The king frowned. "In that case, I'll have the King's Council draw up orders to sell off our notes at a low rate for quick liquidation."

"Impossible, for the notes have been converted into mortgages and the mortgages have been leveraged, with the debts divided into so many parts and resold that the original note could never be reconstructed."

Louis, upset, was walking back and forth, frowning. "But if it's as you say, Monsieur Colbert," he said, stopping suddenly, "wouldn't I be ruined before I've even reigned?"

"That is, in fact, the case, Sire," replied the impassive compiler of figures.

"But surely, Monsieur, there's some money somewhere?"

"There is, Sire, and as a beginning, I bring Your Majesty an account of funds that Monsieur le Cardinal de Mazarin wasn't willing to list in his last will and testament, or in any testament at all, but which he entrusted to me."

"To you?"

"Yes, Sire, with instructions to deliver them to Your Majesty."

"What? Money beyond the forty million in the will?"

"Yes, Sire."

"Monsieur de Mazarin had even more money?"

Colbert bowed.

"What a bottomless pit that man was!" murmured the king. "Monsieur de Mazarin on the one hand, Monsieur Fouquet on the other, and maybe a hundred million between them! It's no wonder my coffers are empty."

Colbert just waited.

"And is the sum you bring me worth the trouble?" asked the king.

"Yes, Sire, it's a goodly sum."

"Amounting to . . . ?"

"Thirteen million livres, Sire."

"Thirteen million!" cried Louis XIV, trembling with joy. "Did you say *thirteen million*, Monsieur Colbert?"

"I said thirteen million, yes, Your Majesty."

"That nobody knows about?"

"That nobody knows about."

"And which are in your hands?"

"In my hands, yes, Sire."

"And when could I have it?"

"Within two hours."

"But where is it, then?"

"In the cellar of a house that Monsieur le Cardinal had in the city, and which he was good enough to leave to me in a particular clause in his will."

"You're familiar with the cardinal's will?"

"I have a legal copy signed by his hand."

"A copy?"

"Yes, Sire. Here it is." Colbert drew the will from his doublet and showed it to the king.

Louis read the article relative to the gift of the house. "But," he said, "this is only about the house, and doesn't mention any money."

"Your pardon, Sire, but that part was confided to my conscience."

"And Monsieur de Mazarin confided that to you?"

"Why not, Sire?"

"Him, the most suspicious of all men?"

"He wasn't so with me, Sire, as Your Majesty can see."

Louis paused to admire that face, vulgar but expressive. "You're an honest man, Monsieur Colbert," said the king.

"It's not a virtue, Sire, it's a duty," replied Colbert coolly.

"But isn't that money intended for his family?" asked Louis XIV.

"If that money were for his family, it would be listed in the cardinal's will with the rest of his fortune. If that money was owed to the family, I, who drew up the deed of bequest in favor of His Majesty, would have added the sum of thirteen million to the forty million already offered to you."

"What!" said Louis XIV. "It was you who drew up the bequest, Monsieur Colbert?"

"Yes, Sire."

"And yet the cardinal trusted you?" added the king naïvely.

"I told His Eminence that Your Majesty would never accept it," said Colbert in his usual tone, calm and rather solemn.

Louis wiped his hand across his brow. "Oh, how young I am," he murmured under his breath, "to think I can command men!"

Colbert waited until the end of this interior dialogue and Louis lifted his head. "At what time should I bring the money to Your Majesty?" he asked.

"Tonight, at eleven o'clock. And I don't want anyone to know that I have this money."

Colbert made no reply, as if he preferred to talk as little as necessary about secrets.

"This sum, is it in ingots or in coins?"

"In gold coins, Sire."

"Good."

"Where shall I bring it?"

"To the Louvre. Thank you, Monsieur Colbert."

Colbert bowed and left.

"Thirteen million!" whispered Louis XIV when he was alone. "It's like a dream!"

He leaned his forehead into his hands, as if he were preparing to sleep. But after a moment he raised his head, shook his shining hair, rose, and throwing open the window, bathed his burning forehead in the brisk morning breeze that brought him the bitter scent of the trees and the sweet perfume of the flowers. A resplendent dawn was rising on the horizon, and the first rays of the sun gilded the young king's brow.

"This golden dawn is the first of my reign," murmured Louis XIV. "Is this an omen that you send me, Almighty God?"

L

The First Day of the Reign of Louis XIV

That morning the news of the cardinal's death spread throughout the château, and from the château to the city. The ministers Fouquet, Lyonne, and Le Tellier went to the King's Council chamber for a meeting; the king, hearing of it, sent for them immediately. "Messieurs," he said, "while Monsieur le Cardinal lived, I allowed him to govern my affairs, but now I intend to govern them myself. You will give me your opinion when I ask you for it. Now go!"

The ministers looked at each other in surprise. If they managed not to openly smile it was with great effort, for they knew that the prince, raised in absolute ignorance of affairs, had taken on, out of pride, a burden far beyond his abilities.

Fouquet took leave of his colleagues on the staircase, saying, "So much the less work for us, Messieurs." And he went cheerfully to his carriage. The other two, rather anxious about this turn of events, returned together to Paris.

The king, around ten o'clock, went to visit his mother, with whom he had a long conversation, and then, after the midday meal, he called for a closed carriage and went straight to the Louvre. There he received a great many people, taking a certain pleasure in their curiosity and hesitation.

Toward evening, he ordered the gates of the Louvre to be closed, all but one that opened onto the river quay. He sent as sentries to this gate two of the Hundred Swiss who didn't speak a word of French, with orders to admit all bearers of deliveries but no one else, and then to let no one leave. At eleven exactly he heard the rumbling of a heavy wagon outside the river gate, then another, and finally a third, and then the gate squealed on its hinges as it closed. Shortly thereafter someone scratched at the door[123] to his study; the king opened it himself to find Colbert, whose first words were, "The money is in Your Majesty's cellars."

Louis then went down personally to see for himself the barrels of coins, gold, and silver, that, under the eye of Colbert, four men had just rolled down into a vault the key to which the king had given Colbert that morning. His inspection completed, the king returned to his rooms, followed by Colbert, whose chilly demeanor seemed not the least bit warmed by the satisfaction of this personal success.

"Monsieur," said the king, "what would you desire as your reward for this devotion and integrity?"

"Absolutely nothing, Sire."

"What, nothing? Not even the opportunity to serve me?"

"If Your Majesty doesn't give me an opportunity, I will serve him nonetheless. It's impossible for me not to serve the king as well as I'm able."

"You will be my Intendant des Finances, Monsieur Colbert."

"But isn't there a superintendent, Sire?"

"Indeed."

"Sire, the Surintendant des Finances is the most powerful man in the realm."

"Oh?" exclaimed Louis, flushing. "Is that what you think?"

"I won't last a week under him, Sire, unless Your Majesty gives me independent authority. An intendant under a superintendent has none."

"You don't think you could depend upon me?"

"As I had the honor to tell Your Majesty, while Monsieur Mazarin was alive, Monsieur Fouquet was the second man in the kingdom; now that Monsieur Mazarin is dead, he's the first."

"Monsieur, I'm willing to tolerate hearing you say such things to me today, but tomorrow, believe me, I won't put up with it."

"Then I shall be of no use to Your Majesty?"

"You're already useless, since you're afraid to compromise yourself by serving me."

"The only thing I fear is not having the *means* to serve."

"What do you want, then?"

"I want Your Majesty to give me some assistants to serve in his intendancy."

"Won't that diminish your position?"

"It will add to its security."

"Name your colleagues."

"Messieurs Breteuil, Marin, and Hervard."

"They'll be in place tomorrow."

"Thank you, Sire!"

"Is that all you need?"

"No, Sire, one thing more . . ."

"What's that?"

"Allow me to empanel a Court of Justice."

"A Court of Justice? To do what?"

"To try the corrupt tax-farmers and debt collectors who've been cheating the treasury for the past ten years."

"But . . . what will we do to them?"

"We'll hang two or three of them, which will make the rest come clean."

"But I can't begin my reign with a spate of executions, Monsieur Colbert."

"On the contrary, Sire, better to begin with a few executions than to end in mass upheaval."

The king said nothing to this.

"Does Your Majesty agree?" said Colbert.

"I'll think about it, Monsieur."

"A delay to think about it will render it too late."

"Why?"

"Because we're dealing with men whose positions, given time to reinforce them, are stronger than ours."

"Empanel your Court of Justice, Monsieur."

"I shall do so."

"Is that all?"

"No, Sire, there's one more important thing. What authority does Your Majesty give to this intendancy?"

"Well, I don't know . . . the usual authority, I suppose."

"Sire, I need this intendancy to include the right to read any correspondence with England."

"Impossible, Monsieur—that correspondence isn't even shared with the King's Council. Monsieur le Cardinal handled it personally."

"I thought Your Majesty had declared this morning that he would handle such affairs *without* the council."

"Yes, I did declare that."

"Then let Your Majesty himself be the only one to read such correspondence, particularly from England; I must emphasize the importance of this."

"Monsieur, you shall handle that particular correspondence, and give me a full account of it."

"Now, Sire, what shall I do regarding the finances?"

"Everything that Monsieur Fouquet doesn't do."

"Then that's all I need from Your Majesty. Thank you, that puts my mind at ease." And with these words, he took his leave.

Louis watched him go. Colbert wasn't a hundred paces from the Louvre when the king received a courier from England. After a quick look at the envelope the king opened it and found within a letter from King Charles II. Here's what the English prince wrote to his royal brother:

Your Majesty must be very anxious about the illness of Monsieur le Cardinal Mazarin, but this imminent danger must serve to inspire you, as the cardinal is given up for dead by his own physician. I thank you for your gracious reply to my communication regarding Lady Henrietta Stuart, my sister, and in a week the princess will leave for Paris with her court.

It warms my heart to acknowledge the fraternal friendship which you've shown me, and which makes you all the more my brother. And it's good, moreover, to prove to Your Majesty just how warm my feelings are. You are quietly fortifying Belle-Île-en Mer.[124] This is a mistake; we will never make war on one another. This measure doesn't upset me, it just makes me sad. You are spending millions there uselessly and can tell your ministers as much. As you can see, my intelligencers are well informed, and I hope, my brother, that you can render me a similar service if the chance arises.

The king tugged violently on his bell pull, and his valet de chambre appeared. "Monsieur Colbert just left and can't have gone far," he cried. "Call him back!"

The valet was about to follow this order when the king stopped him. "No, never mind," he said, and then continued to himself, "I see what Colbert was up to. Belle-Île belongs to Monsieur Fouquet, and fortification of it implicates Fouquet in conspiracy. Discovery of this conspiracy is the ruin of the superintendent, its discovery would be reported in correspondence from England, and that's why Colbert wanted to handle that correspondence. But, oh! I can't rely solely on this man—he's a brain, but I also need brawn."

Louis paused, then gave a cry of satisfaction. He said to the valet, "Didn't I have a Lieutenant of Musketeers?"

"Yes, Sire, Monsieur d'Artagnan."

"Who recently left my service?"

"Yes, Sire."

"Find him for me, and make sure he's here for tomorrow morning's lever." The valet bowed and went out.

"Thirteen million in my cellar," the king said, "Colbert holding my purse and d'Artagnan wielding my sword: I am king!"

The End

~ The story continues in Book Six of the Musketeers Cycle,
Court of Daggers ·

Historical Characters

ANNE OF AUSTRIA: *Anne of Austria, "Anne d'Autriche," Queen of France* (1601–66). Eldest daughter of King Philip III of Spain and sister to King Philip IV, Anne was wed to King Louis XIII of France in a political marriage at the age of fourteen. A Spaniard among the French, unloved by the king, proud but intimidated, and vulnerable to manipulation by her friends, she wielded very little influence until she finally gave birth to a royal heir, the future Louis XIV, in 1638. After Louis XIII died in 1643, with his heir still a child, Anne was declared Queen Regent and thereafter came into her own, holding France together against threats both internal and external until Louis XIV was old enough to rule. Anne was intelligent and strong-willed but not a skilled politician; in that she was aided by her close association with her prime minister, Cardinal Mazarin. Were they lovers? Anne's exact level of intimacy with Mazarin is a matter of conjecture; Dumas the novelist prefers the juiciest possible interpretation.

ARAMIS: *Aramis, Chevalier René d'Herblay, Bishop of Vannes*, is based loosely on Henri, Seigneur d'Aramitz (1620?–1655 or 1674), but Dumas drew the character from Courtilz de Sandras's fictionalized *Memoirs of Monsieur d'Artagnan* (circa 1700). In his pseudo-biography of d'Artagnan Sandras had made Aramis the brother of Athos and Porthos, but the historical d'Aramitz was a Gascon petty nobleman, an abbot who spent at least the first half of the 1640s serving under his uncle, Captain de Tréville, in the King's Musketeers. Sources disagree as to the date of his death. The sly and ambitious Aramis of the Musketeers Cycle is entirely an invention of Dumas.

Artagnan see D'ARTAGNAN

ATHOS: *Athos, Comte de La Fère,* is based loosely on Armand, Seigneur de Sillègue, d'Athos, et d'Autevielle (c. 1615–1643), as filtered through Courtilz de Sandras's fictionalized *Memoirs of Monsieur d'Artagnan.* Though Sandras had made Athos the brother of Aramis and Porthos, the historical d'Athos was a Gascon petty nobleman who joined his cousins, Captain de Tréville and Isaac de Portau (Porthos) in the King's Musketeers in 1640. Little is known of his life; he was killed in a duel in December 1643. Dumas invented Athos's character and personality from whole cloth to suit his storytelling purposes.

BERNOUIN: *Monsieur Bernouin* or *Barnouin.* Little is known about Mazarin's premier valet de chambre Bernouin, except that he may have been a Provençal who came north to Paris with his master when Mazarin became a protégé of Richelieu.

BRAGELONNE: *Raoul, Vicomte de Bragelonne.* The young viscount, son of the musketeer Athos, is almost entirely Dumas's invention, based solely on a single reference in Madame de La Fayette's memoir of *Henriette d'Angleterre,* which mentions that in Louise de La Vallière's youth in Blois she had once loved a young man named Bragelonne. Raoul embodies all of Athos's noble virtues, even those unsuited to Louis XIV's less chivalrous age. His relationship with Louise de La Vallière—and her relationship with King Louis—are central to the final volumes of the Musketeers Cycle.

BUCKINGHAM: *George Villiers, 2nd Duke of Buckingham* (1628–1687) was the son and heir of the Buckingham who figured so prominently in *The Three Musketeers,* and an important secondary character in the later volumes of the Musketeers Cycle. A committed Royalist, he fought for Charles II and supported him during his exile, though Buckingham and Charles had a falling-out before the Restoration. After Charles regained the throne, however, Buckingham was soon restored to favor, but he was smitten with the king's sister Princess Henrietta, and scandal followed (as we will see in *Court of Daggers* and thereafter).

CHARLES: *King Charles II, Charles Stuart, King of England, Scotland, and Ireland* (1630–1685) was the exiled son of that King Charles I whose 1649 execution was depicted in *Blood Royal*. Dumas alluded to the intrigues and adventures of Charles II on his long road to Restoration without going into detail, but it was a full ten years of melodrama, reversals, frustration, and hairbreadth escapes. At first Charles had hopes of French support, but when Mazarin allied France with Cromwell in 1655, Charles and his exiled royalists on the continent were driven into the arms of Spain, and he actually led English royalist troops on the side of the Spanish against the French at the Battle of the Dunes in 1658. The 1660 visit to Louis XIV in *Between Two Kings* is fictional, but the role of General Monck in facilitating Charles's return and restoration is basically accurate. Dumas portrays Charles as a young Romantic Era melancholy hero, but by contemporary accounts he was more impatient and entitled than tragic and resigned.

COLBERT: *Jean-Baptiste Colbert* (1619–1683) was a government administrator in various roles starting in 1649 and was about ten years older than depicted by Dumas in *Between Two Kings*. He served Mazarin throughout the 1650s, became interested in financial reform, and early on warned the minister that Superintendent Fouquet was peculating the state's tax money, though Dumas delays the conflict to link it with the rise of Louis XIV. What Dumas got right is that Louis recognized Colbert's talents and ambition and, mistrusting Fouquet, put Colbert in charge of his financial affairs.

CONDÉ: *Louis de Bourbon, Prince de Condé, "Monsieur le Prince,"* later *"The Grand Condé"* (1621–1686). One of the most celebrated military commanders of his time, while he was still the Duc d'Enghien he won two signature victories in the long war against Spain, those of Rocroi in 1643 and Nördlingen in 1644. Upon the death of his father in 1646 Enghien became

Prince de Condé, First Prince of the Blood and third in line for the throne, but he continued his role as France's leading general, further cementing his military reputation with the victory at Lens in 1648. This was followed by his successful leadership of the royal troops in the first half of the Fronde, but then he turned to plotting against Mazarin, who in 1650 had Condé, his brother Conti, and his sister the Duchesse de Longueville arrested, thus triggering the Second Fronde. In the confusion that followed, Anne was forced to release Condé and his siblings, but Monsieur le Prince was by then her sworn enemy, and after the Fronde ended he left France to fight for Spain. Once the long Franco-Spanish war finally concluded in 1659, Condé was rehabilitated by Louis XIV and welcomed back to France, where he served with distinction until his death.

D'ARTAGNAN: *Charles de Batz de Castelmore, Chevalier (later Comte) d'Artagnan* (c. 1611–1673). The historical d'Artagnan was a cadet (younger son) of a family of the minor nobility from the town of Lupiac in Gascony. Like so many other younger sons of Gascony, he followed his neighbor Monsieur de Tréville to Paris to make his fortune, and by 1633 was in the King's Musketeers at a time when Tréville was a lieutenant. D'Artagnan spent the rest of his life in the musketeers, except for the periods when the company was briefly disbanded, when he soldiered with the Gardes Françaises. He gradually rose through the ranks until he became Captain-Lieutenant (in effect, Captain) of the Musketeers in 1667. During the Franco-Dutch War of 1673 he was killed at the Battle of Maastricht. Dumas famously borrowed d'Artagnan from Courtilz de Sandras's highly fictionalized biography, *The Memoirs of Monsieur d'Artagnan,* but his personality and character in the novels of the Musketeers Cycle are entirely the product of the genius of Dumas.

DE GUICHE: *Guy Armand de Gramont* or *Grammont, Comte de Guiche* (1637–1673). Armand de Guiche, son of the Duc de Gramont, was one of the leading playboys of the Court of Louis XIV and a frequent favorite of both the king and his brother Monsieur. Dumas portrays him as a romantic cavalier with a touch of melancholy and makes him Raoul de Bragelonne's closest friend. A lover of both men and women, the historical de Guiche was one of Monsieur's leading bedmates before he was supplanted by the Chevalier de Lorraine, after which he took up with Monsieur's wife Madame. (This Comte de Guiche, by the way, is the same historical personage who serves as the villain in Edmond Rostand's *Cyrano de Bergerac*.)

Du Vallon see PORTHOS

FOUQUET: *Nicolas Fouquet, Marquis de Belle-Île, Vicomte de Melun et Vaux* (1615–1680) was a Parisian of the political class, precocious enough to join the Parliament of Paris as an *avocat* at age thirteen. At age twenty-five he married a wealthy heiress, who died a year later, and by twenty-seven he was a financial intendant in the province of Dauphiné. When Mazarin became Queen Anne's prime minister, Fouquet attached himself to the new regime, serving the cardinal ably throughout the 1640s. During Mazarin's brief exile near the end of the Fronde, Fouquet looked after his interests in Paris, and as a reward the cardinal made Fouquet Superintendent of Finance. Dumas portrays him as a gallant cavalier, dashing and magnanimous, and Fouquet certainly spared no expense to convey that impression. He could well afford to do so: as a finance minister, he was at least as corrupt as Colbert makes him out to be in *Between Two Kings*.

GASTON: *Prince Gaston de Bourbon, Duc d'Orléans, "Monsieur"* (1608–1660). Younger brother to Louis XIII and first heir to the throne, favorite son of Queen Marie de Médicis, Gaston seems to have had no redeeming characteristics whatsoever. Proud, greedy, ambitious for the throne but an arrant coward, he was the figurehead in one conspiracy after another against Louis XIII and Richelieu. These plots failed every time, after which Gaston invariably betrayed his co-conspirators in return for immunity from consequences—because as the healthy heir to a chronically unhealthy king, he knew his life was sacrosanct. Banished to internal exile in Blois in 1652, he lived out the remainder of his life in luxurious boredom.

GUÉNAUD: *François Guénaud* or *Guénault* (1590?–1667) was Queen Anne's chief physician and an object of mockery by the young wits at the French Court. In Molière's play *L'Amour Médecin* (1665) he's represented by Monsieur Macroton, one of the five foolish doctors who present contradictory diagnoses and ridiculous treatments.

Guiche see DE GUICHE

HENRIETTA: *Princess Henrietta-Maria Stuart, Henrietta of England* (1644–1670), the youngest child of King Charles I and Queen Henriette-Marie, was born during the English Civil War and raised in exile in France, where she and her mother lived for many years in poverty. Though bright and observant, she was disregarded as a child, one royal orphan too many, and it wasn't until after the Restoration of her brother Charles II that she was suddenly recognized as someone who mattered. In 1660 she was wed in a political marriage to Philippe de Bourbon, younger brother of Louis XIV, and became one of the leading ornaments of the French Court. Vivacious and beautiful, Henrietta was loved, or at least desired, by both Buckingham and de Guiche, but she set her romantic sights higher than that, as we'll see in the next volume, *Court of Daggers*.

INFANTA: *Marie-Thérèse of Austria, Infanta of Spain and Portugal, Queen of France* (1638–1683), was wed to her cousin King Louis XIV in 1660 in a marriage that sealed the end of the long war between France and Spain. Raised in the rigid and insular Spanish Court, timid and retiring, she had little worldly experience before her marriage and would have been lost and alone in Paris if her mother-in-law, Queen Anne—herself a Spanish princess married young to a French king—hadn't taken her under her wing.

She adored her new husband Louis and was happy while he was faithful to her, a period of almost a year.

La Fère see ATHOS

La Vallière see LOUISE

LORRAINE: *Chevalier Philippe de Lorraine* (1643–1702), a young nobleman of the House of Guise, was a courtier who was the friend, favorite, and lover of Prince Philippe, the younger brother of King Louis XIV. Handsome, clever, jealous, and vindictive, by age sixteen he had the young prince wrapped around his finger, where he kept him for decades.

LOUIS XIV: *Louis de Bourbon, King of France* (1638–1715): The only Frenchman of his century more important than Cardinal Richelieu, the Sun King consolidated all power in France under royal control, thus ending centuries of civil strife, but creating a political structure so rigid it made the French Revolution almost inevitable. Dumas and his assistants did considerable research into the life of Louis XIV, and his depiction of the king's character and personality is mostly spot on. The final volumes of the Musketeers Cycle chart Louis's rise to maturity and power through the eyes of the Four Musketeers, Dumas's most enduring characters.

LOUISE: *Françoise-Louise de la Baume Le Blanc de La Vallière* (1644–1710). Louise de La Vallière was raised in Blois at the Court of Prince Gaston, and after coming to Versailles in 1661 became the first long-term mistress of King Louis XIV. Louise was introduced in *Twenty Years After* as a girl of age seven and returns here briefly as a young woman of seventeen. As the love of Raoul's life, she will be a central character in the next three volumes, *Court of Daggers, Devil's Dance* and *Shadow of the Bastille.*

MALICORNE: *Germain Texier, Comte d'Hautefeuille, Baron de Malicorne* (1626–1694), an ambitious courtier and the lover of Mademoiselle de Montalais, is still largely offstage in this volume, though he will come to the fore in the next book, *Court of Daggers*. Though the historical Malicorne was a petty nobleman, Dumas makes him a bourgeois, an aspiring lawyer, to add the drama of class difference to his romance with Montalais.

MARIE DE MANCINI: *Marie de Mancini; Anna Maria Mancini* (1639–1715) was the middle-born of the five nieces of Cardinal Mazarin that he brought over from Italy to find them politically advantageous marriages in France. Though not the most conventionally pretty of the sisters, Marie was by all accounts the liveliest and most intelligent, and when they were teenagers, she became the first real love (of many) of Louis XIV. He explored the idea of making her his wife but was forcefully dissuaded by the queen and cardinal. Unlike her sisters, who were found influential French husbands, Marie was married off to an Italian, Prince Lorenzo Colonna, possibly to put her farther away from Louis.

Mancini see MARIE DE MANCINI

Marie-Thérèse see INFANTA

MAZARIN: *Cardinal Jules Mazarin*, born *Giulio Raimondo Mazzarino* or *Mazarini* (1602–1661). In 1634 the Italian-born diplomat became a protégé of Cardinal Richelieu and in 1639 was naturalized French and entered the king's service. Through Richelieu's influence he was made a cardinal in 1641 and brought onto the King's Council. After Richelieu and Louis XIII died, Mazarin made himself indispensable to the regent, Anne of Austria, and basically stepped into Richelieu's shoes to become France's prime minister. He was probably intimate with Queen Anne and functioned as her co-ruler until Louis XIV attained his majority. Mazarin was an extremely able diplomat, negotiating an end to the Thirty Years' War, maintaining royal authority through the chaotic years of the Fronde, striking an alliance with Cromwell, and maneuvering the fractious French nobility back into compliance with the crown in time to hand an intact and flourishing state over to King Louis XIV. He was widely disliked for being a foreigner and arriviste who presumed to place himself above the native nobility, feelings basically endorsed by Dumas, who preferred men of heart to men of mind.

MONCK: *General George Monck* or *Monk, 1st Duke of Albemarle* (1608–1670) was a career soldier who worked his way up through the ranks, fighting on the Continent, the Scottish border, and against the Irish in the rebellion of 1641. When the English Civil War broke out, he served as an officer on the Royalist side, but was captured and imprisoned for two years, and then released to command troops for the Parliamentarians. He became one of Oliver Cromwell's most trusted commanders and proved to be as canny at political strategy as he was at warfare. After Cromwell's death, he consolidated his position in the north of Britain and began a waiting game, biding his time to see how matters would play out. When Richard Cromwell and John Lambert both showed themselves too weak to govern effectively, he finally threw his support behind Charles II and was instrumental in the Restoration that put the Stuarts back on the throne. He was rewarded with a peerage and, eventually, the admiralty.

Monsieur see GASTON *or* PHILIPPE

Monsieur le Cardinal see MAZARIN

Monsieur le Prince see CONDÉ

MONTALAIS: *Aure* (actually *Nicole Anne Constance*) *de Montalais* (c. 1641–?). Mademoiselle de Montalais was a maid of honor at the Court of Prince Gaston, and later dame d'honneur to Princess Henrietta in Paris, where she helped arrange an affair between the princess and the Comte de Guiche. Though she is said to have had a taste for intrigue, little else is known about her, and her personality is largely an invention of Dumas.

Orléans see GASTON

PHILIPPE: *Prince Philippe de Bourbon, Duc d'Anjou,* later *Duc d'Orléans, "Petit Monsieur," "Monsieur"* (1640–1701), was the younger brother of Louis XIV, but to keep him from assuming the fractious role his uncle Prince Gaston had taken under his brother Louis XIII, Philippe was never trained to rule or consider himself entitled to assume the throne. He was openly homosexual but did his duty to the dynasty and married twice, producing six children. Though he was a capable military commander, his first concern was always luxury and ease, which he pursued without stint.

PORTHOS: *Porthos, Baron du Vallon,* is based loosely on Isaac de Porthau (1617–1712), as filtered through Courtilz de Sandras's fictionalized *Memoirs of Monsieur d'Artagnan.* Though Sandras had made Porthos the brother of Aramis and Athos, the historical de Porthau was a minor Gascon nobleman who joined his cousins, Captain de Tréville and Armand d'Athos, in the King's Musketeers in 1642. When his father died in 1654, he left the musketeers and returned to Béarn, where he served as a parliamentarian and local magistrate until his death in 1712. His character and personality in the Musketeers novels are entirely the invention of Dumas.

Queen Anne see ANNE OF AUSTRIA

Queen Marie-Thérèse see INFANTA

Queen Mother see ANNE OF AUSTRIA

Raoul see BRAGELONNE

ROCHESTER: *John Wilmot, 2nd Earl of Rochester* (1647–1680) was an accomplished poet and one of the leading playboys of the Restoration Court of Charles II. His father, Henry, who had supported Charles during his exile, had been created 1st Earl of Rochester in 1658 and died shortly thereafter, passing the title to his son. At the time of *Between Two Kings* the young Rochester was still a student at Oxford, but Dumas, who loved aristocratic writers, backdated him a few years to fit him into his story.

SAINT-RÉMY, MADAME: *Françoise Le Prévôt de la Coutelaye, Madame de Saint-Rémy* was an oft-married lady of the Touraine who was the wife of Laurent de la Baume le Blanc when she gave birth, in 1644, to Louise de La Vallière. Her third husband, the Marquis de Saint-Rémy, was First Chamberlain to Prince Gaston in Blois.

SAINT-RÉMY, MONSIEUR: *Jacques de Couravel, Marquis de Saint-Rémy*, was First Chamberlain to Prince Gaston during his internal exile in Blois, and stepfather to Louise de La Vallière. After Gaston's death he moved to Paris and performed the same function for the new "Monsieur," Prince Philippe.

Vallon see PORTHOS

Notes on the Text of *Between Two Kings*

1. CHÂTEAU DE BLOIS: Blois was an old medieval city on the Loire River about 120 miles southwest of Paris. The sprawling Château de Blois, which dominated the city, was a royal castle occupied by Prince Gaston from about 1620 until his death in 1660.

2. 'MONSIEUR': By tradition at the French Court, the younger brother of the king and heir to the throne was always referred to as "Monsieur." At this time "Monsieur" is Prince Gaston, the Duc d'Orléans (see GASTON under Historical Characters).

3. HALL OF THE ESTATES GENERAL: Under the Ancien Régime the Estates General was an extraordinary gathering of representatives of the three classes, or Estates, of French society: the clergy, nobility, and commoners. The Château de Blois had hosted the Estates General in 1576 and 1588, during the prolonged crisis of the Wars of Religion.

4. CHAMBORD: Just upriver from Blois, Chambord was the largest château in the Loire valley, built for King François I early in the 16th century as a hunting estate. Still stunning today, it's one of the finest examples of French Renaissance architecture.

5. "MADAME": At the Royal Court, just as the younger brother of the king was called "Monsieur," so his wife bore the informal title of "Madame." At this time Madame was Prince Gaston's second wife, Marguerite de Lorraine, Duchesse d'Orléans (1613–1672).

6. QUEEN MARIE . . . CLIMBING DOWN A FORTY-SEVEN-FOOT DROP: The Italian heiress Marie de Médicis (1575–1642) was the second queen to France's King Henri IV, who married her in 1600 in a desperate quest for an heir after the infertile Queen Marguerite was set aside. Exiled to Blois by her son Louis XIII in 1617 for rebellion, with the help of other conspirators she escaped in 1619 by climbing out a high window, after which she returned to plotting against the throne.

7. 'MONSIEUR LE PRINCE': Louis de Bourbon, Prince de Condé (1621–1686), cousin of Louis XIV and second heir to the throne after the king's younger brother, was known at Court by the informal title of "Monsieur le Prince" (see CONDÉ under Historical Characters).

8. THE VICTOR OF ROCROI AND LENS: Renowned as a general, the Prince de Condé was widely regarded as the military savior of France for his victories over the forces of Spain at the battles of Rocroi (1643) and Lens (1648). The Battle of Lens, recounted in *Twenty Years After,* was the young Vicomte de Bragelonne's first military action.

9. MY SISTER-IN-LAW: Prince Gaston refers here to Queen Anne, widow of Gaston's elder brother King Louis XIII and mother of Louis XIV (see ANNE OF AUSTRIA in Historical Characters).

10. BILLET-DOUX FROM THE BODICE OF MADEMOISELLE DE HAUTEFORT: This refers to a famous incident in which Louis XIII, jealous of the affections of Marie de Hautefort, one of the few women he ever coveted, concealed a presumed love letter in her bosom, whence the king was too shy and prudish to remove it. Dumas provided an amusing depiction of the scene in chapter 74 of *The Red Sphinx.*

11: WE LIVE HERE IN THE PAST LIKE POLES: The Royal Court of Poland, east beyond the Germanies, was proverbially backward by French standards, though by intermarriage France provided monarchs to Poland in the 16th and 17th centuries. Poland returned the favor in the 18th century, providing a queen consort to Louis XV.

12: DON LUIS DE HARO: Luis Méndez de Haro (1598–1661) was a Grandee of Spain who succeeded the Count-Duke of Olivares in 1643 as King Philip's favorite and leading minister. He negotiated with Mazarin the Treaty of the Pyrenees that ended the long war between France and Spain and led to the wedding of the Spanish infanta to Louis XIV.

13. WE SHALL RE-CROWN THEM WITH MYRTLES: In ancient times, military victors were crowned with laurel leaves, but a crown of myrtle, associated with Venus, was a symbol of love.

14. THE ESTATE OF THE COMTE DE LA FÈRE: Athos's modest estate just outside Blois had first been introduced in *Twenty Years After,* where it was referred to as Bragelonne, presumably to explain Raoul's noble name. (All French nobles were known by the names of their domains.) In *Between Two Kings* and subsequent volumes, Dumas referred to the estate as La Fère, apparently forgetting that he'd previously stated that Athos's domain of La Fère was a county in the province of Berry.

15. THE TURMOIL OF THE FRONDE, OF WHICH WE FORMERLY ATTEMPTED TO RECOUNT THE FIRST PHASES: The first half of the multi-year rebellion of the Fronde formed the basis of the political intrigue between the musketeers and Mazarin in *Twenty Years After* and *Blood Royal*. See Note 45 below.

16. LOUIS DE CONDÉ HAD MADE A FRANK AND SOLEMN RECONCILIATION WITH THE COURT: After serving Queen Regent Anne of Austria and Mazarin as their general in the first half of the Fronde (1648–1649), the Prince de Condé had gone over to the Nobles' faction in the second Fronde (1650–1653), ultimately losing when the nobles were defeated, then defecting to Spain. He commanded Spanish troops against France until his defeat at the Battle of the Dunes in 1658, which led directly to the end of the war and the Treaty of the Pyrenees in the following year. After that treaty, Condé was rehabilitated and accepted back into the French Court by Mazarin and Queen Anne.

17. PRINCIPLES OF LOYALTY TO THE MONARCHY, AS HE'D EXPOUNDED ONE DAY TO HIS SON IN THE VAULTS OF SAINT-DENIS: Athos swore Bragelonne to lifelong loyalty to the king in chapter 24 of *Twenty Years After*.

18. MONSIEUR DE TURENNE: Henri de La Tour d'Auvergne, Marshal and Vicomte de Turenne (1611–1675) was, after the Prince de Condé, the other great French general of the mid–17th century. After Condé went over to the nobles' faction in the Second Fronde, Turenne, his former associate, stayed with the royal party, thereafter repeatedly defeating Condé until the Fronde was concluded with a victory for the royals.

19. A NOTEBOOK, ENTIRELY FILLED WITH HIS HANDWRITING: These are presumably the fictional memoirs of the Comte de La Fère, whom Dumas in his preface to *The Three Musketeers* had pretended to consult as a source for the story.

20. GOOD OLD GRIMAUD: The laconic Grimaud has been Athos's "lackey," or manservant, since *The Three Musketeers*. Like the musketeers' other lackeys, Grimaud appears throughout the Musketeers Cycle, and eventually one gets the impression that this stoic but caring and utterly reliable man was Dumas's favorite of the four.

21. MARSHAL D'ANCRE: Concino Concini, Maréchal d'Ancre (1575–1617) was a handsome Italian courtier who was a favorite of Queen Marie de Médicis. During Marie's regency after her husband King Henri IV was assassinated, the arrogant Concini

was showered with posts and preferment; he lorded it over the French nobility and they cordially hated him for it, no one more so than the youth King Louis XIII. Luynes, the young king's favorite, engineered Louis's rise to power (and his own) when he orchestrated Concini's public assassination in 1617.

22. THE SCHOOL OF RAPHAEL AND THE CARACCI: Raffaello Sanzio da Urbino, "Raphael" (1483–1520) was a painter and architect of the Italian Renaissance, one of the "Old Masters" along with Michelangelo and Leonardo da Vinci. The three brother artists of the Caracci family of Bologna in the late 16th century rejected the dull Mannerist style then prevailing and hearkened back to the more naturalistic painting of Raphael, founding an art school called the *Accademia degli Incamminati* that pointed toward the innovations of the Baroque era.

23. MADAME LA MARÉCHALE D'ANCRE: Leonora Dori Galigaï (1571–1617), wife of Marshal d'Ancre (see Note 21), was like her husband a favorite of Queen Marie de Médicis. After the young Louis XIII had the marshal assassinated, his wife was arrested, charged with using witchcraft to enchant the queen, convicted, decapitated, and burned at the stake on the Place de Grève in Paris.

24. BRONZINO: Agnolo di Cosimo, (1503–1572) called "Bronzino" probably for his dark skin tone, was a Florentine painter in the Italian Mannerist style, and the portrait painter of the ruling Medici family.

25. ALBANI: Francesco Albani or Albano (1578–1660) of Bologna was a Baroque painter and student of the Caraccis (see Note 22) known for his bright, decorative paintings illustrating classical themes.

26. ANACREONTIC SIRENS: The Greek poet Anacreon (5th century B.C.E.) was known for his songs celebrating love and conviviality, implying the queens on the sign looked amorously inviting.

27. AS THEY REALLY DIVIDE INTO TWO RACES, THE BLACK AND THE WHITE: For Dumas, whose father was born a half-black slave in the Caribbean, the matter of race was complicated. Dumas burned with outrage at the injustices his father suffered in the Napoleonic years, and though he never pretended he wasn't one-quarter black, the author was deeply hurt by the racist attacks of those Frenchmen who derided his "African" aspects. But young Alexandre had been raised in the bourgeois society of

a small conservative French town, and though he flirted with rebellion and revolution as a young man, he craved even more the approval of the establishment. Deep down, he never really questioned the establishment's fundamental belief in the overall superiority of the "white race." Dumas was a man ahead of his time in many ways, but he could only go so far.

28. A PHYSIOGNOMIST: By which Dumas means the innkeeper can read men's personalities from their faces and expressions. Physiognomy was an ancient pseudoscience that was revived in 1643 by the English physician and philosopher Sir Thomas Browne (1605–1682) that was often invoked to justify the prejudice of first impressions. Browne also brought the word "caricature" into the English language, which should give some indication of physiognomy's lack of subtlety and nuance.

29. KING'S MUSKETEERS: A company—later two—of elite soldiers, the musketeers were the personal guard of King Louis XIII and after him Louis XIV. They were founded in 1622 when a carbine-armed company of light horsemen was upgraded and given the new, heavier matchlock muskets as primary arms. Though their function was mainly ceremonial and to serve as royal bodyguards, they were sometimes deployed on the battlefield, where they fought either mounted as cavalry or dismounted and relying on their muskets. They are often depicted wearing their signature blue tabards with white crosses, which were adopted sometime in the 1630s.

30. MONSIEUR DANGEAU: Philippe de Courcillon, Marquis de Dangeau (1638–1720) was a longtime ornament of the Court of Louis XIV and one of his early favorites, liked for his wit and because he was such a dedicated cardplayer.

31. THE GORGET AND BUFFCOAT: A gorget was a semicircular plate of armor that covered the neck and upper chest; the buffcoat was originally an arming doublet worn under plate armor, but when full armor became obsolete due to firearms, it evolved into a leather jerkin typically made of thick ox or cowhide. The buffcoat of a gentleman of high rank was often heavily embroidered.

32. PARRY: The old man who served as the loyal body servant to England's King Charles I and then his heir was first introduced in *Blood Royal.* He is an invention of Dumas.

33. PISTOLES: Pistole was a French word for a gold coin of the 16th and 17th centuries, usually Spanish in origin. The leading European states liked to mint their own coins,

but gold was hard for them to come by—except for Spain, which flooded Europe with gold from its possessions in the New World, making the Spanish escudo the de facto base currency of European trade for two centuries. When Dumas's characters refer to pistoles, they are mostly Spanish escudos. One pistole is worth about ten livres or three French crowns (écus).

34. A CROWN THAT WAS ALREADY SLIPPING FROM THE VALOIS TO THE BOURBONS: France was ruled by the House of Valois from the 14th through 16th centuries; Henri III, who ruled from 1574 to 1579, was the final king of the Valois line, followed by Henri IV, the first of the Bourbons and grandfather of Louis XIV. Henri III "stooped to betrayal and assassination" when he had the Duc de Guise murdered—see Note 35 below.

35. THE VERY SPOT WHERE THE DUC DE GUISE RECEIVED THE FIRST THRUST OF THE PONIARD: In the previous century, during the French Wars of Religion (roughly 1562–1598), the hardline Catholic members of the nobility, who wanted to crush the Protestant (or Huguenot) faction, were often held in check by the more moderate Catholics who were usually allied to the then-current Valois king. In 1576 a powerful and ambitious Catholic peer, Henri I, Duc de Guise, founded the Catholic League to organize opposition to the Huguenots and to King Henri III, who was regarded as too conciliatory toward the Protestants. The League was heavily armed, and more than a few battles were fought before Henri III had the Duc de Guise assassinated in 1588 in the Château de Blois.

36. LA PORTE: Pierre de La Porte, Cloak-Bearer to the Queen (1603–1680) entered Queen Anne's service in 1621 and was for decades one of her most trusted confidential servants. The 1839 edition of La Porte's *Memoirs* was one of Dumas's primary sources. La Porte will reappear in an important (albeit nonhistorical) role in the final book in the Musketeers Cycle, *The Man in the Iron Mask*.

37. THE SCOTS . . . HANGED LORD MONTROSE, MY MOST DEVOTED SERVANT, BECAUSE HE WOULDN'T BECOME A COVENANTER: James Graham, 1st Marquess of Montrose (1612–1650), had been a Covenanter, or Scottish Presbyterian, and in the civil wars was initially opposed to Charles I before coming over to the Royalist side in 1644. One of the best of Charles I's generals, he was a master organizer who won a number of battles but met defeat at Philiphaugh in 1645 and escaped to Norway. To support Charles II, he returned to Scotland in 1649, but was

defeated, captured, and hanged by Parliament in Edinburgh—ironically, shortly before the Scottish government changed sides and declared for Charles II.

38. RICHARD ABDICATED THE PROTECTORATE ON MAY 25, 1659: Richard Cromwell (1626–1712), son of Oliver, became Lord Protector when his father died in 1658, but he lacked both experience and will and held the position for less than a year before being forced by the military to step down.

39. MONSIEUR DE RETZ: Jean-François Paul de Gondy or Gondi, Bishop Coadjutor of Paris and later Cardinal de Retz (1613–1679) was a political and militant churchman who was one of the most important leaders of the Fronde, and an important character in *Twenty Years After* and *Blood Royal.* He was awarded a cardinal's hat in 1652 in an attempt to pacify him, but the gambit failed and he was exiled; Louis XIV eventually recalled him to Court in 1662.

40. FOUR FRENCH GENTLEMEN DEVOTED TO MY FATHER: That is, d'Artagnan, Athos, Porthos, and Aramis, who nearly saved Charles I from execution in the preceding volume of this series, *Blood Royal.*

41. MONSIEUR DE BRIENNE: Henri-Auguste de Loménie, Comte de Brienne (1594–1666) was the Secretary of State for Foreign Affairs from 1643 to 1663, reporting to Mazarin. A diplomat from a family of diplomats, he was a stable and steadying influence for decades, plus his wife was a close friend of Queen Anne's, which helped maintain him in his influential position—until Louis XIV, eager to flex his own diplomatic muscles, replaced him in 1663.

42. CARDINAL RICHELIEU: Armand-Jean du Plessis, Cardinal de Richelieu (1585–1642), Louis XIII's incomparable prime minister, was one of the two most important Frenchmen of the 17th century, exceeded only by Louis XIV. Richelieu has been the subject of scores of biographies (including one by Dumas), and his life and works have been analyzed in excruciating detail, starting with his own *Memoirs.* His deeds were momentous, but it was his character and personality that interested Dumas, who loved historical figures who were great but also greatly flawed. After deploying Richelieu in *The Three Musketeers* as the worthy antagonist of his most enduring heroes, Dumas couldn't resist revisiting him as a protagonist for *The Red Sphinx.* Though gone from the Musketeers Cycle after *The Red Sphinx,* Richelieu nonetheless casts a long shadow over the rest of the series, all the way through *The Man in the Iron Mask.*

43. YOUR FATHER'S BROTHER-IN-LAW: A reminder that King Charles I had married Princess Henriette of France, sister of King Louis XIII.

44. THE RUMP PARLIAMENT: After England's Parliament was purged of royalists—half its number—by strongarm commanders loyal to Cromwell in 1648 (in order to try to convict Charles I), its remaining members in the House of Commons were referred to as the "Rump Parliament," and so it was called until replaced by the "Convention Parliament" during the Restoration.

45. THE FRONDE: A number of social and political conflicts combined in France to cause the messy and intermittent rebellion of the Fronde from 1648 to 1652. King Louis XIV, still in his minority, was too young to rule, and the realm was ruled by a queen regent and her foreign-born prime minister, a leadership regarded as weak by the opportunistic *Grands* of the high nobility.

46. *MAZARINADES*: Dumas uses the term *mazarinade* to describe the cardinal's political machinations, but it originated ten years earlier, during the Fronde, to describe the scurrilous pamphlets insulting Mazarin illicitly published during that political unrest. The cardinal responded by funding a flurry of opposing pamphlets supporting him, and eventually these became known as *mazarinades* as well. The pamphlets that publicized the cardinal's deceits and diplomatic half-truths eventually lent their name to the machinations themselves.

47. ARMORED IN TRIPLE BRASS, AS HORACE SAYS: In Book Three of Horace's *Odes,* he refers to a Tower of Brass, with "locks, and bolts, and iron bars." This might also be an allusion to Cromwell's armored cavalry, who were known as the Ironsides.

48. LOUIS XI: France's King Louis XI (1423–1483), nicknamed "the Cunning" and "the Universal Spider," was as renowned for his diplomatic brilliance as he was notorious for his lack of scruples.

49. MONSIEUR DE BEAUFORT, MONSIEUR DE RETZ, OR MONSIEUR LE PRINCE: The three main leaders of the uprising of the Fronde: François de Vendôme, Duc de Beaufort (1616–1669) was the grandson of King Henri IV and his mistress Gabrielle d'Estrées, which made him a Prince of the Blood; Jean-François Paul de Gondy, Cardinal de Retz (1613–1679) was a political and militant churchman (see Note 39); Monsieur le Prince was the Prince de Condé (see Historical Characters).

50. A BIRETTA OF VELVET: That is, the red velvet beret of a cardinal.

51. PROUD PROFILE OF AN EAGLE FACING THE SUN: Dumas invokes Louis XIV's later adoption of the appellation the Sun King.

52. LIKE A FIGURE FROM CALLOT: Jacques Callot (1592–1635) was an artist, engraver, and printmaker from Lorraine who drew expressive portraits, street scenes of Paris, and images of battles and atrocities from the Thirty Years' War. Dumas refers here to Callot's famous sketch of a cavalier with a great plumed hat, which he also references as a description of the swashbuckler Etienne Latil in *The Red Sphinx*. (The sketch is reproduced in this editor's edition of that title.)

53. AN EPIC OF TASSO OR ARIOSTO: Italian authors of 16th-century chivalric romances; Torquato Tasso (1544–1595) wrote *Jerusalem Delivered*, a knightly epic of the First Crusade, while Ludovico Ariosto (1474–1533) was the celebrated author of *Orlando Furioso*, a romantic saga of Charlemagne and his paladins battling the Saracens.

54. MESSIEURS DE RICHELIEU, DE BUCKINGHAM, DE BEAUFORT, AND DE RETZ: D'Artagnan's mighty adversaries and allies in the events of *The Three Musketeers* and *Twenty Years After*: Cardinal Richelieu (see Note 42); George Villiers, the first Duke of Buckingham (1592–1628); and the Frondeurs the Duc de Beaufort and the Cardinal de Retz (see Note 49).

55. CAPTAIN OF THE MUSKETEERS: The position d'Artagnan refers to was technically *Captain-Lieutenant* of the King's Musketeers since the ultimate rank of "Captain" notionally was held by the king himself. He is right about the prestige and precedent the position commanded at Court due to its propinquity to the Crown, though it was less prestigious as a battlefield rank in times of open warfare.

56. MONSIEUR DE TRÉVILLE: Jean-Arnaud de Peyrer, Comte de Troisville or Tréville (1598–1672) was Captain-Lieutenant of the King's Musketeers from 1634 to 1646, the first to hold that position, but had been forcibly retired by Mazarin when the cardinal temporarily disbanded the elite company.

57. A MORNING LEVER: The *lever* (rising) was an official morning reception held at the bedside of every adult member of the royal House of France, and by other important members of Court as well. The relative importance of a person could be told by the

quantity and quality of those who attended their lever; Louis's here is described as a "pretense" to indicate that he is, as yet, insignificant in his own Court.

58. MAY GOD FORGIVE HIS MURDERER: As related in *Blood Royal*, the king's executioner was Monsieur Mordaunt, son of Milady de Winter, and his "murderer" was none other than Athos himself.

59. BAZIN: Throughout the Musketeers Cycle, Bazin serves as the loyal lackey and assistant of Aramis. Just as the scheming Aramis is the least sympathetic of the musketeers, his servant, the pompous and selfish Bazin, is the least likeable of the lackeys, mainly serving as a butt for Dumas's jokes about churchmen.

60. OR DO I MEAN THE VICAR GENERAL?: A vicar general is a bishop's deputy, so d'Artagnan is joking here about the ambitious Aramis's ambitions for ecclesiastical rank. But his joke is short of the mark, as he soon finds.

61. MOUSQUETON: The loyal servant of Porthos throughout the Musketeers Cycle. As related in *The Three Musketeers*, his birth name was Boniface, but his master renamed him with the more martial French word for musketoon, a large-caliber musket cut down to the length of a carbine.

62. MONSIEUR RACAN: Honorat de Bueil, Seigneur de Racan (1589–1670) was a poet, playwright, and founding member of the Académie Française. The play *Les Bergeries* (1619) was his first great success. Mousqueton is quite wrong about the author having "died just last month."

63. PLANCHET: Like his counterparts who serve the three musketeers, d'Artagnan's stalwart lackey appears throughout the novels of the Musketeers Cycle, eventually becoming less servant to the Gascon than friend and partner.

64. USURY: Lending money out at interest was widely considered immoral; it was forbidden by the Church and was strictly controlled by law. Jews, who were outside of Catholic law, could engage in moneylending, but it was a perilous enterprise, as a Christian's accusation of predatory lending could result in exile or execution.

65. ENCOUNTERS ON THE BOULEVARD: Duels, in other words. For a Christian, to be accused of predatory usury was a serious matter, and Planchet was defending his reputation as an honest businessman.

66. YOU NEVER LEFT THE PLACE ROYALE: During the Fronde, Planchet was an officer in the Frondeur militia, and as shown in *Blood Royal,* commanding a unit during the Battle of Charenton that stayed in Paris and missed all the fighting.

67. LIKE TWO ATTORNEYS' CLERKS: As a youth, Dumas had served an apprenticeship as a law clerk, and the experience was the source of many humorous scenes.

68. MONSIEUR COQUENARD, THE FIRST HUSBAND OF MADAME LA BARONNE DU VALLON: In *The Three Musketeers,* Porthos's mistress was Madame Coquenard, the wife of a wealthy, and elderly, Parisian attorney. After Monsieur Coquenard died, Porthos, elevated to the rank of Baron du Vallon, had married the wealthy widow.

69. PERFIDIOUS ALBION: The French regarding their longtime adversaries the English as treacherous and deceitful is an attitude with a long history, and the phrase *la perfide Albion* has been attested as far back as the 13th century.

70. DOUBLE-LOUIS: The louis d'or was a French gold coin introduced into circulation in 1640 by Louis XIII (who put his face and name on it). In size and weight it was an imitation of the Spanish double escudo (or "doubloon"), which was also the pistole so frequently mentioned in the Musketeer novels and the most common gold currency in Europe. A pistole was worth ten or eleven livres, or about three crowns (*écus*); the louis d'or was worth the same or slightly more. A double-louis, therefore, was a doubloon.

71. REMINISCENT OF HIS ARRIVAL AT THE INN OF THE JOLLY MILLER IN MEUNG: A reference to Chapter I of *The Three Musketeers,* and the commotion caused by the young d'Artagnan's arrival at an inn.

72. NEPTUNE PRONOUNCING THE *QUOS EGO:* In Virgil's *Aeneid,* Neptune quells the gales of the rebellious Aeolus with this famous curtailed threat, basically Latin for "Why, I ought to . . . !"

73. THE PIRATES OF TUNIS: The so-called "Barbary Pirates" of North Africa, who operated out of the ports of Tunis, Tripoli, Rabat, and Algiers, crewed their fast galleys with slaves taken from European ships and shore towns.

74. SAILOR OF THE PONANT: The *Ponant* was an archaic French term for the Western Sea, i.e., the Atlantic, and was the opposite of the *Levant,* or Eastern Mediterranean.

75. WILLIAM II OF NASSAU, STADTHOLDER OF HOLLAND: Dumas has his dates and Dutch rulers wrong here: William II, Prince of Orange and Stadtholder of the United Provinces, had died in 1650 and been succeeded by Jan de Witt, who ruled the Dutch Republic until 1672. It is true, however, that Charles II had long been living as an exile on the Dutch coast.

76. GENERAL LAMBERT: John Lambert (1619–1684) was an officer in the Parliamentary army under Oliver Cromwell who rose to the rank of general. Following the victory at Worcester, he was appointed Lord Deputy of Ireland and thereafter was a prominent politician, leading the military wing of the Protectorate, often in rivalry with Cromwell. After Cromwell's death he led the faction that forced Cromwell's son, Richard, to step down, outplayed all his competitors, shut the members out of parliament, and assumed the rank of Major-General of the Armies. He then set out north with his troops to challenge his only remaining rival, General Monck.

77. AT COLDSTREAM, ON THE TWEED: Dumas makes it sound like Newcastle and Coldstream are next to each other when in fact they're fifty miles apart, but the advance elements of the two armies were close enough for near encounters.

78. NEWCASTLE ABBEY: This abbey, and its very convenient location, are Dumas's inventions.

79. THE MUSKETEERS' FORMER HOST: Dumas named him in *Blood Royal* as Señor Perez, though without giving his inn a name, which he calls the Hartshorn here. Dumas wrote quickly in his rush to get chapters out for weekly publication, and in sequels didn't always take the time to look back at what he'd written before.

80. THE *MEMOIRS OF D'AUBIGNÉ*: Agrippa d'Aubigné (1552–1630) was a Huguenot supporter of King Henri IV who wrote a memoir published in 1729 with which Dumas was doubtless familiar. Agrippa was the grandfather of Françoise d'Aubigné who appears in *Twenty Years After* and went on to become Madame Scarron and then Madame de Maintenon, Louis XIV's final mistress and secret wife.

81. LUYNES, BELLEGARDE, AND BASSOMPIERRE: Favorites of Louis XIII who were rewarded with position and privilege, though Athos's compliment in comparing

d'Artagnan to them has perhaps an unintended sting to it, as all three ended their lives out of favor and in disgrace.

82. EXCEPT FOR MONTROSE: See Note 37.

83. KNIGHT OF THE GARTER: The Most Noble Order of the Garter was an English knightly order founded in 1348 by Edward III; it was highly prestigious, and only the monarch could induct new members into its ranks.

84. CHEVALIER DU SAINT-ESPRIT: The Ordre du Saint-Esprit, Order of the Holy Spirit, was a French knightly order established by King Henri III in 1578 during the Wars of Religion as a counterweight to the Order of the Golden Fleece, whose members largely supported the fractious nobility of the Catholic League.

85. ORDER OF THE GOLDEN FLEECE: A Catholic knightly order established in 1430 by Philippe III, Duke of Burgundy, and later adopted by the Hapsburg dynasty of Spain and Austria as their highest order of chivalry. There could never be more than fifty living members of the order at a time.

86. THE KING OF FRANCE . . . ON THE OCCASION OF HIS RECENT MARRIAGE: Dumas had his dates slightly off: Charles II entered London on May 29, 1660, and Louis XIV married the Spanish Infanta Maria Teresa shortly thereafter in France, on June 9, 1660.

87. VICEROY OF IRELAND AND SCOTLAND: Dumas overreaches a bit; Monck was named Lord Lieutenant of Ireland (but not Scotland) in August 1660.

88. FABRICIUS: Gaius Fabricius Luscinus was a Roman patrician of the 3rd century B.C.E. who was renowned for his frugality and incorruptibility.

89. *THE SECRET WIFE OF MONSIEUR DE MAZARIN*: It was widely rumored that Queen Anne and Cardinal Mazarin had been secretly married in a private service, but there is no solid historical confirmation of this.

90. THIS PREPARATION FOR COMBAT, WHICH THE ROMANS CALLED *ACCINCTION*: in Latin, *accinctio* means to gird on one's weapons, to arm up.

91. THE QUALITIES OF FABIUS AND HANNIBAL: That is, the complementary skills of two opponents, Carthaginian general Hannibal Barca (247–182 B.C.E.), a wily aggressor, and Roman general Fabius Cunctator (280–203 B.C.E.), who resisted Hannibal's advance with innovative delaying tactics.

92. IRUS: In *The Odyssey*, Irus (Latin) or Arnaeus (Greek) is a poor Ithacan beggar who makes the mistake of challenging another beggar who's new in town, and who unfortunately for Irus is Odysseus in disguise. This ends badly for Irus.

93. THE POSTILION: The post horse system was a way of hiring horses by stages, turning in a rented horse at a "post" and hiring another one, if necessary, for the next stage. Packhorses, carriages, and wagons could also be rented by post, usually coming with a hired driver who rode the lead horse and was called the *postilion*.

94. THAT GOOD OLD WINE OF ANJOU THAT ONE DAY NEARLY COST US SO DEARLY: A reference to Chapter XLII of *The Three Musketeers*, "The Anjou Wine," in which Milady de Winter sent d'Artagnan an entire case of the vintage—all poisoned.

95. PALAIS ROYAL: Cardinal Richelieu started building his Palais Cardinal in 1633 and completed it in 1639. When Richelieu died in 1642, he willed his grand Paris residence to the king, and it was renamed the Palais Royal. Upon the death of Louis XIII, Queen Anne moved her family—including Cardinal Mazarin—from the Louvre into the more modern Palais Royal.

96. THE COMTESSE DE SOISSONS: The cardinal's niece, Olympe de Mancini (1638–1708), Marie's elder sister, had been a countess of high rank since marrying the near-royal Comte de Soissons in 1657.

97. HE, WHO NEVER PREVENTED ANYONE FROM SINGING, PROVIDING THEY PAID: A reference to a famous remark Mazarin is said to have made during the Fronde about the satirical songs of the Frondeurs, quoted by Dumas in *Twenty Years After*: "If they sing the song, they'll pay the piper."

98. MY FATHER: The Comte de Guiche's father was Antoine III, Duc de Gramont or Grammont (1604–1678). A capable military commander, he was made a marshal in 1641, and for his victories—and because he was married to one of Richelieu's nieces—he was elevated to the peerage and became Duc de Gramont in 1643.

99. THE DAYS WHEN MONSIEUR CROMWELL WAS SENDING US CUTTHROATS AS ENVOYS: Mazarin refers to the events of *Twenty Years After* in which Cromwell sent the murderous Mordaunt, the son of Milady de Winter, to Mazarin as a diplomatic messenger.

100. THE PLACE DE GRÈVE: In Paris, the broad square on the Right Bank of the Seine in front of the Hôtel de Ville where convicted criminals were publicly tortured and executed, commoners by hanging and nobles by decapitation.

101. BOILEAU'S SATIRES: Nicolas Boileau-Despréaux (1636–1711) was a French satirist and critic of poetry; he mocked Guénaud for supposedly poisoning his patients with antimony in his *Satire IV* (1664).

102. HE TREATED THE PATIENT AS A TURK TREATS A MOOR: In other words, without any special consideration for his status. In *Don Quixote* Cervantes complained that the Turks treated the Spanish Moors as badly as they treated Christians.

103. I'M BARELY FIFTY-TWO: Mazarin shades his age downward; born in 1602, the minister was fifty-eight.

104. HE WAS THIRTEEN YEARS OLDER THAN LOUIS XIV: Colbert was nearly twenty years older than the king, but Dumas often played fast and loose with the ages of historical characters to suit his dramatic purposes; here he made Colbert slightly younger to match his depiction as ambitious and aspiring.

105. THE CHÂTELET: A medieval keep in central Paris on the Right Bank at the Pont au Change, the Grand Châtelet contained the offices of the Provost of Paris and the city's civil and criminal courts.

106. MICHEL LE TELLIER, THE SECRETARY OF STATE: Michel Le Tellier, Marquis de Barbezieux (1603–1685) was a protégé of Mazarin who served as Secretary of State for War from 1643 until the minister's death. He made the transition to continue to serve under Louis XIV and was appointed Chancellor in 1677.

107. THE THEATINE FATHER: The Theatines were a monastic order dedicated to reform and austerity founded in Italy in the 16th century. Cardinal Mazarin sponsored

their expansion in France, and in 1644 gave them permission to build a Theatine church across from the Louvre.

108. AS THE SON OF A FISHERMAN: It was a common slander that Mazarin was a mere son of a fisherman, but though the cardinal plays along with the joke, it was just exaggerated wordplay on the fact that his family came from Piscina.

109. ALL FOUND IN THE CHRONICLE OF HAOLANDER: Mazarin did make overblown claims about his ancestors, but the Chronicle of Haolander is an invention of Dumas.

110. CASALE: The Siege of Casale in northern Italy was one of the key episodes in the War of Mantuan Succession, fought between France and Spain on the territory of Savoy. Mazarin first made his mark there as a negotiator and envoy for Rome, and you'll find the entire affair described in detail in Dumas's *The Red Sphinx*.

111. MONSIEUR DE BEAUFORT, WHOM I TREATED SO HARSHLY IN THE DUNGEONS OF VINCENNES: Mazarin's relations with the Duc de Beaufort, and the duke's escape from Vincennes, are recounted in *Twenty Years After*.

112. TO ATTEND HIS *COUCHER*: The *coucher* was an official evening reception held at the bedside of every adult member of the royal House of France. Like the morning lever, the relative importance of a person could be told by the quantity and quality of those who attended their coucher.

113. HIS CONFIDANT SAINT-SIMON: Louis de Rouvroy, Duc de Saint-Simon (1675–1755), ornament of the late-reign Court of Louis XIV and son of that Saint-Simon who was a favorite of Louis XIII (and who appears in *The Red Sphinx*) was a mediocre diplomat and soldier whose fame rests primarily on his voluminous memoirs, a primary source for anyone who studies the French Court in the early 18th century.

114. CANCER THAT WAS EVEN THEN GNAWING AT HER BREAST: Six years after this scene Queen Anne would die from breast cancer, though it's not clear that it would already have been afflicting her in 1660.

115. FROM VAUX TO THE LOUVRE: A distance of almost forty miles, or sixty-some kilometers.

116. UNDER THE GOLDEN SUN OF THIS ROYAL LUXURY GROWS THE LUXURY OF INDIVIDUALS, THE SOURCE OF WEALTH FOR THE PEOPLE: What we now call the "trickle-down" theory of economics is an old idea and has a long history among the apologists of both monarchy and capitalism.

117. THE SAME TONE WHICH MARIE ANTOINETTE MUCH LATER SAID, "YOU TELL ME THAT MUCH?": *Vous m'en direz tant!* An exclamation from Queen Marie Antoinette (1755–1793) in a similar situation, as attributed in the memoirs of Lucien Bonaparte.

118. VINCENNES: The Château de Vincennes, a grim 14th-century royal fortress just east of Paris, was used by the French monarchy as a refuge in wartime and as a prison for their enemies in times of peace.

119. THAT SUBLIME JEST FOR WHICH THE SAD GRUMBLER BOILEAU DARED TO CRITICIZE MOLIÈRE: Scapin is the roguish lackey of his reprobate master Don Juan in Molière's 1665 play of that name; at the end of the play, once his master has been dragged down to Hell, Scapin complains that he never even got paid, a remark the critic Boileau considered vulgar.

120. *FLORA* BY TITIAN: A masterpiece of feminine beauty by the great Renaissance painter dating from around 1515. In the 17th century it was mainly passed around between various royal Hapsburg collectors, so putting it in Mazarin's possession in 1660 is rather doubtful. Today it's in the Uffizi Gallery in Florence.

121. THE HUNDRED SWISS: The *Cent-Suisses*, a company of mercenary soldiers from Switzerland, had served the French Crown as a ceremonial palace guard since established by Louis XI in 1471.

122. A TEN-GUN FLUTE: The flute (Dutch: *fluyt*) was a medium-sized and relatively nimble merchant ship of the 16th through 18th centuries; as Colbert alludes, they were often mounted with guns to fend off pirates and privateers.

123. SOMEONE SCRATCHED AT THE DOOR: At the French Court in the 17th century, it was considered proper etiquette for inferiors to scratch at the door to request admittance rather than knock.

124. *BELLE-ÎLE-EN-MER*: Belle-Île is a medium-sized island in the Atlantic about ten miles off the south coast of Brittany, renowned for its mild summer clime and the dramatic cliffs along its *Côte sauvage*.

Acknowledgments

The cover painting is "The Arrival of d'Artagnan" by the 19th century Belgian painter Alex de Andreis. The interior illustrations are by Alphonse de Neuville, Frank T. Merrill, E. Van Muyden, Edmund H. Garrett, Félix Oudart, and Iain Lang; many thanks to John Armstrong for digitizing and formatting these old engravings.

Thanks also to my literary agent Philip Turner, the good shepherd who has guided this series to publication.

And many thanks, once again, to Claiborne Hancock, Maria Fernandez, and Victoria Wenzel at Pegasus Books for another handsome edition in the Musketeers Cycle. They make these books look so proud on the shelf!

For your benefit, reader, I'd like to welcome you to my website, Swash-bucklingadventure.net, where you'll find news and information about this book and others, plus additional related matters of interest. I hope to see you there!

—Lawrence Ellsworth